Ivan panicked as he imagined Zephyrus dying minutes before their arrival. His fingers tightened on the reins. Rivulets of sweat made their way down the sides of his face, wetting his collar, chilling his neck. After all the challenges he'd endured, risking his life and his beagles, the thought of failing now left him shaken.

"The Dark Army is advancing," Sebastian wailed, breaking Ivan's tortured thoughts. "We can't risk losing another second."

Praise for Vicki D. Thomas

Just when you think you've read every plot line, there comes another, one that's so distinctive it makes you hope it will become a series. *The Long Dark Cloak* contains a plethora of vibrant, unique characters that remain true to their personalities throughout the book. At first Ivan appears to be a normal fifteen-year-old farm boy, and then he's thrown into life situations that would test even the strongest adult. This book is wonderful for anyone who loves action, adventure, and true emotion. What a delight it was to learn this would become a series!

~ Cindy Davis, https://cindydavisauthor.com

Author, Vicki D. Thomas, has given words that turn imagination into a fantasy journey you can't wait to finish and look forward to the next book in the series.

~ Sunny Marie Baker, Multi-published Author

The Long Dark Cloak

by

Vicki D. Thomas

The Relics Adventures
Book 1

The Long Dark Cloak

Contact Information: info@thewildrosepress.com

Cover Art by *Jennifer Greeff*

The Wild Rose Press, Inc.
PO Box 708
Adams Basin, NY 14410-0708
Visit us at www.thewildrosepress.com

Publishing History
First Edition, 2022
Trade Paperback ISBN 978-1-5092-4074-6
Digital ISBN 978-1-5092-4075-3

The Relics Adventures, *Book 1*
Published in the United States of America

Dedication

This, as well as future books in this series, is dedicated to my parents. Although they have both passed, my mom and dad are the best examples and inspirations in my life. They instilled the value of perseverance, hard work, and the importance of following your dreams. If you have a dream, grab hold and make it happen.

A dark-haired lad will come seeking and find maturity, wisdom, and friendship. He will risk his life for the forest's survival. He will find himself in his search. Your duty is to keep him alive.
    - The Black Book of Pearls. Chapter 77, Verse 7

Chapter One

Southern England, 1947
Ivan

Ivan leaned into the schoolhouse door and pushed with his shoulder. He shoved harder, but it scarcely budged. Snickers and shuffling feet sounded against the floorboards on the opposite side.

Not again. He drew a deep breath. *Why can't they just leave me alone?* With teeth clenched, he took several steps back, ran, and crashed against the door. It swung open, and Ivan fell into the classroom, catching himself before dropping to his knees. His books scattered onto the floor. Dirk Mackle laughed at his prank and gave Ivan's history book a swift kick with his ragged boot.

"Go fetch it, you stupid foreigner." Dirk's eyes narrowed.

"Yeah, go fetch it, you dog," said Mackle's cousin, Gussy. Ivan's hands tightened at his sides.

"Coward. Ya don't fight back, do ya?" Gussy put up his fists, his brow creased. "Try, just try an' hit me."

Breathing hard to hold back his anger, Ivan remembered his mother's words: *Always show good manners. Don't fight or cause us troubles. It is best to avoid attention to ourselves. Do you understand?* Ivan would nod, but he didn't understand at all.

His parents cautioned him and his older brother, Peter, not to speak of their royal Russian heritage. "There are those who hunt us for the secrets we have." His mother would put her index finger to her lips and say, "Sssh. Don't tell."

"I-I don't fight," Ivan said, trying to hide his stuttering.

"Sissy. No guts." Mackle's face twisted with disgust.

Bonnet raced forward with stringy brown hair flying. She picked up Ivan's books, clutching them to her chest. "You're such a bully, *Mackerel*—that's an ugly fish, you know?" she said with a sneer. "Why don't you pick on me instead?"

"Cuz you bite," Gussy said quickly.

"My name's Dirk Mackle. You'd better remember that."

"You look like an ugly fish to me." Bonnet lifted her nose and stuck out her tongue.

Funny, Ivan had to agree. Dirk did have a fish-like face, with his jutting chin and squinty, almond-shaped eyes.

"He can't fight for himself." Eddie Rample stepped forward. "He needs a girl to fight for him."

"Boys!" Mrs. Hambuckle stomped into the room, her voice cracked the air. "Dirk, Gussy, Eddie, take your seats at once. It seems I can't leave the classroom for a minute, but you three are always causing trouble." She faced Ivan and said in a low voice, "Why don't you knock them on their rear ends?"

Ivan shook his head, and he met his teacher's sympathetic eyes. "I…I can't. My parents…they wouldn't allow it."

Mrs. Hambuckle replied gently, "Your parents are dead, Ivan. You're on your own now. You'll have to fight for yourself." Her voice quivered with sadness. "If there's ever anything I can do—please. You have only to ask."

"No, I…there's nothing." He turned away, wishing she'd stop.

"Well, then." She exhaled, brushing her hands against her black dress. "Take your seats now. Bonnet, give Ivan his books. It's time for our history lesson."

"Here you are." Bonnet smiled brightly and handed them to him, touching his fingers lightly.

Behind him, Eddie Ramble whispered, "He's a Russian spy, I'm sure of it. No Russian has a last name like Kimble."

"Shush now." Mrs. Hambuckle held up the palm of her hand. "You must know that Russia was our ally during the war. This is no way to treat our friends." Glancing at Ivan, she said, "You're the tallest in the class, would you please pull down the map?"

Ivan stood, gave a short bow, and unrolled the map of England from its wooden dowel. A voice hissed behind him. "Aaah, teacher's pet. Hee-hee."

"Enough." Mrs. Hambuckle spun around, her jaw set hard. "To the cloakroom with you, Dirk. I've had enough of your rude behavior. Go!"

Dirk rose and hesitated as though testing her. He glanced around looking for allies, but no one would look at him.

"Now!" The teacher's voice rang out even louder. She shook her finger toward the cloakroom.

Dirk bared his teeth at Ivan. "You'll get yours, rat." He slouched away, where he disappeared into the small space that held coats, boots, and umbrellas, along with the students' lunchboxes.

"Thank you, Ivan. Please take a seat in front." His teacher pulled back a stray lock of light brown hair and tucked it under her hair bun. She took a deep breath and pointed the rubber-tipped stick at the map. "I'm not sure what your substitute teacher taught you while I was sick—ah, absent last year, so I'll begin with the most rudimentary history lesson. This is Southern England, where you live." She half-turned and glanced at the students. "You do know that, don't you?"

When no one answered but all bobbed their heads, the teacher went on.

"This entire area is the West Forest." She circled the green wedge-shape with the pointer and turned once more to face the students. "This is the Solent, and farther south is the Isle of Wight." She tapped the areas for emphasis.

Looking over the rim of her glasses, she continued, "The West Forest is one of the largest remaining forests in England. It encompasses about one hundred and forty thousand acres within its boundaries and is ruled by Lord Richard Graydon. I understand he's a fair and just person, though few people have ever met him. A long time ago, his father willingly released Graydon Village from his kingdom, wanting us to rule ourselves and take responsibility for our own welfare. All in all, this was sensible and has worked quite well."

"My daddy says the forest is haunted with vicious creatures—like dragons and mad weasels," Mercy said, her eyes went wide.

"I heard there are trolls in the forest that eat little children and horses," said a boy in the second row.

When a girl frantically waved her hand to speak, Mrs. Hambuckle shook her head. "Enough of this." And that put an end to their ridiculous statements.

Ivan glanced at the boy who mentioned the trolls. Peter had claimed trolls existed, along with many other odd and dangerous creatures when he'd sneak into the West Forest. Rather than sound crazy, Ivan stayed silent.

"You may know from history that William the Conqueror left his home in Normandy, along with an immense army, and conquered England. He became king in 1066. William was a brutal man, stopping at nothing to steal, burn, and slaughter the townspeople." She paused. "That usually sums up the picture of war, doesn't it?" She let out a small sob and pulled a hankie from her pocket, dabbing her eyes.

"I'm sorry your husband didn't come back from the war," Mercy said. "My daddy got killed, too. The Germans shot him right here." She touched her forehead with her fingers.

Mrs. Hambuckle's face froze, and she turned away quickly. "Please excuse me," she stammered and hurried from the classroom.

"Why'd you have to go and say that?" Bonnet jumped from her desk and yelled, "You know her husband was lost in the war."

Ivan watched his teacher from the window where she wandered slowly in the schoolyard, wiping her eyes. Some students had learned that Mrs. Hambuckle had suffered a nervous breakdown when her husband didn't return home after the war. He knew the sadness of losing someone in World War II. Peter, his older brother, hadn't come home either. A sharp pain of loneliness flashed through his heart, and it caused him to gasp.

Dirk peeked out from the cloakroom, snickering. A chalkboard eraser sailed through the air, hitting Ivan on the side of his head. It bounced off Mrs. Hambuckle's desk where it left a mark and dropped to the floor. Chalk dust fell on Ivan's shirt collar and shoulder. After a moment, he picked up the eraser and placed it in the tray. Ivan stretched his lips taut, but he said nothing as he remembered his mother's warnings. Ivan sat down, grinding his teeth.

When Mrs. Hambuckle returned, she removed her eyeglasses and examined the white dust on her desk and floor. She shook her head, frowning. "It's after two o'clock." She sniffled. "Classes are over. Please read the second chapter of *The Norman Conquest* in your textbooks, and tomorrow we'll take up where we left off."

The students rose from their seats in a mannerly way and filed out, getting rowdier as they neared the exit. Dirk and Gussy, along with a couple other boys, whooped and hollered, pushing smaller students out of their way.

"Such hoodlums," Mrs. Hambuckle muttered. "Oh, Ivan, could you stay for a few minutes?"

"Yes, ma'am." He bowed slightly.

"Bring a chair closer to my desk." She gestured with a sweep of her hand.

"The eraser, Mrs. Hambuckle, I didn't—"

"Oh, I know that. I wanted to talk to you about something else." She sat down, blew her nose into her hankie, and tucked it into her dress pocket. "You may think it's none of my business, but I'd like to help you if I can." Her eyes were pale blue, and her cheeks had red blotches from weeping.

Ivan chanced a look at her, feeling more comfortable in her presence now that his classmates had left. "What did you want to talk to me about?"

"How are you managing all alone?"

"Well enough," he replied, not wanting to seem weak. "Peter will be coming home soon, now that the war is over. He'll be a big help on the farm."

"Have you heard anything from him?" Mrs. Hambuckle absently arranged papers on her desk.

Staring out the window, Ivan saw Bonnet standing in the schoolyard next to her horse, while holding the reins of his chestnut gelding. She smiled, waving vigorously. Ivan returned the smile, wondering if she could see him inside the schoolhouse.

"No," he said, looking down at the floor. "I haven't heard anything. But Peter must know our parents were killed in a train accident and is on his way home."

"Ivan," his teacher said softly, placing her hand on his. "You haven't heard or seen Peter since he left our village four years ago. Maybe, like my husband Aaron, he won't be coming home. What will you do?"

"I can manage the chores by myself." His voice broke, and his throat grew tight.

Mrs. Hambuckle shook her head slowly and then took a deep breath. "Ivan, listen to me. You're fifteen now. You can apprentice with a professional, just as you've always wanted. I know an engineer in London who will take you on and teach you everything you need to know. It's a wonderful opportunity, and you certainly have the aptitude for math and engineering. Your father thought so, too." Her eyes locked intently on him. "Here." She pulled open the top desk drawer. "I've had these papers of recommendation prepared and signed for several weeks. I was waiting for the right time to show you."

Ivan avoided her eyes, studying his fingers.

"You do want to go, don't you?"

"Oh, yes. I've thought about building bridges, roads, or houses, ever since I was a little boy."

Mrs. Hambuckle smiled, and her eyes turned glassy. "Now your dreams can come true, and it would bring me such joy."

"But what about the farm? The spring planting, the weeding, the harvesting? Who will care for the animals?"

Leaning back into her chair, Mrs. Hambuckle laced her fingers, tightening them. "I don't have all the answers for you, but I'm sure we can find solutions."

Ivan grinned, hope overtaking him. Here was his chance to make his dreams come true. If only Peter were home, he'd know what to do.

"It's nice to see you smile, Ivan. You don't do that very often." She hesitated and then coughed into her hand, blushing a bit. "Well, you're a serious young man."

They were both quiet for a moment. Ivan didn't know if he should explain his shy behavior or stay silent. "It's my accent, ma'am. They...the students resent me because my parents were foreigners."

"Well, I'm not so sure. When Peter was my student, he told me your family came from high society Russia and perfect manners were the call of the day. But this is rural England, far from high society protocol. I don't believe bullies like Dirk and Gussy know what to make of you."

Ivan nodded, knowing Peter told Mrs. Hambuckle about their family and that she had been sworn to secrecy. But she was only partially right. Peter warned him many times not to be so passive. He always said, "Stand up and fight for yourself. You are so much more than you believe." Now, his teacher was telling him the same thing. He felt he was a disappointment to everyone.

"Thank you, Mrs. Hambuckle, for the good news." Ivan stood and returned his chair to its place. "I have to go now and take care of chores."

"It's my pleasure to help. I'll make the arrangements when you're ready." His teacher glanced out the window and winked. "I think someone is waiting for you."

Bonnet stood on the school lawn stroking Bounty's cheek.

"Oh—and Ivan," Mrs. Hambuckle's voice was suddenly sharp. "I meant what I said when I told you to smack Dirk the next time he bullies you. Otherwise, he'll just become a bigger bully, hurting people wherever he goes. You'll probably run into a lot of his kind in your life."

"Yes, ma'am." Ivan lifted his dark eyebrows. He scooped up his books and went into the cloakroom where he grabbed his jacket and lunchbox. Liquid, smelling like urine, leaked out. He gritted his teeth and opened the box, dumping its contents into a dustbin near the front door. There was no question who had done such a barbaric thing. *Someday. Someday*, he promised himself.

"Hi, Ivan," Bonnet called sweetly, waving for his

attention. "I fetched Bounty for you."

"Thanks," Ivan said. "How'd he get loose from the stable?"

"Take a good guess." She dropped the horse's reins and scratched her head with both hands.

"The Mackerel?" He gave a short laugh, liking the new nickname for Dirk.

"Yeah. What a bloody bloke." She scratched her head again. Ivan jumped back. *Lice?* He mounted quickly and said, "Thanks for getting Bounty for me."

"Anytime," she sang.

Nudging his horse in the ribs, Ivan rode to his farm home. He thought of all the things Mrs. Hambuckle had told him. Then he imagined his balled fist smashing into Mackle's fish-face, knocking him on his bum. That made him laugh out loud.

****

The next morning, Ivan went into the barn grinning as he considered Mrs. Hambuckle's advice. His whole future looked cheery. For the first time in a long while, he believed he could become an engineer. Someone would help him. Someone cared.

There were stanchions for seven cows on each side of the walkway, although Ivan had only five, they kept him busy enough. He hung a kerosene lantern on a hook where the rays illuminated the walkway and the reclining cows. One by one they hauled their heavy bodies upright, puffing foggy breath into cold air.

Grabbing a milk pail, he sat on a wooden stool, positioning himself near a Friesian cow. It dawned on him that he wouldn't be going to London or anywhere else unless Peter came home to take over the farm—if he was still alive. A rush of despair and loneliness covered him. His eyes prickled with moisture. Where was he? Why hadn't Peter come home?

"Feeling sorry for myself won't get the chores done." Ivan squared his shoulders. His callused hands reached for the cow's back teats, and he pulled rhythmically. His thoughts drifted as the dull splash of liquid filled the pail. There was a time, not so long ago when he was surrounded by his family, feeling safe, feeling loved, and worthwhile.

War was ravaging Europe when Peter left to join the British Army. Even now, years later, Ivan remembered Peter's last words to him, "Listen, little brother of mine, you must be brave while I'm gone. I won't be here to protect you. Take care of Mother and Father and be a good lad." Ivan nodded and promised. "And please, don't weep. You're too old for that."

Their mother heard Peter's scolding tone as their father drove them to the train station. She turned from the front seat of their automobile. "Oh Peter, let him cry." Her fine Russian words, with a mix of English, were still spoken with the crispness of a once noblewoman. "It's a very sad day, and I'll cry too when you step onto the train."

Peter boarded the big, huffing beast from the platform and waved energetically, wearing a big grin on his face.

Then he was gone.

A few years later, his parents died in a train accident just outside London. Ivan's pain and loneliness deepened. Now he lived alone in their old limestone farmhouse in the small, rural community of Graydon Village. He hadn't heard from Peter in all that time. Not one word. World War II was over now. Why hadn't he come home?

Everyone Ivan loved was gone.

Daydreams quickly vanished when the barn door burst open and quick steps sounded on the walkway. He peered around the back of the cow. His legs squeezed the milk pail. Dare he hope that Peter was there? Instead, his neighbor Mueller McKay hurried toward him, his eyes flashing with urgency.

"Aye, Ivan."

"What are you doing here so early, Mule?"

"I got news for you," he said, breathing fast. "Good news. I came soon's I could."

"What is it, then?" Ivan glanced up and continued milking.

"Well, I was at the Rouster last night having a little tip-o-the tankard. Lars Benton was there. Said he saw Peter yesterday in the West Forest. Peter's alive!"

Ivan shot to his feet, yanking the pail with him. "Peter—in the forest?" He couldn't believe what he was hearing.

Mule nodded quickly.

"What was Lars doing in the forest?" Ivan asked just as the cow jumped, shoving him against a barn post. He moaned from the pain in his already injured shoulder.

"Seems Lars was picking up free firewood when he saw this tall, blond-haired fellow. Claims it was Peter throwing wood into an old wagon."

Ivan frowned. "Was Lars sure it was Peter?"

"I reckon so. Went to school with him, you know? Peter's hard to miss, being tall like you with good enough features—and a scar—here." His finger traced an imaginary crescent shape on his own chin.

Ivan drew a deep breath, and his chest swelled with heat. He knew about the scar. When Peter was twelve or so, he told Ivan a troll had bitten him after he snuck into the West Forest. The nasty bite caused a dangerous fever, left a mark, and took weeks to heal. He was more apt to believe the story Peter told their parents, that a mad dog attacked him. Yet, Peter secretly confided in Ivan that it had been a troll, supplying details, except why the creature had done such a vicious thing.

"Did Lars talk to him?" Ivan asked Mueller.

"He called his name real loud, and Peter turned to look. Said it was him all right. That he looked surprised and a little scared at the same time. Then he jumped on his horse and pulled the wagon away in a big hurry."

Ivan didn't know what to think, scarcely believing his brother was so close. *Is it possible Peter is living in the huge forest and is only an hour away?* Now Ivan didn't know what to believe.

"Did Lars know Peter went to war and no one has heard from him?"

"Aye, he knew. That's why Lars was shocked to see him there, nice as you please, tossing wood into a wagon."

"It makes no sense." He slowly lowered himself to the hard stool.

"Maybe he got some of that amnesia-stuff and forgot where he lived."

"I've often wondered if he'd gotten a rifle butt to his head during the war and lost his memory."

"Possible." Mueller swept his arm through the air.

Staring across the walkway, Ivan imagined Peter there.

Memories dashed through his mind. Their milk

fights in the barn, chasing through the oat fields, or racing their horses to school, laughing and hollering their heads off. *My brother has survived the war and is only an hour from our farm.* "Why wouldn't he come home?"

Looking sympathetic, Mule hunched his shoulders.

Hope misted Ivan's eyes. He desperately wanted to believe what Mule told him.

"Something dreadful must've happened. I'll go find him as soon as my chores are done."

"I'd offer you a hand," Mule said, "but I got my own herd to milk. My boys started the job when I left, and you can be sure they'll be squabbling before I get back."

"Thanks. I'll be on my way soon." *Did I actually say I'd go into the forbidden forest? Dangerous creatures lurk there, vicious trolls that could take a bite out of me like they did Peter. Everyone has heard the stories.*

Taking a deep breath, Ivan decided that whatever it took, he'd find his brother and bring him home.

Grasping the cow's front teats, he milked feverishly. The quicker he was done, the quicker he could leave. The animal turned her head from the stanchion and looked at him with her big brown eyes.

Mule waited silently, rocking on his feet, as though he wanted to say something.

Finished, Ivan gave the cow an affectionate slap on her rump. His thoughts tangled with excitement and fear as he moved to the milk strainer in the middle of the walkway.

"Better be careful," Mule said. "I hear there are all sorts of dangerous things in that forest."

"I've heard the rumors." Ivan let out a nervous laugh. "But I've always thought they were tall tales." Thinking on it, he added, "When we were young, Peter would ignore our father's warnings and the *No Trespassing* sign at the entrance and sneak into the forest." Ivan almost mentioned something about the troll who'd bitten Peter but then remembered he'd promised never to snitch.

With a snort, Mule said, "Peter never was good at followin' the rules. Why didn't you go, too?"

"I was too scared." He shook his head. "Sometimes Peter made up fantasies about a golden tree that talked or cats that could fly. He wanted to lure me into the forest with him. In that way, Father wouldn't be quite so angry if we were both caught."

Stooping, Ivan washed the Guernsey's teats, a fawn-colored cow in the same row. He moaned and grasped his right shoulder.

"What's wrong?"

"I tripped over some fencing wire this morning near the chicken coop." His face strained as he massaged his injury.

"Be more careful where you step," Mule said, and Ivan gave a conceding nod.

"I may need someone to look after things here. I hope I won't be gone long, but if so, do you know anyone who could lend a hand for the day?"

"Yeah, come to think of it." He paused and stroked his chin stubble. "There's this boy north of the village. He's wanting work before and after school."

"Is he reliable?" Ivan asked.

"Seems responsible enough, I reckon. About your age—maybe a bit younger. I'll go see him soon's my chores are done."

"Thanks. He can stay here until I get back if he'd like."

"Sure," Mule said. "I hope you find Peter. It'd be good to have him back helping you. I know it's been hard since your mum and dad died. I miss 'em terrible." He lowered his face, bottom lip protruding. "It's not right, you being so young and all alone."

"I'll manage."

"What about school tomorrow? You skippin' out?"

"If Peter's in the forest, I need to find him."

"Sure. I'd do the same if I were you." Mule turned and said goodbye over his shoulder.

His friend's footsteps moved away, and the barn door closed behind him. Ivan buried his head against the cow's soft hair, holding back his tears.

Finished with his chores, he hurried toward the house and fed Alfred and Canute. The brother beagles jumped up on the porch and gobbled down their breakfast, but Ivan skipped his.

He stepped inside and reached for his cloth cap, pulling it over his thick dark hair. Carefully, he pushed his sore arm through the sleeves of a warm jacket and envisioned Peter following him home. He wondered if his brother was afraid for some reason to come home and had taken a different name. Surely someone in the vast forest would know where to find him.

Or was a magical spell cast on him, holding him prisoner there? Ivan shook his head. "Ridiculous."

In the stable, Ivan tightened the girth strap on Bounty, his four-year-old chestnut gelding. Lifting the saddle sent a shooting pain through his shoulder. He clenched his teeth, cried out, and dropped his arm to his side. Soon, the pain eased.

Bounty turned, dipping his flaxen-colored mane, swishing his tail in protest.

"We're traveling to the West Forest to search for Peter and fetch him home. You were only a colt when he left." His lips stretched into a cheerful smile at the thought of finding Peter.

Encouraging his horse toward the west, Ivan tried to ignore his sudden fears of mythical beasts or getting lost in the wilderness. Instead, he imagined going to London to become an engineer. With his brother beside him, they would travel the world, explore big cities, and sail deep oceans just as Peter had promised years ago.

Ivan rode at a steady pace, leaving his farm behind. Alfred and Canute followed, their tails swinging crazily. He slowed Bounty to avoid prickly gorse bushes that grew near the road leading to the forest while sand lizards darted for cover in the long morning shadows. Birds broke from the trees, twittering as they flew into the violet-gray sky. Taking a deep breath, Ivan tried to brace his courage.

Farther ahead, he saw turquoise-shadowed birch trees that marked the edge of his farm and the entrance to Lord Graydon's West Forest. "This is it, Bounty. We can't turn back now."

What would Peter say if he knew I was going into the forest to search for him? He'd believe I'm very brave. Then he remembered Peter's words when he left for the war, "You'll have to learn to fight back. I won't be here to protect you." Ivan shrank at the thought of fighting anyone—even Dirk or Gussy.

It looked like rain before early afternoon, though Ivan hoped he wouldn't need to stay that long. The threatening storm billowed huge clouds shaped like dragons, exposing their dark purple underbellies. Drawing his jacket closed, he realized he didn't know much about dragons. He'd never seen one, but Peter talked about them several times.

"I think the stories Mule and Peter told me are only fantasies. But still...I wonder if witches, goblins, and wizards are waiting in the woods." He prodded Bounty on, his hands turning colder as they neared the West Forest entrance.

Chapter Two

The Golden Tree

A dark-haired lad will come seeking and find maturity, wisdom, and friendship. He will risk his life for the Forest's survival. The oath of the Forest is to keep him alive.
- The Black Book of Pearls. Chapter 77, Verse 7

Zephyrus, an enormous Kingwood Oak, knew the sounds of the West Forest. He had listened to their messages for over a thousand years. He knew all things since the time of the Seven Kings. He saw far into the woodland. He knew every leaf on his brother oaks' crowns. He knew their saplings and all the trees throughout the vast forest. When he called the birds, they came and curled their toes around his branches. He could predict the weather seven days out. Zephyrus was The Master and The Peacekeeper of the Forest.

He tried to remember what it was like to be a man who walked on two legs, but that was over a thousand years ago. He pushed his bright green eyes from his bark, and a mouth formed right where it belonged under his nose. It had all changed when his brother, Tereus, declared war on Zephyrus and his kingdom. Greed, hate, and jealousy drove him. Now Tereus, a mad bull of a man, was confined to the fiery underworld, and

Zephyrus, the Great Oak, ruled the above ground. So much division, so much resentment. He sighed with sadness.

A twig snapped. The rustling of footsteps behind him moved stealthily in his direction.

"Who's there?" Zephyrus asked in his commanding voice. He stood in the center of a wide circular clearing surrounded by a thick grove of trees. The other trees' boughs suddenly lifted. Faces formed noiselessly in their charcoal-colored trunks. Eyes flew open as they watched their master.

"Who moves behind me?" Zephyrus asked again. His eyebrows twitched, looking like a mass of tangled twigs. He scanned the area…waiting. "Do you seek my counsel?"

No one answered. The sound of the stranger's quick, shallow breathing intensified as he moved closer, crushing brittle leaves. Someone threatening stood near. *Why?*

Cra-aack. His bark split, followed by a hellish burning in his side. Zephyrus bellowed with pain. His golden leaves quivered, then fell, spinning to the ground around him. Frightened birds pushed off from his branches, squawking, taking flight in scattered directions. The glint of an axe head struck him again, penetrating his side just above the first gash. Another thud, a third sharp blow from the powerful tool.

"My High Intervener, God of the Forest." His scream broke the silence. His eyes pressed tightly. "The axe burns hot like fire." He remembered from a thousand years ago when he had been a man, a king of the ancient kingdom of Helvaka, the burning in his throat from swallowing poison. This was the same feeling.

No response from the axe wielder.

"Who strikes me? I'm not to be taken down." Zephyrus roared with white-hot pain. The poison shot through his woody fibers, traveling up into his branches. From the corners of his eyes, he saw a tall man in a sleeveless gray cloak, a hood shadowing his face. "Who are you? Why do you try to destroy me?"

"You have outlived your usefulness," said a low, contemptuous voice.

In his agony, Zephyrus couldn't determine who spoke, but the voice sounded vaguely familiar.

The assailant lifted his lethal weapon for another blow when Zephyrus caught a glimpse of the tool. In disbelief, he shouted, "You hold the Silver Axe—an Ancient Relic. This is treason."

"The axe is part of my prize," the hooded man answered. "It's time for a *new master* of the Forest."

Ravaged with pain, Zephyrus cried out again, "Who are you?" As his attacker moved closer, he saw the outline of his nose—straight and strong. *Who is this that would betray me?*

****

Raising the Silver Axe, the hooded man gripped it firmly. His treachery nearly accomplished, he pulled back the weapon for the final assault. He gnashed his teeth, shutting out all feelings, forcing himself to go on.

Once, the hooded man had loved Zephyrus dearly. He still did. But now, he had chosen a new direction. A path that offered him what he felt he deserved. His family had been Russian nobles before they left their country, and now he would regain their status. His only assignment was to kill Zephyrus with a poison-edged axe. Then, Tereus would grant him the throne. With Zephyrus destroyed, they'd rule the rich, ancient kingdom of the West Forest.

Frozen mid-swing, the hooded man cocked his head. He paused. His jaw muscles tightened. The echoes of barking dogs and clomping hooves signaled that someone on horseback was approaching. Who could it be when all the Forest's inhabitants were at the castle attending the Annual Festival? He gave the axe a toss, not daring to get caught with it.

Rushing north toward a stand of elms, the man grabbed the reins of his black horse and threw his weight up into the saddle. Turning for only a moment, he viewed the awful crime he'd committed. Remorse shot through him, but it was too late now. His crime could not be undone. Galloping away, he didn't look back.

****

Heathland lay between Ivan's farm and the entrance to the West Forest. Its acidic soil allowed little to grow except straggly trees, gorse, and sparse grasses that clung to life with all their might. The stark appearance served as a natural barrier to those who would dare enter.

Near the woodland's border, where the tall birches grew, a sign read:

Lord Richard Graydon's Kingdom

No Trespassing. Absolutely No Guns. No Motor Cars.

Land grant issued by King William I, 1079

No Swearing Permitted

Ivan gave a quick, nervous smile. He didn't swear. Nor did he have a gun or a motorcar. Though people had cars after the war, petrol was still scarce. He *was* trespassing, but only until he could find Peter. Then he'd gladly leave.

From his recent school studies, Ivan had learned that William the Conqueror, Duke of Normandy, seized this forested area as his royal hunting province shortly after his arrival. A little more than a decade later, Mrs. Hambuckle explained that King William granted the land to the Graydon family. It was eventually inherited by Richard Graydon, who presently owned the entire West Forest and the South Castle.

Clutching Bounty's reins, Ivan hesitated at the woodland's edge. No one guarded the gatehouse, and there were no signs of patrolling garrisons. *Where is everyone?*

Perhaps Peter never came here. Having lost an eye in the war, Lars could've been mistaken. *But Lars had seen the scar.*

"I shouldn't have come." Ivan blew on his hands to warm them. Then, remembering his purpose, he squared his shoulders, took several deep breaths, and rode on.

Soon, he came to an old fence post where a weathered plaque was nailed. It read, *Oakhurst.* He was in the forest now. A frightening place he never wanted to visit, not even with Peter. But it was time to put his childish fears away. Peter would want that.

Adjusting his cap, Ivan shivered from a sudden breeze. A ground fog mysteriously appeared, pushing and tumbling over itself along the forest floor. *Where had it come from*? Silence followed. Closing in, the fog caused his teeth to chatter, his breath to quicken. He turned, judging the distance to the border's edge, almost deciding to go home.

But he needed to find Peter.

"You must help me be brave, Bounty." Nudging his horse's ribs, they moved on.

"Hello, I'm looking for my brother," Ivan called into the moist air, hoping to catch someone's attention. There was no response. Not even a bird peeped. If the fog became thicker, rising higher, he might lose his way.

He heard a groan. The long, throaty sound came from the north, sweeping down and encompassing him. He couldn't figure out what it was. An animal or human? *Is someone trying to get my attention?*

"Peter. Peter," he called, "is that you? It's Ivan." Then he realized how ridiculous it was to assume it was his brother. It could be anyone—*or anything.*

Leaning forward, Ivan strained to hear. He jerked back when an alarm of birds broke the stillness from the surrounding trees, flying in every direction, squawking, and fluttering. He looked skyward, where the birds and dark clouds moved swiftly against a pale gray sky. The whispers of wind seemed to say, "Hurry, hurry, hurry."

Alfred and Canute stopped and plopped on their haunches. Their wide eyes stared up at their master. *Had they heard the leaves murmuring their worried song?* Ivan wondered if the groans were hostile, warning him that he had no right to be on Lord Graydon's property. If it had been Peter moaning for help, he would surely answer back—if he could.

"Where are you?" Ivan waited. Cupping his hands around his mouth, he yelled louder, "Do you need help?"

The Forest hushed. Ivan felt as though hundreds of

eyes were watching him. He raised himself from the saddle, knees quivering. He searched distant trees for a sign, troubled that someone needed him, maybe Peter. *Perhaps it was only a stiff breeze sweeping like a cry through the leaves.* After a long silence, he shrugged, bringing on a sharp sting of pain to his injured shoulder. He grumbled.

Imagining trolls hiding behind bushes and crouching dragons glaring at him through the pattern of dark tree trunks, Ivan's jaw tensed. He thought he heard things—beech masts crunching underfoot or the squeak of mushrooms growing through a rock crevice. All sorts of creatures could be biding their time, waiting to attack and eat him alive. A little whimper left his throat. "I don't believe that nonsense," he said, burying his fears. "If only someone could tell me where to find the free wood," he said to his beagles, "it would give me a clue where Peter was last seen." He had questioned Mule about the location, but the information was second hand, and Mule's directional sense had never been very good.

Another long groan, louder and more desperate drifted through the woods. Ivan scratched his head, looking from side to side. And then, the creeping mist thickened to bluish-gray fog. It rushed forward, becoming thicker and thicker. Mounds of cold and dampness covered the ground, curling up dark trunks. It clung to low oak limbs, elms, and chestnut trees, while scrub undergrowth took on gray, ghostly shapes.

Ivan buttoned his jacket to his neck, shaking with icy fear. He tried to calm himself by taking deep breaths, but doubt clawed at his courage.

Just as he turned Bounty's head with a nervous

yank, Ivan saw something shiny on the ground. He slipped from his horse and recognized an axe. Before it was lost in the fog, he picked it up and studied it. The ancient hickory handle was indented where many hands had gripped it over time. The edge was sharp, and he was tempted to test it with his thumb, but for some reason thought better of it. *Is the axe handle quivering, or am I imagining it?*

A thundering roll sounded, followed by a flash of lightning that shot through the trees' canopy. Bounty jumped and slammed into him. Ivan stumbled, nearly losing his balance. He did his best to still his pounding heart by pressing a fisted hand against his chest, but it didn't help. Everything in him screamed to leave this frightening place. "No!" he shouted, "not until I've found whether Peter is here.

A loud, painful cry echoed through the trees. It was followed by a gust of warm wind that blew an open path through the fog. Up a grassy slope, surrounded by mostly old growth, Ivan noticed a brilliant light. An enormous oak tree stood alone in a large circular clearing, illuminating its surroundings with a golden glow. It was the biggest tree Ivan had ever seen. Its thick girth and wide-spreading branches grew up and outward in great expanse as though reaching for the heavens. The warm wind seemed to come directly from it. Ivan's trembling hands gripped the axe. He waited a few moments until his heart hit regular beats. Clutching the reins even tighter with his free hand, Ivan tugged Bounty toward the huge tree. "Let's take a closer look."

"Good heavens," Ivan cried, his eyes swept through the jumble of branches. "Mule was right. There really is a golden tree in the West Forest—a magnificent tree whose leaves sparkled like priceless jewels." Taking a few steps forward, he placed his hands against the rough, creviced bark. It was hot under his palms. Then he smelled something rotten, with a faint fishy odor. *Where is it coming from?* Just as he removed his hands from the trunk, another groan tapered to a mournful cry.

Ivan's mouth dropped open. Feeling quite foolish, he said, "Are you making that noise?"

A long, deep sound came from the tree. Leaping away, Ivan wound his fingers around Bounty's coarse mane, ready to swing up into the saddle and gallop away. He hesitated, more curious than scared.

"I'm in dreadful pain." The tree's glow flickered.

"But trees don't talk or moan." *This must be some kind of trick to scare me away and keep uninvited visitors out of the Forest.*

He glanced about, searching for the person who'd spoken, but he saw no one.

High above Ivan's head, eyes had somehow formed through the giant tree's trunk. A large nose broke through the wood and protruded above a mustache fashioned from a mess of twigs and moss, just like the eyebrows. Then, a pair of thick wooden lips pushed through and pressed hard together. His heavy, woody brows pulled in with a grieving expression.

"Please," the tree said, "be careful with the axe you hold in your hands. The head is coated with a mysterious poison. It went deep into my side."

Ivan stared at the talking tree, his mouth gaping. How could this be? He glanced at the sharp edge of the axe, glad he hadn't tested its sharpness when he'd found it. With wavering steps, he moved around the massive trunk. The bark had been split several times with a sharp tool—the very axe he now held. A foamy, yellowish substance oozed from the deep gashes.

Ivan's sympathetic nature won over his doubt and fear. "Wh-what can I do to help you?"

Am I really talking to a tree?

"You can see," said the oak, his voice strained, "I have many subjects in the Forest. They would come to my aid if they could."

Glancing all about, Ivan gulped to see a forest full of other trees staring at him with terrified eyes. "I've never seen trees with faces before." Ivan's voice quivered as he studied them. Each appeared to have different characteristics, whether it was the color or shape of their trunks or the positioning of their features.

"We have always been here," the tree slowly replied. "For hundreds and hundreds of years, observing all things."

Ivan opened his mouth, but no words came.

"My name is Barkay. King Zephyrus Westwind Barkay. The tree gritted his teeth until, it seemed, a spasm of pain had passed. "My brother oaks created the rolling fog, and I blew a path for you to find me. I am a Kingwood Oak, The Master and Peacekeeper of the Forest. The entire woodland and its creatures are my loyal subjects."

Ivan shook his head, frowning. He felt he was part of a bizarre dream. "What happened to you?"

"Someone axed me," Zephyrus replied with effort. "It all happened so fast, I couldn't see who did such a terrible thing." He focused on Ivan. "Who are you? And why are you here?"

"I-I am Ivan Kimble, sir," he said, embarrassed for

stuttering. He removed his hat out of respect to an elder, even though it was a tree. "My family owns the property bordering Lord Graydon's land. I've heard my brother Peter is somewhere in the Forest. I've come to find him."

Blinking, Zephyrus's eyes opened wider. He repeated, "Your name is Kimble, and you are searching for your brother?"

"Yes, sir. Have you seen him?"

The pained look returned. "I may not be the one to ask."

Puzzled by the strange answer, Ivan explained further, "Peter could be hurt or has lost his memory during the war. It's possible he's forgotten his way home."

"What makes you believe he's in our vast woodland?"

"I was told he'd been seen here throwing free wood into a wagon."

"Free wood?" Zephyrus's eyebrows lifted. "Ah, yes. We offer it to veterans who need help."

Ivan nodded. "I know that Lord Graydon owns this property, and I've come to ask him if he has seen Peter."

"Many come to have an audience with Lord Graydon."

It was a wary answer to his question. *Does Zephyrus believe I intend to do him harm? After all, I am clutching the handle of the poisonous weapon.*

"You would be prudent to set the axe aside and safely out of your hands." Zephyrus's half-closed eyes looked into the distance. "There behind you, near those three birch trees."

"Yes, of course." Ivan shuddered, careful not to touch the toxic silver head. Taking hurried steps just past the clearing, he propped the axe against the angled birches that grew side by side and rushed back to Zephyrus.

"Perhaps we can help you find your bother if he's in our Forest." Zephyrus released a low moan.

Flashing a grateful smile, Ivan filled with hope. "Th-thank you, sir, for anything you can do."

Canute pawed at Ivan's trousers, making small whimpering noises. "These are my beagles, ah…sir. This is Canute and his brother, Alfred, named after early kings of England."

Zephyrus closed his eyes with a show of understanding. "I knew both kings well." A tiny turn of his broad lips showed the pleasure of his memories. "I ask for your help, lad." The tree gave a great sigh. "Deep into our Forest, there is a remarkable tree called Fungoda. He produces a special sap for healing, though I don't know if it will cure me. The poison used is unknown, but Fungoda's sap is my only hope for recovery. Will you go to him and get the antidote? Bring it back to me as quickly as possible."

Ivan didn't answer at once. "Sir, with respect, I want to help, but I'm not the one to wander through the woods looking for a healing tree. I don't have any knowledge of this place. Besides," he argued, "I'm here to find my—"

"Yes, I know," Zephyrus interrupted softly. "I beg you to make this journey on my behalf. You should know that if I die, the Forest will be lost forever."

Ivan brought his eyebrows together. "How can that be?"

"Sebastian will tell you these things."

Who is Sebastian? Ivan wanted to ask, but Zephyrus had closed his eyes tightly and winced.

After some hesitation, Ivan stammered, "Well, I-I suppose I could look for the Fungoda tree and ask anyone I happen to meet if they've seen Peter. How will I know the healing tree? Which direction should I go?" For a moment, Ivan doubted his own sanity. He was asking directions from one tree to find another tree that supposedly had a cure for an unknown poison. *Am I hallucinating?*

Zephyrus opened his eyes. With labored breath, he said, "Your journey begins on this road before me and continues to the west. You must take the Long Dark Cloak to guide you through the mysteries of the Forest."

"Mysteries?" Ivan swallowed a lump that went down like a handful of acorns. *How can this become more mysterious than it already is? A talking tree? A cloak to guide me? It gets stranger by the moment.*

Ivan's questions were lost amid sounds of rumbling and crunching. A door drew open from the center of the tree's trunk as if by its own power. Ivan lifted his brow in wonder. The trunk had seemed completely solid, and now it showed a large door that slowly opened.

"Please step inside to get the cloak. He will be your guide."

Releasing Bounty's bridle, Ivan stepped into the chamber while his beagles stayed crouched under a holly bush, growling. The immense cavity was cool and dark, where he breathed in the pleasant smell of damp earth, spicy bark, and something else. Yes, a strange fishy odor. A light streamed down from far above, like dazzling rays of sun, warming the top of his head and shoulders.

Toward the back of the cavity, Ivan spotted the dark cloak hanging on a peg that Zephyrus had mentioned. *How will it guide me?*

Ivan counted five empty pegs on the north wall and an ornate silver shelf that held a scarlet cushion with a short, gold fringe. He wondered where the other garments were and what valuable thing once rested upon the velvet cushion. Ivan was about to ask where he would meet Sebastian, his guide when Zephyrus spoke.

"Put the cloak on and tie it securely." His voice trailed weakly.

Slipping it around his shoulders, Ivan's shaky hands knotted the strings at his neck. He rubbed the old fabric between his fingers, realizing it was made from fine broadcloth. It had a deep hood, empty side pockets, and the hem brushed just below his knees. At once, soothing heat penetrated the ache in his shoulder and his scraped elbows. The areas tingled like hundreds of fingers tapping against his skin. When it cooled, Ivan no longer felt the pain from his earlier injury. He opened his eyes wide as he left the tree's cavity. Grinning, he stepped into Zephyrus's sight.

"Yes," Zephyrus said with a small smile, "the Long Dark Cloak has great healing powers, and that's why it's so valuable. But it cannot heal me. Always remember, don't remove the garment unless it asks. When you have the healing sap, return it here to the Sanctuary of Truth."

Though nodding in agreement, Ivan thought it ridiculous that the cloak could talk. But then, *he* was talking to a tree. He quickly dismissed it as Zephyrus's confusion.

"Is that what you call this?" Ivan gestured toward the closing door. "The Sanctuary of Truth?"

Zephyrus's heavy bark lips trembled, his twig mustache quivered. "It's a most important place and even more powerful when all the pegs and the cushion are occupied. The safety of the Forest depends on the items that were once kept here." His groan went deep. "Now the relics are all gone except the cloak. And...the Silver Axe."

Fingering the ties at his neck, brow furrowing, Ivan wondered why the other five cloaks had been lent if they were so valuable and why they hadn't been returned. Did Zephyrus realize the sanctuary would be completely empty when he left with the hooded cloak? And what they had to do with the safety of the Forest, Ivan couldn't guess.

Squeaking hinges sounded where none existed, and Ivan stepped away. The huge door slowly closed. It locked into place with a great click that disturbed Bounty who spooked at the sound. He raised his head and whinnied. Canute let out a bark. No one felt more confused than Ivan at that moment.

He reached for the reins and stroked his horse's nose, murmured reassuring phrases. *Is someone trying to make a fool of me? How can a giant tree talk?* Glancing around, he gave his head a quick shake.

"You must go now." Dull green eyes closed for a moment and then opened with noticeable effort. "My pain is so acute that I must force my dormancy until your return. Though I leave myself in a vulnerable state during this time, I have no choice." His voice grew thin.

"The Long Dark Cloak will direct you on the path to Fungoda. Give my best regards and deepest thanks to my cantankerous friend to the southwest."

Zephyrus's smooth, wooden mouth drew downward with a soft grinding noise. His eyes shut tightly, pulled in, and sank into his bark. Rough facial features disappeared. Golden colors faded from the leaves and lost their luster. The enormous Kingwood Oak stood with drooping boughs, still and silent.

Ivan gawked until, at last, he forced his legs to move. He slowly backed away, trying to grasp what he'd seen. Inhaling deeply, he turned and strode toward the birch trees. His final task before leaving to find grumpy Fungoda was to retrieve the Silver Axe. He'd take it with him on his search. Having no stomach for violence, he hoped desperately he wouldn't need it for his own protection, but he'd take it just the same.

Rotating his arm, flexing solid muscles, he tested his shoulder. It felt completely healed. He stopped and turned. "Thank you for healing my…"

Zephyrus did not speak.

Moving briskly, Ivan approached the three-angled birch trees not far from the now-dormant Zephyrus. When he reached for the axe, six eyes sprang open on white faces with long, sharp noses and mouths twisted into disapproving grimaces. Their glares caused Ivan to sputter for breath. *Another oddity in the Forest?*

"Get your hands off that axe!" demanded an impatient voice. "Who do you think you are?"

Ivan stumbled, tangling his feet in the weeds. His arms windmilled wildly until he caught his balance. Overcoming his sudden shock, he stared up into a pair of dark-brown eyes recessed into a white trunk. At first, he would've believed it was the voice of a ventriloquist that had yelled at him, except he saw the tree's mouth move, smelling breath like the odor of decaying leaves.

Ivan excused himself and explained, "I-I've been sent on a mission to get a special healing sap to save Zephyrus Barkay's life." He turned, pointing at the giant tree which now stood silent in the clearing.

"Oh, is that so?" The middle tree's voice was sharp with sarcasm.

The Long Dark Cloak, resting over Ivan's shoulders, spoke for the first time. "Meet the triplets, Ivan. This center tree is named Dorset. The one on the left is Winchester, and the other is Bristol. I'm afraid their manners are nothing to boast about."

"My word, what's going on around here?" Ivan twirled to see who talked behind him, but he could see no one. "Trees talk. A cloak talks. I must've eaten some bad porridge this morning." Then, he remembered he'd eaten nothing.

"What is this intruder doing here?" Dorset spoke as though insulted by Ivan's presence.

"And why does *he* have the cloak tied around his neck?" Bristol said.

"Is he an outlaw or a thief?" The high-pitched voice belonged to Winchester.

"Weren't you just watching and listening?" The cloak sounded irritated. "This young man, Ivan Kimble, is telling the truth. He has agreed to travel through the Forest and bring back the special healing sap from Fungoda to save Zephyrus's life."

Ivan raised his chin and nodded.

The cloak's raspy voice dropped to a whisper. "The triplets saw and heard every word between you and

Zephyrus, but they mistrust all foreigners."

"He's an outsider," Bristol snapped. "How do we know he wasn't the one who axed our master? Now mount your horse, take your nasty dogs, and get out of our forest, Mr. Thimble."

Ivan wanted to correct the pronunciation of his name but decided not to bother.

"Pay them no mind," the cloak said. "They are a bitter trio and perhaps for good reasons, but they are unquestionably loyal and protective toward Zephyrus. The best Root-Underground communicators the Forest has, and that's no small advantage to our master."

Ivan stared from one birch to another. He thought they could use some lessons in good manners. He swallowed their insults because the cloak seemed to feel they had some redeeming value. Ivan felt a strong urge to reach up and tweak their peaked noses, but he held himself back, hearing his mother's words of warning. The same reason he hadn't kicked Dirk Mackle in his bum.

"Do you know who swung the Silver Axe at Zephyrus?" the cloak asked the birch trees.

"We all screamed frantically for help," the triplets chorused at once, "but no one came to drive the culprit away."

"This young lad came," the cloak replied, sounding almost smug.

"The axe wielder had his back to us. It was impossible to tell who he was through the fog," Winchester said.

"He wore a gray cloak, and a hood shadowed his face," Bristol added his opinion. "I could see nothing,"

Winchester's eyes darted back and forth. "Where

did that rolling fog come from so suddenly?"

"It was conjured by the surrounding trees so Zephyrus could blow a path for this lad to find him," replied the heated voice from the cloak. "You should've realized this."

Dorset raised an eyebrow—an arching mark appeared on the surface of his bark. "The attacker was tall, just like this outsider, and he was holding the Silver Axe in his very hands. We saw him strike Zephyrus three times."

All eyes glared at the lad.

"N-no," Ivan stuttered. "I-I didn't. I wouldn't harm—"

"That's plain ridiculous," said the cloak in a curt voice. "Dorset, you must send Fungoda a Root-Underground message *now* so he will expect us and release his sap. Sometimes it's a lengthy process, and we can't afford to lose time. Tell him what happened to his good friend Zephyrus, that he's been poisoned and has forced his own dormancy. Do this immediately."

"I will," Dorset answered at once.

"Why would anyone do such a horrible thing?" Winchester whined.

"It's unforgivable." Bristol rolled his eyes.

"Then contact the South Castle," the voice from the cloak demanded further. "Find and release the Emergency Underground Distress Signal that Zephyrus automatically sent you. Route it forward to Lord Graydon. Have him dispatch his garrisons without delay."

Dorset agreed to relay the message that would pass from root to root until it reached the castle.

"You know," Bristol said, "Fungoda is a most ill-tempered tree. He may not allow the lad near him or his precious sap."

The cloak snapped back. "He will not question the request if you let him know I accompany Ivan on this life-saving mission."

"But…" Dorset narrowed his eyes to slits, his brows angled at the interloper. "The Silver Axe stays with me. It's an Ancient Relic, illegal in outsider hands. That means you!"

"Oh, let's go, Ivan." The cloak's voice rose in volume and disgust. "There's no reasoning with these leafy knot-heads. We have a long journey ahead."

Ivan moved toward Bounty, mounting hurriedly. He eyed the axe propped against Dorset, feeling uneasy about leaving it exposed. Anyone wandering by could confiscate it.

With a squeeze of his legs, a tug on the reins, he encouraged Bounty to follow the road west.

"We are deeply grateful for your help," the cloak voiced humbly. "If Zephyrus dies, the entire Forest will be lost, as Zephyrus told you."

"How's that?" Ivan shifted in the saddle and looked back to be sure Alfred and Canute were following.

"The Forest will be overtaken by a dark evil that will enslave the people and creatures that live here. We would not recover until the time of a thousand years when peace visits upon the earth. This agreement was forged between Zephyrus and the High Intervener, our Forest's God, when the Great Transition occurred. I'll explain these things to you as we travel together. At the least, I owe you an explanation."

Ivan's head rattled with doubt and confusion as he

thought about the statement. *The High Intervener? The Great Transition?* It's a heavy burden to carry. An uncertain journey lay before him.

Chapter Three

The Long Dark Cloak

Ivan kneed his horse, anxious to be on his way and retrieve the sap that would heal Zephyrus. When the job was complete, he could search for Peter.

Bounty took off with a jolt, throwing clods of dirt and stones behind fast hooves.

The voice from the dark cloak yelled, "Slow down."

"We must hurry if we're to find Fungoda and save Zephyrus's life," he said while his own quest to find Peter burned in his heart.

"That's true, but there are people, creatures, and shy wildlife in the Forest that use this well-traveled road to go about their daily business. You'll dash over them if they step into your path."

What animals? There had been no signs of life. Ivan pulled back on the reins. He accepted the warning, knowing his beagles couldn't keep the fast pace for long.

"I think it's time I introduce myself," the cloak said. "My name is Sebastian."

"Oh," Ivan blurted. "So you're Sebastian. Zephyrus said I'd meet you on my travels."

"And so you have."

"Pleased to make your acquaintance, Sebastian,"

Ivan said formally, making a slight bow from his saddle. But to whom he spoke, he couldn't tell. "Who are you?"

"I'm the spirit of a man that's imbued in this cloak. A very old man, as you can hear by my crackling voice."

"I wouldn't know," Ivan said politely, "since I can't see your face."

"That could be disturbing. Would you feel better if I showed myself?"

"How would you do that?" Ivan raised his eyebrows, and they twitched.

"I will appear to you ghost-like, an apparition at first. After a few minutes, my horse and I will become solid, just like you."

Ivan gave a bemused shake of his head. "Okay. You make me nervous talking behind my back."

"So be it." Sebastian chuckled softly. There was a sudden tug on the cloak's front hem and a pulling on the hood. Ivan slowed his horse to a walk, wondering if someone was yanking off his clothes.

A misty, ochre-colored apparition separated from the garment that lay over Ivan's shoulders, followed by a swishing sound. An elderly man with a gaunt whiskered face materialized, sitting none too steady on a ghostly horse.

"There. How's that?" Sebastian slapped his thin hands together. He straightened his tan-colored tunic, tugged up his leggings while his face broke into a wrinkled grin. Sebastian swept his thin fingers through wiry white hair that went in all directions. He pushed his spectacles up over a slight bend in his nose, while a look of satisfaction registered on his face.

Glancing from the old man to the cloak that he wore and back to Sebastian again, Ivan squinted, and then he, too, grinned. "That was an amazing trick."

"Now you see how it's done. My spirit resides in the garment that you wear, and when needed, I force myself out along with my horse into the open. Within moments, my form solidifies, and here I am. Likewise, when I want to disappear, I dissolve, so to speak, and return into the Long Dark Cloak."

Ivan rounded his eyes, his mouth opened. "I've never seen anything like it in my life."

"Most people haven't." The sly spirit wiggled his bushy eyebrows.

Ivan stared curiously at Sebastian, watching as the wispy apparition solidified more and more. Gray, watery eyes behind wire-rimmed glasses met with Ivan's gaze. The spirit, now a fully recognizable man, smiled mischievously.

Bounty turned his muzzle toward Sebastian and shook his head, snorting.

"Stuck-up," Ivan murmured.

They rode side by side, silent for a time until Ivan could absorb the strange phenomenon.

"The Forest is in your debt, Ivan Kimble. You are very generous to help our most-esteemed Zephyrus. He is our master, our lawgiver, our peacekeeper."

"Anyone would do the same," Ivan said, though he wasn't sure. The bizarre situation hit him right then. "In my world, outside this Forest, only people talk. How can a cloak and a tree have thought and reasoning while speaking with a spirit inside them? What's more, I couldn't see your eyes, and yet you must have sight and ears to hear. Better than mine, it seems."

Sebastian threw back his head with a whoop of laughter. "These are things I plan to explain as we travel. The oddities won't seem so out of place when I'm finished."

Ivan mulled this over silently and then spoke, "First, you must tell me where I can find the free firewood."

"What? Why would you want firewood?"

"I'm looking for my brother Peter Kimble, and I've heard he was last seen loading wood into a wagon. I don't know where else to begin, but that seems like the most logical place."

"Oh, I see." The spirit brushed the sleeve of his tunic with the side of his hand. "The location is northwest of Zephyrus. We offer the wood to veteran families for the coming winter. It's our way of thanking them for their service for protecting us."

"Do you know where I can find Peter?"

"I heard Zephyrus tell you we could search for him on our journey. We'll ask everyone if they've seen him. If he's here, we'll find him." Pressing his lips into a thin line, Sebastian averted his head and stared down the road.

Ivan drew a deep breath. "Did you know my brother?"

Sebastian pulled back on the reins until he brought his old mare to a halt. "I've met him many, many times."

Bounty stopped, too.

"You have?" Ivan exclaimed.

"There's not much to tell. Peter visited Zephyrus, and they talked. It's as Zephyrus has told you, Fungoda will answer all your questions."

"But…why?" Disappointed, Ivan's anger crept up, but he forced himself to stay calm, remembering his parents' teaching about patience and good manners. *Why hadn't Peter come home? Where is he now—in the Forest or traveling?*

"My place is in the sanctuary," Sebastian said. "I seldom leave, not since a decade ago. You and I are together today because of our mission to save Zephyrus. I do say, Peter came often from the South Castle where he stayed, and here he met with Zephyrus. They were famously close. There's much to explain. In time you'll understand it all."

"But…"

"Please, my young friend, be patient." Sebastian threw his arm forward. "We need to make haste."

"That means he's okay…he must have amnesia, just as my neighbor said. Where do I go to find him? Does he still live in the South Castle?"

Sebastian turned a grim face toward Ivan. "All things will be revealed in time."

Ivan bit his lip. Taking a deep breath, his eyes blurred, but he forced his tears away.

"Now, we must hurry."

Staring far into the distance, Ivan thought, *Peter is somewhere in this vast forest. He is alive.*

With that, Sebastian and his horse took off. Ivan followed, smiling, feeling hopeful once more.

Canute and Alfred raced ahead with their tongues hanging out. They seemed only too glad to run, leaving the strange tree that wailed and moaned. After a time, the dogs stopped and barked and growled between the roots of a rotted tree stump. The tree's decayed wood spread over a pile of gray rocks.

Something dark and slender like a weasel paused a moment and then quickly slipped under the stump. The creature had a creamy mane and matching tuft at the end of its long tail. Small rounded ears were set back on its hairless pink face. The beagles began woofing—more of a baying.

"What's that?" Ivan yelled.

Stopping abruptly, Bounty reared. The dogs scratched and pawed at the ground where the strange animal had disappeared.

"Alfred, Canute, stop!"

"It's a harmless fra-hak," Sebastian went on to explain. "He eats bugs, snails, and his favorite, stag beetles. He also consumes fragments of wood. Just how his stomach manages to digest it, I wouldn't know."

"I've never heard of a fra-hak," Ivan said. But he'd never heard an oak tree cry out in pain either or had a black cloak guide him to another tree with healing sap.

"There are many things that will mystify you in our woodland home." His companion frowned.

Ivan reminded as they continued their journey, "You were going to explain some things about the Forest." The surrounding trees seemed to shift their broad, leafy crowns and watch the travelers pass by on Zephyrus Barkay Road. Ivan cast a worried look. *Or am I just imagining this?*

"Yes, yes, and I shall." Sebastian fumbled. "It's just knowing where to begin and how much to tell, because…well, it can be a bit overwhelming if consumed in one big lump." He hesitated a moment as though struggling to collect his thoughts.

Ivan raised his brow, wondering how it could be more bizarre.

"Well…" Sebastian took a quick breath and exhaled. "I was a friend and trusted noble advisor to Zephyrus when he was king of a now-abandoned city called Helvaka."

"Then Zephyrus was once a man just as you were?" Ivan rubbed the back of his neck and frowned. "Where would I find this city? Was it located in Southern England?"

"Yes," Sebastian said, his gray eyes twinkling. "It's part of our Forest, some distance from here. If we were to continue west on Barkay Road and then turn north at the junction of the western ridge, we'd come upon the once great but now ruined kingdom."

"What happened?"

Sighing ruefully, Sebastian replied, "The city fell when Tereus and Zephyrus's armies divided and declared war on each other, just as Zephyrus has told you. You know a country cannot survive if it divides on itself? Well, they fought a fierce battle, driven to annihilate each other."

"Why?"

"It was several years after Zephyrus was proclaimed king. He inherited the throne from his father, you know."

"I've never read anything about it." They'd been riding for some time, and Ivan's rear was sore, his body weary, and his head throbbing.

A distant rumble reminded the travelers that ragged-edged rain clouds were collecting in the far west, moving steadily toward them. Sebastian looked worried. "I believe we should find shelter from the storm soon, or we could both be drenched within the hour. It's too dangerous to ride when it rains."

"I think we should go on regardless of the weather," Ivan said with urgency in his voice. "A little rain can't hurt us. We must get the sap from Fungoda and return to Zephyrus right away. The sooner we complete our mission, the sooner I can search for Peter."

"We'll see. Maybe the storm will be only an irritating sprinkle. I could probably survive that."

"Survive?"

"I don't do well when I'm wet." Sebastian threw Ivan a sad, defeated look. "I seem to lose my inherent powers of appearing and disappearing."

"And your powers to heal?"

"That is a fine gift to have, isn't it?" Sebastian wiggled his eyebrows.

Reality and truth must have left me since I entered the Forest. Ivan shook his head. Shyness often prevented him from speaking up, but he recognized common sense when he heard it. At the moment, he seemed to have almost none.

Yet here he was, listening to a tale about a fallen city from an apparition who'd been a dark piece of cloth only an hour before. He felt himself blush at the absurdity. *Am I actually that gullible, like the students at school, or my neighbor, Mule?*

Ivan massaged his temple, considering for a moment. Curiosity won him over. "Then how did Zephyrus become a Kingwood Oak? Did he die, and his spirit was reborn into a tree?"

"I was just getting to that." Sebastian waved his hand as if to grant him time. "When Zephyrus's father died of an infection, about 900 AD, Tereus, being the firstborn son, held the right to inherit the kingdom. This was the accepted method of succession, you understand. But in this case, it would've been a disaster."

"Then that means…" Ivan gasped in disbelief. "Zephyrus is over a thousand years old. How can that be?"

"Well, let me refigure my calculations. I could be off a few decades." The old man scratched his whiskers, mumbling. "What year is this?" Ivan answered that it was September 1947. Sebastian counted on his fingers, obviously struggling with his subtraction. "You're right. We're both over a thousand years old. Who'd think so much time has gone by so quickly?" He smiled and winked.

Ivan whistled softly.

"Zephyrus and Tereus vied to occupy the throne after their father died," Sebastian explained once more. "Naturally, this caused conflict between them. The majority of citizens, laborers, tradesmen, and merchants knew Tereus was vicious and greedy. They recognized his tyrannical plans to pillage their homeland. And so, the people pledged their loyalties to Zephyrus. Furious to be cast out, Tereus commandeered the most ruthless, power-hungry men to join his army."

"I wouldn't want to be king." Ivan frowned. "Too many enemies waiting to do you in."

"So it would seem." Sebastian tipped his head. "Well, the inevitable happened. The brothers gathered their armies and went to war against each other. Both demanded the right to rule the Kingdom of Helvaka and the Forest's incredible wealth." He gave a proud lift of his chin.

"I see."

"They fought a terrible, bloody battle. Even now, I shudder remembering the senseless loss."

"What happened?" Ivan asked. "Did Zephyrus kill his brother and defeat his army?" He couldn't imagine going to battle against his own brother.

A zigzag pattern of lightning flashed, brightening the entire western sky. It was like a crescendo before some great announcement.

Sebastian's face tightened. Drawing a quick breath, he plunged on. "I'm considering how to tell you this, but there's only one truth of how the events unfolded. I was there, so I know. We discovered the city's supplies were running low, the royal treasury dwindling quickly. The two armies were evenly matched, and after seventy-seven days of warfare, with countless dead and wounded, a powerful and, let's say, an unusual intervention occurred. Here's where the story gets a bit sticky." Sebastian hunched his shoulders, sounding apologetic.

"What happened?"

"The High Intervener came forth and put an end to the war. It was finished. All the weaponry grew fiery hot and dropped from the hands of the soldiers, untouchable for a hundred years." Sebastian stopped talking, bending his head slowly toward Ivan as though waiting for his response.

After some moments, Ivan said, "I assume the High Intervener is God...of sorts?"

"He is, precisely." Sebastian clapped his hands once. "That's the Forest's name for He who intervenes to help us."

"I've never taken the myth of God seriously myself." Ivan removed his hat and ran his fingers through his hair. He scowled, wondering what kind of fable Sebastian was dumping on him. *Does he think I'm that naïve?*

"You must believe what is right for you," Sebastian said. "I wouldn't try to influence your belief. God is someone you find in your own personal search, in your own time of need."

"How did Zephyrus become a great oak?" Ivan asked again.

Sebastian held up his hand in a halting gesture. "I'm getting to that." He took a shuddering breath. "The High Intervener did the right thing. The fighting couldn't go on, or an entire kingdom would have perished under the sword. Neither side could have claimed victory."

A cool, moist breeze blew through a green glade. Limbs shook overhead, scraping against each other, creaking, and groaning, while leaves tumbled and scattered about the ground.

Glancing over the tops of trees, Sebastian continued, "It was proclaimed by the High Intervener that Zephyrus Barkay's spirit would reside in a magnificent Kingwood Oak after his natural life had ended. He would rule the above world of the Forest with love, fair-mindedness, and his keen sense of justice. And it was fated that Tereus, his wicked brother, would remain a man and rule the fiery underworld in any manner he pleased.

"I see." Ivan rubbed his temples.

"I don't expect you to believe this simply because I told you."

"And you...how did you become part of this story?"

"I was chosen by Zephyrus, as were five other men in his kingdom, to continue as his advisors in our new roles of inanimate objects—each imbued with our individual spirits and special gifts."

"Why did Zephyrus choose your spirit to reside in a cloak?"

"Well, I suppose I could've become anything, but Zephyrus selected his own traveling cloak for my spirit-residence. I reckon familiarity and convenience were probably the best reasons I can think of." Sebastian chortled softly. "I could've inhabited worse objects."

Ivan threw back his head with a burst of laughter as he, too, thought of the possibilities. "How about a crooked stick?"

"How about a loo?"

"How about a troll?"

"How about a fra-hak?"

By now, both Sebastian and Ivan were holding their bellies from laughing. Ivan wiped the tears from his eyes and felt more comfortable in his companion's company than he had since their journey began. He couldn't remember laughing like this in a very long time. Only Peter made him laugh this way.

"Now, let's hurry," Sebastian said with a wave to the west. "The sky is turning ornerier by the minute."

Chapter Four

The Goddess Anna-Iza

Sebastian turned his horse from Barkay Road, veering diagonally to the southwest where it connected with Sheepherders' Path Road. "This should be faster, although the ride may be a little rougher in places," he said. "We can find shelter from the storm if need be."

"Wait," Ivan shouted. "I saw someone peeking through the bushes just off the main road." Twisting in his saddle, he glanced back at a copse of holly bushes. "It's a young lady." He was excited because she was the first *real* person he'd seen since he entered the Forest. "She's standing alone, looking abandoned. There, Sebastian, do you see her?"

"I believe I do, yes."

Ivan raised himself in the stirrups, straining to see into the thickets. The girl wore a woolen, royal blue traveling cloak that covered her long skirt. Soft, auburn curls beneath the cloak's hood framed her face. She stood motionless, but her intense eyes followed his every movement. His breath caught in his throat, his words were scarcely a whisper, "She's beautiful."

"That she is." Sebastian glanced at the girl in the thickets. "She's the High Goddess Anna-Iza."

"The Forest has its own goddess?" Ivan lifted his dark brow. "We should go back and check if she's in danger."

"Anna-Iza doesn't travel alone. Her retinue of Twelve Protective Goddesses is surely standing nearby," Sebastian assured him. "All are beautiful with pleasing natures."

Ivan's heart beat a little faster. "Is she costumed for a special event, a party of some kind?"

"Party? Why I don't think so. The goddesses always dress that way."

The lovely girl in blue was lost from sight. Ivan reluctantly turned. "Are you sure she doesn't need our help?"

Sebastian gave a little laugh. "I suppose it's a natural question for a handsome lad to ask about a stunning young lady. Did you see what stood next to our Anna-Iza?"

"It was a-a light-colored horse, wasn't it?"

"Certainly not an ordinary horse. It's Anna-Iza's personal *flying silver stallion*. Had it stepped out from the cover of bushes, you would've seen an extraordinary animal with a huge pair of wings."

"Wings? A horse that flies?" Ivan's voice pitched. "I thought they were creatures of myth from long ago. Are you sure about this?"

"They are real." Sebastian grinned and nodded. "I believe the girls stable thirteen of these grand beasts, one for each of them. Gifts from her gods. Her circle of goddesses is quite unique, you see."

"I'll say," Ivan whispered. "How did they become part of the Forest?"

"They were invited to join Zephyrus's kingdom soon after the Great Transition. That's how it's referred to when Zephyrus's spirit went into the mighty oak, and he became the Forest's new ruler." Ivan looked at him, waiting for more.

The spirit lifted his face to the sky. "I think we'd better leave this story for later."

Disappointed not to hear the full account, Ivan took a moment to gaze into a long grassy lawn bordered by woodland and a small flowing stream. Wishing to see the lovely Anna-Iza again, he scanned the area but didn't see her. Ahead, a small herd of fallow deer looked back at him with dark, worried eyes. They moved slowly in the shadows of the trees. Ivan was glad his beagles were far ahead drinking from the stream, and they didn't disturb the animals.

A few raindrops fell on Ivan's nose, sliding down his cheeks. The uneasy quiet since they'd left Zephyrus clung in the air like dried fungus on a rock. It was as though the entire forest grieved for the great Kingwood Oak.

"The High Goddess has many special gifts," Sebastian said, as though suspecting where Ivan's interest lay. "The most remarkable one is that she can tell what kind of person you are with only a single kiss."

"Aah, then I'd like to volunteer and take her test," Ivan said with enthusiasm, puckering his lips and smacking them. He grinned broadly, flashing straight white teeth. "It's what faery tales are made of."

Sebastian chuckled. "I'm afraid it can't happen that way, my friend. Nothing could develop between a goddess and a mortal man. It's forbidden to put your hands upon them, especially a High Goddess. Anna-Iza is untouchable."

"I'm sorry to hear that." Ivan cast down his eyes,

his bottom lip stuck out. He guided Bounty through a dry ravine cluttered with brush and dried reeds. Field mice scattered across the rocky bed and hid in their secret holes.

Sebastian must've seen Ivan's sad expression. "What's wrong?"

He shrugged, turning his face away.

"Tell me, what is it? I can't help you unless I know."

"Here…this," he mumbled, sweeping his hand in an arc.

Sebastian looked around, adjusting his glasses on his sharp nose. "What?"

"I don't know what I'm doing on this journey. I came to find my brother and to take him home with me."

Reaching for Bounty's reins, the old man pulled Ivan's horse to a halt. "I'm sorry about delaying your plans. You're so young, and if I might say, you seem an unusually somber person. Isn't your life a happy one?"

Ivan shifted uneasily in his saddle. No one had ever asked him if his life was happy. He pressed his lips together, not knowing how to answer.

"Your feelings are safe with me."

Lowering his head, Ivan felt a need to share his deepest thoughts. He was sure he could trust Sebastian not to make fun of him.

"It's lonely on the farm all by myself. That's why I need to find Peter. He makes me laugh with his stories and larking about. He was always there to look after me and be sure I was safe. We did everything together."

"What about your mum and dad?"

"They died nearly two years ago in a train accident

outside London. It was a terrible time, and I'll never forget the pain of it. Peter was off to war."

"Then you've been all alone, doing the farm work by yourself?" Sebastian's voice wobbled with compassion. "No relatives?"

Shaking his head, Ivan answered, "My parents were Russian nobles. They fled to escape the tyranny of the Bolsheviks and other political renegades fighting for power. They came to Southern England when they were very young, always looking over their shoulders for their enemies.

"You were born in Russia?"

"No. Peter and I were born here." He glanced quickly at Sebastian, wiping his eyes with the heel of his hand. "Sorry...I didn't realize I was tearing up. How childish of me."

"It's understandable. Don't scold yourself for grieving over your losses. I'd behave the same way and have done just that many, many times in my long life."

Sniffing, Ivan gave a feeble smile. "Thank you. I think we should go now."

"Were you upset because I told you about Anna-Iza and that she's unavailable?"

Ivan sighed. "I came here with high expectations but encounter delays and more problems. I only want to find Peter and go home."

They started slowly down the gravel road, staying close to each other. "Perhaps things will become clearer as time passes," Sebastian said, "but I'm here to help you however I can."

Ivan rubbed his sore back and gave a brief grimace. "Why is it forbidden to put your hands on the goddesses? It seems a peculiar code to live by."

"You'll taint them, I guess." Sebastian brought his bony shoulders together as though at a loss. "I've never asked the question before but have only accepted their ways."

Removing his cap, Ivan shoved it into the cloak's deep pocket. He raked his fingers through his hair several times, trying to understand. It seemed nothing was going as he'd hoped or expected.

"Don't despair. You may meet Anna-Iza again. I'm sure she's wondering why I'm here in solid form with my cloak draped over your shoulders. It's a rare occurrence, as I've mentioned. She's sure to report to Zephyrus that there's a stranger in the Forest. Then she, too, will discover that Zephyrus is seriously wounded and sleeps to avoid pain."

Ivan and Sebastian moved slowly on the angled road to the southwest as the gray sky turned darker. "Where's the wildlife?" Ivan squinted into the depth of trees. "The rabbits, foxes, and deer? I don't hear any birds, either. Where are the soldiers? I thought the garrisons patrolled the Forest."

"Humph! That's just the problem." Sebastian tightened his scrawny legs around his horse. "Absolutely everyone, including the Forest's servants, is at the South Castle where Lord Graydon is hosting his Annual Fall Event of Feasting and Celebration."

"It's a special Forest holiday, then?"

"Of sorts, you could say. It's the castle's competition for the Shield of Honor. You know the fun kind. Our own garrisons participate in games of jousting, mock war battles, archery contests, and sword fighting amongst the teams. The spectators and the soldiers talk about it for a full year before the event and then brag until the following year. Now, all communication has been interrupted in our Root-Underground system, and there's no way to send an alarm for help."

Ivan stroked his forehead. "You send messages through the tree roots?"

"It's one of the fastest and most reliable," Sebastian said, "except for now."

The road had narrowed. Beyond the trees, Ivan took in the wide meadow dotted with bushes and violet heather scattered in gay patches of color. Then the heavy clouds returned, bullying away the sunlight.

"Watch out for the fallen branch just in front of you," Sebastian pointed, giving a nod of his head. "It could cause Bounty a nasty stumble."

Carefully, Ivan maneuvered his horse around the broken limb. Its leaves, bright green on their front, almost fresh, had not yet curled. Canute inspected the leafy limb with a sniff. Finding nothing to eat, he woofed and moved on.

"Wait up a moment." Sebastian half-stood in his horse's stirrups. "Look into that glade. What do you see?"

"It looks like a violent struggle took place there, maybe ten or twelve hours ago." Ivan moved his head from side to side. "*Pee-whew!*" His hand shot up to cover his nose. "Something smells terrible."

"Must be that huge pile of scat." Sebastian leaned to the side of his horse to examine the ground.

"See this." Ivan reluctantly dropped his hand from his nose. "The soil has deep gouges, and rocks have been pushed aside. There's been recent damage to this elm tree and several more broken branches. What do you think happened?"

Sebastian stopped his horse and looked around for clues. "The trees have shut down, showing no faces. They're either unable or too frightened to communicate. We'll have to report this to the castle. If only a functioning tree could send an urgent message for us."

Suddenly a flock of strange, ungainly birds lumbered from the edge of the thickets, squawking in a most terrifying way. Blue and white rings circled their elongated necks. Other than thick orange legs, they were unremarkable in their brownish-gray plumage.

Ivan gulped. "What are they?"

"They're called kaleido-birds. I expect you'll learn why in a few moments."

The more colorful male made a frightful hissing sound. His thick beak opened wide showing a sharp point. Large, well-lashed eyes looked suspicious as the bird tipped his head this way and that.

"They look like a rhea with three toes and tough legs." Ivan pointed. "And they are large, like an ostrich. Look at that tail." Feathers of green, citrus orange, and yellow lifted, fanning bands of color. Spellbound, Ivan questioned, "Is his display a signal of defense against intruders like us? Are we trespassing in kaleido-bird territory?"

Sebastian shook his head. "Don't worry, they're quite harmless. Fetters, this is our guest, Ivan Kimble. His farm borders our Forest."

This seemed to put the big bird at ease…somewhat. "The male kaleido-bird is named for his unique tail," Sebastian explained with a wave of his hand. "Tiny pin feathers vibrate nervously, causing the colors to change by the second."

Ivan returned a faint smile.

"What do you want, Fetters?" Sebastian's voice was edged with impatience. "We really are in a hurry."

What have I wandered into? Ivan wiped his brow. *Is this a children's book fantasy?*

Sebastian quickly explained, "We're on a mission for Zephyrus. He's been severely injured, and we must get help."

"Who would do such a thing?" Fetters rapidly blinked his large eyes.

"We don't know," Sebastian said. "But the culprit will be found and punished severely."

Ivan fought to calm his excited horse. "Whoa, boy!" The animal shook his light-colored mane, raising his hoofs high. "It's more than just the noise. It's also the putrid smell in this area. Notice how wide Bounty's nostrils are and running with mucus."

Sebastian's brow wrinkled. "The pile of scat?"

Patting his mount's quivering neck, Ivan calmed him. "It reeks of urine, a peculiar stench that's causing him to behave in this way."

"I can't imagine." Sebastian tapped his nose. "But then, I possess no ability to smell."

"Your good fortune," Ivan mumbled.

Fetters let out another rasping squawk just as Ivan brought his animal under control. "If your horse is this flighty, you will never leave the Forest alive."

"What's that supposed to mean?" Ivan tightened his face and decided he didn't appreciate the bird's poor manners.

Sebastian's patience fizzled. "Oh, shut up, Fetters. We're on an urgent quest, and you're wasting our valuable time."

"That's just it, don't you see?" The bird shrieked and flapped his wide wings. "I went before Zephyrus, but he wouldn't wake. It's too early for the Big Sleep, isn't it?"

"Why did you want an audience with him?" Sebastian said.

"It's like I'm trying to tell you." Fetters' voice shook. "Some hens are missing. We've been searching but can't find them anywhere."

"How many?" Sebastian swiveled his head around, examining nearby bushes.

One of the hens ventured from behind the thickets, answering boldly, "Eight of my sisters in two nights' time." Her neck stretched long, showing her bright blue and white bands. Other females, peeking through the shrubbery, bobbed their heads up and down in agreement.

"The bird-napping, did it happen here?" Ivan pointed at the clods of grass, the bruised and broken trees.

"Yes, we believe so," the same female answered. "That's why we're here looking for clues. Just ahead, we've found splattered blood and a lot of unattached feathers. We're certain this is where our sisters were captured."

"The hens disappear at night, then?" Ivan asked.

"That's right," volunteered another female. "But last night, I heard huge wings flapping overhead and muffled grunts. Something large and dark flew over our colony."

Another hen batted her large eyes. "I think I heard two giant beasts."

"I'm not certain," the first conceded. "It could've

been two."

"When we took a headcount this morning," Fetters raised his voice. "More hens were gone, snatched right under our very beaks."

"It does seem suspicious." Sebastian thought on this a moment. "Have you contacted Commander Simon and his garrison or Commanders Gifford and Greendyn about this matter? The mystery of missing persons—or birds, falls into their department."

"I went to talk to Zephyrus about it." Fetters raised his wings and flapped them. "But he sleeps soundly, so I'm looking for the soldiers to help me."

"There's a good reason," Sebastian exclaimed. "I'm surprised you don't remember."

"Remember?"

"Why, it's the South Castle's Celebration and Competition for the Shield of Honor. All garrisons and, indeed, nearly every person and creature of the Forest is there right now, sitting comfortably in the bleachers watching the games."

"Oh, poof." Fetters shook his head. "I'd forgotten. We don't much care for the Games of Battle at the castle, so we never attend."

"We really must be on our way." Sebastian stroked his horse's neck with impatience. "And Fetters, keep trying to send messages to the garrisons. Ivan and I will notify anyone we chance upon about this most unfortunate situation."

"It was that nasty dragon!" Fetters blurted. "Zello's been sneaking into our feeding ground at night, plucking out my prize hens and eating them in one gulp."

"What in bloody blazes are you saying?"

Sebastian's face twisted from shock.

The other hens gasped. "Do you mean Zello is eating our sisters?" a stricken female said. "The South Castle's dragon has turned into a-a carnivore?"

"Well," Fetters said with a snap, "he's a dragon, ain't he? Dragons eat meat, don't they? That means helpless kaleido-birds."

Shivering with fear, the females fluttered for cover.

"You are mistaken," Sebastian said with forced calmness. "Zello would never eat one of the Forest's own. Look here before you go accusing him. He's a hero. One of Lord Graydon's most revered and trusted creatures. It's simply not possible."

"Even good dragons can go bad." Fetters stomped his large foot for emphasis.

The beagles jumped and then hunkered onto their bellies.

Stretching, Ivan flexed his long legs. *I've quite had enough. I don't know about kaleido-birds or missing hens or carnivorous dragons.* "Let's go," Ivan said, jerking his head.

Fetters stood gawking, blinking back obvious disappointment.

"One last thing." Sebastian wagged his finger at the broken trees. "There's been some serious damage here. Contact the Forest faeries to come immediately and seal all wounds. That should stop any insect invasion."

Lumbering away, Fetters muttered bitterly.

As they continued their ride down Sheepherder's Road, Ivan asked Sebastian, "Do you believe Zello was responsible for the missing hens?"

"No, no, this is not the doing of our illustrious dragon. Nor would it be the female dragons, Jezebel and Hemple. Lord Graydon feeds them well enough at the castle."

The realization of Ivan's incredible situation returned to smack him. A bird-eating dragon and little flying people with squeaky voices and sparkling magic wands.

"So there are three dragons, then?" he asked meekly. "And faeries inhabit the Forest as well?"

"But of course. Where else would these unique birds and mages go if it weren't for Zephyrus's generous invitation to live unharmed in our Forest? Do you think the rest of the world would welcome such oddities without making a sham of them? There are very few safe havens left on any continent for the unusual." He gave Ivan a sympathetic look. "Are you all right?"

Returning a wry shrug, Ivan shook his head. "This is too much for me. Tell me, am I under some kind of hallucination from something I've inhaled?"

Sebastian laughed lightly. "I can understand your puzzlement. Most of the time, nothing dangerous happens here. But Zephyrus has been attacked. His very life is in question, as is the safety of the Forest. We've never experienced an interruption like this, when our trees couldn't send messages to each other. I simply can't explain these strange and unfortunate happenings except to say that the culprits' timing has been totally to their advantage."

"How do you mean?"

"Well, *they* knew the Forest lacked any protection or safeguards," Sebastian replied. "All the soldiers are playing out their prowess at the castle."

"They? Do you believe there's more than just the

axe-wielder then?"

"I'm sure of it." Sebastian scrunched his face. "The man in the gray cloak is just a minor player in a network of dark forces that have gathered for the purpose of taking over the Forest."

"I don't know about your dark forces, or your communication system, or about dragons or faeries." Ivan scratched his head, pausing to pick a worm from his hair that had probably fallen from a tree.

The travelers moved on. The good news was that the rain had held off.

"I'm not sure I trust that bird," Ivan said. "Did the missing hens tire of him and simply wander away?"

"Ah, Fetters is all right. Sometimes he's a bit witless, dizzy—even vain—but he has his place in our Forest. Someone is abducting his females, and it most definitely is *not* Zello."

"How can you be so sure?"

"I've known Zello since he was as small as a sand lizard. He was a gift to Zephyrus from the Gods of Mount Olympus. It was their way of thanking him for accepting the Order of Goddesses into his Forest. The same order that Anna-Iza belongs to yet today."

Ivan called his beagles and urged Bounty into a trot. Thinking about his own deficiencies and lack of courage, he frowned.

He knew he came up short.

Chapter Five

Shelter from the Storm

Ivan rubbed his tired eyes. When his stomach growled, he pressed his hand against it. He worried whether he and Sebastian would ever reach their destination. Canute and Alfred lagged behind, tongues dangling out. They were weary of travel. Wanting to eat and drink, they snarled at each other.

The sky grew darker and more threatening as the afternoon crept on.

Ivan was about to remind his guide he hadn't eaten that morning when Sebastian turned to look at him. "There's a hamlet for The Aged and Destitute about a mile from here. We'll chance a visit to a retired commander of the South Castle's Garrison. I'm sure ol' Tom Shiffert will welcome our company, especially your beagles."

"I would like that." Things were looking a little brighter in spite of the disagreeable weather. They passed rolling green hills scattered with cows, sheep, a pair of fine-looking workhorses, and even a few donkeys. Clusters of whitewashed cottages and farms dotted the landscape to the west.

"We'd better move faster, Old Bones." Sebastian clicked his tongue and shook the bridle.

The beagles followed as they sped down the trail

crossing small hills of poor acidic soil devoid of trees. Gorse grew thick. Their yellow flowers were nearly gone with the coming of fall, but the colorful Dartford warbler still perched on the spiky thorns calling to the rain clouds.

It began to drizzle. The Forest critters, wise in their knowledge of weather, hurried to seek shelter. Several rabbits scampered away, heath lizards darted under shrubs, and, to his surprise, a wild boar chewing on beech masts looked up blandly and grunted. At last, Ivan saw more wildlife and felt reassured.

"It's turning dark and growing late," Ivan said. "How will we get the healing potion from Fungoda and give it to Zephyrus yet tonight?" He was discouraged that the storm would delay them, especially if they were to be Commander Shiffert's guests. If the Commander invited them in, surely they would have to impose on him and stay the night. A short moan escaped Ivan's throat.

"We can't possibly travel to Fungoda in the dark." Sebastian pressed his lips together. "The untimely interruption by Fetters and the coming storm will prolong our journey until early morning, I'm afraid."

"B-but…I'd hoped to find Peter, and we'd be home by late afternoon."

"I'm sorry. That's impossible." Sebastian's bushy eyebrows rose. "Do you have someone who will care for your farm animals and do your chores?"

"Yes." He sighed with disappointment. "My neighbor knows of a lad who will milk the cows and feed my cats and chickens. I'd hoped we'd be done with this, and I could find Peter right off. I don't know how long the lad can stay…"

"I am sorry the journey isn't as you planned. Perhaps it will improve when we arrive at our evening destination. It's possible old Shiffert will have some information for you about Peter."

Ivan gave a single nod, feeling his chest constrict.

Riding on, Sebastian pointed. "Ahead, past that grove of lime and fruit trees, there's a southerly entrance into Hurst-on-the-Vert."

Drops of rain replaced the misty drizzle of late afternoon, while the wind skittered through the tree branches. Water beaded on Ivan's eyebrows, and long drips slid down his cheek and onto his jacket collar.

"We've arrived none too early. The drenching rain is only minutes away." Sebastian's prediction proved accurate. "Turn here on this gravel road, and we'll follow through until we reach the first cottage."

Approaching a tall, open, wrought iron gate, Ivan squinted through his wet eyelashes to read the weathered old sign:

Welcome to Hurst-on-the-Vert
Community of the Aged and Destitute
No Swearing Permitted

"Hurst means *wood* in Anglo-Saxon, and *vert* is green, or an enclosure of vegetation—in private hands, I believe," Ivan said. "Our teacher, Mrs. Hambuckle, explained this to the students."

"That's right," Sebastian replied at once. "The community includes an old brick Norman manor, part of a long and enduring history of the Norman Conquest more than nine-hundred years ago."

"We're studying King William's invasion of England in school." Ivan pulled the Long Dark Cloak closer to his neck.

"Ah, yes," Sebastian responded. "A rather large portion of the Forest was granted to the Graydon family in 1079 in return for Knight Wallace Graydon's brave fighting service." Snorting, Sebastian added, "What King William didn't know was that Knight Wallace was not on his side. He did everything he could to sabotage the foreign intrusion."

"I know. The date is posted on the sign at the entrance to the Forest."

"Oh, is it really?" Sebastian glanced over the rims of his rain-spotted eyeglasses. "I didn't know they advertised such an ancient bit of history there."

Ivan chuckled. "You have to get out of the sanctuary more." His companion grinned.

"After we pass this parade of old oaks..." Sebastian leaned forward, his open palm held above his head as if testing the rain. "You'll see the stately Harold Manor that sits atop a large knoll."

Ivan caught an enticing aroma, like something delicious to eat. Alfred and Canute must've smelled it, too, for they bolted from their slow pace and dashed ahead.

Chestnut and willow trees screened the cottages from view while white columns of smoke twirled from chimneys. The smoky whiffs brought back a pleasant memory of his farm. He was homesick.

As they approached, a faint voice called through the trees.

"Tie your horses near the first cottage and hurry if you don't want to get soaked." Though the voice was vague in the drizzling rain, it was obvious it belonged to a young lad.

Dark clouds burst open, and rain poured steadily

down. The boy stood waiting under an old oak by the hitching post already drenched to his skin.

"You staying for dinner, sirs? With Commander Shiffert?" The boy, about seven or eight, yelled through cupped hands around his mouth. "The commander said he was expecting company. You must be it."

"Well, I-I don't know," came Ivan's startled answer. He was about to ask if he—they—would be intruding on another dinner guest when the boy grabbed the horses' reins and reached to stroke Bounty's wet nose.

"I'll take your horses and stable them with our ponies. What's his name?"

"Bounty." Ivan dismounted. "This is Sebastian, and my name is Ivan."

"Yes, sir. I live up in the big house." The boy waved his arm vigorously toward the brick manor that Sebastian pointed out earlier. "My name is Colin. Your dogs can go in the cottage, even if they're wet. The commander loves dogs like I do. They're beagles, aren't they?"

"They are indeed," Ivan said, impressed.

"What are their names, then?" He stooped down with a happy grin to pet them. The lad didn't seem to mind the pelting rain through the branches. He swept the wetness away from his face.

Ivan introduced his pets.

"Oh!" Colin's eyes opened wide. "You named them after early Kings of England. King Canute was a Dane who ruled all of England once, even Denmark and Norway in the eleventh century. I learned about him in my history lessons. Up there." Colin turned to the large house on the hill again.

"You live way up there?" Ivan pulled the cloak's hood over his head, thinking it would be wise to get out of the downpour.

"Yes, sir, I'm a servant to the Harold manor. Me and Martin. We're both orphans, you know. So we have a guardianship."

"I see," Ivan said, feeling a bit sorry for him.

"Go on in." Colin swung his free hand at the door. Then the small boy, with horses in tow, moved toward the stables. "I'll start a fire in your cottage, so it'll be nice and warm by the time you go to bed," he yelled over his shoulder.

Ivan and Sebastian stepped up onto the stone stoop, ducking under the overhang. Several times Sebastian knocked the metal ring against the door, shaped like a dragon in flight.

"Oh, my!" Tom Shiffert cried, easing the door open. "Sebastian, you finally came to see me. I've been looking forward to your visit for a very long time. Come in out of the rain now."

Ivan reached to take the commander's extended hand. "I'm Ivan Kimble, sir."

"Aye." Tom glanced down. His heavy-lidded brown eyes stared at Canute. "I'm happy to see you brought Roman, too. Oh! There are two beagles." His bushy white eyebrows came together.

The dogs dashed into the warm cottage, where a blazing fire sparked in the large fireplace sending cinders up the chimney. Ivan and Sebastian followed. Just then, the rain thundered down, pounding against the roof.

"Looks like we just made it." Sebastian wiped his wet hands on his traveling cloak. He greeted his old friend and introduced Ivan to the white-haired man with age spots on his forehead. "Tom, this young man is from outside the Forest."

"Ah, yes." Tom squinted, looking a little confused. Leaning his head closer, he inspected Ivan. "You're right. I was expecting Simon and his beagle, Roman. But no matter, company is company, and I'm only too glad to make you at home."

Tom turned and shuffled to a battered cabinet made from dark wood, where he pulled out several towels. He handed them to Ivan and Sebastian to dry themselves and his pets. He smiled broadly at the animals. "I miss having Simon and his beagle."

Untying the cloak's strings, Ivan draped it over a chair next to him to dry. He breathed in the aroma of what smelled like stewing venison. His hungry eyes scanned the cottage where a large, black cauldron rested on an iron arm over low flames in the fireplace. His stomach lurched with an embarrassing growl. His mouth watered as he imagined such a delicious meal. Alfred and Canute scampered from one corner of the small cottage to the next, sniffing for food.

Ivan sat down at the table where cutlery and a cotton napkin lay. He reached for the full glass of milk that had already been poured and then stopped mid-air. His face felt warm as he remembered the good manners his mother had taught him. "Is this milk for me?"

Old Tom confirmed with a nod. "What brings you here, Sebastian?" he asked, coaxing his eyeglasses over the ridge of his nose. "It must be mighty serious for Zephyrus to release you from the sanctuary. Tell me, what is it?"

Sebastian took a seat and related the sequence of

events that led to Zephyrus forcing his own dormancy. "If it weren't for Ivan's unexpected visit this morning, I believe it would've been Zephyrus's death. This young man is a blessing to the Forest and has kindly agreed to help us save Zephyrus's life."

The heat around Ivan's neck intensified, and he was sure his face was bright red.

Tom gave him an approving look. "I've always worried about the lax guarding and patrolling during this annual event. I've warned Zephyrus a hundred times that he should keep a few good soldiers close at hand to watch over him, but he wouldn't hear of it. He has too much trust in the hearts of men."

"I feel the same as you, Tom." Sebastian shook his head, blinking rapidly. "I've cautioned him about the many dangers in the Forest, just waiting for the right moment. And then this happens."

Tom turned away as though hiding a frightened look. "What do you make of it? Who'd attempt such a brutal act of treason—trying to bring down our great master?"

Sebastian scrunched his face into a scowl. "We don't know."

With effort, Tom rose from his chair and ladled steaming stew for Ivan into a large bowl and set it before him. He cut thick slices of homemade bread, plopping them onto a pewter plate that also held a mound of fresh butter. Meanwhile, Sebastian settled back in his chair as if in deep thought.

"The water's boiling for tea." Tom glanced absently toward the stove.

Waving aside Ivan's offer to help, Tom scraped more stew from the caldron into heavy ceramic bowls.

"I'd like to feed your dogs," he mumbled. "My friend Simon, who replaced me when I retired as Commander of the South Garrison, often brought Roman when he visited. Now I remember, his beagle died. Simon doesn't come anymore. I sure do miss their company terribly." Tom wiped wetness from his eyes with the sleeve of his robe.

Ivan lowered his head. "I'm sorry about Roman."

Placing the teapot in the center of the table, Tom Shiffert sat down and leaned over, stroking the dogs affectionately. Shortly, Tom must've noticed his guest's disciplined method of eating and asked, "The stew to your liking, then?"

"It is." Ivan raised his eyebrows and grinned. He gently blew on a spoonful of stew and put it in his mouth. After a bit of chewing, he said, "The best I've ever eaten."

Leaning forward with his elbows on the table, Tom whispered, "So, who was this scoundrel that dared to use our own Silver Axe to strike Zephyrus?"

"The man wore a gray cloak, and his face was hidden under the hood." Sebastian reached for his cup of tea and even took a sip. "I heard his voice, but I'm sure it was disguised. Unfortunately, the attacker landed three disastrous axe blows into Zephyrus's side before fleeing. He must've seen or heard Ivan approaching."

"I think he heard Canute and Alfred barking." Ivan smiled at his beagles, who growled and pushed at each other for the last of the stew.

Tom gazed ahead with a concentrated look. "Do you think Fungoda's sap will save him?"

"It was Zephyrus's suggestion." Sebastian raised his shoulders. "He was suffering terribly until he forced his own dormancy. We hope to get the potion before…"

"If only he will survive until our return," Ivan said, meeting Tom's puckered brow.

****

Zello and the Discovery

They left Tom's warm home. Ivan licked his lips with satisfaction and smiled. His beagles frolicked, turning in circles, dashing through the puddles. The rain had eased up for the time being, and Sebastian and Ivan moved as fast as Sebastian's old legs could carry him.

"The guest cottage isn't too far from here." Sebastian pointed, leading the way. "We'll follow this road around the bend. I remember it being tucked away real cozy-like amongst a thick stand of oaks."

Raising the lantern Tom had lent them to light their path, Ivan saw a large stationary shape on the wet lawn. It was a fountain carved from gray stone of a fierce-looking dragon clenching a king's scepter in his claws.

"So, that's the dragon they call Zello?" Ivan tugged the hood of the Long Dark Cloak over his forehead to keep away the drizzle that began once more.

"He's really not as threatening as this work in stone shows." Scarcely had the words left Sebastian's lips when a series of loud crashes and thumps rumbled through the trees.

"Watch out, you big oaf," screamed an angry voice.

"What are you doing here pushing your way around?" shouted another.

Ivan searched through the dark spaces between the tree trunks. "What's that racket?"

Stopping to listen, Sebastian yelled, "Is that you, Zello?"

Ivan sucked breath into his lungs and froze. "Zello, the dragon?" He strained to see into the darkness.

"Zello, it's me, Sebastian. Show yourself."

A cavernous voice vibrated through the trees, and the pounding of heavy feet halted. "I'm leaving, and I'm not coming back."

"Oucheee."

Squeals and furious shouts echoed through the depth of the Forest.

"Who's screaming?" Ivan cocked his head following the noise and commotion.

"The trees," Sebastian said. "The dragon is tromping on them, and they don't like it."

"I wouldn't think so."

"What's the matter, Zello?" Sebastian's frail voice heightened.

"I was accused of something I didn't do, and I'm mad," he shouted. "I didn't eat those stupid chickens."

"Chickens?" Sebastian asked. "Do you mean the kaleido-birds?"

"Yeah, that's what I mean. I don't like feathers getting caught in my teeth."

The dragon-beast snorted and spit. His footsteps moved in the opposite direction.

"Wait a minute, let's talk." Sebastian cupped his mouth with his hands and shouted, "Then who did eat the hens?"

"Ask Lord Graydon," Zello hollered back.

"What's he got to do with it?"

"He spoils his gryphons, and they mock his generosity," the dragon blurted.

"Gryphons?" Ivan opened his eyes wide.

"I can't believe it." Sebastian lowered his face,

sober as a stag beetle. "Are you sure of this?" he yelled into the moist darkness. "Zello, are you still there?"

The pounding of Zello's feet had faded and disappeared.

"Drat, he's gone. What can that spoiled dragon be talking about?"

"Where are these gryphon-beasts?" Ivan ducked his head as though expecting the creatures to burst through the forest and attack them.

"Well, they're actually—how do I explain?" Sebastian stroked his beard, frowning. "They are the stone pillars that hold up the pediment at the entrance of the South Castle. They *are* stone."

"Then how..." Ivan was even more bewildered.

"The gryphons are permitted to leave their posts at midnight and transform into living winged creatures and take to the sky. Their purpose is to patrol the Forest after dark."

Ivan gasped and swallowed. "I've never seen such a thing in my life."

"Most people haven't," Sebastian murmured.

Shaking his head, Ivan said under his breath, "Gryphons. Who'd believe? Do they look like the pictures I've seen, with heads and wings of an eagle and the body of a lion?"

"Something like that," Sebastian replied. "Not eagles, exactly. More like vultures."

"Why do they steal the hens and take them away?"

Sebastian was quiet for a time before he answered. He stared at the treetops silhouetted against a charcoal-gray sky. "The gryphons may have been solicited by Tereus's Dark Army to provide kaleido-birds to feed them. Otherwise, I don't know where the army would get food to fill their bellies. Just a theory, you understand."

"That's a terrible thought," Ivan said with a shiver of fear. "Tereus has his own army?"

"Army?" Sebastian had been distracted, staring into the distance as though Zello might reappear and give more information. "Tereus is still a man, although imprisoned to the fiery underworld. Remember I told you? So, others must do his dirty work."

"Aren't the gryphons Lord Graydon's property?"

Sebastian turned toward Ivan and raised a bushy eyebrow. "They're among his favorite beasts, and he'll be heartbroken if the accusation is true." Sebastian huffed. "But I believe Zello may have hit on the answer."

"How so?"

"You said you smelled strong urine at the kaleido-bird's feeding ground, didn't you?"

"Yes, Bounty reacted to it most disagreeably."

"The gryphons are known to have such a strong odor after they relieve themselves that even skunks rush away."

"I wouldn't argue with that." Ivan wrinkled his face. "Will you tell Lord Graydon about this?"

"When the time comes, we must tell him. But I don't look forward to his reaction."

Ivan stopped and scanned the trees. "I don't hear Zello's footsteps. Where did he go?"

"He left the back way. Mad as a rhino stuck in a snowbank."

"What?" Ivan swung his head.

"Nothing…just a meaningless expression." Sebastian sighed, his eyes cast down.

"Should we follow him? I'd like to see the dragon close-up."

"Not after he's been insulted and is raging mad. I want to wring Fetters' scrawny neck for blaming Zello for eating his hens."

Powerful wings beat overhead. Zello's gigantic black shape moved swiftly—the biggest flying thing Ivan had ever seen. Wings flapping rhythmically, rising ever higher, the dragon disappeared into the dark clouds.

Ivan gawked until he could no longer see the shadowy speck.

"Dang it all." Sebastian's shoulders sagged. "Zello could've helped us get the sap to save Zephyrus. A hardheaded creature if I ever saw one."

They returned to the gravel path. Sebastian dragged his feet as they continued toward the cottage. There was nothing more they could do.

As his companion predicted, the rains came down in a torrent as they reached the bend in the road.

"Bloody nuisance!" he said. "After I've just dried off properly, too."

The instant Ivan opened the arched wooden door, the rush of heat from the blazing fire Colin had made warmed them. A hasty glance around the guest cottage showed a small bed, a pitcher, and a washbasin sat on a marble-top table. Clean towels, along with a new cake of lavender soap, were provided. He was grateful for the toothbrush.

Dead tired, Ivan removed the cloak and placed it over an old wicker chair. He stripped off his wet clothes and draped each piece on hooks near the fireplace. Stifling a yawn, he shoved his arms through the sleeves of a clean blue nightshirt he'd found and plopped on the bed.

"The Hurst-on-the-Vert is a welcoming place," Sebastian said. With that announcement, he eased his thin frame into the chair, releasing a weary breath. Ivan bobbed his head in agreement.

Canute settled near the fireplace while Alfred curled up on a braided rug near the bedpost. They were soon snoring.

Before Ivan slipped under the covers, Sebastian said, "It may be wise to place the cloak over your shoulders. Once the fire dies down, the cottage will chill quickly. It will provide you with extra warmth." He handed Ivan the garment, and he put it around himself, tying the strings.

Extinguishing the lantern, Ivan crawled beneath the flannel sheets. Yawning twice, he nestled his head against the soft pillow. "Thank you, Sebastian," Ivan mumbled sleepily. "A dragon and gryphons and talking birds. Who'd ever believe such things?"

An hour before dawn, Ivan sat upright on the bed, stretching his arms wide. Outside, crickets tried to out-sing one another. The slow clanking of distant cowbells sounded. Inside, the tumble of smoldering logs in the fireplace clunked as they dropped from the grate and turned to ash.

"Sleep well?" Sebastian straightened from the wicker chair near the bed with his arms folded on his lap.

"My night was filled with frightening dreams."

"What were they?"

Ivan lifted his shoulders, averting his eyes for a moment.

"Your dreams are safe with me."

"I...well," he hesitated. "I'm searching for Peter. When I find him, he's burning in a pit of fire, screaming my name and begging me to save him." Ivan's eyes fluttered. "My arms aren't long enough to reach him. The fire tears at me, scorching my clothes. I back away and abandon him." Ivan covered his face with his hands. "It's too horrible to talk about."

Sebastian sat next to Ivan on the bed. He put an arm around him and patted his shoulder. "We all have bad dreams, it doesn't mean they'll come true. In fact..." he raised a bristly eyebrow. "I'll guarantee it won't come to be."

"How can you be so sure?"

"I know by mere observation. That is, I know you only want to find Peter, whom you need and love. You genuinely want friends and to help save Zephyrus. And—you want Anna-Iza to admire you."

Ivan scratched his head. "How do you know these things? It's like you read my mind."

"Simple. We all wish for friendships, helping others, and being admired." A smile tugged at the corners of Sebastian's mouth.

This day was like any other, except Ivan wouldn't be doing his farm chores. He settled his feet onto the cold floor, his lips pressed together. Worry lines etched his forehead. *Will the boy Mule suggested come this morning to milk my cows? Will Mrs. Hambuckle worry about my absence?* Ivan glimpsed in the mirror above the washbasin and blinked several times to dislodge the gummy stuff around his lids. He washed his face and combed his hair, feeling a bit better now that he was presentable.

"I wish I had a change of clothes," he addressed his image in the mirror. "I never wear the same clothes two days in a row." He wrinkled his face as if something unpleasant had assaulted him. "Come on, Canute, Alfred. Let's go and say our goodbyes to Tom. Then we'll be on our way to get the healing sap."

Sebastian pushed up from the chair, threw his own traveling cloak over his thin shoulders, and followed.

A thick mist hung in the cold air. Ivan's breath turned white when he exhaled into the morning twilight. He pulled his jacket closed, buttoned it, and retied the cloak's strings around his neck.

After the rainstorm, the gravel pathway had collected numerous puddles. Ivan hopped back and forth from the path to the moist lawn to avoid getting his boots wet. "I feel like a little kid," he chortled, tipping his head skyward.

"It's good you can still feel the playfulness of youth," Sebastian said with a trace of sadness in his voice. After monitoring Ivan's dreams, Sebastian had learned that Ivan rarely laughed or showed much emotion. He'd been dominated by his older brother Peter, and Ivan was shy about being a foreigner. It was a bleak testimony for one so young.

The rich smell of chimney smoke wove long, wavy plumes through the mist and trees. Ivan again scolded himself for feeling a sudden stab of homesickness. He wished he and Peter were returning to their farm, absorbed in conversation, sharing memories, and discussing their future.

Colin swung open the door before Ivan had a chance to knock. "Good morning, sirs," the boy said with a swift bow. He squatted to his knees and hugged

Canute and Alfred, giggling away.

Ivan's lips curved into a smile, and he too laughed. The scene reminded him of times he and Peter spent together enjoying their own pets.

Tom gave a brisk wave from the cooking stove. "Come in, come in. I'm making a hearty breakfast for you. The Forest's own homemade sausages. Eggs from the manor's chicken coop, brought here just this morning. Fresh, real fresh. And these potatoes are fried in pork lard."

"It all sounds scrumptious," Ivan began. "Thank you, but…"

"I believe you'd better stay for the meal." Sebastian went toward his chair. "There's little assurance you or your beagles will have the chance to eat again until our return. But we'll need to hurry."

Alfred and Canute scampered around the kitchen area, nosing for any signs of food.

Ivan nodded, not wanting to refuse Tom's hospitable offer or to deny his hungry stomach. He wondered just how long their return would be. A full day? Many days? How could they not eat for the entire time? He sat in the same cushioned chair he'd occupied the night before and reached for the glass of warm milk that Tom had placed before him on the table.

Unfolding a tattered-edged napkin, Ivan smoothed it over his lap and then began rearranging his food with scientific precision. He sliced the sausages into button-sized pieces and moved them to the top of his plate. Fried potatoes, glistening with grease, were carefully separated to the east side, while the remaining entrée of eggs was escorted by knife to a neat mound to the west. He was uneasy when he noticed Tom watching with effort and shaking his head.

"There's a reason for such a procedure?" Tom asked with a skeptical grin.

Glancing up, Ivan said after his first mouthful, "Nothing unusual."

"I believe we should hurry along if we're to reach Fungoda before it gets too late," Sebastian said.

Tom ignored Sebastian's words. "You have family?"

"A brother. Peter's seven years older than me and went off to war while I stayed on the farm to help Mother and Father. Have you ever met him?"

"Once, as I recall."

"You did?" Suddenly alert, Ivan leaned forward, his chest pressed hard against the table's edge as his heart beat faster.

"Seemed like a decent sort of fellow." Tom adjusted his glasses. "I see the resemblance now that I study your face. Your hair is dark while Peter is blond."

"Is he all right? When did you last s-see him? What's he doing here in the F-Forest?" Ivan stuttered with excitement that he couldn't contain. His lips stretched into a long, hopeful smile.

"I believe he's okay, though I haven't seen him for some time. Don't know his purpose or motivation— never seemed to have much. Happy enough, I suppose."

"He must have suffered amnesia, and that's why he hasn't come home." Ivan bobbed his head, convinced it was the answer. "I miss him so much."

"Sorry." Tom's eyes shone with moisture.

"If he comes by, will you tell him I'm searching for him?" The old man said he would.

When the Commander asked about Ivan's parents,

he told him they'd died two years ago.

"You're all alone then?"

"Yes." His head lowered, holding back his tears.

"There's no wonder you want your brother home with you." Tom's voice was low and sad.

"Must be tough."

"Peter will know what to do," Ivan said with determination. He returned to eating, swallowing with difficulty past the obstruction in his throat.

"We'd better hurry if we're to reach Fungoda," Sebastian said again.

"What route do you plan to take?" Tom glanced at Colin, his youthful servant.

Colin had moved to the kitchen and was making sandwiches for their journey. This unexpected consideration pleased Ivan. At least, he could count on another meal for himself and his pets.

Sebastian spoke quietly. "We need to make up for valuable time lost because of the storm last night. But we don't dare get too close to the dwellers in Lake Gorgon."

Tom nodded in solemn agreement. "You've little choice, I'm afraid. You can't go around to the south, or you'll get trapped on the backside of the lake between the high ridges. You'll have to stay on the road next to the river, to the north, and remain alert every minute. Then, you might be all right."

"Pretty risky." Sebastian shook his head. "After those heavy rains, the river will be high and the edge soft for both hoof and foot."

"Dwellers? What kind of dwellers?" Ivan gulped.

The commander sighed, deep in thought. A heavy frown buried his eyes. He lowered his fork that held a bite of tomato. At last, he asked, "Are you suggesting you'll use the narrow track near the lake's shore? Why, that's plain foolhardy. I won't sanction it. If anything happened to either of you, there would be no one to get the sap, and it would be too late to save Zephyrus."

Ivan tugged nervously at the cloak's ties around his neck. "There must be people at the Harold Manor—the servants who delivered the eggs for our breakfast. Could they go to the South Castle for help?"

"I pleaded with a delivery servant this morning to make the trip," Tom said, "but he absolutely refused to leave the Hurst Community without his master's permission. He's not in the best of shape, anyway. And, of course," Tom added, "Lord Harold and his family left two days ago, including most of his staff, to enjoy the Competition for the Shield of Honor. Confounded event."

"You couldn't take the rigors of travel, either," Sebastian said to Tom.

"I know," he replied with a hint of embarrassment.

They had no choice, it seemed.

Ever more perplexed, Ivan asked meekly, "Could we ride to the castle and summon the soldiers?"

"There's not time for that." Sebastian combed his fingers through his thinning white hair. "If only we could send a message from here to the castle with a dependable Root-Underground tree. I know Lord Graydon would dispatch every man to save Zephyrus. Why, I'll bet Richard would strap on a weapon and join us on the quest."

"You're right." Tom closed his eyes in agreement."

A long moment of worried silence followed.

"What's in the lake?" Ivan's throat tightened.

Chapter Six

The Spine-Back Swamp Dragons

"Aberrations," Tom said. "We're not sure how the creatures came to inhabit our once-pristine Lake Emerald, but now..." Tom's rueful gaze met Ivan's worried eyes. "It's a puking cesspool. We call it Swamp Gorgon."

Ivan remembered a ghastly mythological tale his mother had read to him and Peter when they were just boys. "A gorgon is the name of a kind of vicious creature. I recall from the story that Medusa had writhing snakes on her head, a frightening image if there ever was one."

Both men appeared surprised that Ivan knew this and exclaimed in unison, "That's right!"

"Well, this is not myth or legend." Tom's scowl was more pronounced. "These beasts are real, and I'm sure they were planted in the lake through dark magic. Those swamp-buggers just showed up one day, grew and grew, and became giants. They ate everything in sight and kept on multiplying. We knew they were a hazard to our livestock and woodland animals, but the council turned a blind eye and a deaf ear."

"There's no way to destroy them?" Ivan's voice had a pleading wobble.

Tom Shiffert snorted. His wrinkled face twisted

with disgust. "We have rules here, Ivan. We don't kill our own. So, while these monsters grow and threaten anyone close to the lake, our illustrious Council of Seven does nothing but talk about it."

Sebastian said brusquely, "I might remind you that I'm one of the council members."

"Humph! Well." Tom's retort was just as sharp. "Our garrisons have about six hundred men at their disposal. Just how long would it take to rid the lake of those menaces?"

"Now, don't get all a-lather." Sebastian waved his hands. "Commander Simon will soon find a way."

Tom wasn't easily calmed. "If I were still leading my garrison, why, I'd slaughter and burn those filthy reptiles at once. I'd never feel guilty over it, either."

"Amphibians. The swamp dragons are amphibians," Sebastian blandly corrected. "They move about on land and in the lake, having both gills and lungs."

Tom pressed his lips hard together. "I don't care what you call them. They're a hazard to the area and should be exterminated."

"Wha-what do they look like?" Ivan squirmed in his chair.

The commander sat back and released a painful groan as though the images nearly made him ill. "Colin," he suddenly called, "leave the kitchen-work for now. Go saddle Ivan's horse. Martin can help you. And be sure to pull the girth strap tight."

"Yes, sir." The boy was obviously thrilled to get out of kitchen chores. He gave the towel a careless toss. Calling Canute and Alfred to follow, the boy skipped his way out the front door.

"I'll send the lads to the castle right after Colin brings your horse to the front." Tom rubbed his temple, hesitated, and then looked satisfied with his decision.

"Good idea," Sebastian said. "The sooner, the better."

Ivan asked again, "What are the monsters?"

"We call them Spine-Back Swamp Dragons. They are like a…"

"They're dragons, then?" Ivan's eyes widened with curiosity and a healthy dose of fear. "I mean like Zello, with huge wings and blasting a breath of fire?"

"Well, they're lizard-like in some ways, I reckon." Tom chewed the last of his forkful of tomato. "But they don't fly, and they don't blow fire. Their skin is milky, thin, and more translucent—a bit like a frog's belly. Yeah, maybe that's it. They have a row of highly poisonous quills that run along their backs. That's partly why we call them aberrations. Nothing quite like them in all the British Isles."

"Or in the entire world." Sebastian lifted a bushy eyebrow.

Tom ran the palm of his hand over his thinning hairline and scratched. "They're difficult to describe. They have large heads with wide mouths lined with sharp teeth. The male is noticeably larger. I remember when I saw one some time ago. I stared into its round eyes—reddish, with thin membranes that can lower to protect their eyes during a fight. It nearly scared me to death. Those stiff spines begin from the top of his head and gradually taper to the end of his long tail. We call that one Porcupine. Nasty creature if I ever saw one."

"They are confrontational and temperamental," Sebastian added, having heard plenty of accounts from

Commander Simon. "You'd never want to catch a swat from those poisonous quills."

Ivan gulped, going weak. He was certain he wouldn't have the courage to fight a Swamp Dragon, male or female.

Bounty whinnied outside the cottage. "We'd better go," Ivan said, afraid he'd lose his courage to continue the journey.

"Wait, Kimble. I want you to take a weapon for your own protection." The commander rose from his chair and shuffled to the stone fireplace. He reached high to lift a lethal-looking sword from the brackets. "It was always at my side for the many years I commanded my garrison."

Tom's pale-blue eyes watered. He stroked the shiny blade, pointing to the engraved name, *The Protector*. Caressing the spiral groove on the hilt, he whispered, "This should give you a good grip."

Ivan kept his hands at his sides. He didn't want to take a dangerous weapon on the mission. "Why do I need this if Sebastian and I go around Swamp Gorgon?"

"I'm not sure we can avoid the narrow road between the lake and the river," Sebastian said, hinting at an apology. "We really must make up for lost time, and no other route will offer us this."

Ivan reached for the sword, trembling. *I wish it was over and I could go home.*

"Oh, and here…" Tom released The Protector into Ivan's unsteady hands and turned to search under a pile of yellowed newspapers. "You'll need this, too." He handed the sword's sheath to Ivan.

Strapping the long leather belt at his waist, Ivan

located a hole for the metal tongue. "I don't know how to use a sword," he said, feeling helpless and embarrassed. "Even if I did, I'm not sure I'm brave enough to use this."

Unexpectedly, Tom reached and embraced Ivan around his shoulders. "Godspeed, son." His voice cracked, and tears collected at the rims of his lids. "Sebastian and the High Intervener will take care of you."

"Y-yes sir," Ivan replied.

Sebastian faced the commander. "Meanwhile, if you can find anyone besides Colin and Martin that can ride to the castle and call for help, then do it with haste."

"At once," Tom said crisply and saluted as he followed Ivan and Sebastian to the door. He stopped and exclaimed, "Ah, your lunch. I don't want to forget that." The old man retrieved a burlap bag and handed it to Ivan. "Colin put in several sandwiches, a couple of apples, and I see a liter of milk for you and your pets. It's glass, so be careful."

Ivan grasped the bag and turned to Tom. "If you see Peter, would you please tell him I'm in the Forest looking for him?"

"I'll do that."

Bounty stood tethered at a post outside the cottage, and Ivan hooked the bag that held his lunch onto the pommel of his saddle. Colin ran this way and that way on the lawn, slipping and sliding on the wet grass, coaxing the beagles to chase him. His boyish laughter and squeals of play caused Ivan to smile with delight. A stab of loneliness rushed through him as he again recalled the fun he'd shared with Peter. *I must find him.*

Ivan complained. "How am I to walk with this sword bouncing against my leg with every step?"

Apparently, thinking he'd spoken to him, Colin looked up with questioning eyes. "I dunno, sir. I never wore a sword that long before."

Ivan grinned. "Thank you, Colin, for all your help during our visit."

The boy's eyes sparkled with joy. It occurred to Ivan that Colin hadn't often received compliments or praise from the brusque old commander. His thoughts surprised him as he'd never considered such a thing before.

Gripping his horse's reins with cold hands, Ivan mounted. He repositioned the sheath, so it lay comfortably at his side.

Sebastian mounted Old Bones with some effort, and they left Hurst-on-the-Vert, passing through the wide wrought iron gate. The sun climbed higher, and the day promised warmth, but for now, Ivan felt the cold and dampness after Tom's cozy cottage. As they rode on, Ivan became more and more unsure of himself. The description Tom had given of the Swamp Dragons made him quiver. He broke the silence. "I'm not right for this job. Even this piece of metal strapped to my side won't change that."

"Oh, you'll be all right, my lad," Sebastian said with a reassuring glance.

"I should warn you, I'm not very brave or aggressive. You may be bitterly disappointed in me. Even Peter often told me I needed to be bold and stand up for myself."

"Please, don't worry how much courage you think you have. We sometimes surprise ourselves with hidden strengths. Let's just pray we complete our mission safely and return to Zephyrus in time."

Ivan fell quiet, but his self-doubt gnawed on him as they rode south.

They followed the well-marked groove of wagon wheels and horse tracks for several uneventful hours. Sebastian stared intently ahead and gave no additional encouragement.

The road wove southward through the moist woodlands of oak and ash trees, skirting holly bushes with shiny green leaves and clusters of red berries. Quick lizards and poky beetles skittered across the road. A kind of rabbit with small rounded ears, red squirrels, fra-haks, and feral cats, darted through the thickets. There were plenty of animals that inhabited the region, and this brought an amount of calm to Ivan.

Birds chirped as they flitted from bough to bough. Squinting, Ivan pointed to an unfamiliar bird on a gnarled oak limb. "What is it?"

Sebastian shielded his eyes from the glare of the sun. "A fenner whip. Odd-looking little thing, isn't it? They never leave the Forest when the seasons change like many of our birds."

Slowly nodding, Ivan said, "I've never seen a black and white striped bird with a brilliant red beak before." The top of his head was marked with a perfect yellow circle and a black dot in the center, looking much like a young schoolboy's hat.

"The fenner whips are reporters." Sebastian gave the bird a passing glance. "They monitor what goes on in the Forest and report to the Elftens who keep a carefully written account. Only a few of us understand their chirping messages."

"Then, please tell him to contact someone at once and send help."

"I was just going to." Sebastian cupped his thin hands to his mouth, calling several times. "Fly to the castle, little bird! Tell Lord Graydon that Zephyrus has been axed, and he's in grave danger. Tell him to dispatch his garrisons at once and travel to Zephyrus and protect him."

After a moment, the fenner whip turned his head and seemingly stared at Sebastian. Then he left his lookout branch and flew away.

Sebastian's eyes blinked with disappointment. "I don't think he heard me."

"Whoa, boy." Ivan pulled back on leather reins and dismounted to give Bounty a few minutes' rest. His lungs filled with fresh, crisp air. He felt assured for the first time since he heard Tom Shiffert's account of what lurked in Swamp Gorgon. He gazed at the lake in the distance that appeared harmless enough. "A breathtaking sight designed for an artist."

Stretching his legs, Ivan remounted and surveyed the lawn that lay between the lake and the high rocky ridge that loomed on the north side of the river. It had overflowed its banks during the heavy rains, narrowing the area they'd hoped to pass through.

The terrain was exactly as Tom and Sebastian said. It appeared to be the only choice they had.

"What lies beyond the rocky ridge?" Ivan motioned with his arm. "Could we cross there?"

"There's no easy or safe way to cross it," Sebastian replied. "It would nearly double our time."

With a chilling shudder, Ivan nodded. "Then, I suppose we must travel along the corridor."

"I'm sorry, it does look that way. But if we move slowly and quietly, I'm sure we'll be safe."

"Follow close behind, boys," Ivan called to his beagles. "I don't want you wandering off and causing trouble."

Canute looked up, meeting his master's stern eyes with a shy, guilty look.

"Tell me, Sebastian, why have I never heard about this lake? Peter often visited the Forest when he was young, but he never mentioned it."

"The lake's existence is kept secret by magically removing the memory from the minds of men who trespass here. Many things are kept hidden in this way."

Ivan closed his eyes, considering the comment. "I'm sure Peter has lost his memory. Otherwise, I know he'd come home."

"This lake was a favorite vacationing place for the many guests visiting Graydon Castle." Sebastian's wrinkled face beamed. "Boating, fishing, and swimming were available to all. But after those beasts appeared, no one in good mind dared venture here."

Ivan's Adam's apple lurched. "Tom mentioned something about the use of dark magic that created the Swamp Dragons. Do you think it's true?"

"I happen to agree, but just who the offenders were, we don't know. The fallen wizards would be suspect, except some were sent to prison, and the others are no longer welcome in our Forest. We drove them away and asked that they never return." Stroking his whiskers, Sebastian continued, "Although several disgruntled wizards could've placed a dark spell on the lake more than a decade ago in order for the dragons to have grown to such a hideous size."

"Why would they do such a thing?"

"I've asked myself many times." Sebastian scowled. "Anger and revenge, maybe? I can't say. They were a proud lot, especially their leader, Maloof."

"Look, Sebastian." Ivan raised himself in the stirrups. "Up ahead!" He broke into a cheerful smile, spotting about a half-dozen sturdy ponies grazing on the shimmering wet grass that lay between the lake and river. He lowered himself to his saddle and peered through the sunlight that glowed warm and silent on the still water.

Worry lines etched Sebastian's face. It was a dangerous equation that couldn't be shared: dogs-plus-ponies-equals-Swamp-Dragons-disturbed-in-the-lake.

"Yes," Sebastian cleared his throat. "We do see wild ponies and horses from time to time all over the Forest. They prefer to stay together in isolated areas away from the disturbances of people and dogs."

At first, nothing interrupted the lake's glassy-gray surface except a few ripples far off shore, traveling ever so slowly toward the shoreline.

When the lake's pungent odor swept on a breeze in their direction, Ivan held his hand firmly over his nose and gagged. "What's that wretched smell? It seems familiar." Then he remembered the fishy smell from Zephyrus's wounds. Could there be some kind of connection?

"Tom did say the lake stank like a cesspool, didn't he? But as a spirit, I wasn't awarded the gift of smell or taste. Not needed, I suppose."

"So you've told me." Ivan coughed, shaking his head roughly. As they moved closer, the corridor narrowed with the flooded marshland that had encroached upon the narrow path. Appalled, Ivan realized with a jerk of his head, the swamp's shoreline wasn't white sand.

"Those are bones, aren't they?" His chest quivered when he recognized weather-bleached rib cages, femurs, and skulls from various hapless animals that littered the shore. A large pile of fowl skeletons lay snarled together where you couldn't distinguish which bones belonged to which birds.

"I'm afraid so," Sebastian replied sadly. "Domestic and wild animals have had the misfortune to stop and drink here."

"I'm feeling doubtful about this route. There must be another direction we could travel that would be safer, even if it took a little longer. What do you think, Sebastian?"

More ripples moved closer to the shore and trailed a long string of bubbles.

Sebastian gazed at the green corridor as if thinking heavily on Ivan's suggestion.

The wild ponies were just beyond the tightest stretch of land, moving slowly and enjoying a peaceful morning of delicious grass when Canute spotted them. The beagle shot away like a flash of lightning, barking in a mad frenzy.

"Stop him!" Sebastian shouted. "Ivan, you must stop Canute at once."

But it was like holding back the wind and rain during a violent storm. Ivan yelled over and over, "Stop, Canute. Please stop!" He pressed his hands around his mouth, screaming louder.

The headstrong beagle raced straight toward the ponies barking all the way, his legs a blur against the green lawn.

Within moments, Alfred took up the chase and helped stampede the peaceful animals up the corridor and into the woodland.

Ivan gritted his teeth, muscles constricted in his jaw. Furious as he was, he was more frightened about his pets' safety than the ponies stampeding.

All six of them shot off at a run, swishing their tails, with hooves pounding the ground.

There seemed little reason to continue calling. Ivan's throat was already raw from the strain.

When Sebastian caught up with Ivan, he groaned. "The noise will alert the Swamp Dragons resting on the bottom of the lake."

At the narrowest distance between the lake and the marshes, the first creature emerged from the fetid waters and moved toward the shoreline. Another, and then another. Seven Swamp Dragons lined up, front feet planted on the bone-strewn shore while their back-quarters and tails remained submerged.

Ivan got a good look at the creatures. They were positively grotesque.

In spite of all the commotion, the Swamp Dragons hesitated, watching with hungry eyes.

The creature with muscular shoulders and deadly-looking spines must be the male.

Ivan's heart lurched, thumping in his chest.

"That's the one they call Porcupine," Sebastian said, confirming Ivan's fears.

The beast was far worse than any nightmare Ivan could've imagined. It didn't look like any amphibian he'd ever seen. Its head was huge with red eyes and two round cavernous holes for nostrils at the end of his snout. Their skin looked almost transparent, especially on their underbellies. Ivan remembered that Commander Shiffert had told him this. Extra rolls of pale, pink flesh surrounded their forelimbs and curved around their necks. Ivan surmised this was to trap air in the grooves of their flesh while submerged. He jerked back and quivered when Porcupine opened his mouth wide and showed two rows of sharp teeth.

The ponies understood the danger, for they galloped away, but Canute and Alfred were not as careful. The beagles turned and rushed toward the howling Spine-Back Dragons.

The dragons watched and waited, moving their heads from side to side.

Canute's barking increased, and Ivan felt a sharp flash of panic. Porcupine's long red tongue darted in and out as though testing the air for evidence of prey. He released a threatening hiss, followed by a guttural roar.

"I'm turning ba-back," Ivan shouted over the noise. Fear gripped him, pressing hot across his chest and down his limbs. With a jolt, he realized this was what worried Tom and Sebastian so profoundly. This was why Tom warned Sebastian about avoiding the shorter route through the corridor by the lake.

"Yes, we must leave at once." Sebastian's own horse reacted nervously, turning in a full circle. "Confounded animal." He pulled hard on the reins until he brought his horse under control.

"We can't leave without Alfred and Canute." Ivan's voice trembled. His body shook with fright.

Other heads emerged from the swamp as more hungry females moved to the white shores anticipating a meal.

To make matters worse, Bounty sidled, snorting loudly. He blew mucus while tugging against Ivan's hold. Frightened and confused, his horse reacted to the overpowering odor and the incessant barking dogs. Ivan leaned forward and stroked his animal's neck. He coaxed with a strained voice, "Whoa…take it easy, boy. Alfred and Canute need us now." Sweat drizzled down Ivan's face. His heart pounded.

Though untrained in swordsmanship, Ivan withdrew The Protector from its sheath. He wasn't worried the beasts would attack him while he sat atop Bounty. They appeared slow, almost lethargic as they waddled upon the beach of broken bones.

The dogs yelped at the huge male dragon as it moved closer and closer. Porcupine hissed, lowering his eye membranes. The Swamp Dragon backed away as though intimidated by the frenzied dogs.

Ivan recognized Porcupine's ruse to lure his prey closer.

Sebastian raised his voice above the noise, "Call Canute before it's too late!"

Giving Bounty a swift slap on the rump, the horse raced forward and then stopped abruptly, rearing. He panicked and screeched. His hooves hit the mud. His thin pasterns tangled in sun-bleached rib bones, terrifying him even more.

Ivan felt a strange movement. "Something is dreadfully wrong," he said, just as his saddle slid back toward Bounty's flanks. Colin and Martin hadn't tightened the girth strap. Ivan was furious with himself because he'd forgotten to check. The burlap bag holding their lunch slipped from its hold and crashed to the ground. The liter of milk shattered with a muffled clunk, spilling its contents where it puddled in the mud.

As his feet left the stirrups, his body slid backward. When the reins jerked from his sweaty hands, he reached for something solid to grab hold of. There was nothing.

"Sebastian!" Ivan screamed. "Help meeee…"

It happened so fast he had no time to think. Tumbling over Bounty's rump, Ivan's frantic glance showed Porcupine shoot forward with an unexpected burst of energy. He grabbed Canute in his powerful jaws. The dog let out a high-pitched cry, but Ivan could do nothing as he crashed to the ground, landing with a loud crack on a bed of bones.

The Dark Cloak flared out behind him. A sharp bone drove itself into his back, penetrating deeply into his flesh, and he yelled a blood-curdling wail.

Bounty stood on hind legs, twisting his body until the saddle slipped over his rear. It moved down his legs and hit the dirt. Clumsily, the horse escaped his binding and bolted toward the open corridor. Ears flattened against his head, he raced away as though a demon was in pursuit.

From the corner of his eye, Ivan saw Sebastian rush toward Porcupine, shaking his angry fists, shouting at the top of his voice. The dragon didn't react. Seemingly, the spirit was invisible to the beast.

Several female Swamp Dragons strained forward, ready to lunge and grab the prize in the burlap sack. Their saliva-dripping tongues hung out while their bulging eyes stared at Ivan, who held shiny metal in his hand.

Ivan gritted his teeth to hold back the throbbing pain. His surroundings lost focus, turning ghostly gray.

Chapter Seven

Saving Canute

Canute cried a piercing wail. Alfred dashed into the fray, howling madly.

Sebastian yelled something, but Ivan only heard his own screams. He twisted his body to the side, wincing with pain. He took quick gulps of air and shook his head, trying to think straight.

For a moment, he couldn't determine where he was. He grabbed a handful of sand and clenched it in his fists until his brain brought him back to the dire situation.

A sheep's rib had driven into Ivan's back. Blood oozed out, soaking his shirt, trickling down his trousers. He was paralyzed from the burning that threatened to plunge him into darkness. He blinked against flashing pale lights behind his eyes.

A human-like skeleton lay near his elbow. Had the horrible beasts eaten a helpless youngster? Its large, deformed cranium was detached from a severely curved spine. Thick, distorted arm and leg bones protruded through the mud. Revulsion overtook him, and he vomited atop it all.

Ivan's right arm and sword were snarled in a heap of bones, and a streak of pain shot from his wrist to his neck. He groaned and released The Protector from his hand. Sweat dripped from his forehead, and his whole body shook with teeth-rattling tremors. He fought the urge to scream for help from Sebastian but instead forced his lips together until his teeth cut into them. He tasted hot blood.

"Don't scream," Sebastian cautioned in a directed whisper. "The predators will hear you and know your vulnerability."

With great effort, he rolled onto his side and propped himself on his elbow, where he struggled to dislodge the ragged-edged bone from his lower back. He wrenched his torso until the bone pulled free. Panting, he collapsed onto his shoulder and shivered. Darkness crept around him. He was afraid he'd pass out and die right there in the mud.

A female dragon's eyes stayed fixed on Ivan. She moved cautiously from the shore, watching over her shoulder as her competition followed just behind. They raised their snouts, sniffing the air, picking up the powerful smell of spilled milk.

Only one thing stayed them. Ivan realized by their tentative motion—the glint of silver that lay beside him. He concluded the Swamp Dragons feared metal and shiny things.

Sebastian's image and horse turned smoky, whisking into the cloak so quickly that only a puff of wind swept across Ivan's ears and around his neck.

"Help Canute, please." Ivan squeezed his eyes closed and cried, "Save him, or he'll be eaten alive by Porcupine."

"I'll heal your injuries first," Sebastian said from the cloak, "or they'll tear you apart too. Your wrist is badly broken. The bone you fell on has punctured your back. Thank goodness, it missed your kidney, but only by a fraction."

"I-I'm cold, s-so cold." Ivan's teeth chattered.

"You're going into shock. Wrap the hem of the cloak around your wrist," Sebastian said. "I'll heal it first. Hurry, you'll need your fighting arm to protect yourself."

Ivan's hand and wrist were turning red, swelling quickly. His head felt as though it was ready to burst open and spill onto the muddy shore just as the bottle of milk had.

Grinding his teeth, he reached back, tugging the hem of the Long Dark Cloak. It had spread out behind him when he fell and hooked onto a bone embedded into the ground. He stopped to stifle a shrill cry, gulping air to stay conscious. "I don't have the strength to pull the cloth. It's wedged tight behind me."

"Try! You must help me to heal you so you can save Canute. He has little time left."

Again Ivan clutched the cloak's fabric, twisting harder still. Shifting his body, he pulled at the cloth, but it stayed lodged. "I can't." He tipped his head back and wailed.

"Pull!" Sebastian shrieked. "Ivan, yank it with all your might."

Breathless, Ivan gripped the fabric, gave it one last hard tug, and finally jerked it free. His head throbbed as darkness surrounded him. Then, within seconds, came the rush of warmth and the cloak's healing power. The pain vanished.

Ivan bent his wrist, flexing his fingers several times. Watching through his half-closed lids, he saw the swelling go down. He groaned with relief. Now his back burned with pain, and he begged Sebastian to bring relief.

Canute's terrifying cry cut the air.

Porcupine dropped Canute to the ground and lunged toward Alfred, who'd been nipping at the dragon's forelegs. Alfred leaped away from the deadly snapping jaws and barely dodged the attack.

It was Canute's chance to escape.

"Run, Canute, run away!" Ivan shouted across the boneyard. His beagle ran. Bleeding, he dragged his injured leg behind him and headed toward a rock pile where he wedged his trembling body between two large boulders, whimpering all the way.

Ivan watched, horrified, unable to help. "Stay hidden, Canute."

"Don't come out," Sebastian bellowed to the dog.

"My back, it's throbbing like a thousand arrows stabbed into me." Clamping his teeth, Ivan's jaw grew numb from the pressure. "Help me…"

"Pull the cloth around you closer," Sebastian said. "Hold it tight, so I can send my healing powers and repair the damage." After a moment, it felt like a hot bath on a cold day. He lay there, the fog from his eyes cleared, his breathing returned to normal.

Ivan stood on wobbly legs amongst the litter of bones. He reached for The Protector, where it lay half-buried in the mud. His hand was a little stiff, but otherwise, it was all right. He grabbed his weapon and wiped the sword's muddy blade on the cloak's fabric. Swamp Gorgon was an appalling hellhole, Ivan bitterly decided. He wanted to grab Canute and leave, vowing he'd never set foot near the stinking lake again.

Canute cried, reminding Ivan of their terrible

plight.

Porcupine pawed viciously at the rocks and shoved his snout between them, sniffing ravenously at his next meal.

Clutching The Protector, Ivan dashed toward Canute, tripping across skeletons, rocks, and mud. As he drew closer, the Swamp Dragon raised his menacing red eyes. He snorted and hissed a warning for Ivan to stay away. Then he resumed pounding at the large boulders with sharp webbed claws. Several rocks broke away. Stones flew like darts, pinging as they struck other boulders.

The smaller females watched. Their long tongues stabbed at the air. Straining forward, they waited for a sign from their male leader.

"How will I fight them if they decide to attack?" A cold shiver of fear sped through Ivan in his moments of indecision. "The sun is warming the beasts. They're more agile now. What am I to do?"

"Move closer toward Porcupine in short, careful steps," Sebastian said in a whisper from the cloak. "Don't take your eyes off him. The females will wait for their leader…I hope."

"Sebastian, can you help me?" Ivan moved closer.

"I can do nothing. Porcupine didn't react to my hollering and fist-shaking. I'm a spirit, and these beasts cannot see me."

Ivan could wait no longer. Terrified, he crept toward the male. His quivering hands flashed the shiny reflection of The Protector, but Porcupine made no move toward him.

The Swamp Dragon loomed tall with stiff spines atop his head, graduating in length down his tail.

Sunlight caught the tips of the deadly quills, reminding Ivan of what Tom Shiffert had said about their fatal toxin. Facing the beast, Ivan gripped The Protector and raised it high. He hesitated, considering if there was any other way. "Get away from my Canute!"

The hungry beast swung his big head and stared at Ivan. Then he returned and tore viciously at the rocks, raking with front claws. His maw pushed between the cracks. Canute howled.

Porcupine raised his head, a mouthful of dog hair dangling from his sharp teeth. He was getting closer.

"Canute, Canute. Stay where you are! I'll save you." Sweat shot down Ivan's face. The salty liquid dripped into his eyes. His heart thumped with white-hot fear.

Alfred barked ferociously, feigning an attack at Porcupine. Ivan thrust The Protector forward just as the beast raised his head and swallowed the clump of hair. Ivan had missed. Not wavering, he swept his weapon full force at the beast's throat. Porcupine seemed to anticipate the strike and stepped back, shaking his head violently. Then he plunged his snout between the rocks. They split apart. To Ivan's horror, the dragon caught Canute by his flank and dragged him out of his hiding place. Blood streamed from the beagle's hind leg. His tortured whine sounded almost human.

Porcupine dangled his prey from his mouth and swung him as though to toss and gulp him whole.

Canute stopped struggling. His cries ceased.

Fury like Ivan had never known filled him until it boiled inside. He moved with the speed of lightning, and with all his strength, the flash of sharp metal swept through the air with a sizzle. The powerful thrust of The

Protector entered Porcupine's fleshy neck, where Ivan shoved the blade deep. Up, up, it went until the tip reached the creature's skull. The beast opened his mouth wide in a deafening roar and released Canute. The beagle dropped into the bend of Ivan's arm, where Ivan held him tightly against his chest.

A wobbly echo sounded, guttural and terrifying, as the dragon tried to shake free from the lethal weapon that impaled him. Porcupine struggled to pull away from the razor-sharp edge of the sword. Forcing his head downward, he charged Ivan and thrust his deadly quills at him.

Ivan leaped back and arched his body just in time. The beast's strength surprised him, but Ivan returned with equal might. Gnashing his teeth, he stayed The Protector into Porcupine's skull and twisted the metal. A grayish-white substance mixed with blood poured from its mouth, flowing along the blade, onto Ivan's hand and down his arm.

"Will this horrible thing never die?" Ivan screamed through his clenched jaws.

Holding Canute's limp body with one arm, Ivan yanked his sword away and jumped back.

Porcupine's forelegs gave out. The huge monster crashed to the ground, expelling a long, raspy breath. His slithery red tongue lay writhing like a snake upon the wet shore.

The females watched, unmoving.

Canute's half-opened eyes looked up. Was he begging for his master to put him out of his misery or asking forgiveness for his disobedience?

Backing away slowly, Ivan clung to The Protector with a slippery blood-soaked hand.

At once, a female dragon shot forward, her eyes locked onto the furry meal cradled in Ivan's arms. Starvation drove her as she followed the smell of blood. She opened her mouth and hissed hot, stinky breath into Ivan's face. He lifted his sword, slashing a powerful arc with his weapon. For a second, he thought he'd missed his new attacker. But it was the female who had erred. The Protector's tip sliced across the bridge of her nose, splitting her large, ravenous eyes. A gelatinous substance leaked down her pale cheeks. Raising her head high, she shook it vigorously and shrieked in agony. The dragon buckled, landing with a heavy thump, crushing the bleached bones beneath her. She rubbed her face into the cool mud for relief, but nothing could save her now.

The dying beast's earsplitting screeches stopped the other dragons. They stood frozen. Ivan watched, terrified by their next move. Several flat-finned tails slapped the water as though relaying messages to each other.

Porcupine lifted his large head from where he lay. He snorted, blowing blood from his nose, and a low rumble left his throat, and then his eyes rolled up into their sockets. His head hit the pile of bones under him with a crunch, and there he took his last breath.

"They've just realized their only male is dead," Sebastian said.

Ivan nodded and gulped air.

Another dragon, near the middle, crumpled and fell to the ground. She let out a long exhale, and she, too, died on the shore.

Startled, Ivan didn't know what was happening— he didn't care. He just wanted to get away from this horrible place.

Ivan avoided tripping over the saddle that Bounty had abandoned on the edge of the grassy corridor. He left it, favoring to comfort Canute in his arms.

Alfred gave the saddle a brief sniff. Showing no promise of something to eat, he ignored it and turned to yowl at the beasts.

"Please, Sebastian, save my Canute." A sob left Ivan's dry, aching throat. "Just like you healed my broken wrist and closed the wound in my back. I can't feel his heartbeat. He can't be d-dead!"

"I've never tried to save a dog's life before," Sebastian said. "Quickly then, wrap the cloak around Canute. Hold him close and share your warmth."

Ivan prayed that Sebastian possessed enough healing power to restore his beagle. The awful sight of his dog's torn hind leg with the bone exposed nearly caused Ivan's knees to give out. He wrapped the cloak's muddy hem around his pet, leaving only his head and nose showing. Ivan begged, "Please live, Canute. Please."

"Keep moving toward the river." Sebastian increased his step, which wasn't very fast. "I can't bring Canute back from the dead if we lose him, but— he *is* alive!"

"He is!" Ivan cried. "I feel his faint heartbeat against mine."

"Barely. I'll mend the broken bone in his leg and fix his dangling paw. This will take some time."

"I'll wait as long you need. Only, please, please, don't let him die." Hot tears rolled down Ivan's cheeks and dripped from his chin.

Before long, the Swamp Dragons overcame their

fear and crept toward the spilled milk. A half-dozen creatures rushed forward at once, fighting each other for the right to lap up the white liquid. It meant survival for one or two of them at most. Ivan noticed they had discovered the burlap bag held sandwiches, and their sharp teeth tore it apart from three different directions.

"Don't turn your back to them just yet." Sebastian held up his hands in a halting gesture. "Hold onto The Protector and move carefully. Alfred has done an excellent job holding the beasts at bay, but he must not stay behind."

As Ivan moved cautiously away from the lake's edge, a female rushed toward the bag. With the last of her strength, she seized it. The dragon nearest her turned abruptly and sank vicious jaws into her shoulder. Another gave her a hard shove. The injured dragon collapsed onto her belly, and there she stayed. Several raced to the corpse, tearing at her flesh, consuming huge chunks with hungry jaws.

"They're eating her." Ivan's mouth dropped to his chin.

"Starvation," Sebastian replied. "That would explain the pale color of their skin. It would explain their madness."

Ivan's only thought was of his dear Canute, who lay so still in his arms.

Another female dragon with several quills missing from her head sniffed at the dead male. She raised her snout to sound a woeful yodel from the back of her throat. All dragons turned toward her. They blinked, and then the ghostly-gray creatures seemed to understand. Their only male, their leader and defender, was dead.

Bounty was nowhere in sight. If Ivan had any energy left, he would've been angry at his horse for abandoning him when he needed him the most. "Phooey." He spat.

For now, they were safe, Ivan hoped. Exhausted, he lacked the strength to fight another swamp monster. As he strode the distance to the aisle of green, he assessed the carnage that lay behind him. The bunch of them were attacking, clawing, and ripping at each other—a feeding frenzy, meat to fill their empty bellies

"Alfred!" Ivan called and kept walking. "Come." The dog obeyed. "Please live, Canute." Ivan choked back tears. "I love you and would miss you terribly." He bent his head to touch the dog's blood-matted ears with his lips. "Alfred would miss you too." Ivan lowered himself onto a patch of downed reeds near the river's edge, leaving the terrible lake behind. Tired legs could not resist the soft cushion of the grasses. With his sword sheathed at his side, he held his bundled patient in his arms.

Silently, Sebastian worked his magical healing powers on Canute.

Ivan thought about Zephyrus, whose very life teetered on the edge. He thought about his quest to find Peter, and here he was, more concerned about his beagle than his brother or the safety of the Forest. A stab of guilt flashed through him, but he would never sacrifice Canute.

Alfred went to drink at the clear flowing river. Although parched, Ivan stayed and held Canute. He tried to relax, but his mind whirled with the sounds and images of the Spine-Back Swamp Dragons. Inwardly, he thanked Commander Shiffert for loaning him The

Protector. Without it, he didn't dare think about the possible outcome.

Time passed, perhaps an hour or so. Fretting, Ivan peeked under the cloth several times, only to see Canute's eyes tightly shut. He wished he could do something to help, but it was Sebastian who had to heal his pet.

Ivan dozed under the warm sun and the soothing, musical rippling of water. His chin dropped and rested upon his chest. He probably snored a little. Alfred snuggled against Ivan's hip waiting for his brother to wake and come play.

Suddenly squirming, Canute gave a stiff kick into Ivan's belly and let out a sharp yip.

Ivan's eyes shot open. Memories flooded back through a sleepy haze, and he swiftly caught up to his surroundings. He lifted the corner of the Long Dark Cloak and peered beneath just as Alfred jumped to his feet, alert.

"Canute is healed," Sebastian said with a tired sigh from the confines of the cloak. "Porcupine damaged him badly, and it didn't help that I know nothing about the physical makeup of a canine. He will be fine and able to chase wild ponies once again, though I suggest he not do it around here."

Ivan's smile turned into a burst of laughter. He threw back the dark broadcloth, now caked with dried blood, and looked down at his beagle nestled on his lap. He folded Canute in his arms and lavished affection. The sight was such a delight that Ivan chortled and cried all at once.

Nudging his brother with his nose, Alfred licked him with a warm darting tongue while Canute struggled to escape the cocoon. He managed to raise himself to Ivan's chest and slathered his face with kisses. He pushed from Ivan's arms, dropped to the ground, and shook his hind end.

The dogs chased each other. They raced around brown rock piles and scraggly bushes with no cares in the world, it seemed. Ivan nodded, grinning.

"Sorry, I didn't match the hair quite right," Sebastian said from the confines of the cloak.

"Thank you so much. It's doubtful he'll care."

"It's the least I could do for all you've done for the Forest."

Returning a weary grimace, Ivan inhaled joyful tears. He rubbed something that had dried and clung to his cheek, a mixture of mud and blood. This reminded him that he needed to wash himself and Canute before they left. He could scarcely bear the dragons' stench that permeated the both of them.

"It'll only take a minute or two for me to scrub my beagle." Ivan again thought about his mission, his promise to Zephyrus, the urgency to find Peter.

Sebastian conceded with a brief nod, though he didn't appear really pleased about yet another delay.

Ivan washed the filth and blood from Canute in the river flowing by the high ridge. The dog was not fond of bathing to begin with, and the water was cold, moving swiftly. He complained and squirmed and then shook the water from his coat and sped off to nip at his brother's ear.

Stepping farther into the chilling river, Ivan shivered from the cold. He removed the cloak and pulled off his shirt, dunking them both, trying to rinse off the bloodstains. Bath completed, he waded to shore, and with a swirl of black, he draped the soaked garment over a nearby bush.

Ivan felt the gnawing pangs of hunger, but there was nothing to eat. The milk and sandwiches Colin had prepared for their journey were gone, sacrificed to the voracious beasts.

With bare shoulders warming under the sun, Ivan took several deep breaths. "We'll never save Zephyrus if I wait here to dry. Wet clothes or not, we need to leave this dreadful place."

Sebastian agreed. Drawing his fingers through his disheveled hair, he shifted his stance. His tired face wrinkled and scrunched up, causing him to look a bit guilty. "I'm sorry for this, and I'm even sorrier I didn't tell you everything. I encouraged you to travel in this direction, believing it would be safe enough, but I left out some important information."

"Oh?" Ivan turned with a worried expression.

"The part where Porcupine ate Commander Simon's beagle," Sebastian said quickly. "That's why Simon can't bear to come here to do his duty and rid this swampland of its gruesome predators. The thought of losing Roman still brings him to tears. He really loved his dog."

"I certainly understand. It's over now, and the outcome can't be changed. I'm just grateful Canute is alive, running on all four legs again."

Gazing westward, Ivan sighed. They had a long distance to travel before they would return to Zephyrus. His brow bunched, and his left eye twitched anxiously. "Tell me," Ivan asked, "about the youngsters' deformed skeletons there on the shore."

"Youngsters? Oh. Yes—that. I saw them too. They

actually belong to trolls."

"Trolls?" It was the last answer Ivan expected.

"I remember several of the squat little fellows escaped from our Troll Transformation Prison about three or four years ago." Sebastian scratched his forehead. "I suppose I can now report with certainty they ended up here."

"T-trolls actually exist? Just like Peter tried to tell me, but I doubted his stories. He told me one of the trolls bit him on the chin. You can see the scar yet today."

"Yes, I know about Peter's scar and, yes, trolls really do exist," Sebastian replied. "They live in squalid prison conditions. I'll speak to you about our shameful troll population as we travel. It's more complicated than you would at first think."

It seemed to Ivan that everything in the Forest was more complicated than he'd first thought.

With that announcement, Sebastian strode up the slight incline from the river. "Now, we should leave at once." He rotated his arm slowly, and with little effort, it seemed, the smoky fragments of a horse appeared. The animal soon solidified while Sebastian called soothingly, "Stand still, Old Bones," and he mounted.

Ivan pushed images of skeletons and trolls aside and wondered glumly how far he'd have to go to find Bounty and then return to the shore to retrieve his saddle. "Can you take the saddle if I put it over your legs?" he asked. Sebastian assured him he could.

Just as Ivan reached for his wet shirt draped over a holly bush, he heard animals snorting behind him. His heart thumped wildly, fearing a Swamp Dragon had caught up with him, seeking her dinner. Grabbing The

Protector's hilt, he whirled around and jerked the sword from its sheath. He leaned forward, prepared to do battle and slash the hungry dragon to pieces.

To his surprise and delight, he found himself looking up into the blue-green eyes of a stunning young girl.

A gentle, melodic voice spoke, "That's quite a welcome, sir."

Chapter Eight

A Telling Kiss from a Goddess

Ivan stared at the lovely lady and saw a sweet smile, the glint of gold in her eyes, and long dark lashes. She was the High Goddess Anna-Iza, the same girl he'd seen on Barkay Road.

She sat atop her horse wearing a forest green riding cloak and gazed down at him. Her thick auburn curls were covered with a hood bordered with creamy white trim.

Ivan relaxed his rigid stance, feeling a hot flush spread down his bare chest. Slowly, he lowered his sword. He stood before her like some barbarian prepared for battle with wet, stained trousers and a mortified expression.

Remembering his manners, he cleared his throat. "Please excuse me, your Highness, I wasn't expecting company." He turned his back and hurriedly shoved his arms through the sleeves of his damp shirt and tucked it into his trousers. His embarrassment continued when he noticed his shirt had rusty blood stains that had refused to wash out. A button was missing from his sleeve's cuff, so he rolled them both to his elbows. Reaching for the Long Dark Cloak, he twirled it around his shoulders, hoping it would hide the soiled spots on his clothing.

Sebastian's eyes opened wide, and he gave a friendly wave.

Anna-Iza slipped quietly from her horse where the soft whisper of her boots came to rest upon the ground. "It's lovely to see you again, Sebastian," her melodic voice sang.

"And so it is with me, your Highness." Sebastian moved toward her and embraced her.

Ivan stared past the girl and toward the horses, too shy to meet her eyes. He recalled what he'd admitted to Sebastian—that he hoped for a test of her *kiss.*

"He is called Rainier." Anna-Iza followed Ivan's gaze. She stroked the horse's charcoal-gray nose and patted his cheek with her slender hands. The reins she held didn't belong to her winged silver stallion but rather the most elegant, pure white Andalusian Ivan had ever seen.

At last, he found the courage to face the girl. Her beauty nearly stole his breath away. She was slender under the gentle folds of her riding garment, revealing a green empire-fit dress with gold piping and floral embroidery that edged the garment's high neck.

Ivan greeted her with a broad smile but couldn't find his voice.

Returning a polite, though apprehensive nod, her inquisitive eyes moved from Ivan's face to the cloak he wore. And then she peered curiously at Sebastian. "I saw you on Sir Barkay Road yesterday. I became concerned and changed my journey's destination to make your acquaintance."

"Dear Anna-Iza," Sebastian said, "this is Ivan Kimble, and he is traveling with me." He added gravely, "We are in a hurry to see Fungoda."

The goddess's bright eyes widened, and the arch of her brows rose. For a moment, Ivan wondered why his name seemed to astonish her.

"You are from the outside then, Mr. Kimble?"

"Yes, my farm borders the east side of Graydon Land Grant." *How does she know I'm from the outside?*

Anna-Iza pressed her soft lips together. A worried look caused a wrinkle in her otherwise smooth forehead as she studied Ivan's face.

He felt he owed her an explanation since Sebastian hadn't said more. "I came to find my brother Peter. Do you know him? Have you seen him?"

"Yes, I have met Peter—"

Before she could finish her sentence, Ivan jumped toward her excitedly. "W-where? Are you sure he was my brother?"

"Oh, yes," she insisted. "Most people in the Forest know him. He shares some of your physical traits."

"Does he have blond hair and blue eyes, and his jaw is quite angular?" He traced his own jaw as an example when he asked the question.

"Yes. And his nose is strong and straight like yours."

Ivan breathed rapidly. He wanted to ask more questions, but Anna-Iza looked away and seemed reluctant to go into further detail. Was there some deep secret about Peter that she was trying to avoid answering?

"It's been a long time since I've seen him. Perhaps you should ask Fungoda. He is wise and knows all things."

"We'll ask him." Sebastian raised his arm as though that ended the matter. "In fact, we should be on our way."

A loud snort from a horse in the meadow caused Ivan to turn his head. Blinking, he pretended to shield the afternoon sun, not wanting Anna-Iza to see his uncertainty. To his amazement, lined up some distance away were at least a dozen stunning Andalusian horses. Young ladies clothed in colorful traveling cloaks sat silently upon their mounts, staring at him. *No beauty compares to this in my own village.* He stifled a grin. *Surely not Bonnet, who Mrs. Hambuckle hinted has a crush on me.*

Gesturing with a graceful sweep of her hand, Anna-Iza said, "These are my sisters. We are thirteen Protective Goddesses, and as our name suggests, we are guardians. When it becomes necessary, we protect and defend the Forest with our spells and chants."

Ivan's heart warmed to learn of their magic, dedication, and courage.

"We found a saddle." Her voice rose excitedly as though just remembering. "One of my sisters holds it. Does it belong to you?"

Ivan didn't want to explain how Bounty's saddle slipped over his rump, and Ivan went flying along with it, falling on a heap of bones. How could he reveal his own lack of bravery at the very end when it was almost too late to save Canute?

"That would be mine." Ivan eased up a reluctant hand.

"It sadly lacks a horse," she said with light humor, showing beautifully shaped lips that framed small white teeth.

Ivan laughed and answered with his own subtle wit. "I'm sure my spoiled horse doesn't even realize his saddle—or his rider—is missing."

It was the goddess's turn to laugh. Her musical laughter enveloped him. He knew he was grinning widely because his teeth felt the chill, and his chest turned warm.

"How did you find it?" Sebastian asked.

She turned to point. "It was there, near the shore. We were dreadfully worried its owner and his horse were victims of those awful Swamp Dragons. Thank the Gods of Olympus that was not the case."

"I thank you, Anna-Iza." He gave a graceful bow.

"We were curious why the shore is littered with fresh carcasses of the Swamp Dragons." Anna-Iza reached her delicate hand to tug at a curl, twisting it anxiously around her small fingers. "What do you suppose happened to them?"

Giving the lake's shore only a brief glance, Ivan shrugged and peered in the distance as though he had no knowledge of the incident. He certainly wouldn't confess his tumble over Bounty's rump to this charming girl.

Sebastian shook his head indifferently and clasped his hands behind his back.

Changing the subject as quickly as he could, Ivan motioned toward the rocks and green ferns where the dogs played. "Those little rascals are my beagles, Canute and Alfred. They were named after early kings."

Anna-Iza beamed. "They have a great deal to live up to."

"I'll say." Ivan thought back on the catastrophe that nearly took Canute's life.

The goddess became serious. "Why do you wear the Long Dark Cloak?"

"We are on a desperate mission." Sebastian took the question and answered it abruptly as though to hurry the conversation along. "Ivan Kimble has agreed to help us."

"What is your mission?" Her dark lashes fluttered.

Sebastian briefly told the story. "The Silver Axe was laced with a devastating poison and used to axe Zephyrus in his side. It may yet take his life. The pain has caused him to go into dormancy. Now he sleeps to preserve what strength he has. We must hurry to get the healing sap from Fungoda, or surely Zephyrus will die."

The goddess pressed her hand to her mouth, holding back an anxious cry. "That explains why he hasn't responded to my Root-Underground messages today." Her voice quivered. "We, too, must hurry to protect the Great Oak."

Sebastian dipped his head thoughtfully. "Yes, that sounds prudent."

"You still have a long distance to travel." Anna-Iza glanced over her shoulder in a westerly direction.

"I know," Sebastian said, "and that's why we really must be going." Grasping his horse's mane, Sebastian tucked his boot into the stirrup and pulled himself into the saddle. He turned to stare at Ivan and rolled his eyes in an impatient way.

Anna-Iza shook her head. "I regret we came on our common horses instead of our winged stallions, or I would go fetch the sap myself."

"How far away are your flying horses?" Ivan suddenly saw the answer to shorten his journey, to be free and search for Peter.

"The stables at our Crystal Palace are quite a distance from here. But more importantly, we are needed at Zephyrus's side to chant and pray and keep him safe."

"Sorry, I didn't realize." Ivan gave a half-bow, feeling the heat rise from his neck to his cheeks.

The lovely girl bit her bottom lip. "Who do you suspect is responsible for committing this terrible crime against our dear Zephyrus? I can't imagine anyone so cruel." She frowned.

The serious set of her mouth caused his heart to quicken. Her blue-green eyes sparkled with the touch of the afternoon sunlight. His breath seemed trapped in his lungs, and it was most difficult to breathe.

"We don't know the identity of the man or his reasons for axing Zephyrus." Sebastian squirmed in his seat, making quick motions with his head. "The attacker's face was concealed in shadow under the hood of a gray cloak. According to the three birches, the culprit is tall, at least Ivan's height."

For one awkward moment, Ivan saw a skeptical rise in Anna-Iza's brow. *Does she think I'm the perpetrator? Why would I be here wearing the valuable Long Dark Cloak and accompanying Sebastian on an important mission if I were the axe-wielder?* He hoped to reassure her that he was only here to help when...

The goddess raised her face and looked deeply into his eyes. "May I kiss you?" she asked, as though it were the most ordinary question to put to a young man she'd never met before.

Ivan answered at once without stammering, "I would like that."

Her warm hands came to rest on Ivan's bare forearms. She stood on her tiptoes and closed her eyes. Ivan stooped, bringing his lips to hers.

With a start, he realized this was the Kiss of Discernment that Sebastian had told him about. It was the goddess's method of testing him. Touching the High Goddess with his hands was prohibited, he'd been warned, but Sebastian said nothing about returning her kiss with enthusiasm, and that's exactly what he did.

What would the kiss tell her about his character? His lips pressed against hers while his senses spun crazily, soaring skyward. It was like no other kiss he'd ever felt in his fifteen years—not that he'd had other kisses—because he hadn't.

Her breath was a soft, musical whisper against his lips.

The girl did not move away but seemed to linger. *Did her fingers squeeze my arms even tighter?* He wanted to pull her closer and their kiss to go on forever.

Gazing back at him, Anna-Iza's smile lifted the corners of her sweet mouth. "You have made a wise choice, Sebastian. Ivan Kimble is a fine and trustworthy person."

Anna-Iza turned her head and gave a brief nod to where the twelve goddesses waited patiently. One came forward on her stallion, where she held a covered basket on her lap.

"This is Diana, my Goddess Advisor," Anna-Iza said. "She holds lunch for you."

Ivan bowed and thanked the girl. "May I take it?" He took several steps closer to Diana.

Frowning, Anna-Iza reached for the woven basket from Diana's hands. "Thank you, but I can do this myself."

He dropped his arms to his sides and waited, wondering if he'd done something to offend her.

"He knows about your non-touching rules," Sebastian said, and Ivan confirmed this with a tip of his head.

"Oh." The two goddesses raised their eyebrows. "We didn't realize," Diana said and smiled in a friendly manner.

"Our kitchen eunuchs have prepared a midday meal for you." Anna-Iza offered the basket to him. "I believe it contains the kinds of food you and"—she glanced at the dogs –"your beagles will enjoy."

Ivan thanked the goddesses as he reached for their lunch. Although eating wasn't on his mind right then, no doubt, the gnawing pangs of hunger would soon return.

"I hate to interrupt," Sebastian whispered as he leaned from his horse and fidgeted, "but we really must be on our way."

Ivan's gaze remained on the girl. "Where are you going now?"

"We'll travel to Zephyrus. There, we'll dance and chant our prayers, surrounding him with our Protective Spell. We'll keep him safe until you return with the sap. But please, do hurry."

"We will," Ivan promised.

She suddenly looked overcome with worry when Rainier galloped to rejoin his mistress. His golden reins jingled while his brilliant white tail whipped behind him. He raised his head and shook his mane.

Ivan memorized her every movement. The swing of her long green skirt, the drape of her riding cloak as she mounted, and her pleasing fragrance.

"Is there more we can do for you before we leave?" she asked.

"If you hear anything about Peter, anything at all, will you please get word to me?"

"I will," she replied.

"And, if you happen to find a chestnut horse that sadly lacks a saddle..." Ivan grimaced. "Would you send him back in my direction?"

Anna-Iza laughed delightedly. "I'll do better than that." She turned to call one of her sister goddesses and introduced Lanee. Yellow-haired, wearing a pale violet-hooded cloak, the girl held Bounty's saddle over her lap. Ivan thanked her and pulled it away.

"Lanee, please lend Ivan your horse. He and Sebastian are on a most important mission."

The girl appeared startled as though she might protest. After a moment, she nodded with a slight tug of her eyebrows. She dismounted and strode toward a sister goddess where she nimbly hopped on behind her.

Sliding her hood over soft curls, Anna-Iza brushed the strays from her face. "We will see you when you return to Zephyrus. Do hurry. His life is in great peril."

"Yes, and I'll look forward to seeing you again," Ivan said politely. His gaze held steady on her face.

The goddess swept onto Rainier's back with almost no effort and urged him into a fast trot. Her retinue followed in formation. Soon, only the sound of muted hoof beats echoed through the open meadow.

Ivan stood there gawking at the galloping horses fading into the distance. He was convinced Anna-Iza found him just as fascinating. He could tell by the way she looked at him and held his eyes with her own. He knew by the way she laughed at his joke. He knew by her lingering kiss, and that was the most telling of all. Ivan sighed. "She's a beautiful girl with a kind nature."

"That she is, but we must go now." Sebastian stood in the stirrups, searching far down the road. "Maybe we'll be lucky, and your rebel horse will find us first."

"Will you carry the basket?" Ivan asked, and Sebastian motioned for him to place it on his lap.

Ivan settled onto the Andalusian, hefting Bounty's saddle across his own legs. The striking white horse turned his head to stare at Ivan with wide brown eyes.

"Does he talk?" Ivan stared back.

"Why don't you ask him and find out." Sebastian chuckled.

Ivan posed a few questions to the animal, like his name and the capital of India, but he gave no answers. The Andalusian suddenly took off running. Whooping a startled cry, Ivan held on tightly.

They galloped down the strip of land that edged the river with the beagles following. After a time, Ivan slowed the powerful horse to check on Sebastian, who looked a bit weary and worse for wear.

"Ah," Sebastian said, "thanks for waiting up."

"What do the goddesses do?" Ivan stroked the Andalusian's smooth neck. "I mean, what is their importance here?"

"Well, they protect the Forest, of course." Sebastian's rapid breathing blended with the wind that rustled through the boughs. "One of their most important duties is to look after Zephyrus and aid him in any way they can. And it's the High Goddess's duty to teach her sisters and demigoddesses about becoming good stewards of the Forest. All that goddess protocol, you know?" Sebastian's tone unexpectedly turned serious. "Why do you ask? Do you hope Anna-Iza will love you?"

"Yes," Ivan said at once, glancing at his companion with hopeful eagerness.

"And what would you expect Anna-Iza to do for you? The goddesses are not domestic. They know nothing of caring for a home or raising children. Their life is devoted to Zephyrus, his needs, and to the Forest."

"Only that she would love me, and I would love her." He remembered what Sebastian had said about Anna-Iza reaching a certain age, and she would be obligated to marry a nameless god in a faraway country. A terrible sadness swept over him, and he closed his eyes to stop his tears.

Sebastian fell silent. "I'm afraid that would be impossible," he finally said, exhaling.

"Why?"

"Look over there." Sebastian pointed ahead and to the left. "Is that Bounty behind the hedgerows?"

Ivan stared off into the distance. He sensed Sebastian intentionally changed the subject. "No, it's just a shadow." He dug his fingernails into the pommel of the saddle resting over his legs, struggling to hold back tears.

"I'm sorry, Ivan. It's like I told you before. Loving or marrying a goddess can never be, not this goddess, anyway."

"Because I'm an outsider?"

"It's because of their rigid code of behavior, which has rarely been violated during their extensive history." Sebastian nudged his dusty, gray horse next to the Andalusian. "I wish with all my heart it could be as you want, but…"

Ivan's bottom lip poked out. He was unwilling to

accept the finality of Sebastian's disturbing words. "We should eat before we continue on." Ivan pouted. "There's no reason for you to carry the heavy basket, and my dogs are hungry."

They guided their horses toward the side of the road where several downed trees allowed them a place to sit. Ivan removed the saddle and took their lunch from Sebastian's lap. Lifting the starched linen cover, he spotted several thick meat sandwiches, a liter of chilled milk, and two fat red apples.

"There's no cutlery," Ivan sulked. The quiver in his voice betrayed his hurt feelings. It didn't matter that Sebastian saw his helplessness. By now, the spirit had become like a wise and kindly old grandfather.

"Cutlery? Why would you want that when you have a sandwich?" Sebastian turned to look at him. "The bread serves as its own package, doesn't it?"

"I always quarter them." He sniffed. "My mother taught us it was more civilized."

Sebastian was quiet for a time. "Ivan, I'm sorry your feelings are hurt. A High Goddess such as Anna-Iza must set precedence for her sisters. It is her accepted fate in life. Like her goddess mother before her, and her mother before her. The position is inherited, like it or not."

Ivan squirmed on the edge of the downed tree trunk. Removing the milk bottle, he jerked off the cap and drank slowly. He had no appetite. He only wanted to go home and sleep in his own bed.

"I know she favors me. I felt her affection in the way she kissed me. The way her pretty eyes looked at me. I can't explain it. A man just feels it inside."

"I don't doubt she found you agreeable, kind-hearted, and a generous young man." Sebastian tapped his temple. "Kissing you would have revealed these things to her. I'm also sure she discovered things about you that you don't even realize. That's her job—to learn about our visitors before they are an accepted part of our Forest. That's why it's called a Kiss of Discernment."

"I know what I felt." His dour mood unchanged. "I trust my feelings."

Sebastian gave a heavy sigh.

Delicious, Ivan decided, after he'd carefully torn off a small chunk of his lamb sandwich, chewing deliberately. *Maybe I am a fool, seeking love in a mystical Forest where I understand so little. This is a place of strange rules, talking inanimate objects along with some very odd creatures.*

Canute and Alfred gobbled their portion, unaware their master was falling in love with the highest goddess in the land. Ivan could do nothing to stop the feelings that enveloped him.

Anna-Iza had captured his heart.

Chapter Nine

Illegal Fireballs

Riding on, Ivan moved between joy and resentment. Sebastian threw him a glance from time to time but gave no more advice.

As the afternoon sun lowered, they hesitated at a crossing where someone called Sebastian's name.

"Who is it?" He raised his spectacles and scanned the treetops.

"Up here," called a high, thin voice with a meowing edge.

"You scared us, Pousses." Sebastian sheltered his eyes from the sun. He turned his head toward Ivan and said quietly, "The winged skink-cats are unfriendly, stuck-up, and always selfish. The only friend this breed of cat can claim is Lord Richard Graydon, and that's probably because of his generosity when it comes to feeding and housing the short-haired little freeloaders. Well, that's the opinion of most Forest people, and I happen to believe the assessment."

Ivan smothered a laugh.

"Pousses, meet Ivan Kimble. He lives near the border of our Forest."

The cat snarled and ignored the introduction.

"Are the games at the castle over?" Sebastian raised his head once more to speak.

"How should I know, and why should I give a piddle?" Pousses said brusquely.

Ivan stared. *A talking cat! It can't be true.*

"What's he doing here?"

"He's a friend and a visitor."

Pousses huffed.

"His face is even more disagreeable than I remembered, with a disposition to match." Sebastian scowled and lowered his voice. "Pousses is a funny little creature with paws that look like fancy white boots. His feathery wings are tucked back against his charcoal-gray fur. He has a pushed-in face that resembles the Algerian sand cat, and indeed, so the folklore goes, they'd descended from the breed long ago. When the gods first created the skink-cats, they forgot to give them the keen eyesight generally awarded to felines. They constantly flew into tree trunks and other hard surfaces until their faces became painfully flattened. Finally, the gods took pity on them, accepting their oversight, and granted them exceptional vision. But the cats' unwelcoming and sour faces haven't changed through the generations."

Ivan raised an eyebrow, enjoying the story about the stuck-up cat.

"It's a *cat*-astrophe!" Pousses stood on all four paws, twitching his white whiskers. "Zephyrus sleeps and didn't wake when I called his name. Why are there no guards? No servants? I'll tell you why." The feline's fur bristled, his tail stretched high. "Because they're playing their stupid games at the South Castle, that's why."

"We know the danger." Sebastian crossed his arms over his chest.

"Humph-foe." The angry cat grunted. "No messages can be sent. Have all the trees been struck dumb?"

"Communication between them has been interrupted." Sebastian cleared his throat. "We're in a hurry to save the Great Oak."

"What's wrong with Zephyrus?" The cat cocked his head, eyeing them suspiciously.

"Some maniac hacked him with the Silver Axe. It had a type of poison we can't identify." Sebastian's scowl deepened.

Ivan chanced giving the information, hoping it was okay. "We're on our way to draw a special sap from Fungoda and bring it back to save Zephyrus."

Pousses hissed. He didn't seem to care much for Ivan.

"Fly to the castle and tell Lord Graydon about this." Sebastian's eyebrows came together, almost touching each other.

"But I just came from there. I hate all that raucous clamor. The people swarm everywhere in drunken stupors. Noisy braggarts, the lot of them. I couldn't stand another minute, so I left."

"Pousses, tell the garrisons to come," Sebastian said through clenched teeth. "Explain to Richard Graydon that Zephyrus's life is in jeopardy. They must put their games aside and leave at once."

The cat looked away as though weighing his decision.

"And one last thing."

"Eh? What would that be?"

"Stop for nothing, and hurry as fast as you can. This is our master we're talking about."

The cat meowed unpleasantly. He stood and spread his furry wings and leaped into the air, barely missing a jumble of branches. He didn't even bother to say goodbye.

"Brat." Sebastian spat after him.

****

Pousses soared, legs outstretched, flapping his wings, veering southward toward the castle. Soon, he passed over the mid-part of the Forest where the trees thinned in an open meadow. Two ponies browsed in the dappled sunlight, unattended. The cat flew fast, banked, and swerved to take a closer look.

Spotting ponies in the Forest was not unusual, but the sharp-eyed cat saw something below that bothered him. There, sprawled in the shadows on the damp grass, lay two boys, silent and unmoving.

Flying lower, the wary cat tightened his circle. He spiraled down further still, landing on soft paws only a few feet from the boys. It was Colin and Martin, the orphan servants from the Norman manor. An odd sulfur smell mixed with the odor of singed hair filled the area. The boys had been knocked from their mounts by the fireballs still lying on the ground, emitting thin strands of gray smoke.

The cat rubbed his eyes. He hissed and snarled, furious to learn that the horrid balls of flame had returned to the Forest. Only powerful wizards had been approved to possess these dangerous weapons for protection. But the Forest no longer had wizards—only trolls. When Maloof disgraced himself, the Order of Wizards left in shame.

Buzzing sounds and popping noises, like acorns hitting hard ground, interrupted the silence. After only a second, something hot smashed against his head. Vivid red, yellow, and green spots zigzagged across his eyes. His mind exploded into shards of pain and confusion. He smelled his own fur and skin burning, and he screeched in pain.

With a last conscious effort, the cat caught a moving shape. A squat form with a big round head peeked from behind a tree. The face grinned menacingly and sneered. Then Pousses had no thoughts at all. Only darkness.

****

Drawing a deep breath, Ivan's lungs filled with the earthy freshness of the Forest. He marveled at the delightful scenery as he galloped along with Sebastian behind him. Everything around him seemed more bedazzling than he'd ever remembered. The sky was brighter, the lawn was greener, and the crowns of the trees were full and lush.

A wide grin spread across his face. *This must be the feeling of love. Sebastian is wrong about Anna-Iza. She really does favor me.*

Sebastian turned his head and called, as he came next to the Andalusian. "Don't get too comfortable on the goddess's stallion. You'll have to release him eventually so he can go home to his mistress."

Ivan laughed. "As soon as I find that vagrant horse of mine, I'll let this one go."

Just as he finished speaking, Bounty broke through the bushes, running toward the elegant white horse where he raised his legs and bared his teeth.

"Bounty!" Ivan cried.

The angry chestnut horse came to a stone-crunching stop and reared, pawing the air with dangerous hooves. He snorted wildly, blew mucus from his nose, and screamed. Ivan watched in horror as Bounty pawed at his rival and tried to take a bite out of him. But the Andalusian jumped to the side, unharmed.

"Whoa, Bounty," Ivan yelled.

"Stop him!" Sebastian flailed his arms overhead. "He's mad with jealousy."

Ivan spun off the white horse and hit the ground hard, pulling Bounty's saddle with him from his lap. Making a show of it, he shouted, "There, are you happy?" He grabbed the crazed horse's reins and held them firmly. "Hold your horses. I'll strap on *your* saddle."

Rolling his upper lip over yellowed teeth, Bounty snorted spitefully. He leaned forward, twisted his head, and blew a glob of mucus toward his muscular competition. The Andalusian jumped away and whinnied.

Slinging the saddle over Bounty's back, Ivan pulled the girth strap tight and buckled it. After he caught his breath, he glared at his horse, who seemed temporarily satisfied. Bounty would probably stay angry at him for hours and into the evening.

The Andalusian gave Ivan a gentle nudge on his shoulder. He thought the horse was trying to say *goodbye*, or maybe, *good riddance*.

"Go," Ivan said. "Go back to the goddesses who are now at Zephyrus's side. Tell my sweet Anna-Iza I'll be joining her soon and that I... Well, tell her to stay safe until I can be there to protect her. Will you remember all of that?"

After a nod of his large head and a mean snort at Bounty, the white horse took off up the road, throwing stones and a long trail of dust. "I think he understood me." Ivan raised his brow until wrinkles appeared.

"You're definitely privileged. These horses have never had a man, much less a total stranger, on their backs."

Ivan mounted and grinned, calming Bounty by stroking his throbbing neck.

"That was a close one." Sebastian wiped his forehead.

They passed fields dotted with sheep, donkeys, and Friesian cattle. A few long-haired bulls raised their heads and looked quite disinterested as two horses and two beagles passed. Ivan and Sebastian galloped for a time and then slowed to a walk to allow the animals some relief.

Hedgerows and crumbling stone walls from ancient times broke the now-fading colors of late afternoon. Beech trees grew thickly atop lush rolling hillsides. Clustered villages edged the rushing water that raced through rocks and rapids to join King William's River.

Ivan took it all in, his heart swollen with affection for Anna-Iza. He would make the Forest safe for her. Memories of her were still fresh in his mind. Her lavender scent, the soft ringlets of her copper-tinted hair that brushed her delicate shoulders, her full but small pink lips. *Is she thinking of me, too?*

Dusk would soon claim the day, and he knew they wouldn't return to Zephyrus until late the next afternoon, barring any unforeseen delays. Their journey to find Fungoda seemed a marathon of interruptions.

Sebastian's voice snapped Ivan from his reverie. "Something peculiar's going on. Do you see it?" He pointed in the distance. "There's a brilliant light."

"What could it be, so isolated out here?" Ivan squinted, staring ahead. "A traveler with a torch…a lantern?"

Ivan gave Bounty several reassuring pats on his sweaty neck. His horse was still mad at him for the loss of his saddle. Somehow, to Bounty, everything bad was Ivan's fault. Rubbing his forehead, he sighed.

"The light seems to be coming from an old stone shed in the distance." Sebastian threw his arm toward the building, pointing. "The structure dates from the time of the Norman hunters when they kept extra supplies here. It's in bad condition, and I can't imagine anyone living in it.

Canute and Alfred held back, making short whimpering sounds. They dropped to their haunches and looked at each other. Ivan and Sebastian continued on, and not to be left behind, the beagles soon caught up.

The closer they came to the stone building, Ivan realized, the warmer and more brilliant the area felt. He tugged at the cloak strings around his neck, but he didn't untie them.

Lowering his voice, Sebastian leaned forward on Old Bones. "Someone is inside the shed. I wonder…the light…but it can't be."

"What?" Ivan asked.

Sebastian murmured, "Oh, my blessed High Intervener."

"Is there danger?" Ivan held his breath.

"Listen to me carefully." Sebastian's voice grew softer. "Dismount and tie Bounty next to this tree. Tell your beagles to be quiet and stay put. We need to get closer to the window so I can see what's throwing the light. And if it's what I think…"

Ivan slipped silently from Bounty. He repositioned the sword's sheath to his side, where he could release his weapon fast. He commanded his beagles to be still, though he didn't put much faith in their obedience. They rarely listened to him even in the most dangerous circumstances as he'd just experienced at Swamp Gorgon.

"Let's take cover behind these trees." Sebastian motioned, stepping gingerly. "Then we'll move in closer."

Shivering with apprehension, Ivan wondered what kind of mythical beast lurked behind the weather-beaten wooden door. He'd had enough surprises for the day, though it was probably too late to opt for safety.

"Maybe we should leave the poor soul and go about our business," Ivan said in a pleading tone. "What do you think? Sebastian, did you hear me?"

Gasping, Sebastian replied, "I never would've believed our good fortune after all these years. No wonder the light glows far and radiates heat. It's the Golden Lantern!" His voice cracked, sounding as though he was about to cry with happiness.

"Isn't that a-a—?"

"Yes, it's one of the Ancient Relics stolen from the Sanctuary of Truth nearly a decade ago. Imagine how thrilled Zephyrus will be when we return it to him."

Ivan was just as excited, knowing there were seven relics, not counting Sebastian, who'd never been lost. The Silver Axe had been found and was left propped against one of the three triplets. Now, the third relic, the Golden Lantern, is hidden in the old shed. *Is it possible the other four relics are inside?*

"Then who's in there holding the relic captive?" Ivan moved closer, squatting and hunching his shoulders. He wondered if it was the thief who'd stolen the lantern or a thoughtful benefactor who held it for safekeeping.

He couldn't have guessed Sebastian's answer.

"It's a troll. I just caught a glimpse of his ugly face peering through the window."

"A troll! What kind?" Realizing his noisy blunder, Ivan slapped his hand over his mouth.

"Keep your voice down, or you'll give us away." Sebastian turned his palm downward to indicate silence.

"Oh, I'm sorry. Is he a vicious meat-eater or a vegetarian? A very big troll or a small troll?" His fingers curved around the hilt of The Protector. He wondered how dangerous the troll was. They could bite you on the chin, but what else?

Canute barked. He either saw the creature's face against the window or caught his scent. Ivan shushed him. Only the crickets fiddled their legs as though forewarning the travelers of what was to come.

Just then, the troll pressed its big nose into the windowpane. Stumpy fingers cupped around his beady eyes and strained to see through the dirty glass. He looked this way and that, scanning the darkening surroundings.

"It's Maloof." Sebastian ducked low. "I think he spotted us." His voice shook with excitement. "We'll have the advantage if we wait for him to come out."

"Maloof is a fallen wizard, isn't he? You were talking to Tom Shiffert about him."

"That's the one. He was once highly regarded and a powerful wizard in the Forest. Long ago, Maloof enjoyed the love, praise, and admiration his followers lavished upon him, but then…"

Ivan studied the troll staring out the streaked window. "He doesn't look very tall or powerful to me. Judging from his small hands and shoulders, he must be the size of a child." Then Ivan remembered the whitened skeletons lying on the lakeshore. *Trolls really do exist.*

The lantern's light drenched the creature's broad face and thick brow, revealing dark spots and scars all over his nearly hairless head.

"How on earth did he become that way?" Ivan puckered his face with disgust.

"Most likely from disease," Sebastian said in a casual tone. "Those bumps are festered boils along with a large collection of parasites that have attached themselves to a perfect host. They suck blood, multiply, and then move on to another victim. Trolls, the lot of them, are ideal candidates because they never bathe. Too lazy or stupid to understand sanitation, I'd guess." Scratching his ear, Sebastian explained further. "Maloof became stunted after serving his ten-year sentence in Troll Transformation Prison. You'll remember I mentioned this earlier. The prison is located farther north from here behind those trees and surrounded by a thick stone wall. A dreadful place—absolutely putrid."

When a commotion came from inside the shed, like slow shuffling feet, Ivan dropped to his knees and cringed. *Had the troll seen them?*

Sebastian squatted near with some effort.

But Maloof did not leave the shed. He just stood there watching from behind the window, his drooling mouth hung open,

"I'm going to move toward the door to see if it's unbolted." As Sebastian rose to his feet, his body changed into a ghostly, foggy-brown color disguised as a wisp of smoke.

Ivan watched, spellbound, as the spirit glided to the shed.

After a short minute, Sebastian returned and became solid once more. "Funny, I would've bet my whiskers Maloof wasn't smart enough to bolt that door."

"Why was he sent to prison? Was it because of the Circle of Enchantment you and Tom were discussing?"

"It's disheartening, but yes. Maloof created the Circle, placing an enchantment on it. I might as well fill you in on some of the morbid details since we have to wait here." Sebastian leaned back on his heels. "Our Great Wizard of the Forest was revered for his wisdom, intelligence, and benevolent guidance. Zephyrus and Maloof were excellent friends. They shared long and meaningful conversations about the Forest, about its inhabitants, and about the entire world. I must say, it was sometimes quite beyond me."

Thinking on it for a moment, Ivan said, "It sounds like Maloof had it all—power, love, and respect. What happened to cause his fall, then?"

"What happened was that which always happens to men who give in to their own vanities. His Circle of Enchantment turned on him, allowing his own betrayal. Self-righteousness and arrogance replaced spiritual harmony in his heart. And with these destructive characteristics, Maloof committed an unforgivable crime against the Forest."

"What was it?" Ivan's curiosity rose.

Sebastian didn't answer the question but went on to explain, "Maloof plummeted from his lofty position in the Wizard Village. Most of his counselors and supporters left the Forest, disgraced. We've never invited them back—can't accept that kind of betrayal to corrupt our woodland."

Ivan let out a low whistle. "You're not going to tell me what Maloof did, are you?"

Shaking his head, Sebastian said, "It's a sensitive subject. Only members of the Forest Council of Seven are allowed to know the full details."

Ivan speculated what the wizard's offense could've been. Maybe he murdered someone while he was in the circle, or stole something valuable from Lord Graydon, or even betrayed a treasured secret to an old enemy. But it must've been a terrible crime to warrant a ten-year stretch in prison.

The fuzzy yellow disk of the sun had dropped near the horizon, taking on streaked colors of twilight. Pale fuchsia fused against blue-gray clouds with a splash of golden pigment peeking through.

"How long does it take to become a troll once behind the prison gates?" Ivan searched Sebastian's eyes.

"It varies a bit with each person depending upon their resistance." Sebastian tapped the side of his temple as though trying to recall. "About nine months, a year at most. In Maloof's case, the transformation took much longer than expected. He resolutely held onto his powers of magic and spells. He was a strong one, that's for sure. Even today, I have an uncomfortable feeling about his magical abilities."

Ivan considered Sebastian's statement. A tremor of

uncertainty rushed through him. *What have I gotten myself into?*

"I may have to force him out." Sebastian glared at the face that stared through the glass. "We can't wait here all night."

Nodding wearily, Ivan rubbed his eyes. He studied the troll's stained, jagged teeth and inwardly cautioned himself not to be bitten—like Peter had.

Sebastian quieted and sighed. "Now considered harmless, Maloof is a free troll with a dark past."

"It's illegal for him to have the relic in his possession, isn't it?" Ivan stretched his numbing legs. "I remember the triplets were quite firm on this when the Silver Axe came into question."

"Yes, a crime punishable by our strict laws." Sebastian struggled to lift his frail form onto his feet. He reached out, and Ivan pulled him upright.

"Thanks," he mumbled. "I don't think he's smart enough to hold the lantern for a reward. Sneaky, yes, but does he look smart to you? I'm sure there are others coaching him in his thievery."

Just as their conversation lulled, Canute growled and Alfred barked. Something had set them off.

A metal bolt jerked back from the shed door. Hard-soled sandals whacked against wooden floorboards as the door creaked open. A snorting sound like that of a pig sounded behind the door. It flashed a memory from when Ivan was about nine years old. He remembered how frightened he'd been when he heard shuffling feet—more than one pair—in the back of their barn where the calving pens were located. After a few moments, the barn door latch had lifted and opened. A short figure scrambled out and disappeared. Whoever had been there so many years ago had left. Ivan never figured who it was or what they wanted. He didn't dare tell Peter, who would've laughed at him for being a scaredy-cat.

The now unbolted door suddenly slammed open, and a blast of white light shot from the storage shed, sending a gush of hot air that shook bushes and limbs. Leaves swirled and scattered to the ground.

"Watch—the light!" Sebastian shook a bony finger above his head. "You're not going to believe this."

Ivan folded his arms and snickered lightly. "Most everything I've seen here is unbelievable."

Sebastian kept his focus on the light from the lantern, glowing brighter and brighter. "There, it whirls up and around the shed, over nearby trees, traveling between the branches heavy with foliage. Are you following this? It moves at the speed of light, rushing across wide meadows, down small valleys and marshlands, lighting and warming its path." Sebastian sighed and grinned. "It has a thinking process all its own, guided by Joseph, the spirit inside the lantern." He flashed a wink at Ivan.

Ivan's mouth dropped. "Light shouldn't b-behave this way," he stammered in a hushed voice. "How does it do that?"

"The Golden Lantern has announced itself." Sebastian smiled broadly.

"How do you know about this?"

"Simple, really. I know what Joseph can do."

Sebastian tipped back his head, his arms wrapped snugly around himself. Then he called softly, "Joseph, my dear and excellent friend, we are here to reclaim you."

"Joseph? A-a man inside the lantern?" Ivan's mouth dropped open.

"A spirit, just like me." He nodded.

Standing on the stone stoop, Maloof raised the Golden Lantern by its ring, swinging it to and fro. He seemed just as amazed to see a light beam take off over the treetops and fade from sight. His big head turned right and left, searching with piercing eyes for the barking dogs. The troll snorted mucus through his thick nose.

Ivan was certain it had been Maloof who'd visited their barn years earlier. There was no mistaking that sound.

The troll stood about four feet in height, not much more. Shirtless, his tattered brown jerkin breeches and button-less vest were stiff with filth.

"Don't expect to have an in-depth conversation with him," Sebastian said with sarcasm.

In spite of their tense situation, or maybe because of it, Ivan allowed a quick burst of laughter to escape. He slapped his hand against his mouth. "Sorry. What do we do now?"

Another squat figure appeared at the door. The second troll wore a dirty vest over a shirt and loincloth that looked soiled. Wet and stained, it drooped and would have slipped to the ground except the troll held it in place with one hand. He shoved Maloof aside and dashed toward the tree shadows.

Turning away, Ivan threw his arm over his nose. Sebastian didn't react.

"Who's that?" Ivan gawked at the second squat figure as he disappeared into the woods.

"Cecil." Sebastian hissed when he said the name.

"That dirty little bugger. He's the instigator. I should've guessed it."

"Who?"

"Cecil was Maloof's wizard counselor. We can do nothing now, but I know he's the troll behind this conspiracy."

Confused, Ivan dropped his arm from his nose.

"Remove the cloak." Sebastian reached for the garment and helped pull it from Ivan's shoulders. "When Maloof leaves the stoop to check on the noisy dogs, throw it over his head and hold your arms tightly around him. I'll put the troll under a harmless Stupor-Spell."

"I didn't realize you could cast spells." Ivan waited for further instructions.

"I seldom do, but I think I can remember this one. Be sure to grab the lantern's ring just as you drape the cloak over his head. Don't let it fall to the ground."

"Sure." Ivan pressed his lips together, creating a thin line.

"You're ready then?"

"Ready as ever," he replied quivering.

Maloof shuffled around to the east side of the old stone shed, searching. The glow of the Golden Lantern lighted the path, the bushes, and expanse of lawn. The light flickered swiftly as though signaling its rescuers.

The troll examined the lantern. Looking puzzled, he snorted. Mucus trapped in his throat sounded like a tug-of-war. Now Ivan was positive it had been Maloof in his barn long ago, and Cecil had been the other trespasser.

The stink of urine and excrement caused his stomach to lurch. Ivan fought a sudden need to heave the lamb sandwich he'd eaten earlier. He swallowed hard, focusing on what he was supposed to do. His breathing quickened, while beads of sweat collected on his forehead. "I've never done anything like this," Ivan said. "I-I can't harm another person."

"This is a necessary matter." Sebastian dissolved into smoke and dove into the cloak, becoming one with it. Canute gave a sharp woof.

Maloof scuffled to search the north edge of the Forest where Cecil had disappeared. Ivan sprang from his hiding place behind a wide tree trunk. Moving stealthily, he zigzagged through the trees until he reached the building's side. There he lowered himself to one knee, waiting for Sebastian to give the signal to throw the cloak over the troll.

"Get ready," Sebastian whispered from the cloak.

Ivan rose to his feet, drawing closer. Just as he was about to throw the Long Dark Cloak over the troll, Maloof turned around clumsily. Staring up at his captor, his eyes went wild with fear and surprise.

"*Now!*" Sebastian shouted.

Chapter Ten

Captured

Ivan threw the cloak over Maloof. One strong arm held the troll while his free hand shot forward and grasped the Golden Lantern's ring. He tugged and jerked, but Maloof would not release it. Tightening his hold around the troll's chest, Ivan squeezed harder. At last, the lantern was in Ivan's clenched hand. The struggling creature fought beneath the fabric making all kinds of grunts and snorts. Rolls of extra flesh made it difficult to get a solid grip.

"Watch for sharp teeth," Sebastian yelled from his confines.

"Blast it!" Ivan screamed. "Put him under. I can't hold him much longer."

Finally, the troll went limp, collapsing onto the gravel pathway, nearly dragging Ivan with him.

Gasping for breath, Ivan's heart pumped madly.

"Lower your light, Joseph. You're in safe hands." Sebastian gave a small chuckle.

With this victory came elation. Ivan realized he'd helped to find a valuable Ancient Relic. The heavy, rectangular lantern had a name, Joseph, the spirit of a man from long, long ago.

"Capital job, Ivan, ol' boy." Sebastian sounded pleased. "That wasn't so hard now, was it? Maloof should sleep for several hours." Easing his wispy image from the cloak, Sebastian raked his fingers through disheveled hair. He patted his own shoulder, congratulating himself. "I wasn't sure I could still perform a Stupor-Spell."

Ivan coughed and stood straight, averting his head from the unbearable smell. "I know him." He stepped away from the heap.

"What?"

"I mean, I heard him...them. Maloof and probably Cecil, too. When I was about nine years old, they were in the back of our barn. That noise, a kind of snorting, as though some poor creature was choking on his own phlegm. I was so scared I couldn't move until Peter came whistling through the barn door."

"They're not allowed outside the Forest." Sebastian gasped in surprise. "You saw them?"

Ivan shook his head. "I didn't see him, exactly, but I'd recognize that snorting if I heard it in my sleep. It was Maloof, I'm sure of it."

"What did Peter do?" The shock stayed on Sebastian's face.

"I never told him, or he would've accused me of being a scaredy-cat and making up stories."

Canute growled, barking sharply at a safe distance, snapping at empty air. Alfred howled and ran in a wide circle.

"Be quiet!" Ivan shouted, but they continued to bark.

"Maloof is foul." Sebastian wrinkled his face. "The dogs won't go near him."

Taking several gulps of fresh air, Ivan set the Golden Lantern down near a tree. Joseph's light sputtered, his warm glow faded.

"It's wise not to alert other trolls or marauders," Sebastian said for Ivan's benefit.

Ivan understood the warning. "What should we do with him?"

"Pull him inside the shed and shut the door. We'll be far away before he wakes up."

Ivan peeled the cloak from the troll's limp body.

"I think every infected pustule on Maloof's body broke." Sebastian stared at the pus clinging to the garment.

Coughing, Ivan dashed behind some holly bushes where he threw up. When he returned, he pulled his eyebrows together, and his eyes turned watery. Dabbing his mouth with his handkerchief, he managed to get control of himself.

It was impossible to imagine how Maloof looked as a man. A proud, tall wizard admired by all. Now, there was almost no hair on the rumpled body. Only a few wayward strands amongst the lichen-like growths clustered over his head. Ivan felt deep pity for the odd creature.

Dragging the troll over the threshold, Ivan dropped the deadweight body onto the hard boards. Maloof groaned and kicked his feet, and then he fell into the Stupor-Spell.

As the door shut behind him, Ivan stepped out holding the cloak at arm's length, his face puckered. "You don't expect me to put this on, do you?"

"Sorry." Sebastian held up both hands. "You can wear it inside out until we rinse it in a creek."

"Must I?"

"Yes. You need to keep the cloak on at all times

until it's safe to remove it. You heard Zephyrus say this." Sebastian's eyebrows slanted. "I've waited a long time to get even with this hideous little maggot. And now I realize it wasn't Maloof's doing at all, but rather it was Cecil."

"What should we do?" Ivan moved away, gritting his teeth.

"As soon as the trees can communicate, we'll send an alert for Cecil's capture. He'll be brought before the High Court Trial in a couple of weeks, and I suspect the outcome will not be in his favor."

Ivan blew air over his lips. "I smell just like a troll." He turned the cloak inside out, swung it over his shoulders, and tied the strings loosely around his neck, trying not to think about what clung to the garment.

Whimpering, Alfred and Canute backed away from their master. Canute sneezed, flattened his belly to the ground, and folded his paws over his nose.

Sebastian and Ivan rushed to the tree where Sebastian grasped the lantern's golden ring and lifted it at eye level. He greeted his old friend with enthusiasm. "My dear Joseph, how I've missed your clever wit and company for these past ten years."

"The honor is mine." Joseph's voice was gravelly-rough, as though he'd been asleep for ages. "I knew it was only a matter of time before I beamed the light amongst my blessed friends."

Sebastian spoke into the beveled glass panels. "Can you come forth? I'd like to see what you look like after these many years and to introduce you to my new friend here."

Joseph wheezed. "I'm a little weak at the moment, but I'm sure I'll manage to appear after a short while."

"Then we'll be on our way." Sebastian walked toward the tethered horses.

"So who are you, young man?" Joseph's raspy voice echoed from the lantern.

"I'm Ivan Kimble. I live on a farm near the east border of the Forest. I'm here searching for my brother."

"This brave lad has agreed to help save Zephyrus," Sebastian said for clarification. He handed the lantern to Ivan while Sebastian took hold of his horse's rein and mounted.

"What happened to our Great Oak?" Panic rang in Joseph's voice.

Sebastian told the horrifying story that led to their journey, seeking Fungoda. "We have to hurry," he insisted, clapping his hands. "I don't know the nature of the poison used on the Silver Axe or how long Zephyrus will live."

Ivan jumped into his own saddle, clutching the lantern in the crook of his arm. He was surprised how cool it felt against his side. It was as Sebastian had said…made of pure gold. The lantern was oblong and heavy, with small, carved lion's feet at its base. An etched design of oak leaves, vines, and acorns appeared on the four-sided panels.

"It's quite fancy and ornate." Ivan smiled at the glass lantern.

"*Oooh,* you're going to make me blush," Joseph cackled from inside. "It was crafted by a very talented druid, especially for Zephyrus when he became our king."

Ivan ran his index finger along the frame's gold edges and the tiny acorn door latch, appreciating the craftsmanship and precision of the Ancient Relic.

They rode on, climbing a rocky path. The beagles followed and seemed happy to leave the Norman shed and the smelly troll.

As they talked and traveled, Joseph interrupted Sebastian several times to express his outrage over the events of the past couple of days.

"It looks like I showed up at the right time," Joseph said. "Maybe I can be of some help. But why weren't the soldiers watching over Zephyrus? Where are the many Forest inhabitants, the servants?"

Ivan told about the Annual Competition at the South Castle. Sebastian had explained it so many times Ivan was almost an expert about it.

"Ah," Joseph said, "what a splendid event. Is it September already?"

Sebastian chuckled. "The years go quickly after you turn a thousand."

Joseph agreed with a chuckle of his own.

There was a low moan. And then another, followed by voices that hummed in hot anguish.

Ivan scanned the treetops. "Is that the wind pushing through the trees?"

"It *is the trees*. They're warning us that Zephyrus is dying, and we must hurry." Sebastian covered his face with his hands.

"Dying?" Ivan stared at Sebastian. "But the goddesses are with him now. They'll protect him, won't they?"

Sebastian shook his head back and forth. "I'm not so sure. The goddesses will stay the evil forces and shadows of dark magic. These things won't enter him, but with this strange new poison, the goddesses may not have the power to keep him alive." Sebastian's shaggy brows bunched together.

Ivan stared into the distance, his chest felt heavy. "We haven't even reached Fungoda, and already another day is passing into night." Ivan turned up his collar, snugging it closer to his neck, feeling more and more dismal. *With all these delays, I'll never find Peter.*

The trees continued to moan, though more softly now. The sounds carried on the stiff back of the wind, sweeping through the valley.

"I know you and your dogs are fatigued," Sebastian said, injecting a sliver of hope in his voice. Ivan figured it was for his sake. "It'll be nightfall soon, and even with the Golden Lantern lighting our way, we'll need to find shelter. The light will attract too much attention."

Sebastian pointed ahead and a bit to the right. "Not far from here, there's a pile of fallen rocks concealing a small cave. I regret it doesn't have the comforts of the cottage in the Hurst-in-the-Vert, but it will keep us safe from any danger for the night."

"What kind of danger?" Ivan turned and gaped at his companion.

Sebastian's brow wrinkled, his eyes narrowed. "I have an uneasy feeling that someone is following us." His gray eyes gazed about. "I believe we need to hide ourselves."

Chewing on his bottom lip, Ivan said, "I think we should continue until we reach Fungoda, even though it's getting dark. If Peter is out there cold and alone, I need to find him." An unexpected lump rose in his throat as he struggled to hold back a cry. But tears came anyway, slipping silently down his cheeks. He was glad it was twilight, so Sebastian couldn't see him.

"I'm dreadfully sorry your search for Peter has been delayed." Sebastian's voice was calm but firm. "These are challenging times, and your help is desperately needed. I've said this before, but I sometimes forget how young you are and, well, I-I'm sorry we must impose on you and your goodwill."

Ivan sniffed and waved the sentiments aside. His mouth was gravel-dry. "I only want to find Peter and go home."

"I know," Sebastian replied in a whisper. "I sense evil from below is following, stalking us. His fingers are long, his sword is sharp, and his intentions are lethal."

"Tereus, the demon of the Dark Underworld." Joseph's voice vibrated from inside the lantern. "A real scoundrel."

Salty moisture blurred Ivan's vision. The joy he'd felt by finding Joseph had faded. Only his thoughts of finding Peter and sweet Anna-Iza's last words sustained him. She'd begged him to hurry back with the healing sap, and yet here they were, delayed once again.

"You're too tired to go on." Sebastian sighed. "If not you, then your animals need rest."

Glancing behind where his beagles lagged, Ivan reluctantly conceded. Although he wasn't pleased they'd stay the night in a cave, he was grateful for a safe place to sleep. He was tired and hungry. His head ached. He felt his goal to find his brother was farther away than ever.

Joseph kept his beam low, showing only a thin shaft of light for the travelers' path. Ancient woodlands loomed ahead, a mix of tall, slender pines and spruce that grew on both sides of the road. Fuzzy shadows cast frightening shapes in the lantern's low illumination. Bounty stumbled in a rut, whinnied loudly, and caught himself.

"We'll stop soon, ol' boy." Ivan leaned back, stretching cramped muscles, and patted Bounty's wide rump for reassurance.

"I don't mean to be..." Joseph's words were garbled.

Bending forward, Ivan spoke into the lantern, "Sorry, will you repeat that?"

"I don't mean to be nosey, but what did you say about your brother?"

Ivan slowed Bounty. "I came here to search for my brother who's been missing since the war." He briefly retold his story.

"Sorry, I don't know anything about him. I've been imprisoned for a long time. I've never heard the name mentioned. What does he look like?"

Ivan repeated the characteristics they shared. That Peter's hair was golden, like the light of the lantern, while Ivan's was black like the cloak he wore. He even mentioned the scar on Peter's chin. Still, Joseph admitted, he didn't know anyone by that description.

"We'll ask Fungoda to tell us what he knows." Sebastian leaned across his horse and said, "If Peter is anywhere in the Forest, we'll find him."

Ivan felt a bit hopeful.

In time, the cave's entrance came into view, obscured by a huge pile of rocks, just as Sebastian had described. Ivan shivered, knowing he'd be staying in the dark tomb for the night.

Grasping The Protector's sheath with one hand, the lantern with the other, his tired legs dropped to the ground. He stared into the dark, vacant cavity and listened. Were wild animals hiding in there? Snakes crawling between the rocks? Flesh-eating bugs burrowing in the crevices just waiting for a fresh meal?

Ivan placed the lantern on the ground and pulled Bounty's saddle away, draping the reins over a tree limb. "Stay put, Bounty."

After Sebastian dismounted, he waved his arm in a circle, reducing his horse to dusty smoke. Swirling through the chilly air, the phantom image vanished into the Long Dark Cloak that Ivan wore.

Alfred and Canute whined the whole time they followed their master down the cavern's incline. "Sorry, fellows," Ivan said, "this is where we sleep tonight, and there'll be no dinner for us."

Ivan set the lantern on a flat, narrow rock and then placed the saddle and horse blanket next to it. He suddenly realized the hard surface would be his bed. "Oh, mercy sake." He shuddered. "I'll go wash the cloak in the stream I saw not far from here," he announced, still thinking on the tough accommodations for the night.

Ivan couldn't wait to wash it clean. When he left the cave, to his surprise, he found Bounty standing where he'd been tied. The horse snorted a friendly greeting, nuzzling the side of Ivan's neck, marking his jacket collar with a slobbering kiss. The gesture meant his horse had finally forgiven him for riding the Andalusian. Alfred and Canute quickly joined them, and they drank at the slow, clear stream that forked off the King William's River.

For the second time that day, Ivan dunked the Long Dark Cloak in a cold river. He turned his face away and scrubbed the broadcloth against a boulder to clean the troll's caked-on pus. Sebastian stood on the low bank watching, his arms folded over his chest, looking amused.

In time, the chore was done, and Ivan spread the cloak over rocks in the cave to dry.

The Golden Lantern turned up its glow and warmed the inside, helping to dry the garment. "I told you I'd be good for something." Joseph chuckled brightly.

Sitting on the rough rocks, Ivan unbuckled the scabbard from his waist. He rubbed his aching legs and back, trying not to moan. He tugged at his boots and puckered his face from the strong smell of his socks. "I need a change of clothing," he said, just as his stomach rumbled. He lay back on the cold, solid surface, resting his head on the curve of the saddle.

Sebastian turned to the lantern and asked eagerly, "Where have you been all these many years? What happened to the other relics that disappeared with you? The King's Scepter, the Bag-O-Bones, the Ancient Scroll of Wisdom, and the Black Book of Pearls. Where are they?"

"Whoa! Hold on," Joseph exclaimed. "I'll tell you what I know. But first, let me release myself from the lantern so we can talk eye-to-eye."

"You're up to the task, then?"

"I think so," was the hollow response.

Ivan propped himself on one arm, watching with fascination as Joseph materialized from the Golden Lantern. The light flickered, and he left his refuge. His head appeared first. His body followed in wispy streams of yellowish smoke until Joseph's form became clear. Somewhat shorter than the average man, his legs dangled in mid-air. His arms held out from his sides, he began to solidify. Then he lowered his feet onto the cave floor, looking a little surprised. He let out a puff of air, smiling at his accomplishment.

"Ah, I did it."

"My stars!" Sebastian gasped. "You've grown old since I've last seen you."

"You're no spring rooster yourself, old friend," Joseph said with a rusty laugh. He stepped forward, embracing and slapping Sebastian on his shoulders a couple of times. Sebastian's eyes glistened while Joseph's tears flowed unhindered down his pale, craggy face.

Joseph was a little bow-legged. His silvery hair, pulled back from a bare forehead, was tied with a leather thong. His brown tunic, quite unremarkable, hung loosely on his frame, but his eyes were sharp and intelligent. Turning stiffly, his smile wide with joy, Joseph bowed to Ivan. "It's an honor to meet a brave lad willing to sacrifice so much with only our promise to help find your brother."

"Your promise is enough." Ivan's expression said it all.

Leaning against the cave wall, Joseph looked thoughtful. His white and gray eyebrows raised high, his gaze swept toward Ivan and moved to Sebastian. The gesture implied he was prepared to tell his story.

Chapter Eleven

The Fall of Lord Henry Graydon

Joseph eased himself gingerly onto a ragged rock that protruded from the cave's wall. Leaning over, he dimmed the lantern's light so Ivan could drift off to sleep if he wanted.

"The person responsible for stealing the Ancient Relics from the Sanctuary of Truth was Richard Graydon's older brother Henry." Joseph paused and then went on, "He was trusted and loved by Zephyrus and the people of the Forest. That is, without doubt, how he deceived everyone."

"If that weren't so," Sebastian said, wagging an angry finger, "we'd be safely hung on wooden pegs in the sanctuary at this very moment and protecting Zephyrus."

"But why?" Ivan shifted and found a new position to lean on his elbow. "The castle and the entire forest belonged to Lord Henry. Why would he risk so much by stealing the very items that kept his kingdom safe?"

"Not all men born to royalty are worthy of their place in the world." Sebastian snorted. "But we're certain Tereus recruited Henry, promising him wealth and power beyond his imagination. Apparently, the West Forest wasn't enough to satisfy his appetite." Sebastian glanced at Ivan and then at Joseph as he pulled an eyebrow high. "We're aware that Tereus had been scheming to rebuild Helvaka ever since he was denied the throne more than a thousand years ago. I'm sure Tereus offered false promises of greatness, and that's how he enticed Lord Henry to deceive everyone." Sebastian shook his head. "How could Henry be so ignorant and selfish?"

"I've thought about it for almost a decade, and still, it makes no sense." Joseph pressed his thin lips even tighter.

Sebastian shrugged his sloping shoulders. "What else could account for such an unexpected and total betrayal? Tereus has always been conniving. He wants to reclaim the kingdom for himself more than anything in the world—and he'll use any method—or person, to attain his goals. Lord Henry became part of his hideous plan like so many before and after him."

Ivan shuddered, wondering if Peter had given into Tereus's promises of greatness.

Several bats left the ceiling, flying out the cave entrance. Ivan snatched the now dry cloak from the rock and wrapped it around his shoulders and neck.

"Who knows what plans Henry and Tereus have conjured?" Sebastian scrubbed a hand over his face. "I could be missing something important, but steal the relics, he did. It was an unforgivable crime against his people."

"After that, everything began to change for the worse, didn't it?" Joseph turned troubled eyes toward his ancient friend.

"It did. Henry disappeared with the relics. Maloof fell from grace, as did Cecil, his wizard counselor. They were sentenced to Troll Prison while his band of wizards left in shame. Both are free trolls, now. Up to no good, if I might say."

Joseph bent his head and stared at the cave floor as though trying to process the bad news.

"How did Lord Henry steal the relics?" Ivan squirmed on his cold stone bed, sighing miserably.

"It was simple, really." Sebastian growled. "So simple, no one ever expected it. Henry and an unknown person who accompanied him asked Zephyrus to open his sanctuary door. They walked in, nice as you please, gathered up the relics, and rode off."

Could the unknown person be Cecil, perhaps disguised, so long ago?

"That's the trouble with Zephyrus's lax guarding policies." Joseph balled his fists.

"I've said that very same thing many times." Sebastian waved a bony hand into the air. "The shock of Henry's robbery and treason left Zephyrus in deep despair for months. I could say nothing to ease his shock and disappointment."

Ivan's eyes fluttered. "Did Richard Graydon take Henry's place and become the new ruler?"

"He sure did." Joseph slapped his knees with joy. "I overheard that Richard is one of the finest lords the West Forest has ever known."

Sebastian confirmed with a swift nod. "He is highly regarded and mightily loved."

"What happened to Henry?" Ivan laid his head on his bent arm, and his voice became a whisper.

"Well…" Sebastian took a deep breath. "We still find it quite odd, but Henry has never been found. After he stole the relics, he simply disappeared, and no one has heard a word from him or his accomplice since. Not a cast-off garment, not a hair from his head. Richard Graydon nearly went mad with shame. How could he make up for his brother's betrayal to his loyal subjects?"

Sebastian asked Joseph, "Where did Henry Graydon hide you and the other relics after he'd stolen you from Zephyrus?"

"We were held captive in the Mountain of Smoke and Fire. Henry was sure his stolen treasures would be safe there."

"Good heavens!" Sebastian's abrupt words caused Alfred and Canute to woof. "I can't imagine any human who would enter that ghastly mountain."

"Henry had a special arrangement with the ghouls that live there." Joseph made a frightening face and stuck out his tongue. "Most likely, Tereus engineered the whole dirty business, though I don't know who carried out his plans since he's forbidden to come above ground." He cleared his throat. "After some time passed, the other relics were taken away one by one. I sensed it when they were no longer imprisoned with me in the uppermost chambers of the mountain. First, the Scroll of Wisdom was taken, and then the Silver Axe disappeared shortly after the Bag O'Bones. The Golden Lantern disappeared, too. Some arrangement made with one of those fallen wizards. Lastly, the Black Book of Pearls, our Forest's Bible, was removed, and I never heard from any of them again. I was sick with grief when the book disappeared. Those filthy ghouls can't even read, much less appreciate the centuries of wisdom and history it holds." Sebastian nodded in a slow, deliberate way.

"The book belongs permanently in the Sanctuary of

Truth, and it must be returned." Joseph clenched his teeth.

"And the King's Scepter. What happened to it?"

"Heaven forbid and rain fiery stones upon my head," Joseph repeated an ancient phrase. "The King's Scepter remains in the filthy hands of Hoxx, the ghouls' leader."

"Ghouls?" Ivan mumbled sleepily.

"I know about him," Sebastian said with a fierce look smoldering on his face. "He's bloodthirsty and savage."

"I can confirm that." Joseph bobbed his head.

Drawing up his long legs, Ivan had a quick dream flash before him where he was brushing his teeth and planning a change of clean clothing. His eyes popped open when Joseph coughed.

"Did you say the Silver Axe has been found and was used in the attempt to kill Zephyrus?" Joseph stood from the rock he was sitting on and rubbed his rear end.

"That's right."

"As for me," Joseph said with a heavy sigh, "I gave my interrogators nothing. I gave no light, no warmth, and no answers to their idiotic questions. They thought I'd extinguished my light when I turned my wick low, but I didn't go out entirely. The ghouls hung the lantern in a small chamber of their cave home. And there, they must've forgotten me."

"How did Maloof gain hold of you—that is, the lantern?" Sebastian growled.

"What a shock seeing Maloof," Joseph said. "I was appalled that our once Great Wizard had been reduced to a slobbering, dull-witted troll. It was actually Cecil who took the lantern because of a deal he'd struck with

Hoxx. Cecil is quite clever still. I always felt he was released too soon from prison. I think you agreed with me at the time."

Sebastian harrumphed. "I knew Maloof wasn't smart enough to plan such a thing."

"It seems that way." Joseph sighed, glancing at Ivan. "You still awake?"

"Barely," he mumbled.

"Tell me, how did Maloof fall so low?" Joseph asked. "What crime sent him to Troll Prison?"

"Mercy me." Sebastian choked.

"What did he do?" Joseph looked strained. "Since I'm not a member of the Council of Seven, I never heard the reason."

Ivan listened carefully.

"Maloof fell by his own self-pride. He gave into the bliss it promised. He thought his powerful standing and reputation would protect him from punishment."

Joseph's response was a painful moan. "The Circle of Enchantment?"

"You guessed it."

"I never trusted that circle. You know I was against it from the beginning, don't you? We talked about it, you and I. I think you agreed it could be misleading and eventually destructive to its participants. Especially if a person was overwhelmed with grief or deep emotional pain and used the circle for an escape."

"I remember," Sebastian said, his voice fading. "There were many of us who thought the same."

"Maloof's intentions may have been good in the beginning," Joseph said in the wizard's defense. "He used his magical skills to design what he called a 'Dwelling Place for Enlightenment.' "

"But it got out of hand." Sebastian finished the statement. "On the morning of the seventh day of his trial, Maloof was found guilty by our own Council of Seven. He was sentenced to Troll Transformation Prison for ten years. After the verdict, he threatened to get even with us all and said he'd make us pay for our shortsightedness." Sebastian's face puckered with fury. "He didn't think any of us worthy to judge him."

"Who'd have guessed Maloof had all that self-righteous pride?" Joseph's expression stiffened.

"Then Cecil's dark magic was used against you from the beginning," Sebastian sounded discouraged.

"Yes. We'll have to search in earnest for the relics. Without them, the Forest has no hope."

Ivan shivered. He promised himself he'd help find the relics. He was thinking of Peter's safety. He was thinking of Anna-Iza and his affection for her. He was thinking about Zephyrus and the wellbeing of all inhabitants of the Forest.

****

For most of the night, Ivan was too exhausted to dream on his cramped rock bed. His mind drifted, not settling in one place for very long. He tried to find a comfortable position, but each turn proved to be painful. He slept fitfully.

Near daybreak, Ivan sat up searching the gloomy cave, momentarily puzzled. *Where am I?* His stare met Sebastian and Joseph, who sat on their hard rock benches protruding from the wall, whispering to each other. Then Ivan remembered where he was. Saying good morning to the spirits, he rubbed the sleep from his eyes. He tugged on his socks and boots, hoping nothing wiggly had crawled inside.

Ivan stepped out of the cave and inhaled a breath of cool, early morning air. Alfred and Canute scampered after him when he ducked behind bushes to relieve himself. He passed Bounty and sighed with relief with his horse standing where he'd been tethered the night before.

Ivan raised his head and inhaled. "I smell something delicious." His stomach growled.

"Funny," Joseph said, "I don't smell anything."

"Neither do I." Sebastian tapped the side of his nose. "We spirits weren't awarded that gift."

Alfred and Canute must have caught the aroma too. They woofed and stood on their hind legs begging for their breakfast.

Just outside the cave, Ivan spotted several baskets with a note attached. In poor penmanship, it read: *We were delivering our goods to the South Castle for the tournament when Anna-Iza met us. She asked us to leave this for you. Very Truly, Whiskers and Muff.*

Ivan smiled, grateful for Anna-Iza's thoughtful gesture. "Who are Whiskers and Muff?"

"They are the little goat men who live in the King William's fertile valley. They are men from the waist up and have goat bodies from the waist down. Like you, they are farmers and always supply a wagon-full of goods to the Annual Tournament."

Ivan frowned and wondered about the creatures. *Goat men.* Soon, his hunger got the best of him, and he hefted himself onto a large, flat rock outside the cave and pulled the basket onto his lap. Lifting the linen cover, he saw a container of milk, a couple of meat pies, and a fresh loaf of bread. The next basket held a bottle of Ickleberry wine and at the bottom rested a small round of cheese. Its cover read: Made by the Wolflords. The Finest Quality Cheese in the West Forest.

"What's a Wolflord?" Ivan was almost afraid to ask.

"A rather newcomer to our Forest…been here about ten years," Sebastian said. "The pack was once werewolves, but they've been transformed into men. Perhaps you'll meet them one day."

Without much enthusiasm, Ivan nodded. *Yet another oddity.* A note appeared in the second basket, written in beautiful script: *Don't worry about returning the baskets. All things in the Forest eventually find their way home.*

Ivan was sure the note had been written by his dear Anna-Iza. Hurriedly, he divided the food between Alfred and Canute. They barely gave their master a moment to set down the meat pies before gobbling up their portion, lapping the milk quickly. The Ickleberry wine was left unopened. He didn't care for such a thing.

They finished eating their breakfast, and Ivan sat staring into the distance. Joseph and Sebastian, who didn't eat, left the cave and sat next to each other on the opposite side of Ivan.

What will the day bring? Doubt crept in, and the chunk of cheese Ivan had eaten threatened to come up on him. He shouldn't fret so soon after he'd consumed a big meal, but his worries intensified.

****

The pale sun rose silently, burning away the lingering fog. The promise of warmth set the Forest critters to chattering. Birds, like yellow warblers and stone chats, twittered and sang their beautiful songs.

171

These natural sounds uplifted Ivan's spirit.

Ivan stretched and twisted, trying to pull the kinks out of his back. He excused himself to Sebastian and Joseph, who were still talking about the changes and dangers in the Forest and made his way to the cold stream. There, with Canute and Alfred's helpful interference, Ivan washed his face and wiped dry on the cloak.

Impatient to leave, Sebastian conjured his phantom horse from the Long Dark Cloak that Ivan wore. Joseph climbed on behind, mounting with the grunts and groans of an old man. Ivan swung onto Bounty, holding the lantern as he did the day before, resting it on his thigh.

They wound their way through a small wooded valley following the King William's River for a time. They crossed over a series of rounded hillocks, and there Ivan stopped a moment to marvel at the dynamic clash of sky meeting the horizon's colorful morning streaks.

Today, Ivan was sure to learn about Peter. Fungoda would tell him. The promise at the end of his long journey gave him the courage to go on. He smiled at his companions.

"There ahead, just beyond that thick stand of timeworn oaks. That's where Fungoda stands." Sebastian's excitement spilled over. "Our destination is near."

"I'm looking forward to seeing our bad-mannered friend." Joseph showed a crooked grin.

"His disposition hasn't improved much since you last saw him." Sebastian chuckled.

Ivan drew an anxious breath, slowing Bounty.

Even now, he wondered if Fungoda actually existed or if this was a challenge to test his endurance. "Is it possible…" Ivan turned to ask. "Could we collect the healing sap from Fungoda and race back to Zephyrus yet today? Then, I could search for Peter."

"If we make good time and aren't waylaid." Sebastian wiggled his bushy eyebrows. "The trip home will be considerably faster. We'll pass swiftly through the White Rocks."

"White Rocks?"

Sebastian simply pursed his lips and teased. "You'll see."

The beagles raced to the bottom of the hill, tails wagging and ears flopping as they sped away, woofing at each other from time to time.

"Now, Ivan," Sebastian began. At once, Ivan didn't like his tone. "You must face Fungoda alone while Joseph and I return into our refuges."

"Why would you disappear at a time like this?" Ivan whined. "I don't want to deal with the bad-tempered tree by myself."

"Too many visitors at once will irritate him," Joseph said and frowned. "We wouldn't want to rile him."

Ivan gulped, wondering what he'd gotten himself into.

Sebastian said, "As soon as he accepts our presence and understands our important mission, I'm sure he'll cooperate." He stared ahead at the dirt path through the dark tangle of limbs.

"I thought Fungoda knew we were coming, and he'd have the sap ready." Ivan's zeal dropped.

"Only if an underground message has been sent

and received." Sebastian's voice sounded doubtful.

Ivan bit his inner cheek. It was bad enough he had to be here at all but to face the tree alone was even more frightening. Hands trembling, he gripped Bounty's reins tighter.

"Sorry, Ivan," Joseph said. "You'll understand why it's necessary after you've met Fungoda." His body turned gray and ghostly, and he rose like a funnel cloud of dust. "Open the glass door and hold onto the lantern, please," he called to Ivan. Joseph's apparition whirled and slammed into the Golden Lantern, evaporating inside. He hit so hard he nearly knocked it from Ivan's hands. A loud, painful groan sounded as if Joseph had crashed through a long tunnel. "Ouch, that hurt. I think I need a bit more practice."

Sebastian let out a whoop of laughter, causing Ivan to chuckle.

"It isn't funny," Joseph shot back.

"You need to slow down." Sebastian demonstrated caution with a hand gesture. "I remember that was your problem long ago."

The spirit in the lantern sniffed and muttered something, but Ivan couldn't translate it.

Ivan spotted a group of oaks ahead, so gnarled and thickly interlocked they seemed to support one another. Their curled faded brown leaves and dark branches closed out much of the sunlight within the grove. Underneath, the ground looked spongy, covered with a carpet of decaying leaves, fungi, and moss. Years and years of build-up had created a layer so dense that neither a blade of grass nor sapling grew.

"Careful." Sebastian shot his right hand upward. "The drooping limbs are brittle and could easily break.

Some of the trees are over a thousand years old. Fungoda himself is nearly five thousand years standing. This area has rarely been disturbed since man first recorded his thoughts and beliefs."

"Fungoda is five thousand years old?" Ivan couldn't believe it.

Sebastian gave a swift nod. "The High Intervener created him long ago."

"It's true," Joseph replied. "His great seeding was written about in the Black Book of Pearls."

"Why was he created?" Ivan stared ahead, expecting a glorious thick-trunked tree with shiny golden oak leaves.

"To keep the Forest safe until Zephyrus became the new king," Sebastian explained.

Turning Bounty's head, Ivan ducked low to avoid a mass of black-spidery limbs and wet leaves holding the morning mist. The deeper they traveled, the darker and eerier it became, with only the creaking of shifting branches and a soft whistling of the wind. Alfred and Canute stopped and sat on their haunches, looking at Ivan and whining.

"What's the matter? Come on, Alfred, Canute. Follow us, or we'll leave you behind." He couldn't blame them. The dark interior of Fungoda's domain put the shiver in him, too. The beagles growled and then hesitantly caught up with their master.

"I haven't seen Fungoda for nearly a decade," Joseph said. "Do you suppose he'll recognize me?"

"Certainly. You're quite unforgettable." Ivan let loose a crack of laughter, which even surprised him. Joseph snorted from inside the lantern.

Bounty gave a quick shake of his head.

"Even my horse is nervous." Ivan soothed him, stroking his neck with icy fingers.

"Stop here for a moment." Sebastian held up his hand. Ahead was a pathway, unhindered by trees or bushes. A single, twisted oak stood alone in a wide, irregular clearing.

"If that's Fungoda," Ivan said, squinting, "he's not as foreboding as I imagined. I thought he'd be huge and magnificent, like Zephyrus."

"He was in his day." Sebastian gave the reins a tug.

"We're all getting old." Joseph's far-away voice sounded rueful.

Fungoda listed dramatically to the left, his moss-covered trunk distorted with various sized burls. Scraggly limbs with only sparse foliage shot out in different directions. An especially large growth protruded on his trunk, giving the impression the tree was hunch-backed.

Ivan halted his horse. His chest quivered with the pounding of his heart. There ahead stood the tree they'd sought for days, Zephyrus's savior—Fungoda.

"Is he as fierce as you say?" Ivan asked Sebastian.

"His temperament can be nasty if his mood isn't just right. But my brave friend, what do you have to fear compared to your fight with the Swamp Dragons? You've accomplished what no one else could. You killed Porcupine."

Ivan's jaw clenched as he remembered the horrifying experience. He tried to summon his waning courage, but it failed.

"By the way…" Sebastian cleared his throat to give a quiet warning. "I suggest you wait before you ask him about your brother."

"Why?" Ivan heard his own anxious response.

"Don't worry. Fungoda will question you, but the timing must be just right."

"How will I know?"

"He will ask you."

"He knows why I'm here?"

"He will inform you soon enough." Sebastian pressed his lips together while new pucker lines laced his forehead.

Joseph growled inside the lantern. "That ancient tree is so persnickety."

"I pray he will be ready and waiting for us, so we can fill the vial with his healing sap," Sebastian said with weariness in his voice. "If not, then we'll be further delayed."

A little cry left Ivan's throat.

After a moment, Sebastian and his horse separated into long spirals of silvery smoke. They disappeared with a swooshing sound into the cloak that Ivan wore. He felt the familiar push and warmth against his back as they entered.

Sebastian called out, "Mystical One. Wake up. We desperately seek your help."

Narrow sleepy eyes pushed out from the dark-gray trunk, opening slowly. A wide nose broke the surface, and then a tightened mouth appeared through the bark. Ivan recognized a shriveled chin and beneath it, a jagged lump shaped like an Adam's apple.

"Heh? Who? What is the meaning of this outrageous disturbance?" Fungoda glared at Ivan.

He tried to answer, but his voice got lost.

"Well, can't you speak, boy? What are you doing here?"

"I-I've come to-to find my—"

Interrupting, the twisted tree roared. "You dare wake me during my winter sleep?"

"It's not even winter yet, you old gruff," a faceless voice from inside the cloak answered. "Where are your good manners?"

"Who speaks to me this way?" Fungoda asked through gritted teeth.

"It's not the man who speaks, but the garment he wears. You should know my voice, or does your hearing fail you as well as your eyesight?"

Ivan squirmed uncomfortably in his saddle. He wished Sebastian would be quiet and not provoke the old tree. After all, it was Ivan who must endure the magic tree's wrath.

Wispy trails of smoke rose as Sebastian's apparition, and the horse he sat upon, pulled from the Long Dark Cloak. Soon they became solid and fully recognizable.

"Sebastian, you terrible jester, is it really you?" Fungoda cried with delight.

"It certainly is. This lad is Ivan Kimble. He lives outside the Forest's boundary. We're here to save Zephyrus's life."

"Zephyrus, you say? What's wrong with my good friend in the north? And you, Sebastian, why were you allowed to leave the sanctuary when you're the last of the Ancient Relics? How can this be?"

Another voice spoke. "Not the last. I've been found." Within moments, Joseph appeared from the confines of the Golden Lantern. He took his place behind Sebastian on his horse. Joseph grinned, giving a frail wave. "I've returned to my friends of the Forest with great joy."

"Joseph! It's a miracle—after all this time." Fungoda's eyes opened wide.

"Then you haven't forgotten me?" Joseph laughed gratefully.

Fungoda's smile spread long across his wooden lips. Then his crusty old face registered some confusion. He glanced from Sebastian to Joseph to Ivan and back again.

"You *do know* we're here for a reason." Sebastian's voice was calm but forceful.

The tree's eyes darted about as though searching for the answer. "Tell me at once. Why are you here, and what has happened to Zephyrus?"

"Didn't you receive my message?" Sebastian exploded with desperation. "We have need of your healing sap."

"To save Zephyrus's life," Joseph replied.

Puzzlement reappeared in the tree's pale green eyes. "I have received no messages. What has happened to my friend?"

Groaning with disappointment, Sebastian released the reins and collapsed against the neck of his horse. "The healing sap remains deep in Fungoda's roots, and we must wait until he brings it up."

"How long will it take?" Ivan griped.

Shaking his head, Sebastian straightened with effort and slipped down from his horse. Joseph threw a bony leg over Old Bones and did the same. Ivan figured it must be safe, and he reluctantly dismounted Bounty, clutching the lantern in the bend of his arm.

Sebastian briefly told the story. "Nathaniel, the Silver Axe, has been found," he said, skipping many details, "but at a terrible price. The axe was used against Zephyrus in a most dreadful way. Through no fault of his own, Zephyrus has forced himself into dormancy to avoid pain. We pray your sap will save his life."

Fungoda stared at the visitors. With a heavy sigh, he asked, "What chance does he have to recover even with the healing sap?"

"I don't know." Sebastian's face turned grave. "There's no way to know until your sap has been administered.

"Does Zephyrus sleep unguarded when he is so vulnerable?" Fungoda raised his thick bark eyebrows.

"Anna-Iza and her sisters are with him." Ivan's neck grew warm as he thought of the dear goddess.

"That's very good protection," Fungoda said.

"Come here, Ivan Kimble, closer to me." The ancient tree's invitation was gruff.

Ivan took several apprehensive steps toward Fungoda, feeling like a condemned man about to hear his sentence. He looked into the tree's piercing eyes. There, Ivan stood mute, his mouth hanging open as he sensed the tree's supremacy.

"You are the *one*," he said.

"Yes, sir, I suppose I am. What is it you want me to do?"

The tree blinked several times as though clearing his thoughts after a momentous discovery. At last, he returned to the present. "Over here on a small burl just to my side, you'll find a latched door. Jerk it open. It may be snug since the recent rain swelled my bark. Remove the faucet and the vial."

Ivan looked inside the dark hole. Feeling around,

his hand touched the cool glass and a metal faucet. He lifted them out.

Fungoda told him where to screw in the faucet.

Straining, Ivan forced the rusty, threaded end deep into the wood's tough old fibers. He pulled the cork stopper from the vial with his teeth and hung it over the spigot by its wire hoop. He stepped back a few paces. Nothing happened.

The old tree sighed with relief. "I'm always glad when that part is over. Now I can concentrate on drawing the elixir from my roots to the surface. It will be a long, tiresome wait, I'm afraid."

Sebastian bent his weary head and muttered something under his breath.

Some time passed with Ivan staring at the vial, waiting. But still, nothing happened.

"Well, is it coming up or not?" Sebastian snapped. He eyed the glass from all directions, scrunching his face. He pressed his fists against his sides.

"Hang it, Sebastian. I'm not a maple tree, you know. I can't bring up sap at a moment's notice. It takes time to urge my lifeblood through my woody vessels."

"We can't wait all day. Zephyrus is counting on us." Sebastian rolled his eyes.

"I know! I'm pumping as hard as I can. Now don't annoy me while I'm concentrating."

Sebastian stepped back, shaking his head while Joseph's face contorted as though he were about to cry. They were more anxious than ever to get the sap and be on their way.

"It's not your fault, Fungoda," Ivan said in a consoling manner. "Root-Underground has been closed off for days now. I suspect it's all been orchestrated by Tereus because of the distraction of the annual games at the castle." *I hope I sound smart and informed, so the gnarled old tree doesn't yell at me.*

"That explains why I haven't had word from anyone." He scowled deeply. "Not one single message."

"Where in heaven's name are those Forest soldiers?" Sebastian grumbled, jerking at his whiskers. "Surely someone has discovered that Zephyrus is silent and unprotected."

"We should never leave him unguarded in the future." Joseph kicked at a clump of wet leaves.

"I've been trying to tell my obstinate friend in the north that very thing for centuries." Fungoda snarled. "He listens to no one."

At last, one yellowish drop splashed to the bottom of the vial. If only the tree had gotten their message earlier, the healing sap would be waiting, ready to be released. Ivan crossed his arms, not knowing what to do with himself.

Two more drops plopped to the bottom.

The wait would be longer than they'd planned—much longer. Sebastian paced, wringing his hands behind his back. Joseph found a crooked stick to lean upon.

Fatigued from lack of sleep in the damp cave, Ivan covered his mouth, yawned, and rubbed his eyes. He was about to ask Fungoda about Peter but realized the time wasn't right. *Sebastian had said the healing tree would ask him.*

It was a quiet, peaceful place. The rich earthy smells of moist dirt and bark were comforting. The morning's light caressed the leaves and branches of the trees. The soothing call of a horned owl sounded in the distance. Only the playful scampering of his beagles running through the matted leaves disturbed the solitude. Bounty seemed satisfied to stand inert near the oak trees, his big head lowered and eyes half-closed.

Placing the Golden Lantern on a pile of flat, mossy rocks, Ivan unbuckled the sheath that held The Protector and propped it against the ancient tree. "I'm going to take a brief nap while we wait." He said this loud enough for all to hear. "I didn't get much sleep last night."

Though Sebastian flapped his hand with approval, he continued to fume over the delay.

Ivan pulled his jacket closer to his chest and tugged at the cloak's hem around his legs. He sank to the ground, resting his head against the old tree's trunk. He sighed with pleasure. Fungoda didn't seem to mind being used as a leaning post.

Sebastian discussed the timing and reasons for the crime and presented Tereus's name as the likely instigator.

"It's no surprise to me," Fungoda snapped. "I've felt his evil stirrings in my roots for a very long time, and I've warned Zephyrus about it."

Their voices droned on, and after several moments, Ivan drifted into a peaceful slumber.

It seemed only a short time had passed when the sound of shattering glass woke Ivan with a frightful start. His eyes flew open as he sprang to his feet. "What was that?" He spun around, searching for the noise. Then he saw it—and was horrified. "Oh, no." He moaned as the muscles in his face fell.

Alarmed at the sound of shattered glass, the beagles darted off to hide behind Bounty's legs. There they stayed, not daring to move.

"Look what you've done," Ivan screamed at the dogs. "You've broken an Ancient Relic."

Joseph's physical image vibrated. Turning brilliant white and with a flash of light, it separated into spiraling wisps of smoke as it shot back into the lantern. He let out a long, agonizing wail and disappeared.

"How did this happen?" Ivan asked.

"Alfred and Canute were chasing a fra-hak through the leaves when it dove for safety under the mossy rocks." Sebastian held his forehead. "The dogs got too close to the Golden Lantern, and the panels shattered when it fell. The light went out."

"That's a pity." Fungoda frowned.

Sebastian's voice dropped to a whisper. He called into the lantern, "Joseph, Joseph, my dear friend. Are you okay?"

"We can always relight the wick, can't we?" Ivan said with hope in his voice.

He patted the pockets of his jacket, checking for a matchstick. But he had none.

Alfred and Canute seemed to understand what they'd done. Not even their sad, brown eyes could erase Ivan's scowl of displeasure. They hunkered down, whimpering, staying close to Bounty.

"A match won't do the trick, anyway." Sebastian waved his hands in frustration. "Only fire from a dragon's breath will relight the wick of the Golden Lantern."

"Did you say…"

"That's right, a dragon's fiery breath, to be

precise," Sebastian said. "Zello, our domesticated dragon, who lives at the South Castle, has done this on rare occasions."

Scratching the back of his head, Ivan stared at the broken panels. "I'll pay for the damage, of course, but how will I find Zello now that he's flown away to the mountains?"

"He will come when he's needed," Fungoda said with confidence.

Ivan lifted the lantern to eye level and examined it closely. The light was extinguished, no doubt. Joseph did not speak when Ivan called his name. "Canute and Alfred didn't mean to break the glass and put your fire out. Dogs play, and sometimes they become rambunctious."

Fungoda spoke, his voice a bit terse, "Never mind that, now. Come here."

There was something about how Fungoda gave his command. Ivan slowly moved in the tree's direction with a trembling in his chest.

"You wanted to ask me something?" Fungoda's squinting eyes seemed to burrow right through him.

Chapter Twelve

The Message

"I-I've heard my brother Peter Kimble is somewhere in the Forest." He continued in a rush, "Do you know where I can find him?"

"Yes, he is here."

Ivan's knees twitched and felt like jelly. "H-he-he's here?" His chest grew hot from the pounding of his heart. His mouth went dry. "W-where?"

The ancient tree seemed to see deep into Ivan's soul. "Peter is not the person you remember."

"I knew it." Ivan blurted with a wide grin while meeting the tree's scowl. "He was hurt in the war, and he's lost his memory. That's why he didn't come home. That's why he didn't attend our parents' funeral, but I'm sure he'll recover."

Fungoda questioned Sebastian. "I last heard Peter traveled north and is staying in the ruined Kingdom of Helvaka. Have you heard differently?"

Sebastian's brow rippled. "I haven't seen him for some time."

Ivan's breathing came quick and shallow. "Helvaka is a frightful place where Zephyrus and Tereus once fought for the kingdom's throne, right?"

"That's right," Fungoda replied.

"What would Peter be doing there? He must be

wandering aimlessly, not knowing who he is. I have to find him, take him home."

"Your brother is not lost." Fungoda's rough eyebrows pulled into a slant. "He has chosen a new path."

"What do you mean?" Ivan stepped back.

"An army is congregating there. In the last few days, I've sent warnings to Zephyrus, but he hasn't responded. Now I realize why."

"What does that have to do with Peter?"

"Your brother has joined them."

"No. I don't understand." Ivan's bewildered voice trailed. "What kind of army?"

Fungoda's gray-bark face tightened as though in pain. "The Dark Army. They are recruiting, expanding their numbers. They plan to declare war against Zephyrus and the Forest's garrisons. They'll fight to take possession of the Forest and the South Castle."

Ivan gave a shuddering gasp.

"Yes." Sebastian's eyes glistened. "Joseph has told me that war would come—and soon." He sighed regretfully. "I was hoping my friend in the lantern was wrong, that he'd been absent too long."

"But Peter? No, my brother wouldn't go to war again. He just got back from World War II a few years before. Especially not to fight against Zephyrus. T-they were—are friends."

"He didn't join the British Army," the tree said, his bark-mouth turned downward. "He stayed at the castle until the war was over."

"You're wrong." Ivan pounded his fists against his thighs, fighting to hold back tears. "My brother is an honorable and decent person. He'd never join any army and plan to conquer the people who live here. It must be someone else." A sob escaped from his burning throat.

"As I have said, he is not the person you remember."

Anger pushed away Ivan's tears. "I don't believe you." He spun to face Sebastian. "What do you know of this? Why is Fungoda telling these lies?"

"Ivan...I...you must understand the importance of..." Sebastian's face scrunched painfully.

"Do you believe it's true?" Ivan's cheeks and neck felt hot with rage and betrayal. "Has Peter joined the Dark Army? You told me nothing, even when I'd asked." His voice broke. His fingernails dug into his hands, but he scarcely felt it. "All this time, I believed I was your friend, that you cared about me."

"You *are* my friend. You *are* special, more than you can understand right now." He moved toward Ivan and wrapped his arms around him. "I do love you very much, like family. We all love you." Stepping back, he placed his hands on Ivan's shoulders.

Ivan shrugged at Sebastian's touch, but the spirit gripped tighter. He loved Sebastian and Joseph too. They'd become like loving grandfathers to him, and now he'd learned they'd kept secrets, making a fool of him. Struggling to control his anger and understand the betrayal, Ivan pushed Sebastian away. "Tell me, tell me about Peter."

Fungoda's eyes rested upon Sebastian. "You should share what you know. It's not fair to keep it from the boy."

Sebastian hunched. Guilt spread over his face. "Peter lived at the castle. Everyone loved him and his humorous, easy ways. Then he changed. He stayed away. And when he did visit, he was evasive and seemed very nervous."

"But that's not reason—" Ivan's jaw muscles tightened, his nostrils flared.

Sebastian shook his head and continued, "I noticed his strange behavior, as others had. He talked about his new power and something about an alliance. We didn't understand what he meant at first, and he wouldn't elaborate. And now…" He looked over his shoulder at Fungoda. "I've just heard it confirmed. Peter has joined the enemy and will fight against us."

"There's been a horrible misunderstanding." Ivan felt winded. "My brother wouldn't do such a thing."

"Perhaps," Sebastian replied, not sounding convinced.

"You knew and yet—" Ivan glared at Sebastian. "You didn't tell me."

"I couldn't. You'd rush off and go looking for him. Ivan, please understand the situation."

Ivan spun on his heel, stomping toward Bounty. "You can take the sap yourself and leave me out of it. I'm going to find Peter."

"Please, listen to me." Sebastian moved quickly, grasping Ivan's forearm and held it with both hands. "Zephyrus must live. Don't you understand? If he dies, the Dark Army conquers the Forest. Everyone will be killed or enslaved. We can't let that happen."

Ivan shook his head, averting his eyes, holding back tears. "That's your problem, not mine." He turned to Sebastian and yelled, "You used me. You used me to get the sap to save Zephyrus. You didn't care one whit about my finding Peter—or my safety."

"That's not so." Sebastian gripped Ivan's arm

tighter, his voice incredibly earnest. "But your services are needed for this single task, and now the job is nearly accomplished."

"Let someone else finish it." Ivan hissed, jerking his arm away.

"You must complete this journey," Sebastian pleaded.

Ivan twirled around, glaring. "I'll find Peter and talk to him. If it's true, I'll tell him he must leave the Dark Army and come home with me."

"You can try." The ancient tree sighed.

"Where will I find him?"

"Your brother will come to you," Fungoda replied. "I can't predict more than this."

Ivan's anger faded a bit, and his face lit up. "Peter will find me?"

"Yes, but…things could change in an instant if someone else influences him. *He* has a strong and evil power over him."

"There." Sebastian crossed his arms, unsmiling. "Fungoda has assured you that Peter will find you. There's nothing to worry on."

The terrible news about his brother left Ivan feeling confused. He stared in the distance wishing he were back home taking care of his farm and his beagles. "What is the evil that influences Peter?"

"It shouldn't surprise you when I say it's Tereus." Fungoda raised one bark-eyebrow. "The demon doesn't want you here to influence your brother's allegiance."

Ivan's head felt drained. His shoulders slumped. *Who should I trust?*

Glimpsing at the vial, Ivan was surprised it had filled to the brim. He walked slowly toward Fungoda and lifted the glass from the faucet, corking it with great care, and slipped the lifesaving sap into his jacket's breast pocket. He unscrewed the faucet, replacing it in its special compartment. His bottom lip stuck out. *More bullies in my life.*

"Now, I encourage you to leave immediately," Fungoda said. "I feel rough stirrings in my roots."

"Let's go." Sebastian pushed gently against Ivan's back.

"I hope you find your brother," Fungoda called, "and that Peter is still who you think he is."

Ivan swallowed and didn't turn to look.

"Come visit me again when circumstances are happier. You are always welcome to my ancient woodland home."

They said their cheerless goodbyes. As Ivan dragged his feet toward Bounty, his horse raised his sleepy head and neighed softly. Alfred and Canute, who'd settled nearby, shot up, looking anxious to leave. Canute's tail wagged crazily.

Head lowered, Ivan didn't want to talk. He took Bounty's reins in shaky hands and swung into the saddle. With an angry shove, he slid The Protector beside his leg and locked one arm around the broken lantern. Turning, he stared at Fungoda and then looked away. His jaw muscles worked, clenching and unclenching. His lips pressed hard with disappointment. He couldn't believe Sebastian hadn't been honest with him. He couldn't believe what Fungoda had told him. He *would never* believe his brother was a traitor.

****

Sebastian's breath came in short deep gulps. "Let's hurry! The goddesses can't dance and chant forever."

Ivan went numb, feeling powerless. *Why didn't Sebastian tell me? Why did he keep Peter's behavior a secret?*

"Are you all right?"

Ivan couldn't bring himself to say anything. It hurt too much.

With Bounty in a full gallop, they left the twisted limbs of Fungoda's domain. *Peter has been living in the Forest, and he's never come home. Why is he with the Dark Army? Does he know our parents died?*

Questions and doubts clawed at him.

After some time, Ivan slowed, allowing his beagles to catch up. He wouldn't meet Sebastian's eyes. It stung to know his friend held back, that Ivan's quest seemed unimportant to him.

The warm disk of the sun cast colorful shadows beneath the trees. Gravel on the road sparkled like thousands of tiny jewels, but nothing sparkled for Ivan. Only anger, sadness, and doubt.

"We'll follow this curve and turn north on King William's Road until we reach the wide notch through the mountains," Sebastian said after a long silence. His eyes swept in Ivan's direction. "Is there something I can say? To explain further?"

Ivan turned his head and said, "I have many questions, but they'll wait. Only one person can tell me the truth—and that's Peter."

Sebastian's brow wrinkled. "You're ready then?" Nodding, Ivan squeezed Bounty's ribs, and they galloped forward.

"If the Rock Gateway is open for us, we'll make excellent time." Sebastian sounded hopeful. He gave his reins a quick shake, and his horse dashed alongside

Bounty.

Ivan's anger eased somewhat. "Who has the power to open and close the gate?"

"Why, it's Pillard, the Keeper of the Rock Gateway, of course," Sebastian replied, as though the answer should be obvious.

"It's his decision, then?"

"Well, not exactly. Old Pillard is guard and protector of the secret corridor. He usually depends on communications from Zephyrus whether to open the passageway to…ah, visitors or trespassers. Since Zephyrus is dormant, we'll have to depend upon Pillard's decision."

"I don't put much faith in the Forest." Ivan's brows pulled together. His tone was curt, but he didn't care. This was no time to hear his mother's cautious advice about good manners.

Wiping perspiration from his neck, Ivan reached under the Dark Cloak and patted the magic elixir in his jacket breast pocket. Reassured, he felt the vial's slender shape. He sighed, releasing what was left of his hurt feelings. *Surely, Sebastian has his reasons.*

"I can't believe what you and Fungoda told me about Peter. Tell me he's not a traitor."

Sebastian hunched his shoulders, pursing his lips. "We don't always know everything. It's possible Fungoda got his information mixed up. It's also possible that Peter came to his senses."

Grasping at thin hope, Ivan wanted to argue in Peter's defense. But what could he say?

"Tereus has instigated this. You can be sure of it. He has the power to manipulate almost anyone and to make them his thrall."

Has Tereus made Peter his slave, forcing him to do things against his will?

"The timing was ideal for Tereus's plan to conquer." Sebastian threw a glance at Ivan and snarled. "He knew everyone in the Forest would be at the castle celebrating and that Zephyrus would be unprotected. He froze the natural electrical currents that pass from tree root to tree root, causing all communication to stop. I'm sure he manipulated the unidentified man who drove the Silver Axe into Zephyrus's side, too.

They rode silently for some time. Ivan shifted the Golden Lantern to his opposite thigh. He asked, "Why would Tereus choose such a cruel manner to end his brother's life?"

"Festering hate and resentment for more than a millennium has caused him to behave like the heathen-madman he's always been. Fungoda suggested that the axe-poison would take only days to reach Zephyrus's core and kill him." Sebastian's bushy eyebrows crunched together so closely they almost covered his eyes.

When Ivan asked the obvious question, Sebastian winked. "While you napped, Fungoda and I talked, and that's how I know these things."

The sun moved overhead, warming the day. Ivan's stomach lurched with hunger and thirst. His beagles needed another stop at the King William's River to drink. "Can we rest soon?" Ivan shouted at Sebastian. "We need to quench our thirst and to do our business in the bushes."

Without answering, Sebastian slowed Old Bones and looked for the best place to pull toward the rushing river's bank.

"There, just beyond those trees." Ivan pointed and took the lead since his motivation was quite powerful by now. Alfred and Canute sped away behind a cluster of gorse bushes still in bloom while Ivan and Sebastian dismounted and stretched their stiff legs. "Would you hold on to the lantern while I relieve myself?" Sebastian agreed.

As he walked away, Ivan heard Sebastian talking and apologizing to Joseph in the lantern, but it was doubtful the spirit could hear anything since his light had been extinguished. Ivan wondered about the dragon whose flame would relight the wick. *How many of these fantasies am I to believe?*

A while later, as they rode north, Sebastian pointed out several notable landmarks. "That's the Wolflord's Village." He waved as they passed, though it was too far away to see any people. Farther up the road, Sebastian said, "And there, inland, is the Elften's Village. You can just make out the flags mounted on their ancient fortress turrets.

Ivan looked with interest, wondering who the people were that lived in the villages on the western border of the Forest. *Wolflords? Elftens?*

Sebastian thrust his hand toward an enormous castle structure that gleamed in the bright sunlight. "And that's the home of Anna-Iza and her sister goddesses—their splendid Crystal Palace."

Now more interested, Ivan raised himself in the stirrups, mesmerized by the palace where his lovely Anna-Iza lived. He remembered her warm Kiss of Discernment and smiled at the memory. If they hurried back to Zephyrus, she would be there chanting and protecting him.

After some time riding and gazing into the distance, Ivan saw the dip in the mountain ridge where they'd soon cross. He wanted to ride faster. He wanted to see Anna-Iza.

Ivan slowed and rubbed the sweat from Bounty's neck and shoulders with his hand. Alfred and Canute lagged behind, their pink tongues hanging out. "We need to walk the horses. The animals are weary."

Sebastian pulled back on Old Bones' reins. "This is a good time to give you a bit of our history."

Ivan turned his head and nodded, pleased he was finally trusted enough to hear information about the mystical Forest.

"Tereus has plans to command his army to take control of the Forest by brutality and force." A muscle jerked in his face. "Our Forest will be lost forever. We need to save Zephyrus and return all the relics to the sanctuary as soon as possible."

"What's the purpose of the seven Ancient Relics?"

"Oh, I thought I told you."

"You said you would at another time. Is this a good time?"

"As good as ever, I suppose." Sebastian leaned back on his horse in a more relaxed position.

"I…that is we, are the items that stand for truth and justice. All six of us possessed these characteristics a thousand years ago when we served Zephyrus as living men. That's why we were chosen. The seventh relic is the Black Book of Pearls, an account of our history—and even future prophecies. I'm sure I told you that much."

Ivan tipped his head and closed his eyes, trying to remember. The information had been sketchy, at best.

"Our purpose is to aid our Master Oak in all affairs. We were awarded special gifts that would help us accomplish these tasks. Without us, Zephyrus is vulnerable and limited in his protection and defense.

"The relics, missing these past ten years, have had me extremely worried." Sebastian twisted the ends of his mustache. "Nathaniel the Silver Axe, Joseph the Golden Lantern, the King's Sceptre, the Bag of Bones, and the Scroll of Wisdom. We all helped to protect Zephyrus. But of course, they were stolen away, except the Silver Axe and the Golden Lantern."

Ivan's brow crinkled. Now he understood the six empty pegs and the velvet cushion inside Zephyrus's trunk. It was the Sanctuary of Truth.

"We each have our own special place. The terms are a little complicated. The High Intervener made an agreement that if Zephyrus were destroyed, all the people and creatures in the Forest would come under Tereus's tyrannical rule. It was only a matter of time before Tereus tried to dethrone our master."

"Why would Zephyrus settle for these terms?" Ivan was quite astonished.

Sebastian shrugged one shoulder. "I believe he agreed to take residency in the tree so that he could save the Forest from his evil brother. These severe rules came from the High Intervener."

"Zephyrus has a very big heart."

"That he does." Sebastian flapped his arm forward. "Let's cross the wooden bridge."

They rode through a lightly forested region that opened to rolling green knolls divided by bushy hedgerows. There, atop the grassy hills, stood hundreds of grazing sheep, Friesians, and Guernsey cows that followed a well-trodden path to their farm homes. Some distance away, a shepherd raised his crook in a friendly gesture, and Sebastian waved back.

The scene conjured a strong longing for Ivan's own farm. *Will my animals be taken care of yet one more day? Will Mrs. Hambuckle worry about me?* He felt differently as he thought about his life before he entered the Forest. He wasn't the same person. His farm life was far away—almost a dream. Only the Forest was real.

"Don't worry," Sebastian said, with a sly look. "I'm sure your animals are being cared for just right."

"How did you know what was on my mind?" Ivan stroked his chin, lifting a dark eyebrow.

"Well…" Sebastian fumbled, and the cunning look quickly left his face. "It stands to reason you'd be feeling some homesickness while enjoying this rural scene."

Ivan shot his companion a doubtful look. *How does Sebastian seem to read my thoughts before I've had a chance to complete them?*

Magpies, black crows, warblers, and starlings flew round and round above, but no sounds came from their throats. Ivan wondered why. Sebastian mumbled something as he also watched the birds. Deep worry lines creased his eyes.

"Sebastian!" Ivan's shriek caused Bounty to jump.

They stopped their horses with a hard jerk. Ivan fought nausea at the sight of hundreds of stiff birds, their tiny feet curled tight against their chests. They lay scattered on the road and in the ditches. Some thrashed in the bushes fluttering their wings to find an escape. Others took flight only to fall swiftly to their death.

"Wha— Oh, no," Sebastian wailed, his body slumped.

"What happened here?" Ivan gasped.

"All those lovely birds—dead." Sebastian ran his hands over his face as though he could shut out the horrible scene before them.

"Did someone poison them? Alfred, Canute, leave them alone. They may be diseased."

"Not diseased." Sebastian turned pale.

"Then what?"

"This is a terrible warning. A sign that Zephyrus is dying."

Chapter Thirteen

The White Rock Creature

"What will we do?" Ivan's stomach pitched, seeing all the dead birds.

"Travel on, we have no choice."

They pushed forward as the sun crept past noon in the high sky. Ivan couldn't get the picture of bird carcasses out of his mind.

It was a torturous climb to the top of the mountain. Ivan encouraged Bounty to move slowly and to choose his steps carefully, but the horse stumbled several times. He had no experience climbing uphill or judging the security of rocks. When they passed through the opening in the mountain, Ivan sighed with relief. He wondered if Anna-Iza and her twelve goddesses had used this same path to reach Zephyrus.

Thoughts drifted back to the lovely girl who had clutched his upper arms, allowing Ivan to return her kiss. He was anxious to see her again. *Will she be happy to see me?* Stubbornly, he pushed away Sebastian's warnings of her unavailability. Embarrassment rushed over him. His worry should be for Zephyrus and the dire warning of the dead birds. He gave his head a rough shake and teared with remorse.

Wiping his eyes, Ivan pretended he'd gotten a bit of debris in them. Things weren't looking much better, though they were closer to their destination. Soon they'd reach Zephyrus Barkay, and Ivan's task would be complete. Then he'd go at once to find Peter.

The scene before him suddenly caused Ivan's jaw to slacken. He rose slowly from his saddle, standing high in the stirrups and clutching the Golden Lantern against his chest. "Joseph, if only you could see this." Cocking his head in several directions, Ivan blinked with disbelief. He eased himself down. "What in Heaven's name is that? It looks like a blizzard of white hills."

"It's quite awesome when seen for the first time," Sebastian said with a grin.

Ivan's mouth hung open as he tried to find the right words. "Like an endless mass of petrified whipped cream."

"That's a pretty good description, Ivan ol' boy. I've often wondered how to describe these mounds of chalk." Sebastian finally gave in to a chuckle. "This is Pillard's domain, our illustrious Keeper of the Rock Gateway."

Bounty's ears flattened against his head as they rode closer. He stomped his front hooves and swished a nervous tail.

"Whoa, boy! Take it easy now."

Another curious sight was dozens of large, pyramid-shaped rock piles. Each rock was about the same size, slightly yellowed, and stacked carefully one upon another. The piles rose to the height of a medium-sized man.

His stomach tightened, turning acid-hot. Ivan opened his eyes wide and shouted, "They're human skulls." He stammered when he tried to speak, and for a moment, no words came. "I-I wouldn't want my head to be put there."

"No one would ask such a sacrifice." Sebastian's response was bland as he stared into the distance.

Pointing a shaky finger, Ivan raised his voice and repeated, "Sebastian, those are human skulls. They were part of a person once."

"They were betrayers, opposing armies who made poor choices in which master they served."

"But Sebastian…" Ivan's knees quivered.

"They're dead—forget it. Now, wait here." Sebastian turned to scowl and left Ivan to ponder the gruesome display. *Why is Sebastian terse with me? I'm not responsible for them.*

"Sorry." Sebastian's scowl left his face. "I'm looking for someone, and I'm never certain how I—we will be received."

Bounty lifted his head and flattened his ears against his head, neighing loudly. Ivan soothed him though he needed comforting himself.

They waited.

Sebastian rode along the ridge, anxiously scanning the white surface, searching for something. Ivan followed slowly, unwilling to be left behind. Soon he drew close to Old Bones. Canute and Alfred raised their heads, gave sharp woofs, and stared at the piles. Alarmed at the sight, the dogs dashed away to crouch in the cool, long grasses.

"Pillard can sometimes be a bit irritable when unexpected company arrives," Sebastian warned, speaking quietly behind a palmed hand.

It seemed everyone is irritable and short-tempered in the Forest. They waited for some time. The air around them went deadly still. Ivan glanced at the pyramids again, visualizing his head resting on top. He tried to swallow past the raw lump in his throat. *Had the betraying soldiers been slaughtered by the Keeper of the Rock Gateway?*

Without warning, an earth-moving rumble shook the ground. Ivan stiffened his back. "What's happening?"

Bounty sidled and jerked his head. He didn't like this place any more than Ivan did.

Sebastian didn't seem disturbed by the ruckus, but his attention was on Ivan.

Shifting hard edges, the rock divided, scoring the ground beneath as it pulled apart. The crack in the mound widened, snapping and echoing into the distance, creating a fissure about a foot wide.

"Who stands at my gateway wanting to pass?" thundered a threatening voice.

Ivan tensed, looking around for the owner of the voice. "Wh-where is this Keeper of the Gateway?"

"He has yet to show himself, and his name is Pillard, like I said." Sebastian seemed preoccupied, scanning the tops of the smooth mounds.

There appeared a huge, bald-headed white form with a snarling, open mouth. It rose from the mass of rocks above their heads. Its dark eyes glared back and forth from Ivan to Sebastian.

"That's Pillard?" Ivan jerked in his saddle. "Good Heavens, why didn't you tell me he was a rock?"

"Oh, I thought I had. Everyone knows what he is."

"Well, I didn't even suspect."

Ivan thought he heard Sebastian chuckle under his breath.

Pillard pushed noisily from the surface with a pair of thin stone arms and hands that extended just below the creature's ears. His big head ended where a jawline and neck would've been—if he'd had any. A heavy overhanging brow chiseled by the passing of time cast a dark shadow over his deep-set eyes.

Pillard's mouth opened to show wide square teeth and a flat white tongue. He shouted, "What business do you have trespassing here?" His lips widened with fury while squinty eyes darted back and forth, locking menacingly onto Ivan.

"You know me. I am Sebastian from the Sanctuary of Truth." He released his horse's reins and folded his arms over his thin chest. His face bunched in a scowl. "We need to pass. Part your gates, now."

"Of course I know who you are," Pillard said with some terseness. "I want to know who the stranger is."

Neither spoke. Ivan didn't know what he was supposed to say, and Sebastian hadn't offered.

Eyeing him with suspicion, Pillard asked, "Is the stranger mute?"

"I can speak," Ivan shot back.

"Oh, so you can," Pillard volleyed sarcastically. "And who are *you* related to in this Forest?"

"No one. I'm from the outside."

"I should've known," the rock scoffed. "You don't belong here. Get out."

"Pillard, hang you!" Sebastian yelled back. "If you don't stop badgering our visitor, I'll dump the dirtiest bucket of slop on your fat head. Now open your corridor at once."

An icy glare spread over his white face as Pillard addressed Sebastian, "Tell me, who is this stranger that you are bound to? What Gray-Spell has he cast upon you while he steals you away from our Master Oak?"

"Spell? Steal away? Whatever in the whip-o-the-wind are you talking about?" Sebastian's tone became even more aggravated.

"Dark Magic has returned to our Forest. You must be aware of this. Gray-Spells, fireballs have infiltrated our Forest, and the dreaded rising of the decayed are coming. And..." Pillard hesitated before adding, "the Dark Army is gathering."

"Are you sure about this?" Sebastian's face froze with horror.

"I am sure."

"W-what does that mean?" Ivan widened his eyes.

"It's worse than I expected." Sebastian lowered his head.

"More frightening than when Helvaka divided and went to war with itself over a thousand years ago." Pillard crunched his stone teeth together.

Ivan leaned sideways toward his companion. "What Dark Magic are you talking about? What's a fireball? And-and..." he forced himself to ask, "who are the decayed?"

"The dead," Sebastian replied.

Ivan's forehead creased. "But how can they rise from their graves if they're dead?"

"They were killed in the War of Division a thousand years ago," Sebastian explained with a troubled look on his face. "But their spirits were forced to rise again by Tereus and his accomplices."

A rush of terror coursed through Ivan's veins. "I'll leave—right now."

Sebastian agreed, and then he asked Pillard, "How

do you know about the rising since communication has shut down and all the inhabitants are celebrating? Even our messengers and spies are being entertained at the South Castle."

"I feel stirrings in the earth." Pillard's demeanor changed to outright misery. "But I did not detect the attack against my friend, Zephyrus."

"Well," Sebastian said, "we don't have time to do anything about it right now. We're on an urgent mission to save him."

"Open your gates," Sebastian said.

"Step back." Pillard raised his thin rock arm and lowered it.

The ground trembled. Trees shook, and strange white birds took flight. Canute and Alfred yelped as rocks crunched and crackled, pulling apart. They dashed away and hid beneath some ragged bushes, whimpering.

Bounty spun around whinnying, raising his front legs, his hooves pawed at the air. Ivan hung on tightly, trying to pacify him. "There now, boy. We'll be on the other side soon." Sidling, the horse gave loud snorts until Ivan brought him under some control.

The rock separated, revealing what seemed an endlessly long passageway. A cold haze blotted out the distant exit—if there was one. Only enough space existed for one horse to pass at a time.

Ivan swallowed, shivering with fright. *Are we to enter this narrow passageway?* Ivan's hands quivered while he imagined being crushed between the hard sides.

"My corridor is open to you." Pillard's eyes squeezed closed as though in great concentration.

"Let's go." Sebastian shot his arm forward, and he called Canute and Alfred to follow, but they hesitated.

Urging Bounty down the unfamiliar corridor, Ivan smelled wet chalk, decaying vegetation, and the stench of rotting meat. Looking behind himself, he called sharply to his beagles, and they reluctantly trailed.

Pillard's eyes opened, following their movement with an unreadable expression. It looked like a cold stare, but maybe it was worry. Ivan had no experience in reading the stolid face of a rock.

"Perhaps we should drop money into this carved bowl as payment for our passage," Ivan suggested, knowing he had nothing in his pockets to give. "I saw several gold coins and a gleaming ruby lying there."

"I don't pay," Sebastian said stubbornly. "That hard-headed, prissy rock needs to be put in his place. People of the Forest shouldn't have to pay to use his Time-Flash route. Besides, I don't have any coins or rubies on me, either."

"What's a Time-Flash?"

"You'll just have to experience it. I find myself quite at a loss to explain such a phenomenon."

"Is this what you mentioned to me earlier? A flash in time? That we'd reach our destination quickly by using this route?"

"Yes. Now let's hurry, hurry," Sebastian called, "in case Pillard's temper flares and he decides to close his corridor, crushing us to mush."

"Would he do that?" Ivan was aghast. "Crush a harmless horse? And my beagles?"

"You can't be sure about a rock, I always say." Sebastian huffed.

Ivan stiffened his shoulders and glanced warily

about. "I have the strangest feeling here.

"Now hang on," Sebastian shouted, grinning like crazy. "You're in for the ride of your life."

Then, something amazing happened. A cool rush of air swept over Ivan's face. Dry leaves swirled, ripping from the branches of ash and beech trees that grew through cracks in the smooth white rocks. Bounty's hooves left the solid ground while he and Ivan were propelled at an incredible speed along the narrow strip of dirt and bone fragments.

Ivan felt as though he was flying, his movements out of control. Wind pushed hair back from his forehead. He squinted to keep debris and stinging wind from his eyes. Long streaks of light mingled with the dark verticals of trees as he was shoved forward—on and on. He tried to turn and question Sebastian but couldn't utter a word. His mouth froze open in an impossible scream.

It seemed like the longest trip Ivan had ever taken. Breath froze in his lungs, his legs squeezed against Bounty's sides, trying to stay seated with the thrust of wind against him.

Once they'd cleared the passageway, the crunch of stone grated against stone as the sides came together and closed the corridor behind them, achieving a perfect fit. Dizzy with relief, Ivan struggled to recapture his breath.

"Wh-what was that wild ride?" He gulped air over dry lips. With a sweep of his hand, he brushed the dirt and shredded leaves from the cloak, thankful they'd reached safety at the opposite end.

Sebastian laughed. "I knew you'd enjoy it. This is quite fun, and the magic allows you to quickly bypass time and space. Now we are closer to Zephyrus and have saved much time."

"It was thrilling." Ivan burst into laughter. He rubbed his fingers over his eyes. "I've never traveled like that in my life."

"Most people haven't." Sebastian trailed a chuckle.

"There, above us—what are they?" Ivan raised his face where the white birds circled in the sky, their long, filmy tails swirling.

"Altiffs." Sebastian's grin quickly changed to a scowl. "Something akin to Song Birds of Grief. They show up at funerals and death ceremonies singing their little hearts out." He shrugged, giving the impression there was nothing to worry about.

Ivan wiped his brow. "I hope their message isn't about *my* death."

Near the east end of the rock mounds, another white boulder forced his head up just as Pillard had done on the west side. This rock was smaller, with a bulbous nose and rounder eyes, giving it a much friendlier face. It spoke, "I've just received a terrifying message from Pillard the Gate Keeper."

"Yes, yes! We know who he is, for heaven's sake," Sebastian shouted with impatience and anger. "What is it?"

"There is tremendous danger." The boulder's eyes squeezed to half their size. "The decayed have been summoned to rise from their graves. They will fight against us."

Sebastian choked. His face tightened, his teeth clamped together. "We know about the rising. Pillard has told us. I hoped we'd have more time to organize." He lifted his eyes and looked to the south. "The garrisons must come, and they must come soon." The boulder hesitated and listened as though deciphering another incoming message. "Pillard says an army of thousands is mobilizing. First, the dead will come to do battle, and then the army of living soldiers will follow to claim victory. Both the dead and living armies are gathering, preparing for war." His eyes rolled up into his head, where they disappeared for a moment.

Moaning, Sebastian's voice strangled with dread. "The Great Rising is here."

Ivan's heart thumped hot in his chest. "I'll leave the Forest as soon as I give the antidote to Zephyrus. I shouldn't be here if you are going to war."

The spirit plucked at his eyebrows, frowning deeply. "Yes, of course," he muttered. "You must go as soon as possible."

Ivan couldn't abandon his friends. He would hide until the battles were over. *But where will I go?*

"Surely this is treason," Sebastian ranted and flailed his arms in the air. "Tereus has gained the alliance of someone who has knowledge of Dark Magic. Whether it's Cecil or another sorcerer that's breached our borders, I don't know. That's the only way the Great Rising could've been accomplished. How could Tereus command those poor souls to repeat the past when they sacrificed their lives for him so long ago? Zephyrus will have his brother's blistered hide for this."

"I don't think Pillard liked me very much," Ivan said. "I've never been hated by a rock before."

"He doesn't like outsiders, nor does he like his pristine domain getting dirtied. Did you see the look on his face when I threatened to dump slop all over him?"

Sebastian roared with hilarity. "I thought the old rock would explode into bits of gravel."

Ivan forced a smile but must have missed the humor.

"Well." Sebastian sighed. "We're done with him now, and we should make excellent time." He raised his fisted hand over his head as though he were leading his own army. "We must leave at once."

They rode on with Alfred and Canute close behind, their ears flapping against their heads.

"Where are we?" Ivan asked, glancing about.

"We are near the west end of Sir Barkay Road. When we reach the juncture of the Sheepherders' Path Road, you'll recognize where you are."

"I first saw Anna-Iza there," he said and opened his eyes wider.

"Yes, she hid in the bushes."

Ivan flexed his white-knuckled hand and strained arm that had held the Golden Lantern during his incredible ride. He raised the lantern to his eye-level as though the spirit could still see and hear. "Take a look, Joseph, past that long grove of oak woods. There Zephyrus sleeps."

The two riders scanned their surroundings for any sign of danger.

"What if we're too late to administer the antidote?" Ivan patted the vial tucked in his jacket pocket, relieved it was there.

"We won't be too late." Sebastian wound the reins tighter around his hands.

Ivan suspected the spirit spoke more from optimism than from facts. "What will we do if the garrisons don't arrive in time to help us fight these ghosts? Tell me, who am I against an entire army?"

"You're expected to do nothing. This war is not yours to fight." Sebastian's face was stark with worry.

"B-but," Ivan stammered, "who will save Zephyrus—the goddesses? If I leave, there will be no one. If I stay, I'll surely get my head removed, unable to hold off a merciless hoard of warriors."

"I don't know how the garrisons will fight the ghost warriors, either." Sebastian wiped his brow. "Maybe Zephyrus will know. Or maybe Nathaniel, the Silver Axe. He was our war advisor in the Kingdom of Helvaka. Tereus has committed a most blasphemous crime by raising the dead."

Ivan gulped loudly, and his heart beat faster. "What are we to do?"

"Zephyrus will know. He'll tell us how to stop them."

"But he's deep in dormancy," Ivan reminded, trying to stay his lips from trembling.

Sebastian nodded slightly. "We must reach Zephyrus and give him the healing potion. He will know what to do against the impending attack."

"If he's still alive," Ivan whispered.

Chapter Fourteen

Pillard's Brilliant Plan

When Pillard, the Keeper of the Rock Gateway, summoned Pousses, he came reluctantly. Grumbling all the way. He twitched his ears as though scrutinizing the ledge and wondered why Pillard would call on him. Didn't he realize he had to cut his lunch short just to be here?

"What are these piles of rocks you're collecting? A new hobby?"

Pillard proudly corrected him. "Those are skulls. Duly earned, if I might say."

"Oh, so they are." Pousses skirted the gruesome display and ran alongside the white mounds of chalk. Pushing off from the grass, he took wing and landed on the top of the rock. There, he settled on his haunches, licking his paw and removing a small pebble between his toes.

"We have big worries, now," Pillard said in a half-whisper. He gazed about and paused. "The Ghost Warriors are coming. They will be followed by the Dark Army of men."

"What?" The cat hissed and arched his back.

"I felt the Great Rising. The Ghost Warriors, or the decayed, as they're sometimes called, have been commanded to rise from their graves and to fight. And then, Tereus's bloodthirsty army of living men will follow."

Pousses seemed to faint. He flattened his body on the smooth white rocks, laying his head between his front legs. "What did I get myself into?"

Pillard surveyed his once-pristine home, now dirtied by leaves, twigs, and pockets of dirt.

Normally, this messiness would've moved him to the brink of fury, but none of this mattered now. Not with the threat of absolute destruction to the Forest looming before them.

At last, he spoke, "Pousses, we need a plan."

"A plan?"

"Let's consider how Ivan can defend Zephyrus as well as the goddesses against all those merciless warriors." The rock rolled his eyes upward.

"He has Tom Shiffert's sword strapped to his side," the cat suggested feebly.

"Phooey!" the old rock spat. "The Protector is ordinary. It can't do anything special."

"Then exactly what do you want me to do?"

"I'm considering the worst." Pillard's thin arms rose, palms opened in an empty gesture. "What are we to do if the garrisons don't arrive in time?"

The cat shook his head. "How would the army fight the ghosts, anyway? I've heard our weapons are useless against them."

With a sudden flash, Pillard hurled an idea. "I want you to fly at once to the ruins of Helvaka where Tereus's hand-picked Commander Kruse Hays is gathering his army." He paused for a second, considering the plausibility of his plan. "You must convince the commander to use the most direct route to

Zephyrus through my Time-Flash Corridor. Tell them it will save time, and they will have the advantage to take the Forest Army by surprise. Emphasize that I have the power to move them through time in an instant. My gateway will be open if only they'd drop a bag of shiny gold coins and precious jewels into my collection bowl for my trouble. I love shiny things." His dark eyes twinkled with delight.

"You're a deceitful creature." Pousses hissed.

"It's not for the coins, you brainless ninny," Pillard snapped and then frowned. "If I gave my services away, they would suspect a trap immediately."

"Oh, I see. Of course."

"Although, I wouldn't mind a few more treasures," he said as his rigid forehead lifted with joy.

The cat let out a sour meow. "I'm not sure anyone will listen to me—a mere cat. Not without getting skinned alive, that is."

"You're right." Pillard's stone-hard teeth grated together. "But fortunately, you aren't well-known in the Forest to any but a few, since you spend all your leisurely days at the South Castle. You may not be recognized."

"I don't think I'm going to like this." Pousses raised his wings and whined.

"I've got it!" Pillard shouted. He brought his stone-fingers together, flexing them. "If I first send Drugan, our bronzed-tipped owl, I think the Dark Army's Commander will believe the oracle's advice."

"Drugan's an oracle?" Pousses shook his head in confusion.

"Yes, of course." Pillard smirked. "He's a bridge between the world of life and death, dark and light, evil and good. Drugan will tell Hays to await your arrival. The wise old owl must convince them you're a mystical cat with knowledge and insight into the future and that your guidance will lead their army to certain victory. Yes, I think my plan will do rather nicely."

Pousses blinked, releasing a weak mew.

"You must persuade Commander Hays to use my *passageway.* Do you understand now?"

The cat frowned and shivered. "I don't know if I'll be believed.

"You are supposed to be Lord Graydon's spy and a messenger, aren't you?" the rock reminded and frowned. "Pousses, we have few choices. War is certain. We must do what we can to defeat these terrible ghosts." Pillard showed his rectangular teeth, speaking forcefully. "It's your time to be brave."

The leaders of men are not fooled easily. Pillard also realized Tereus's army was a mistrustful and suspicious lot, especially Kruse Hays, who was known to subscribe to the Dark Arts and Sorcery.

Pillard hoped his plan would work. He didn't think Pousses would look very dignified without his black fur coat. "Are you up to it, ol' cat?"

Whiskers jerking nervously, he bobbed his head. "What choice do I have?"

****

"Look!" Sebastian's eyes turned bright with eagerness. "The late morning sun has warmed the tips of the trees where the dew sparkles like tiny lanterns. Do you see it, Ivan?"

Glancing up, Ivan nodded. Gently pulling back the reins, he realized Bounty was tired from their difficult journey.

"I used to write a good bit of poetry to keep Zephyrus and my other friends entertained in the sanctuary." Sebastian wiggled his eyebrows. "I don't claim it was very good, but they all seemed to enjoy my modest attempts."

Ivan thought Sebastian was trying to bring lightheartedness to what seemed a hopeless situation, especially after seeing the dead birds and the altiffs flying overhead. Were they portents of the coming Ghost Warriors and the Dark Army?

"Don't worry." Sebastian turned toward Ivan, nodding. "We'll save Zephyrus, and he'll be around for a long, long time to come."

In just a few short days, the trees had begun to lose their moisture, returning sap to their roots. A light breeze shook drying leaves from their limbs. They were changing to the glorious colors of fall. The foliage seemed to quiver a message, like notes from frenzied music, "Hurry, hurry, hurry. Not a moment to lose."

Bounty slowed and swung his head. The Golden Lantern thumped against Ivan's ribs and was heavy in his arms. Then his belly growled, and his ears felt chilled from the breeze. These things irritated him all at once, but he refused to complain.

He turned in his saddle and called to his beagles, "Keep up with us." He soon felt more encouraged when he realized his journey to save Zephyrus would soon come to an end. He reassured himself that he'd travel where necessary, even to Helvaka, to convince Peter to come home with him. His brother would be cleared of any involvement with the Dark Army. Everything would be put right again.

In spite of his best efforts to concentrate on the

road and Zephyrus's condition, Ivan's thoughts drifted back to Anna-Iza. She would be near Zephyrus, swaying as she chanted and danced. He visualized her lovely face framed with auburn curls. He imagined her slender form moving daintily to the songs that the other goddesses sang in unison.

He suddenly worried about how he looked. Would she find him attractive, willing to let him kiss her again? He licked his tongue over his teeth and straightened his collar. There was little he could do about his disheveled appearance.

"I'm wondering," Ivan said, "about the mysterious man who wore the gray cloak and axed Zephyrus. Do you believe he's under Tereus's control?"

Sebastian didn't answer at once. "I'm not sure, but he's either a misguided fool or, yes, under Tereus's bidding. Just what he has to gain is a puzzle, a real puzzle." His voice died away to a soft cry, and he turned his head from Ivan's gaze.

A loud hoot sounded from a nearby tree. And then another. It seemed like an owl calling for their attention.

A small shape with bronze-tipped wings flew near, almost clipping the side of Ivan's head. He ducked. The owl swerved and lit upon the drooping bough of an old ash tree. His eyes glowed yellow with flecks of orange. He fluttered with nervousness.

"I'm Mart-Mart," the owl rasped, trying to catch his breath. "My uncle Drugan sent me to deliver a message."

Sebastian's worried frown reappeared. "I know your uncle. This is Ivan, a visitor from the outside. It's safe to share your message with us."

"Armies are racing on horseback through the Forest." The little owl flapped his wings. "Some are dead, having left their graves, and some soldiers are alive, marching from Helvaka. They're coming this way. Do you understand my uncle's message?"

"We know," Sebastian replied.

"What does it mean?"

"The Forest is going to war." Sebastian's voice quivered.

"Oh, hoot!" Mart-Mart's feathers ruffled, his head twisted, his round eyes darted and rolled. Taking flight, he screeched, "*War!* We're going to war."

****

Galloping hoofs dug into the gravel as Bounty raced eastward on the now-familiar Zephyrus Barkay Road. They passed the holly bushes where they'd first seen Anna-Iza. It seemed like years and years ago.

Ivan panicked as he imagined Zephyrus dying minutes before their arrival. His fingers tightened around the lantern. Rivulets of sweat made their way down the sides of his face, wetting his collar, chilling his neck. After all the challenges he'd endured, risking his life and his beagles, the thought of failing now left him shaken.

"The Dark Army is advancing," Sebastian wailed, breaking Ivan's tortured thoughts. "We can't risk losing another second."

The beagles seemed to recognize the road they traveled on. Their tails wagged as if anticipating their return home—or something to eat. Nipping at each other, they ran carelessly around an alder tree, enjoying their tumbles in the fall leaves. Alfred generally got the best of his brother, being somewhat bigger and perhaps, smarter.

In an instant, something with pink-tinted fur and short rounded ears scampered through the bushes. The strange animal challenged the dogs by dashing past them and disappearing into a tree cavity. It poked out its head, sniffed the air, and then took off hopping and squeaking, making sounds like a mouse.

"A kind of small rabbit?" Ivan watched it hop away.

"Not exactly, but it's in that family. It's a timmerlan."

"I've never heard the name before."

"They are very rare, known to live only in the West Forest."

Canute chased the rabbit-like critter with such speed that his brother spun around, disoriented. Not to be left behind, Alfred joined the pursuit.

Slowing Bounty, Ivan turned and yelled, "Canute, Alfred! Come back." His shouts were ignored, lost in the warm afternoon breeze. Frustrated, he slapped his thigh. "Dang animals." They ran into the Forest, barking their fool heads off.

"Does it bite? Will it sting or put a spell on my beagles?" Ivan flexed his jaw muscles with worry.

"He's quite harmless. And you are right—it does look like a rabbit. A very savvy one, by the way."

Ivan shifted on his mount. "There was something silver around its neck. A name tag or a collar?"

"The thin band you saw has a small, silver ball attached with star-shaped holes. Inside is a special sleeping powder made from dried red mushrooms. It was placed there by faeries for the animal's own protection. When they're chased, the powder is released into the air, and after their enemy inhales, it brings on a peaceful slumber. It has no effect on the timmerlan. This allows him to escape."

Ivan raised his brow in surprise.

"No permanent harm," Sebastian assured. "Better your floppy-eared friends have left you. They'll probably lie down under some bushes and sleep out of harm's way. War is no place for dogs."

"That means I'll be part of your war. I can't leave my beagles," Ivan protested, his words raspy in his dry throat. "Sebastian, I'm not a soldier. I don't know anything about fighting. Please, I-I can't go to war. I couldn't kill a man." Heat spread across his chest and rushed to his neck.

"You aren't expected to fight." Sebastian's tone was blunt. "You should hide in the guest cottages, located behind Zephyrus, before the battle cries are sounded. Is that clear?"

"Yes, but what about Alfred and Canute? How will they find me?"

"Just you watch." Sebastian snorted and waved his hand. "Your pets will come back shortly. They'll give up when they realize the timmerlan is too smart to be caught."

"Unless they breathe the mushroom powder." Ivan's face knotted with worry.

"Well, yes, that's possible."

Bewildered, Ivan wondered how long it would take before his beagles returned. His dogs were now out of sight. He released an aggravated sigh. *Why can't they realize danger and avoid it—at least for my sake? Maybe they will return soon, as Sebastian suggested.*

Ivan abruptly found reason to smile. With a rush of

joy, he saw Zephyrus just ahead. The tree showed no facial features, no golden sheen on his huge trunk, only massive amounts of drooping foliage. The sounds of the goddesses singing renewed Ivan's hope. "Zephyrus must still be alive," he said with profound relief. He patted his jacket pocket once more, assuring himself the vial was safe.

Sebastian's face lit up, and a smile stretched wide.

The goddesses no longer wore their riding cloaks. The swirl of long, unbound hair, multiple layers of organza skirts twirled around them, catching their slender hips and legs. Their haunting whispers of song wove through the trees as the thirteen girls danced with the grace of swans gliding on calm cobalt-blue water. Ivan's ears heated to see his sweet Anna-Iza lead her sisters in complex steps, swooping and swaying around Zephyrus. She knew the words to chant while her sisters echoed with lilting harmony. He brimmed with pride.

Riding closer, Ivan sat taller, squaring his shoulders with a new confidence. He wasn't the same frightened young man Anna-Iza had met at the river. He'd overcome danger, made tough decisions, and was a bolder, braver person. The whirling dresses in warm fall colors were adorned with fresh flowers that fitted their bodices. Vines and blossoms were woven into their hair, with ribbons that matched, swirling with their action.

Beautiful. Ivan's chest expanded, his heart increased its beat. He brought Bounty to a halt. Each goddess held the hand of the next, chanting a sad song in a language Ivan couldn't understand. Anna-Iza gazed vacantly at Ivan and Sebastian as they approached. She didn't seem to recognize them. *Is she that deeply under a trance of her own making?*

When she circled Zephyrus a second time, Ivan realized she was exhausted. Of course, that was it. They'd been performing their Spell-of-Protection, encircling Zephyrus for days. Their pale satin slippers had dots of blood on the toes and heels, their thin ankles were bruised and swollen.

How have they managed? Ivan's heart filled with compassion. He ached to sweep Anna-Iza into his arms, to hold her, to make everything safe.

Raking his fingers through dusty, wind-swept hair, Ivan was again conscious of how he looked. *If only he could wash himself and brush the film from his teeth.* But he needed to be near her even if he couldn't put his hands upon her soft, warm skin.

Leaping from his saddle, Ivan tugged on Bounty's reins while gripping the lantern's golden ring. He walked briskly toward the huge open circle where Zephyrus stood and the goddesses danced.

Sebastian followed, mumbled softly, "If we could only stop the goddesses from their ceremony, allowing them some rest."

"How can we help?" Ivan stared. "The girls are near to collapsing."

"There's nothing we can do," Sebastian replied in a quiet tone. "This is their fate. They must protect Zephyrus even if their ceremony costs them their lives. Please don't interfere or break the ritual until they stop on their own accord. They are keeping the darkness away."

Ivan squirmed, wishing he could say or do something.

With the healing elixir in his possession, he could now save Zephyrus. He chewed on his bottom lip, frustrated he had to wait for a break in the ceremony. Leaning wearily against Bounty, he draped one arm across the saddle and held the lantern by its ring.

While waiting, sounds of quarreling voices, loud grunts, worried clucking, and the scratching of large feet against the leafy ground grabbed Ivan's attention. He supposed the clucking could be from the kaleido-birds and the grunts from trolls. Nearby, the unruly bystanders added more confusion to an already perilous situation. He recognized some of the creatures, but others looked extremely odd. There were feathered rodents, large wild cats with two sets of horns on their heads, and even bovine-type animals with spotted fur collars and short back legs.

Ivan released a flabbergasted breath. "I've never seen creatures like these in my life."

"Most people haven't," Sebastian replied with a scowl. Apparently, he wasn't happy about the peculiar collection of creatures adding to the confusion.

Mixed into the group, serving no useful purpose, a large horde of trolls bickered and snarled, shoving at each other. Maloof was there but his sidekick, Cecil, was nowhere in sight. The fallen wizard lifted his narrow beady eyes and glared at Ivan with a look of pure hate.

"I think Maloof recognized me as the person who covered him with the cloak outside the Norman shed." Ivan grimaced. "How did he get here so quickly?"

"He certainly travels fast on stumpy legs," Sebastian replied. "I guess my spell didn't put him under as deeply as I figured."

The angry troll jabbed his fist into the air toward them, making a series of pig-like snorts, baring dangerous teeth. Ivan presumed he wasn't happy to see him. But Maloof was the least of their problems.

The kaleido-birds appeared from behind a cluster of bushes, making loud squawking noises, and Fetters grumbled constantly. Most likely, he was irritated he hadn't yet gained a private audience with Zephyrus. They kept their distance from the violent trolls.

Sebastian swept his hand toward the weird menagerie of bystanders and shouted, "Get away! This is no place for spectators. Ghost Warriors and the Dark Army are about to storm into Oakhurst riding fast horses and wielding dangerous weapons."

The group stopped and gawked, and to Ivan's surprise, they turned and scampered away. He wished everything could be that easy.

"If I called to the goddesses, would they stop?" Ivan asked.

"Only Anna-Iza knows when it's prudent." Sebastian slipped from his horse and brushed his dusty tunic with the side of his hand. "You could call softly, and maybe she'll hear you."

Striding forward, Ivan begged, "Anna-Iza, please stop a moment." She whirled past him, her head turned to reveal her lovely blue-green eyes, glassy and faraway.

"I have the healing potion here in my pocket. I need to pass. Stop, please stop."

The goddesses locked their hands tighter, increasing the volume of their song. Their feet moved faster. They swooped and whirled. They shook their heads as though defying the black cloud of death surrounding their beloved master. *Do they believe I'm a danger to Zephyrus?*

"Anna-Iza, Diana, listen to me." Ivan tried again, louder. "I have the healing sap from Fungoda. It will save Zephyrus's life. Please stop so I can pour it into his wound."

Sebastian snorted impatiently.

"What can I do?" he cried. "Anna-Iza doesn't know I'm here."

"They are protective goddesses." Sebastian squeezed his eyes shut for a moment. "It's their duty to shield our king while he's in this dormant state. But you must administer the sap without disturbing their performance—and you must do this very soon."

Chapter Fifteen

The Black Knights

"Finally," Sebastian yelled, spotting a servant coming his way. "Eustace, where is everyone? Blast it all! We need help here."

"I am here, sir." Eustace gave a short bow, hindered by the heavy sword he held. He offered it to Ivan, but he stepped back and didn't take it.

"I left the South Castle's celebration a bit early," the servant said. "There is much to do for the Annual Victory Feast before the soldiers and Forest folks return."

With no sheath to house the sword, Eustace lowered the tip to the ground, his hand resting upon the ornately carved hilt. He looked back and forth from Ivan to Sebastian, puzzlement etched in his brow.

Ivan introduced himself.

"I know who you are, sir," said the impeccably dressed servant, standing rod-straight. "Anna-Iza has told me of your coming. I have been waiting anxiously for you." Eustace's worried face was thin and angular. His receding hairline formed an almost perfect M across his high forehead.

"Have any returned from the South Castle?" Sebastian stepped closer to Eustace. "The servants, the commanders, or soldiers?"

"Not that I know of. There was no need for them to leave until the games were over and the final victory celebration played out. No one knows the danger Zephyrus is in. I venture they are unaware that communication is lacking through Root-Underground, too."

Sebastian and Ivan moaned miserably. Ivan bit his lower lip, the feeling of desperation rushing over him. He wondered if Eustace had any idea what was about to take place.

Stretching his neck, Ivan searched the woodland grounds to see if Canute and Alfred were returning. He didn't see them. "Where are those mutts?" He sighed with frustration.

Eustace turned his head and shrugged, not understanding the comment. "I'm sure I don't know, sir."

Sebastian rested his hand reverently on the silver blade. "Why do you hold The Challenger?"

Lifting the great sword, Eustace positioned it across his arms once again. "I present The Challenger to you, Mr. Kimble." He looked Ivan straight in his eyes. "It is to aid you in case of danger." He waited, unmoving, for Ivan to lift the burden.

Ivan set the Golden Lantern onto the ground and reached for the sword. Embedded in the hilt were beautifully carved images of oak leaves, acorns, and vines twisting around the golden cross. It was a striking piece of craftsmanship that reminded him of the embellishment on the lantern, and he wondered how Eustace had obtained it. More importantly, why was it being given to him when he didn't plan to fight?

"The sword is heavier than I thought." Ivan

bounced it on his palms. "But the hilt feels right in the curve of my hands." He hadn't gotten the same feeling from The Protector. On the silver blade, in English Gothic script, Ivan read the name, *The Challenger.* "Why do you offer me the sword?" He was terrified he would have to fight the deadly Ghost Warriors.

"I'm sure I don't know," Eustace replied. "Lord Graydon asked that I bring it with me since the annual games arc almost over and to see it replaced in the Sanctuary of Truth. But now I realize there will be no opening of the sanctuary door."

"Oh, I see," Ivan said, still a bit confused. "I'll be sure this splendid sword is returned to Zephyrus when he wakes."

Eustace pulled on the sleeves of his waistcoat. "If you would be so good, Mr. Kimble, sir, as to give me Tom Shiffert's sword and sheath, I'll see that it's returned to him."

"Quite right." Ivan removed the weapon and handed it over.

Sebastian snapped a hasty order. "Eustace, ride to the castle immediately and get help before the enemies invade us. It seems our desperate messages haven't been delivered."

"That is precisely why I asked for The Protector." Eustace gave an understanding nod as he buckled the belt and sheathed Tom's sword. "I may need a bit of protection myself."

Ivan sighed, giving a frustrated look at the dancing goddesses. "What are we to do?"

Sebastian scratched his beard and then suddenly said, "Ah! I recognize the song the goddesses sing. It will come to an end in a few moments, and I believe they will lower their heads in silent prayer. At that time, it should be safe to slip past them and administer the sap."

Ivan beamed. "I'll hang the Golden Lantern on one of Dorset's lower limbs. In that way," he said sensibly, "it'll remain safe near the axe."

When Sebastian approved with a wave of his hand, Ivan darted across the wide-open circle toward the triplets. He held the lantern snugly in the crook of his arm while clutching The Challenger in his other hand.

There, propped against Dorset, was the Silver Axe, exactly where Ivan had left it. Relief and tightness in his chest eased. He laid the axe flat in the grass where it would be better hidden. He hooked the lantern's golden ring on one of Dorset's sturdy branches, waiting for the triplets' biting comments as it was when he first met them. Their eyes shot open, but they didn't protest or torment him. Instead, they asked questions all at once.

"What took you so long?" they chorused. "Do you have the sap with you?"

"We've been waiting for days," Winchester whined.

"Zephyrus is in a very bad way." Dorset focused on the Great Oak. "It's only because of the goddesses chanting that he avoids the darkness."

"I know," Ivan replied. "The delays were out of our control." He was pleasantly surprised the triplets' behavior seemed friendlier. Holding up his hand, he shook his head as they continued to question him. "Later. Sebastian and I will discuss our journey with you."

Just as he turned away, he saw Eustace's terrified face. His mouth opened, his eyes were wide as biscuits.

The servant waved his arms frantically in Ivan's direction. Sebastian stared to the west, looking as horrified as Eustace.

"There's trouble approaching!" Sebastian yelled.

"Trouble?" Ivan tensed, his eyes straining through the obstruction of thick tree growth. "I can't see anything."

Spinning on a heel, Eustace pointed west on Zephyrus Barkay Road. "They're coming!"

Ivan was sure the Ghost Warriors and Dark Army were approaching fast. He imagined them atop thundering warhorses, great blades drawn, leaving a trail of sparks and flame behind pounding hooves. He tried to ask who was coming but couldn't speak through his swollen throat. He needed to find his pets and get to safety at once.

"Three Black Knights are coming this way," Eustace shouted. "Take cover, Mr. Kimble." He ran, making a swift retreat through the trees behind Zephyrus. Glancing back, he yelled, "Run! Hide while you still can, they'll cut you to pieces."

"Are you sure they're not on our side?" Ivan inhaled a long, hopeful breath, but a sense of foreboding and raw fear ripped through him. Instinctively, his shaky hands gripped The Challenger's hilt. He hoped he wouldn't need to use it.

"I'm afraid not," Sebastian mumbled, his attention still on the knights thundering in their direction.

Suddenly alert, Ivan raced back toward Sebastian. "But I thought knights were men of valor, of loyalty, and courage…men to be admired."

"Not this trio of terror. These are the Black Knights. Their title has to do with their black hearts more than their black armor and attire."

Ivan stared, his mouth dropped open. He couldn't make his legs move and run away.

"They've earned their title, I assure you." Sebastian turned in Ivan's direction, his arms stiff at his sides. "That big gorilla in front is their leader. He's mean, vile, and cruel as they come. His companions aren't much better, not having the guts to defy him."

"I-I don't think I would, either." Ivan gawked at the huge knight. An icy tingle crept up his spine. "What do they want? Are they looking for the Ancient Relics?" He cast a glance to where the lantern hung, and the axe lay in the grass. If only he had hung the lantern on a higher branch, but the three invaders were too close to take such a risk now.

"I believe they're here as scouts for the Dark Army that will surely follow." Sebastian's brow crinkled. "They've come to ensure that Zephyrus will soon die."

"They mustn't learn what I have in my pocket, or they'll kill me." Ivan placed the flat of his hand over the vial and gave it a gentle pat."

"Keep it hidden. Say nothing." Sebastian averted his face from the intruders.

Ivan's heart beat like a thunderstorm with high winds. "What can we do?"

"It's too late for us to hide." Sebastian's voice croaked. "Let's hope they stop only for a moment, and then, seeing nothing to delay them, they keep riding."

Something rose up from the bottom of Ivan's stomach, leaving a sour taste in his mouth. He worried for the goddesses' safety, and he suspected Sebastian did the same.

Slowing, the goddesses' dancing stopped. They

folded their hands in prayer, heads lowered, eyes closed, just as Sebastian predicted. Ivan pressed his lips together and twisted his face. *Can I duck between the girls and save Zephyrus now? No, it's too dangerous, and they could be harmed. I'll wait for the Black Knights to move on.*

Grabbing Bounty's bridle, Ivan held it tightly. He had a good look at what caused the servant to run and Sebastian to freeze. Three riders, armored in black with silver trim, galloped on gigantic shadow-dark steeds toward the circular clearing. The largest knight, powerfully built through his shoulders and chest, boasted a red crest on his breastplate and repeated on his shield. The image was a vicious vulture holding sharp-tipped arrows in his thick beak while his lethal talons were poised to attack. Below the crest was the single word, *Burtack*. Ivan wasn't sure if it was the leader's name or the name of his regiment.

The big Black Knight brought his stallion to a skidding halt. The dust mounded and gravel flew all around him. Through his lifted visor, he burrowed his eyes into Zephyrus and then slowly turned toward Ivan with a steady stare. Burtack's thick lip curled into a condescending snicker. His gaze moved to the lovely girls standing in quiet prayer. Saliva dripped down the side of his mouth.

Ivan remained frozen, afraid he might endanger the goddesses if he moved an inch.

Bounty lifted his head and whinnied while he tugged at the bridle gripped in Ivan's damp hands. "Stay, Bounty. Please, be still," he whispered, between clenched teeth.

Burtack's deep, hollow eyes slowly surveyed his

surroundings as though he were overlord of all that lay before him. His attention returned, locking onto the goddesses. His eyes opened wide, staring at them praying around the huge tree.

Imposing and confident, Burtack seemed preoccupied. His twitching fingers curved around a small scabbard attached to a silver-studded leather belt at his thick waist. His head tilted to the side as though he had changed his mind about the knife and withdrew his hand. He jerked his black-plumed helmet from his head, giving it a directed toss across the lawn.

The helmet thumped and rolled. Ivan jumped suddenly. Now that he could see the knight's pockmarked face and sagging jowls, his blood raced hot through his veins. He was even meaner looking than Ivan first observed.

The exhausted girls reached for their sisters' hands, grasped them tightly, and resumed their dancing, picking up momentum as the minutes passed. They swirled, dipped, and twisted their dainty bodies as they sang their woeful song.

The trio licked their lips, and one of them rubbed his hands together.

Furious he'd missed his chance to administer the anti-poison, Ivan balled his fists. His opportunity to save Zephyrus had come and gone. He'd been too cowardly to act. It was as Peter accused him—he was spineless.

Burtack pursed his fleshy bottom lip. His small eyes stared in a lewd manner at the young maidens.

Imagining the knight's thoughts, the veins pulsated against Ivan's neck. He breathed deeply, making him a little dizzy on his feet.

The big one hooked his giant shield to the back of his saddle and lifted his heavy leg over his horse. Sounds of strained leather, metal clanking against armor, and the jingling silver of his horse's rich riding gear resonated. Grunting, he dismounted and dropped to the ground with a hard thud.

Ivan gulped, and Sebastian hissed between his teeth.

"Look what we have here." The brute laughed. "Beautiful maidens dancing just for me." Striding toward the girls, Burtack's eyes raked over them. Slowly unbuckling armor from his arms and legs, he threw it in the same direction his helmet had rolled. The two scouts sat atop their horses silently, not making a move, valuing their lives too much to oppose their leader.

Bounty snorted at the black horses, not liking them much. Pulling his head back, the reins left Ivan's sweaty hands, and the stubborn animal bolted away.

Clutching the hilt of The Challenger, Ivan moved tentatively toward the big knight. He didn't know what he'd do if Burtack forced himself on the goddesses—on Anna-Iza. But he would protect her with his life.

"Don't you dare touch her." Ivan gritted his teeth until his lips tightened into a slice of white anger.

The Black Knight threw a disdainful glance at him with a low contemptuous growl. He strode closer to the goddesses, and when Anna-Iza came into view, he grabbed her slender upper arm. With one sharp jerk, he yanked her to him, breaking the dancing circle.

Under a deep trance, the other girls rejoined hands and danced on. They chorused a sad, haunting song, unaware of their mistress's absence.

Anna-Iza shrieked. A flash of terror spread across her face. Caught in Burtack's ruthless grip, she looked small and helpless. His free hand pulled the knife from its scabbard, and he laughed menacingly at her futile resistance. She struggled, screamed, and quaked, but she could not break free from his hold. Burtack leaned down to kiss her. She pushed her hands against his chest and twisted her head to the side. She ducked, avoiding his wet lips. "Stop! You must stop," she cried.

"No one will save you, little goddess," Burtack scoffed. "No one dares to oppose me." He glanced at Ivan as though throwing a challenging look.

"You are forbidden to touch me. Let me go!" Anna-Iza dipped her head, but he only snickered in a sinister way.

"We must help her." Sebastian's eyes were wide with horror. He stepped briskly toward the goddesses, pumping his fist at the Black Knight, yelling a stream of harsh threats that Ivan knew he couldn't fulfill. Though Ivan was just as furious, it was Sebastian who rushed forward and offered Anna-Iza his protection. *Why hadn't I done that? I'm chicken—too afraid to challenge anyone.* Ivan gripped his sword until his knuckles turned crimson. *I must do something.*

Sickened, Ivan felt a rush of burning rage. White spots popped in front of his eyes. The merciless brute had threatened the life of his good friend. And much worse, he touched Anna-Iza, contaminating her, violating the laws of her gods. Terror reflected in Anna-Iza's eyes. Ivan caught her look, but he hesitated, feeling helpless to defend her.

"Get away, old man," Burtack warned, "or I'll shove this knife into your skull and crush you flat with my foot."

Lowering his fist, Sebastian moved away toward Zephyrus and the girls. He stood there, his expression tight with anger. Diana pulled from the group and went to his side, placing a comforting arm about his shoulders. He embraced her and whispered something in her ear.

Burtack threatened Anna-Iza's soft white neck with the tip of his knife. She gave a whimpering cry when his weapon pierced her skin. A thin trickle of blood appeared near the bottom of her throat, trailing down her chest. Her lips pressed together as though willing herself not to scream or cry.

Ivan's dark brows pulled together while red-hot fury rose up in him. Burtack shoved his knife back into its scabbard. "I don't need a weapon to get what I want." He jerked her close and crushed her against his hard armor. She closed her eyes tightly where a tear seeped out.

How can I save her? Ivan's anger was replaced with doubt. *I don't know how to wield a sword, and Burtack is so much bigger.* His memory flashed back to Dirk Mackle, the bully at his school who enjoyed hurting others. His teacher said he'd meet more bullies in his life, and she was right!

Sebastian suddenly spun around and marched toward Ivan. "You hold the answer in your hands."

A new voice spoke, sonorous and strong and sure. "I am The Challenger. I will do your fighting for you, Ivan Kimble. I know the training and moves of all Black Knights. Allow me the freedom to contest your opponent."

"By the thunder!" Ivan stared at the sword he held.

"You talk? A blade of silver is guided by the spirit of a man?"

"Yes," The Challenger replied, "I am the spirit of a man from long ago, but I did not choose to become an Ancient Relic."

The other two knights removed their helmets and scanned the area, searching for the source of the deep voice, but they saw no one threatening. They shrugged and shifted uneasily in their saddles.

"Now is our time to fight together, Ivan," The Challenger said. "Tighten both hands around the hilt and approach the knight."

"Y-you don't understand." Ivan felt the blood drain from his face. "I don't know how to use a—I mean, I can't—"

"You have no choice. Fight him or lose your life," The Challenger said. "Grip the hilt and raise your weapon."

Hands trembling, Ivan willed his heart to stop beating so loudly. He had a partner to help him, *but a talking sword*? He was too numb with fear to consider the matter rationally.

The closer he got, the bigger and meaner the Black Knight appeared.

Anna-Iza lifted her wet eyes, trembling like a leaf in a windstorm. He wanted to help her, to take her into his arms and rescue her. But he could only watch as she desperately pushed against her captor, trying to get free. She was no match for his strength.

"Go on, struggle, you pretty little thing." Burtack snickered and bent his head to kiss her again.

She covered her face with her hands, avoiding his lips.

"The goddess is not to be touched!" Ivan yelled. A boiling surge of anger ripped through him. He brought The Challenger upright, gripping it with shivering hands.

"Oh..." Burtack said with mocking amusement. His narrow, malicious eyes glowered as if evaluating the foolish boy poised against him. "And who are you to threaten me, Burtack the Mighty?"

"Take your filthy hands off the High Goddess," Ivan said through a tense jaw, "or I'll remove your arms at your elbows."

Did I really say that? He swallowed hard and prayed he sounded more convincing than he felt, that his trembling knees did not betray his feigned courage.

They glared at each other—the big brute and the young lad.

Anna-Iza mouthed the words, "*Help me! Ivan, please, help me.*"

Burtack eased his hold on the goddess, his reddening face twisting into a livid grimace, but he did not release her. He studied Ivan with a piercing yet befuddled stare. Then, as though he experienced a burst of sudden understanding, the knight tipped back his head and let out a guttural roar of laughter.

"Ah-ha!" he shouted. "She's your girl, is that it? Well, now, that's fair enough. You can have this one, and I'll take the black-haired beauty. That one there, standing near the oak tree. Why, there's plenty for all."

Diana covered her pallid face with both hands, turned, and pressed her face into Zephyrus's rough bark.

The sounds of Anna-Iza's screams had interrupted the other goddesses, who stopped dancing one by one.

They remained in a trance-like state, mixed with extreme fatigue. Leaning their backs against Zephyrus's trunk, they slid down and sat upon the ground, their pretty heads resting upon their bent knees.

One of the black horses snorted, shaking his shiny mane. The scout removed a gauntlet, leaned forward, and stroked his steed. "Pity, the youth seems quite gallant," he said blandly.

"Passionate to his cause," the other black scout replied.

The first scout raised the volume of his voice. "He's sure to die by Burtack's hand."

Unexpectedly, The Challenger rose of its own accord, slashing through the air as a way to warm up. It looked formidable and competent in its maneuvers. Molded in Ivan's hands, the sword lowered itself and pointed at Burtack's heart.

"What's happening?" Ivan stammered. "I'm not ready to fight, I can't, I—"

"The Challenger is prepared to fight," Sebastian replied. "Follow his lead and stay with him."

The sword spoke, "Ivan Kimble, warn Burtack. Tell him he will die here today unless he and his two knights leave Oakhurst immediately."

"Now, for the last time," Ivan said and turned to spit to his right, "let the goddess go!" He hoped the spitting gesture and strong words made him seem tough, but it wasn't the truth.

After a long pause, Burtack released Anna-Iza, giving her a rough shove. "I'd rather fight a man any day and cut his heart out," he jeered. "I'll save the prize of the girl until later."

Anna-Iza stumbled, nearly falling, but moving

briskly, Diana caught her.

Instead of going to Anna-Iza or Zephyrus's aid, Ivan held a talking sword in his hands, prepared—or unprepared—to defend his own life. He felt powerless. *Is there no one who can save Zephyrus?* He couldn't suggest that Sebastian take the vial, though he'd considered it. Realizing this also involved too much risk, he pushed the thought away. The greater danger was that the knights could snatch the sap from Sebastian, shatter the delicate vial, and ensure Zephyrus's death.

"Your job is to fully concentrate on Burtack's first move." Sebastian's cheeks turned pink, his lips quivered. "Don't let any thought interfere."

"But I can't…"

The Challenger spoke: "Watch your opponent. Think of nothing except the position of the weapons and your movements. I will do everything else."

Ivan's response was the chattering of his own teeth. *I know nothing of wielding a sword, much less a magical one.*

With slow ease, Burtack drew his huge sword from its hold. His deadly stare fixed on Ivan, he asked, "You know who you're fighting?"

Ivan could only nod.

"I will now separate your head from your neck." The Black Knight's wide mouth worked into a frightening sneer. He raised his weapon and spread his massive legs for balance. "Time to die, pretty boy."

Sebastian growled at the two knights still on their horses. "No interference. This will be a fair fight between Burtack and the lad."

Fair? Ivan shot a blazing glance at Sebastian.

The two scouts sniggered. "We won't have long to wait. Tear out his heart and feed it to the crows," one said and laughed. The second scout twisted in his saddle and punched a satisfied fist into his comrade's shoulder.

Burtack laughed heartily.

Just then, Zephyrus let out a deep, painful moan.

Chapter Sixteen

Three against One

Burtack's lethal sword halted in an upright position.

Heads turned to stare at Zephyrus's half-opened eyes. He wailed another terrible sound. A warning as if his very life was ebbing away. Ivan's cold, cramped hands clutched his sword to defend his own life. He could do nothing to save the Great Oak now.

Sebastian yelled between cupped hands, "Hold on, Zephyrus, we're here for you!"

The tree's red-webbed eyes fluttered after another pitiful moan. Whether he heard and understood Sebastian's comment, Ivan couldn't say.

"Who will save Zephyrus?" Ivan asked. The huge tree's eyes slowly closed, and his features faded back into his trunk.

"Ivan, watch out!" Sebastian cried.

The Challenger lifted swiftly. Two swords came together with an explosive crack. The force of his enemy's blade vibrated, shooting fiery lightning through Ivan's hands. Pain traveled hot up his arms, biting into his shoulders and across his neck muscles, leaving him breathless and numb. All thoughts evaporated, to be replaced by severe throbbing in his limbs.

Burtack sneered. "Did you see that?" He raised his sword high. "I'm living up to my great legend. Burtack, the Mighty Burtack."

"We saw it, Mighty One," the scouts shouted.

The Black Knight turned to look at Anna-Iza, but disappointment spread across his face. She had lowered her head, her hands clasped together in the stillness of prayer. His obvious wish to impress her with his great strength had failed. He looked like a hurt schoolboy who'd just been rejected.

Again, rising skyward, The Challenger twisted to the right in Ivan's hands. Following through, it crashed against the sharp edge of his antagonist's broadsword. Ivan shrieked in agony, nearly collapsing to his knees, his eyes squeezed tight. His teeth ground together to help bear the raw pain that raced through his arms.

Before Ivan could regain his strength, The Challenger rose, swinging upward, catching the knight's blade a third time—another cracking blow.

Willing himself to stay on his feet, Ivan took deep breaths to clear his head and hazy vision. If he fell to his knees, he would surely die.

He didn't dare cry out for Sebastian's help. It would make him look weak and vulnerable—which he was, and Burtack must've sensed this. Ivan was certain he couldn't recover fast enough to withstand another blow. *This is my end.*

Anna-Iza raised her head from prayer, offering an encouraging, sweet smile. For a moment, it helped to remind Ivan of his purpose and duty. But there was only so much torture he could endure, and he was at his limit. He almost believed he'd be slaughtered as the scouts had predicted—his heart cut out and thrown to the crows.

What will happen to Anna-Iza and her sister goddesses if I die? Who will welcome Canute and Alfred back from their chase in the Forest? Who will care for my farm and animals? "There is no one," he whispered to himself. "I cannot die."

Gasping breath, quick and sharp, Ivan's heart pounded wildly against his chest. He tried to convince himself to go on, to save Anna-Iza.

Why isn't Sebastian taking my pain away? It occurred to him abruptly that there could be no power of healing when Sebastian was absent from the cloak. *Now, what am I to do?*

The Challenger's instructions were clear. "Let me do the fighting, Ivan Kimble. Hold your grip firm, focus on your enemy, and follow me through. I'll do everything else. Is that clear?

"I can't go on," Ivan moaned.

"What's the matter, pretty boy? You can't fight like a man to win your damsel's love?" Laughing, Burtack threw a demeaning glare at Anna-Iza. "Maybe she ain't worth the trouble."

"He's trying to make you angry, so you'll do something careless," The Challenger warned. "Never let your enemy goad you."

"I can't swing the sword." Ivan let out a small cry. "My hands—my shoulders are on fire."

"The girls are depending on you," The Challenger said.

Anna-Iza returned a gentle smile that seemed to say she believed in him—that she cared.

Gathering his courage, Ivan resolved to fight back with all the strength he had. Even if he managed only one more blow, it would be better than simply giving up and being cut to pieces. He remembered Peter saying that he was cowardly, unwilling to fight back. Maybe it was true in the past—but not now.

Ivan squared his shoulders and faced his opponent. "One more blow. One more strike. Bring him down," Ivan repeated quietly.

The Black Knight moved into a fighting position and gripped his sword with thick fingers. "I'm tired of this childish play—a final thrust through your heart."

Ivan trembled. *In a moment, I'll die.*

"Come on, Ivan," The Challenger urged. "We can do this. Remember what I told you."

The encouraging words gave Ivan new strength to raise aching arms and follow the magic sword, ascending for its next strike. He swung at his enemy's blade. A shiny arc of metal whirled overhead as his sword met and parried a strike from Burtack. Sparks flew from edge to edge. Ivan screamed and willed himself to go on.

Taking cautious steps forward, he lifted his sword once again. With tremendous force, The Challenger swung at the enemy in an upward motion. Its tip sliced the metal of Burtack's breastplate, leaving a long, deep gash.

"Ivan, why did you pull back?" The Challenger scolded hotly. "We had him in those moments."

"I couldn't…I can't kill a man."

Howling, the knight hopped back, lowering his sword.

"Ah," The Challenger gloated. "I've cut through Burtack's armor. Now, don't hesitate. Take him down, Ivan Kimble."

Realizing he would die if he didn't act, Ivan knew what he must do. It was exactly as his ancient sword instructed—"Focus, hold on, and follow through." He became one with his weapon, and a new strength entered him.

Burtack's mouth contorted into an ugly smirk. He increased his attack, swinging madly. Ivan jumped back several times to avoid being struck.

When Burtack's sword caught the cloak's hem, Ivan stumbled sideways and tried to catch himself. He balanced himself just as the knight raised his deadly weapon. It swung down and met bone. Ivan screeched in pain as the sharp edge broke his collarbone, spewing blood.

Burtack's blade had slammed just short of Ivan's neck, awarding Ivan a few more precious seconds of life.

"Sebastian!" Ivan cried helplessly. "I've been struck."

"Watch out!" the spirit yelled, running toward him, "Lift your sword and defend yourself."

Ivan doubled over, protecting his injured shoulder bone. His strength waning, his blurry vision saw Burtack charging with his sword clenched in iron hands, his teeth locked hard. With horror, Ivan realized his life would soon be over. He wailed, "Sebastian, you must heal me at once, or I will die."

Throwing himself into the cloak, the spirit disappeared in a flash. Ivan felt the hard push, the enveloping warmth, hundreds of tapping fingers around his shoulder, and the healing touch of magic. Sebastian had reset the bone and sealed the injury with the precision of a fine surgeon.

Burtack stopped, pulled back, and stared with astonishment, unable to grasp what had just happened. Heavy lines creased his sweat-drenched forehead.

In a flash, Ivan raised The Challenger high, and with all his power, all his might, he swung the silver blade at his assailant. His fast comeback and the weapon's powerful return caught the knight off-guard. The sword sliced Burtack just above the bend in his arm. Ivan felt metal against bone and heard his opponent's yowl of pain.

The brute swore, stumbling on his heavy feet. His wound went seriously deep. Blood soaked his arm, staining the carpet of leaves where he stood. Staggering, Burtack tried to find solid footing.

From the corner of his eyes, Ivan saw the other two knights had pushed off their horses, landing noisily on the ground. They jerked their swords from their sheaths.

"You tricked me!" Burtack bellowed. His face reddened. "You." He shook his fist and yelled at The Challenger. "You have put yourself into the hands of a foolish boy who knows nothing about fighting a true champion."

"He seems to be doing well enough," The Challenger said with a calm voice.

In those moments, Burtack must've realized he could lose his life to the revered weapon of magic and to the young novice who held it. He motioned with a turn of his head for his two knights to join him.

"Now, we are even." He laughed sardonically.

The two knights moved into place, standing on either side of their commander. The scout on his left offered Burtack his helmet, but he refused with a single shake of his head. The other offered his shield, but again Burtack refused. A malicious glint flickered in his eyes.

"I want to see the pretty boy go down begging for his life, and then the talking sword will be mine."

Terror knifed through Ivan's chest. "S-Sebastian. The Challenger. How do I fight three armed men?"

Burtack's lips drew back into a terrifying jeer, his eyes flaming with hate. Standing next to him, his two scouts raised their swords.

"Wh-what should I do?" Ivan's hands were so cold he could scarcely hold his weapon.

"Help is on the way," The Challenger said.

Ivan exhaled. Any minute he expected troops to arrive with the crunching of gravel and dust flying behind their horses' hooves. *But soon—they must come very soon.* Even with The Challenger, he knew he couldn't fend off three deadly swordsmen.

His jaw set tight, Ivan stood his ground. He must stay alive to protect Anna-Iza, the goddesses, and Zephyrus.

Burtack ignored his bleeding arm bent tightly against his body.

"Now watch your opponents," Sebastian warned from the cloak. "They all hold lethal weapons and are as dangerous as starving Swamp Dragons."

"But Sebastian, I can't fight three of them. I don't want to fight."

The knights shielded their master, one on each side. Burtack gripped his sword holding it in front of his chest, favoring his injured arm. His grin was icy cold.

Diana nudged Anna-Iza with her elbow. "Mistress, this is where you can invoke the help of our gods."

Anna-Iza responded immediately. "I'm thinking the same thing." She recited aloud: *"The laws of our gods may be called upon by the High Goddess when unfair advantage of man is engaged.* This is one of those times." Diana agreed, bobbing her head.

Moving forward, Anna-Iza stood in the large circular opening making sweeping motions with her arm extended. She made a final snap of her wrist, and white lightning shot forth. It was followed by swirls of blue-violet mist that churned, roiled, and finally thickened. Turning opaque, it formed into three powerfully built men. In only a moment, she had conjured three White Knights sitting atop brilliant white steeds with horns protruding on their foreheads. Anna-Iza tipped her face toward Ivan and gave him a victorious smile.

Burtack froze. His jaw slackened when he appeared to assess the three well-armed White Knights. His two scouts looked as though they'd had a sudden change of heart. Lowering their swords, they moved toward their horses, but Burtack held steadfast, too stubborn to admit defeat. He yelled, "Stay your places. We have a job to finish." The scouts remained.

Help had arrived from a source Ivan hadn't even guessed was possible.

Burtack lowered his sword to his side. He coughed and brought up a slug of mucus, spitting it onto the forest floor. One of his scouts pounded him on his back.

"Leave me be." Burtack's command was like a growl, and the scouts obeyed.

Sliding from their mounts, two White Knights strode toward Ivan, buffering him. Each drew their fine-looking weapons from decorated sheaths.

At once, the White Knights were ready to fight. They raised their swords, understanding the deadly details of the situation. As the code of knighthood demanded, they were ready to defend the cause for which they were summoned.

The captain of the White Knights asked Ivan with a self-assured voice, "Do you wish me to bring him down?"

"Like you have the power." Burtack's snarl was followed by an attempt at laughter.

"No," Ivan said. "I will end Burtack's life here where he committed an unforgivable crime against the High Goddess." Even as the words left his mouth, he couldn't believe he'd spoken them. *Did I just condemn a man to die by my own hands?*

Burtack made a crude response with his tongue and then spit. "Goddesses, my foot! They're babies playing at being women." His face twisted into a mean stare. "And you, pretty boy…" he mocked, "You are not the one to end my life, not even with your fancy talking sword." Inhaling roughly, his weapon rose with a crunching grip.

The conjured men were exceptional fighters. They were acutely alert, strong, and powerful. Calculating their movements, they made each stroke and thrust count without squandering energy. The captain of the White Knights stood aside, statue-still, waiting and watching for foul play.

Now, Ivan followed The Challenger as it rose, swinging harder and longer. The movements felt just right in his hands. He knew this by the feel and sounds of his weapon crashing against Burtack's sword. The sting of pain was not as severe—but bad enough.

"You're doing fine," The Challenger said to Ivan. "Now follow through. Smooth—that's it."

Although Burtack parried each trust of Ivan's powerful weapon, he was tiring, evident by the heaving of his breast armor. His mouth hung open, saliva dribbled down his chin. Favoring his injured arm, he pulled it against his chest for protection. It was only a matter of time before the Black Knight's strength gave out—Ivan hoped.

"Your opponent's not scoffing anymore," Sebastian stated.

A strangling commotion to Ivan's right revealed one of the Black Scouts sinking to his knees, clutching his stomach. He shrieked, falling facedown to the ground. Legs jerking, he succumbed to the throes of death.

The sight of his dead comrade intimidated the other Black Scout, who also showed signs of weakening. He was clumsy against his steadfast rival. Within moments, the second Black Scout folded and dropped his weapon. He flattened to the ground with a loud wail.

Stepping closer, the second White Knight raised his visor. Stoic, he bent to pick up his enemy's fallen sword, nodded, and seemed to study the scout's pierced heart.

A melodious humming of prayer rose from the goddesses, carried on a breeze. "Our Great Master is dying. His spirit is leaving us. May the High Intervener take him and make a place of comfort and peace for our beloved king."

It was odd, but Ivan now understood the goddesses' language, while he hadn't been able to decipher it minutes before. At that instant, Ivan jumped back to avoid the hissing sweep of Burtack's dangerous blade. It had just missed him.

Burtack's laugh turned into a phlegm-invaded cough. Wavering unsteadily, he staggered toward his horse and collapsed against it. He turned his head, looked at the dead scouts, and shivered.

Ivan backed away. *I don't want to kill him. I can't—please just leave.* His stomach knotted tighter and tighter. "Now is my opportunity," he whispered to himself. "I must get the sap to Zephyrus. I heard the goddesses singing a death prayer."

"Yes, you must hurry," Sebastian said.

Burtack straightened. Teeth clenched, with his sword raised high, he stumbled after Ivan and swung. Ivan spun around, hearing Burtack's heavy breathing, and met the strike with The Challenger. He darted toward Zephyrus.

Burtack swore profusely. Anger wrenched his face.

Zigzagging to avoid the next slash of Burtack's lethal weapon, Ivan reached Zephyrus, ducking under the clasped hands of the now praying goddesses. He lifted the folds of the cloak and pulled the vial from inside his pocket. He jerked the stopper. Without a moment to lose, he tipped the liquid into the tree's open wound.

The three White Knights moved in quickly. They poised their great swords, blocking Burtack's path. There the Black Knight seemed to freeze with indecision. He gazed all around, searching for a way past the three White Knights and stop Ivan.

Several seconds passed. Zephyrus's ear-shattering screams permeated the Forest. *Was it too late?* Ivan trembled and stared, waiting and hoping. Zephyrus's wounds spewed a yellowish liquid. The smell was a pungent mixture of damp wood pulp, sulfur, and something musky at the same time, much like the scent inside Fungoda's cavity. White steam curled from the splits in Zephyrus's bark, rising, twisting in long columns until they mingled among his upper branches and leaves.

"Oh, Master," Sebastian cried. "Please live."

Heavy lids opened. Zephyrus's words were faint and mumbled. "High Intervener, have you come to take me away?" Seconds later, the Great Oak's eyes and mouth disappeared into his ancient bark.

Ivan dropped the empty vial, astonished the sap hadn't revived Zephyrus. *Am I too late? Should I have risked my life sooner to save him?* He shuddered at his own inadequacies.

At last, the goddesses stopped praying. They slumped exhausted against the tree, encircling their arms around him, pressing their cheeks into his great trunk. Some grieved, and some wore weary frowns while others broke the circle and held their hands firmly over their ears.

"I have failed." Burtack staggered back. "Zephyrus was to die a horrible death this day. Now he may recover, all because of this intruder, this boy and the magic elixir in the bottle." Furious, Burtack raced toward Ivan, his sword held upward, his face warped with hate.

Their weapons met with a resounding clatter. Metal cracked against metal once, twice, and then again. Ivan ducked and spun so fast that on the third strike, the Long Dark Cloak twirled around him, wrapping his legs, for a moment leaving him trapped—and then it unfurled. There was no slowing Ivan. His rage boiled with vengeance for the rude treatment of Anna-Iza. Ivan parried a strike from Burtack and returned a slash with such ferocity that he gouged a long slit into the knight's chest armor.

Burtack screamed and stumbled. He struggled to stay upright, gasping through dry lips. Looking stunned, his mouth remained open. The slash had intersected the head of the vulture-image emblazoned there. The Challenger swung without letup, forcing the knight's clumsy feet back toward the edge of Zephyrus's circle.

"That's the strategy," The Challenger said. "Exhaust him and end his life."

Ivan saw his chance. With both hands, he brought The Challenger high over his right shoulder. Eyes opened wide, Burtack raised his weapon to block the strike. But he wasn't fast enough.

The Challenger yelled. "Now, Ivan! Swing the blade into his neck."

The magical sword sailed through the air with menacing speed as it sliced into Burtack. Ivan jerked it away quickly, sensing the hot flesh, sinew, and muscle giving way under the razor-sharp edge. A gush of blood spurted from Burtack's neck. Ivan jumped back, gripping The Challenger with horror.

"What have I done, S-Sebastian?" he stammered and faltered, but somehow he stayed upright.

Burtack's sweaty fingers released his weapon. The death gurgle of burning liquid sounded as the knight inhaled his own blood. He hit the ground, his bulky armor twisting. He'd lost his final battle to a talking piece of metal.

Ivan stood near his dead opponent, fatigued beyond

anything he'd ever known. He stared at his wet hands, the front of the cloak, and his shirt splattered with Burtack's blood. *What would my mother say about this?*

"Are you all right?" Sebastian said but remained in the cloak.

The Challenger spoke in a quiet, reassuring voice, "It was Burtack's destiny to die today, Ivan Kimble."

Ivan shook his head from side to side, too stricken to question the curious statement. He couldn't believe what he'd done. Lifting one shoulder in a gesture of hopelessness, revolted by his cold-blooded act, he went silent. He had ended a man's life this day.

Chapter Seventeen

Comforting the Goddess

"You can't think about it now." Sebastian left the confines of the cloak and moved next to Ivan where he placed a consoling hand on his shoulder. "The Forest is a better place without Burtack. No one will grieve for him."

Staring blankly to the West, Ivan wrestled with his shame. "I've killed a man." He felt tears welling behind closed lids. "I've never done anything so terrible in my life."

"I know, but you had to defend yourself. You saved Anna-Iza and the other goddesses from the scourge that wreaked havoc in our Forest. Burtack's brutality was his choice."

Sebastian put his arms around Ivan and pulled him in a tight squeeze. "Listen to me." He tipped his head and met Ivan's watery eyes. "You did what you had to do—the only thing you could. At times we have to do things completely against our beliefs and teachings, but it's necessary to protect those we hold dear, the ones we love. Do you understand?"

"I didn't want to kill anyone."

"Of course you didn't." The kindly spirit released him and stepped back. "I keep forgetting how young you are. So very young. You've had to grow up fast."

Ivan grimaced briefly. "All I could think about was saving Zephyrus and Anna-Iza and not getting my own head cut off. Somehow I didn't really imagine ending a man's life—forever." He moved away in a daze, not knowing or caring where he went. *I'll go home, leave the Forest.* Turning east, he slowly moved in that direction. *Where is that wretched horse of mine? I can't go without him. Neither can I leave Alfred and Canute.*

Following with hurried steps, Sebastian drew beside him. "Can I help you understand this—what had to be done?"

Ivan paused to consider. He shook his head and kept walking. He took long strides with his hands fisted at his sides. "I want to be by myself."

"Certainly," Sebastian replied. "But I should be with you in case you have questions."

"I have done an unforgivable thing." Ivan stared at the ground.

Sebastian sighed, concern etched his face. "I say again, it couldn't be helped."

Ivan stopped and gazed ahead, expressionless.

"You are a true friend of the Forest." Sebastian squeezed Ivan's hand. "You've rid us of a dangerous brute. Now travelers won't fear for their lives."

"I didn't come here to kill your enemies. I came to find Peter, to take him home with me so I wouldn't be all alone."

"I'm sorry. I know you have your own mission."

Ivan confirmed with a nod.

"Well, now you have friends, many friends who deeply care for you." Sebastian released Ivan's hand and smiled. "We love you."

"Only my parents have said they loved me." Ivan

rubbed his eyes.

"I'm telling you, and it's true. I love you. We all love you."

Ivan's nostrils widened, and he inhaled deeply. He composed himself, giving the dormant oak a long stare. "Is-is he dead?"

"I hope he'll recover in time."

"How long?"

Sebastian bunched his thin shoulders. "I don't know. The antidote has its own course to follow. We just wait and see."

Releasing a slow, stuttering breath, Ivan prayed that Zephyrus would recover and reclaim his powerful position in the Forest.

Ivan's eyes came to rest upon Anna-Iza. *What does she think of me knowing I've killed a man?* The thirteen goddesses faced the Great Oak. Their voices hummed delicately, rising and falling in a healing prayer.

"Come here." Sebastian motioned with his fingers to the injured White Knight. "Let's get you cleaned up." He yelled through the tunnel of his cupped hands, "Eustace! Can you hear me? Bring hot water and a towel. We need to wash Burtack's blood away."

"You sent Eustace to the South Castle to summon the troops," Ivan reminded him, wondering how the servant could hear Sebastian's weak command beyond the tree's buffer.

"Oh, yes, so I did." The old man's voice held a tone of regret. They returned to where Zephyrus stood, and Sebastian shouted again, "Then anyone back there in the barracks' kitchen, bring a basin of warm water."

A servant Ivan didn't know came from somewhere behind the trees, yelling, "I've just arrived. I'll put the kettle on."

Ivan wiped The Challenger's blade on his pant leg and dropped it to the ground. He stared at his bloody hands. Rubbing them on the cloak's hem, he tried to stay focused on the present, but he was dizzy and felt faint. When his stomach gurgled, he remembered he hadn't eaten anything all day. Perhaps that was the reason he could scarcely move his legs.

He was devastated by what he'd done. It was different when he killed the Swamp Dragon. Porcupine was about to eat Canute, and he couldn't let that happen. But Burtack was a man, a living, breathing human being. Yet the cruel Black Knight had threatened to hurt Anna-Iza. Ivan's deep sigh sounded like an animal's injured cry.

"First, I'll heal the wound of this brave knight. Come to me," Sebastian called. The White Knight stepped forward, clutching his injured arm.

It was then that Ivan noticed all three White Knights had dark skin and bald heads. The Black Knights were white, and the White Knights were black. For a moment, he was amused over the irony, but it quickly faded when he saw the red stain on the knight's sleeve. "How deep is your wound?" Ivan asked.

The man shook his head, pushing up his sleeve to the edge of the chainmail, and there he held it. "It's not that bad." He tightened his jaw.

Sebastian dissolved into a swirling blue-gray mist and whisked into the cloak. "Wrap the hem around the knight's arm," he said to Ivan, and he did as Sebastian asked. The task soon done, the cut sealed, and the bleeding stopped at once.

"Thank you, sir." The White Knight gave a grateful

nod.

As quickly as Sebastian disappeared, he now reappeared, inspecting the knight's arm. "Ah, good as new." He lifted his chin with pride.

The White Knights located the dark stallions and slung the dead riders onto their horses' backs. They tied them to their saddles with extra rope they'd brought.

This gruesome task accomplished, the captain of the White Knights stood proud. Taking Ivan's hand in his own, he said, "It was an honor to fight by your side, lad."

Ivan returned the compliment. "Thank you for your help."

"And we were daunted by your bravery." The captain rolled his eyes, resting his hands upon Ivan's shoulders. "To take on Burtack the Mighty without armor or the expertise of a practiced swordsman is unparalleled."

"I didn't have a choice," Ivan managed to mutter. "Without the help of The Challenger, I'm sure I would've been cut to pieces and..." He turned toward the goddesses. "They would've suffered a horrible fate."

"All the same," the leader said, "you are a remarkable fighter for one so young and untrained."

"Th-thank you." Ivan felt a blush creep up his neck.

The white horses raised their single-horned heads, shaking their long shimmering manes while the three White Knights mounted. Their purpose fulfilled, they saluted Anna-Iza, who stood watching with a cheerless face. "Take care, little goddess. We will be honored to return anytime you summon us."

They took the reins of the black horses and rode west to connect with the Sheepherder's Path Road.

"Go to her." Sebastian nodded toward Anna-Iza and gave Ivan a gentle push. "She needs you now."

Ivan hesitated and then took a deep breath and walked toward her.

Her eyes misty, she lowered her chin.

Tenderness welled up and stirred through him. "Dear Anna-Iza." He softened his voice with compassion. "You aren't to weep over Burtack. He's not worth your tears."

Her shoulders quivered. She looked up slowly, blinking.

Moving closer, he opened his arms. Comforting the goddess after such a terrible ordeal seemed like the right thing to do. He asked, timidly, "May I hold you?"

Blue-green eyes peered up at him under her moistened lashes. She shook her head, barely speaking above a whisper, "It is not allowed."

"Only to comfort you." His arms stayed open.

Her small shoulders dropped. Holding his gaze, her lids fluttered with tears. Releasing a shaking sob, she went into Ivan's welcoming embrace. He gathered her to him, surprised that he actually held her. She was warm and wonderful in his arms. Everything he'd done, fighting, and ending Burtack's life to save Anna-Iza's honor, was all worth it. She'd kept the darkness away from Zephyrus and conjured the White Knights with a mere flick of her small hand. She made him feel like the bravest and strongest man who'd ever lived.

"I'm so tired. My sisters are weary, too." Anna-Iza shivered, sighing deeply. She laid her head against his chest. Tears fell upon the cloak.

"You are safe now. I won't let anyone hurt you again."

"I'm sorry," she said tenderly. "I shouldn't be crying like this. I still have my life and my honor. My deepest thanks to you."

He caressed her back with gentle strokes across the silky fabric of her dress until her weeping became faint.

"You are a skilled fighter." She pulled back for a moment and looked at him. "How fortunate we are that you were in the Forest to save us, to save Zephyrus."

Ivan's fingertips smoothed her flushed cheek where a tear had lingered. He tipped her face to his, offering an encouraging smile. She sighed and returned her head to the hardness of his chest.

Delighted with the feel of her warmth next to him, he pressed his lips to her forehead. Not exactly a kiss, but very close. *Did she mind?* Her knees trembled just then, and he tightened his arms about her.

Ivan's thoughts soared. He was sure she had affection for him, too. If that weren't so, why would she submit to his embrace and stay nestled against him?

He wanted to ask her many questions about her life as a goddess. But there was so little time to explore the mysteries about her. What would her gods do when they learned she'd been manhandled by Burtack? And what penalty would she suffer because Ivan held her?

Curiosity got the best of him. "How did you make the White Knights appear with only a wave of your hand?"

She raised her head from his chest and looked into his eyes. "I conjure many things. It's part of my gift as a High Goddess. Tables, chairs, and candelabras, even rubies, and riding cloaks are fairly easy to bring forth.

But invoking the White Knights took much of my strength."

"I love you, Anna-Iza," Ivan said with tenderness. "You have taken my heart in only a few days." He wanted very much to kiss her, to seal his declaration of love, but not for the purpose of a Test of Discernment. He held her, wishing this moment could go on and on.

Sebastian wore a look of stunned disbelief on his wrinkled old face. He stared at Anna-Iza and Ivan wrapped in each other's arms. Diana seemed pleased. Her lips bowed from corner to corner.

"Nothing like this has ever happened," Diana whispered. Sebastian confirmed with a slow nod.

A servant hurried through the trees, sloshing water from a large enamel basin, a towel draped over his arm. "Your wash water, sir," he addressed Sebastian.

"It's for him." Sebastian pointed to Ivan.

Easing himself from Anna-Iza's embrace, Ivan smiled at her. She managed to return his smile. As he dipped his hands to wash, Ivan asked, "Are the garrisons coming from the castle to help us, Maynard?"

"I don't know, sir." The servant shifted the basin in his grip. "I passed Eustace as he traveled in that direction. He instructed me to supervise the cooks and kitchen help when they arrive.

Worried about the onslaught of Ghost Warriors due at any moment and the Dark Army predicted to follow, Ivan absently chewed his bottom lip. He finished washing his hands and dried them on the face towel.

With a final bow, Maynard turned and took the basin away.

Suddenly, Ivan was terrified the warriors would arrive soon, and he stood as the only armed person to combat them. To take them on would be foolhardy—one man, one sword—no way!

He wondered how safe it would be to hide in one of the guest cottages when the Dark Army flooded the area.

"You must leave," Ivan said to Anna-Iza.

She nodded. "You must go, too. Our garrisons are better prepared to fight the soldiers of the demon's army. You've already done so much and are not meant to sacrifice your life for the Forest."

With a dramatic flourish, Ivan fanned the Long Dark Cloak's fabric just as he'd done at the river. Bowing, he flashed a wide smile. "Your will, my Lady."

She laughed at his antics, enjoying a brief moment of fun, and then she and her sister goddesses waved a sweet goodbye. They'd started toward the cottages and stables when Anna-Iza suddenly turned and lifted her head. He heard her softly whisper, "Please hurry back to us."

He grinned wildly. *Anna-Iza must be in love with me.* His knees melted. Ivan wished he could run after her, wrap his arm around her waist, and hold her again.

"Sorry, Ivan, ol' boy." Sebastian's puzzled look remained. "You'll have to let her go. They must hurry to avoid the approaching armies."

"I know." Ivan watched her disappear through the dense growth of trees where their horses were stabled. He was certain she felt the same toward him. Now, Sebastian must recognize that things don't always remain the same. People change. Circumstances change. Ivan had changed.

"Hoot, hoot!" The call was familiar. Ivan whirled

around to see Mart-Mart lighting on one of Zephyrus's oak limbs above his head.

"What is your report, little owl?" Ivan said.

Mart-Mart recited his memorized speech, "The Dark Army is riding fast. The Ghost Warriors will come first—they are savage and unstoppable. They can't be killed by arrow or sword, by lance or mace. They'll come from the northwest, crossing the meadow in less than an hour. The living army of men will soon follow." Mart-Mart went quiet, and his bewildered head spun. "I forgot the last part of my uncle's message." Large, round eyes stared at Ivan as if to jog his memory.

Ivan drew a harsh breath.

"Oh, yes! I remember, now." Mart-Mart raised his bronze-tipped wings. "Hundreds and hundreds of enemy soldiers are coming."

Expecting the worst, Ivan clenched his jaw.

"But there's good news, too." The small brown owl left his tree perch, landing awkwardly on Ivan's shoulder.

A glimmer of hope replaced Ivan's desperation. "Tell me, what is it?"

"Three of our garrisons are galloping this way. Commander Simon left the castle first and will arrive from the south, over there." The excited bird pointed his wingtip. "Commander Greendyn will lead his men from the north for an ambush. Commander Gifford will split his regiment from the west, flanking the enemy from two different directions." He jerked his head, snapped his beak several times, and hooted. "I think I got it right."

"That's good news." Ivan slowly exhaled. Help

was coming at last.

Sebastian's lined brow relaxed, and his whiskers stopped twitching. He retrieved The Challenger where Ivan let it drop and inspected the blade. Apparently seeing no flaws, he placed the sword into Ivan's hands and then strode toward Zephyrus with a slight spring in his step.

After examining the Great Oak, Sebastian rubbed his hands over his face. "I think he'll recover." His worried expression stayed.

"Look, look! They're here," Mart-Mart screeched.

Ivan spun to his left. His hand flew to The Challenger's hilt. Terror quickened through his veins as he readied to confront the maniacal army of the decayed. Countless men approached from the south, wearing silver helmets trimmed with blue plumes. Ivan felt a rush of relief when he found they looked nothing like the skeletons of the dead.

Soldiers tromped through the trees toward the large open circle that surrounded Zephyrus. Voices mingled with hoofbeats, metal shields, swords, and chainmail echoing throughout the woodland.

The regiment halted in row formation as their leader raised the flat of his gloved hand. He sat resolutely on a huge bay horse, slowly removing his helmet. The plumage was thick and showy, held fast in a silver cylinder.

"That's Commander Simon." Sebastian twisted his mouth sideways.

Ivan nodded, noticing the commander's breastplate that showed an image of a dark-winged dragon blowing curls of fire. The name "Commander Simon" was written below the icon.

Just behind him, a soldier lowered a long silk banner featuring the same fierce-looking dragon embroidered within a red circle. Bold lettering under the beast read *Zello*.

Commander Simon glanced around as though assessing the situation. He gave Sebastian a cursory nod. Then Ivan became the target of the man's long icy stare. His frown traveled to the cloak and moved to Ivan's bloodied jacket and trousers. Pursing his lips, Simon clenched and unclenched his gloved hand.

Shifting his weight nervously, Ivan was prepared to explain. After all, he was a stranger and knew he looked like he'd just slaughtered a pig.

The commander kneed his bay's flanks, guiding him toward Zephyrus. He circled the wide circumference where white steam climbed slowly from the trunk's open wounds, thinning as it disappeared into the foliage.

At last, the commander dismounted, stretched his legs, and strode toward Ivan. He pulled off his gauntlets, eyeing the gouges in the dirt and the piled leaves splattered with blood. "I see there was some carnage here. Are you responsible?"

Baffled, Ivan wondered if he was referring to Zephyrus's near-mortal wound or the battle with the Black Knights.

"Well?" the commander repeated sharply, his face distorted with impatient anger.

Ivan found his voice. "The Black Knights were removed by the White Knights. They left the Forest taking the corpses with them." Shrugging his shoulders, Ivan looked away for a moment, doubtful he'd given the answer the commander wanted.

"No matter." The commander snapped, slapping his gauntlets against his palm. "We'll get to the bottom of this."

Does he believe I'm responsible for axing Zephyrus?

The commander tugged the ends of his neatly trimmed mustache. His deep-brown eyes held steady with an air of importance. His sandy-brown hair, parted down the middle, was soaked with sweat and covered with dust from his hard journey and three long days of competitive warrior games at the South Castle.

A front-line soldier gasped, "The lad holds The Challenger. How did he get it?"

Ivan didn't trust himself to answer.

"I'm Commander Simon of the South Garrison," he said curtly, his voice heavy with condescension. "That means these two hundred men are under my command. I really don't care who you are or how much clout you think you have with Zephyrus, we're expecting an army of bloodthirsty men very soon, and I want you *out* of here." His brow furrowed as he jabbed his finger into Ivan's chest.

Turning to Sebastian, the commander growled, "You are vulnerable while in your solid state. I suggest you return to the Long Dark Cloak."

"My very intentions." Sebastian saluted. But he didn't jump to follow Simon's orders.

"You have a horse?" Simon's eyebrows pulled in.

"I do." Ivan scanned the area. "Though I'm not sure where he is right now."

"Then find him and leave *immediately*."

"Excuse me, Simon." Sebastian's voice was calm and even. "You might ease your curt temper for a moment and learn the identity of this young man."

Simon lifted one eyebrow, his mouth twisted mockingly. He didn't appear much interested. "Well, who are you, then?"

Before Ivan could explain, Sebastian continued. "This is Ivan Kimble. He risked his life to bring the healing sap from Fungoda to save Zephyrus. I assure you, his journey has not been pleasant or easy. I believe the Forest owes him a great debt."

Commander Simon's face went pale. His mouth tightened. He turned his head to stare at Zephyrus and snarled. "Kimble, eh?"

"And…Ivan killed Porcupine," Sebastian added.

"What?" Simon's head jerked to attention, and his eyes grew wide. "You killed that horrible beast—the Swamp Dragon?"

Sebastian winked at Ivan. "This is your victory story to tell."

"It was terrifying." As Ivan spoke, the pitch of his voice rose. "I've never seen anything like it. Porcupine had my dog Canute locked in his jaws. I had no choice but to kill the beast, or he would've swallowed my beagle whole." He trembled as he recalled the encounter.

Commander Simon appeared to think on this. "Canute is a beagle dog?" His eyes squinted. His voice wavered. "I had a beagle too, but…well…my Roman wasn't so lucky. Porcupine got him." Simon's angry face turned sad.

"I'm sorry for your loss," Ivan mumbled, and he truly was.

Simon lost his stern expression for a moment. With a half-smile, he said, "Why didn't you tell me this before I made a bloody tyrant of myself?"

One of his men holding the banner snickered quietly, as though stopping Simon from one of his tirades was as unlikely as holding back a starving Swamp Dragon.

Extending his hand, Simon said, "Thank you for doing the job I couldn't bring myself to do. You've done my dear Roman and me a big favor. May he continue to rest in peace."

Ivan shook the commander's hand, accepting his gratitude.

"Where is your beagle now?" Simon scanned the area, apparently expecting to see Canute crouched nearby.

"I have two. They are named King Canute and King Alfred." Ivan paused when the commander grinned, suggesting that he knew the history of England's early kings. "They are mischievous brothers who met with a timmerlan and are probably fast asleep under a hickory bush by now."

The comment brought a tense laugh and a swift shake of Simon's head as if he fully understood the circumstances. Within seconds, his grin disappeared. "Mart-Mart!" Simon shouted abruptly. "Go see what's taking Gifford so long and report back to me. One or two of his scouts should already be here. Go now— fly." He wiggled his fingers on both hands, emphasizing the urgency.

"How did you learn that Zephyrus had been attacked, and Tereus's armies were on the move?" Sebastian cocked his head in a quizzical way.

"A fenner whip arrived and reported to Lord Graydon that Zephyrus had been axed and was dying.

He said it was an emergency, and all garrisons were to be dispatched immediately."

Sebastian faced Ivan with a look of satisfaction. "The reporting bird must've heard us talking, after all."

Ivan gave an endorsing nod.

"Not more than ten minutes later," Simon continued, "we met an angry flying cat. Pousses, I think they call him. He had scalded patches on his fur and was as mad as any cat I've ever seen."

Sebastian seemed faintly amused. "I can almost imagine."

The commander shouted an order, "Dismount and walk your horses, men, but don't go too far. We're expecting company soon, and I want to be fully prepared for their visit." He smirked.

Ivan regarded the men with gratitude. Zephyrus's protection was now in experienced and capable hands.

"Two boys were also found in an open glade, not far from Pousses." Simon stopped to wipe grime and sweat from his forehead. "The cat told us he'd been hit by a fireball. He insisted the boys from the Harold Manor had been struck by fireballs, too. But they will recover."

Ivan gasped to learn about Colin and Martin. He didn't know what a fireball was, but it sounded dangerous.

"What? Those confounded things were used against the innocent?" Sebastian trembled, his voice hot with anger. "Dark magic. Dirty, dark magic has returned to our Forest. Someone has brought these weapons, using them against us."

It was too early to accuse anyone, but Ivan was quite certain Cecil, the fallen wizard—now a troll—was still capable of using his powerful skills.

"Sergeant Berkel." Simon barked instructions at a man with a coarse red beard and mustache. "Tell the men to take their horses to the creek to drink. Don't be gone too long."

"Sir." The sergeant saluted. Remounting, he moved forward toward Red Fox Creek. His anxious regiment followed.

"But you, Kimble, must get out." The commander's orders were sharp and non-negotiable. "There will be a war here soon, and I don't want the death of an outsider staining my good record. That understood?"

"Perfectly," Ivan answered at once.

Then…a faraway rumble. Heads rose, eyes widened, soldiers stiffened as they raised their weapons.

Simon heard it right off. He motioned to Ivan and pointed toward the east edge of the Forest where his men had just gone to drink. "Take The Challenger and the cloak with you, Kimble. Hide yourself well."

"Yes, sir." Ivan turned to move away and then froze.

"Listen!" Mart-Mart screeched. "Do you hear galloping horses?"

The soldiers hadn't gone far and now must abandon their trip to the creek. Sergeant Berkel called the men to return at once.

Simon's face went grave, his mustache quivering at the corners. "It won't be long before a horde of ghost warriors descend upon us—right here in Zephyrus's Circle," he yelled and jammed his helmet over his head. Visor open, he met Ivan's puzzled look. "Tereus forced these ghosts to rise from their ancient graves in Helvaka. No other being would dare such blasphemy against the High Intervener, violating the Laws of the Forest."

After a pause, Simon whispered, "Frankly, I don't know how to fight dead men who ride like raging maniacs on ghostly horses."

Chapter Eighteen

Ghost Warriors

As the troops moved into position, an impressive-looking soldier on a shiny chestnut horse came forward.

"This is my war advisor, Lieutenant Pezzuline." Simon motioned. "And the man next to him is Sergeant Berkel, second in command."

Ivan nodded politely, not yet retreating to safety.

Berkel raised his hand in a salute. He leaned forward from his saddle, frowning, and asked Simon, "Do you think our shields will help? Protect us, I mean?"

"Yeah," Pezzuline asked, "will our swords actually kill those ghost warriors, or are we waiting to be slaughtered like the red deer corralled for culling?"

Turning away from both officers, Simon stared distantly. Then... "Mart-Mart!" Simon called sharply. "Go see what's keeping Gifford so long. He should've been here by now. You hear me, Mart-Mart?"

The small owl pushed off the low tree branch where he perched. "Right away, Commander," the bird hooted.

Suddenly, Winchester, one of the three birch trees, screamed, "The Ghost Warriors are coming."

"They're approaching the White Rock Corridor." Bristol's eyes filled with terror. "They're riding fast. I feel the pounding vibrations beneath the ground."

Twisting his head toward the triplets, Simon hollered, "Swamp Dragon dung!" He shook his fisted hand in the air. "Why is that rock-headed creature allowing our enemy to pass through his gateway? Pillard's sole purpose is to keep riffraff like that out of Oakhurst."

Bewildered and angered by Pillard's apparent betrayal, Sebastian and Ivan hesitated before moving on.

A half-dozen soldiers positioned their horses in a tight circle around Zephyrus, weapons drawn and steady. Horses stamped and snorted. Rustling dry leaves interrupted the afternoon's deathly stillness.

The soldiers were all quiet, licking their parched lips with gravel-dry tongues. Soon, Pillard's Time-Flash would propel the merciless warriors into the garrison's midst. Screeching and brandishing their ancient weapons, they would flood the area, mowing down every man and his mount.

Minutes passed. Breath froze in the soldiers' lungs.

Ivan imagined wispy gray images of men from long ago racing on flesh-decayed horses driven by a demonic wail. He pictured the skeletal ghost warriors leaning from their mounts, slashing the soldiers, tromping on their fallen bodies, laughing maniacally.

"Pillard's rock-gates must be wide open by now," Simon growled. "Allowing the warriors to race through the Time-Flash Corridor." All eyes strained, staring through the golden glow of the lowering western sun. The soldiers held their swords and shields in quivering hands, prepared to defend themselves. Prepared to die.

The earth trembled beneath thousands and

thousands of phantom horses, the din increasing from the distant corridor of stone. Driven fearlessly, the Ghost Warriors screamed their bloody war cries of death and destruction.

"They've been commanded to annihilate every soldier and to destroy Zephyrus, leaving nothing behind but a pile of smoldering ash." Simon squeezed his eyes in anger.

The little owl returned, his wings flapping madly. He swooped down and lit on Simon's forearm.

"Well, where are the soldiers?" Simon's quick temper flared.

"It…it seems, sir." Mart-Mart stumbled, giving his report. "G-Gifford stopped to help those two little orphan boys from the Harold Manor. They were unconscious when he found them."

"We know," Simon said.

"How are they?" Ivan interrupted, his brows raised with concern.

"I guess they're okay," Mart-Mart answered. "A couple of Gifford's men took them back to the castle's infirmary. They were promised ice cream if they'd stop bawling." The owl flapped his wings and rolled his eyes. "What a fine treat that would be. We owls love ice cream, too."

"Dark Magic has reentered the Forest." Sebastian shook his head. "That means the rise of the demon's power."

Simon faced Ivan with a chilling glare, as though he'd just realized the visitor was still present when he shouldn't be.

"Kimble, get out."

Ivan didn't enjoy being yelled at. He turned and

walked slowly toward the Forest's east entrance, waiting for Sebastian's old legs to catch up.

"Spread out. Have your weapons at the ready," Commander Simon shouted and raised his fist. "You're in for a treat—killing men who are already dead." His mirthless laugh stopped short and hung in the air.

Mart-Mart made for the sky. Flying high over the treetops, he circled, swooping lower for a closer look. There were rumbles and scraping sounds, like a mountain rising up, dragging its heavy feet. The White Rocks groaned over the gravelly corridor as they always did when they were moving.

Returning swiftly, the owl banked and plunged toward Simon. He screeched, "Closing! Closing! The White Rocks are closing."

"What? Mart-Mart, what did you say?" The commander scowled at the bird's interruption.

"Pillard is closing his corridor on the Ghost Warriors. He's crushing them to death."

Simon listened and cocked his head. He removed his helmet and took a deep breath.

A horse standing near Zephyrus shook his long brown mane, striking the ground several times with his hoof. A soldier muffled a cough behind his closed facemask, or maybe he was choking with fear.

The rough grating of rocks reverberated through the Forest—on and on. Piercing screams from thousands of tortured souls echoed against the crush of stone.

Ivan and Sebastian stopped and listened at the edge of Zephyrus's Circle.

A sound like thunder ripped through the woodland. The two sides of Pillard's rocks jammed together with a bang. In that instant, a flash of lightning exploded, shooting high into the sky. It was trailed by jagged fingers of red and yellow sparks that arched into the atmosphere. Roiling with dark gray clouds, strong winds swept in from the west. Swirling leaves, twigs, and dust tumbled and blanketed Oakhurst in a blizzard of debris.

The Forest filled with distant wails and hollow voices of ancient warriors and their ghostly mounts all smashed together like roaches between sharp-edged stones.

"What happened?" Ivan stepped from behind a coppice of oaks where he and Sebastian had sought safety.

Sebastian gave a gratifying laugh. "Well, I'll be. Pillard came through for us after all. He didn't betray us."

"What did he do?"

"Didn't you hear?" Sebastian laughed, wiping tears from his eyes. "He slammed his white rocks together on the Ghost Warriors. He crushed them all to powder, returning them to skeletal dust."

"He did it He did it." Mart-Mart danced from foot to foot, hooting and cheering on the same tree limb. "Pillard smashed all those terrible dead men. Whooo-hooo-whooo!" he sang.

****

After some time, the howling grew dim and finally ceased. The soldiers lowered their weapons, visibly thankful, wiping their sweaty brows.

"We've won our first victory of the day." Simon removed his helmet and cheered.

Thrilled with their stroke of good fortune, the men

whooped and applauded. Slipping from their saddles, they tossed their shields aside, praising Pillard for his calculating and shrewd ways.

When the final death cry passed away, Commander Simon announced, "You did a remarkable job, men." Rubbing dirt from his eyes, a smile spread across his face until he finally chuckled with relief.

Ivan and Sebastian joined the merriment, offering their praise and joy. At last, Ivan felt welcome. Lieutenant Pezzuline wrapped his arms around him, lifting and twirling, and giving him an affectionate squeeze.

The men picked up their gear and remounted their horses. "This is only the beginning, men," one of the soldiers was heard to say.

"What will happen to the Ghost Warriors' spirits trapped under the White Rock?" Ivan turned to ask his companion.

"They are free of Tereus's hold at last." Sebastian pulled on his beard as though thinking the question through. "Unshackled, they can return to their graves and sleep until it's time for the Great Eternal Rising."

"Why the big concern about them?" Simon looked down from his horse, holding a steady gaze at Ivan.

Ivan shrugged. "At one time, they were men like you and the soldiers in your regiment. They were alive with families and homes. The dead warriors must've contributed something of value to their world when they lived. I suppose that's the reason."

Stroking the blue plumes on his helmet, Simon hesitated before answering. "No one enjoys killing. It's a fact of life—and war. When someone invades your land, threatens your home and those you love, you do what's necessary to protect them."

"I know, but..." Ivan's brow wrinkled, and he lowered his head. He had ended Burtack's life, and it would haunt him for as long as he lived.

"We won't be so fortunate when the Dark Army arrives," Simon said somberly. "There will be no Pillard to crush them between his corridors. It will take them longer to reach us by circumventing the White Rocks, but be assured, they are coming."

"Who commands the army of living men?" Lieutenant Pezzuline asked.

Mart-Mart answered, "My Uncle Drugan said it's Hays, Commander Kruse Hays."

Simon's lips pressed white, his mustache twitched. "I should've known. And how many soldiers?"

"My uncle thought there were about seven hundred, maybe a few more." The owl twisted his head and repeated the number a second time. "Many of them are poorly outfitted, ragged looking, without armor or good weapons."

"I'd like to know how Tereus manages to support an army with that many soldiers." Simon snorted. "How does he feed them? And how does he supply them with horses and weapons of war?" He has no way to create wealth, only to confiscate it."

At once, Ivan remembered the disappearance of the kaleido-birds. Had the Dark Army been consuming the birds, supplied by the gryphons, to feed their army? Glancing at Sebastian, they nodded knowingly.

Leaving his tree limb, the owl flew skyward. "Oh!" Mart-Mart suddenly called, "Mr. Ivan. Your horse is south of here grazing in the meadow. Bounty must've forgotten what I said about pecking a hole in his ear if he didn't get back here."

"Dang him," Ivan growled.

"Private Hambuckle," Simon yelled at one of his soldiers as he swung his hand to the south. "Go fetch Ivan's horse. Give him your sheath, too. If he carries The Challenger around much longer, he's sure to cut his own leg off."

Ivan stifled a laugh, feeling heat rise from his blush. Then he grasped what Simon had just said. There was no mistaking the name—*Hambuckle.*

A friendly round-faced soldier with reddish-gold hair and beard rode forward and saluted. Following orders, Private Hambuckle removed his sword, unbuckled his sheath, and handed it down. He surprised Ivan when he nodded respectfully and said, "It's an honor to meet you, Ivan Kimble. We've learned you risked your life to get that magic sap-stuff, and it will probably save Zephyrus's life. We're all very grateful."

"Sure." Ivan lifted his eyebrows, surprised to receive a compliment from a total stranger.

Before the soldier rode away, Ivan called to the man, "Is your first name Aaron?"

The soldier looked startled, and he nodded slowly. "I don't know much about myself," he confessed. "During the war, a rifle butt to the side of my head knocked all but a few memories away." The private stared at Ivan. "You know something about me?" Before Ivan could confirm that Aaron was his teacher's missing husband, Simon yelled, "Get going, Private. We don't have all day."

The soldier grinned and saluted. He turned his horse and said over his shoulder, "Later. Please tell me later."

Smiling, Ivan envisioned the look of joy and happiness on his teacher's face when she was reunited, at last, with her husband.

Shortly, two scouts approached with crimson-colored plumes atop their silver helmets. Ivan concluded they were the expected scouts from Gifford's garrison. Final proof was the flag that one soldier held proudly. Unfurled, it read in bold, black letters:

Annual Competition for The Forest's Shield of Honor

And in smaller red letters:

Seventh Year—Winners!
Commander Gifford, Garrison 200

Simon bared his teeth, scowling at the flag. He'd lost the competition and the Shield of Honor again. "Next year." He shook his fist and hissed to the smirking scouts, "We'll take the flag from you for certain. Just wait and see."

Both men removed their helmets, grinning widely. "We'll wait—and we'll see," they chorused.

The loss of the flag put aside for more important matters, the men discussed the best tactics to employ as the enemy army advanced.

"Commander Gifford's garrison is moving into position now," the flag-bearing scout stated. "I've heard that Greendyn will approach from the North. No worries there."

"And the dragon, Zello, has he left his castle stable to give his fiery help?" Simon glanced under his eyebrows.

"'Fraid not." The man's brow rippled with regret.

"What?" Simon's rising anger turned his face bright red. "Are you saying Zello's not coming to help us?"

"Well, sir, it seems that dim-witted bird, Fetters, accused him of stealing and eating his hens," the other scout explained. "Zello was insulted. Furious, he up and left a couple of days ago, abandoning his females. I've heard he's hiding out in a cave atop the Azurite Mountains nursing his hurt feelings. It's a pitiful shame it happened now when we so desperately need him."

"I counted on him," Simon said with a weak voice.

Ivan realized with a jolt that he and Sebastian knew of the incident earlier from Fetters, the kaleido-bird. Now Ivan wanted to strangle him, just as Simon did.

"Did Lord Graydon try to talk with Zello?" Sebastian's ancient voice cracked with remorse. "Richard has a way with unusual beasts, you know."

"Too late," the flag-bearing man remarked. "The damage was done by Fetters' sharp and accusing tongue. He gets so excited he doesn't think before he talks."

The second scout straightened in his saddle. With contrived authority, he spoke loudly, "That dragon-bugger is getting old and wimpy. It's a characteristic, I think, of the brown-scaled dragon breed. Their feelings get hurt easily."

"How do you know so much about dragons?" the first flag-bearing scout asked sarcastically. "You've never had a conversation with Zello in your whole life. You big phony!"

"It *doesn't* matter!" Simon threw up his hands. "Who knows anything about a dragon's feelings, anyway? The point is, we have no ally in Zello." Straightening, arching his stiff back, Simon shot off a dozen names from his garrison. The men moved in closer for their orders.

"Stay your guard and protect Zephyrus with your very lives. You all know the seriousness of the coming battle. There's no Pillard to crush this army. There's no Zello to help us. An army of living soldiers is racing this way hell-bent on total annihilation."

Taking Bounty's reins from Aaron Hambuckle's callused hands, Ivan thanked the soldier.

He gave his horse a scalding look and mounted, imagining holes pecked through his ears.

Private Hambuckle put his hand on Ivan's forearm and gripped it firmly. "Tell me—what do you know of me? His dusty face was lined with worry, his eyes wide and fearful.

Ivan replied with a huge grin, "Why, you're my teacher's husband. She's been dreadfully worried about you since you've been gone." He knew not to mention that Mary Hambuckle had had a nervous breakdown because of his absence and hadn't taught the last year.

Aaron Hambuckle looked dumbfounded. "Married? A teacher? Where…where does she live?"

"In Graydon Village, where I live. She's very pretty." He meant to say more about what a fine teacher and person she was when Simon screamed for his men to move into position. Ivan looked at the commander, leaving Hambuckle with his mouth gaping.

"Kimble. Out." Simon jabbed his sword in an easterly direction. "*Now!*"

"I can hardly argue with a jabbing sword." Ivan chuckled. "Come to my village, and I'll reintroduce you to your wife." Hambuckle nodded, still dazed.

Lifting himself into his saddle, Sebastian said under his breath, "We'd better leave at once. I see

Simon glaring at you."

They moved off the field side by side, leaving Aaron Hambuckle behind. Shortly, the man whooped with laughter. "Wait, wait. What's her name?" By then, Ivan was too far away to answer the private's question.

After the soldiers took their positions, the Forest suffered a long moment of chilling silence. They pulled their swords and daggers from their holds with grisly anticipation. Bows and arrows were readied, lances rested on shivering legs. Shields gripped tightly, protected their chests. Soldiers sat rigidly in their saddles. Plumes quivered atop their silver helmets but not from the afternoon breeze.

Trotting past the regiment, Ivan urged Bounty to move faster. The weary soldiers divided, providing an opening for Ivan and Sebastian. One of the soldiers saluted, giving Ivan a bucktoothed smile, disguising the raw look of fear in his eyes. "Take a long drink at the creek for me and me horse," the toothy soldier hollered.

Ivan returned the salute and, for some reason, felt ashamed as if he was a deserter. He kept riding but looked back several times.

The fading afternoon cooled quickly when the sun edged lower to the horizon. "It seems late in the day for a war." Ivan's remark was meant for both Sebastian and The Challenger. He peered at the sky, mumbling, "It will be hard to see anything."

They drew near the creek, and Ivan swung off Bounty tiredly, where he spotted a hungry badger searching for voles. He pulled his horse to the edge of the bank, and there they both drank the cold, sweet water. Sebastian dismounted Old Bones. Holding his back, he groaned.

Time passed slowly. Ivan fidgeted, reaching over to stroke his horse's cheek, down to his fleshy nose. "I wish I could take a pail of water to the soldiers. They must be dreadfully thirsty by now."

"It's only been a few minutes." Sebastian scolded. "Relax and be patient."

Ivan paced, tugging Bounty along by his bridle, waiting for something to happen. The badger had caught a vole, and a red fox moved through the undergrowth looking for a rabbit or a rodent of his own.

Distantly, men's voices shouted and cried, horses whinnied, and the constant clang of metal reverberated through the Forest. Ivan tensed and imagined Hays's army thundering into Oakhurst, like the pounding of a huge sledgehammer against a drum's tight surface. The Forest's garrisons were well-armed and ready for battle. And yet, he fretted.

Silently, he prayed that Aaron Hambuckle would survive the war and return to his wife. He imagined Aaron entering the classroom and grinning. "Hello, Mary. I've missed you terribly." The students would all clap, and Ivan would bow, feeling accepted and proud.

Things were quiet for a time until a jackdaw flew overhead, breaking the stillness with several sharp chirps. It almost sounded like a message.

To Ivan's surprise, there sat a covered basket wedged between the roots of an old tree near the creek.

He leaped up and grabbed it, pulling off the linen cover. "It's from Anna-Iza." Ivan grinned widely. "She thought of us waiting by the stream. I don't know how she knew such a thing, but I'll gladly eat everything she left. He unwrapped the first meat sandwich that was cut into four sections. *How does Anna-Iza know that's how*

I eat my sandwiches? He took his first bite, chewing slowly. *It's delicious.* He licked his lips where sauce had dripped.

Ivan asked The Challenger, "Why didn't you choose to become an Ancient Relic like Sebastian?"

"The answer is simple," the silvery sword replied. "I slew hundreds and hundreds of men as a living warrior and as a spirit imbued in this weapon. I have regretted it for a thousand years. Taking a man's life, even if he's our enemy, has never brought me joy or a minute's satisfaction. I wish to be retired and kill no more."

"Yes, I understand." Ivan lowered his head, thinking about what he had said to the commander. He sat on a rock next to Sebastian and took another bite.

"I heard you say as much to Simon." The Challenger's voice rang clear. "That all men's lives are important."

Ivan nodded. "Yet you joined Zephyrus when he agreed to become the Great Oak."

"I did. To serve Zephyrus is an honor."

Before long, Ivan's thoughts drifted happily to his encounter with Anna-Iza. She had once again thought to bring him lunch, and his stomach was grateful. He bit into a big red apple allowing the juice to run from the corner of his mouth. He recalled how she felt cuddled in his arms, and he was sure she enjoyed being held by him, too. *Would she be proud of me now if she knew I stayed hidden behind the security of Simon's soldiers doing nothing?* The thought grabbed hold and gnawed at him.

Sebastian turned a scowling face. "If you're thinking of joining the battle, you'd better forget it."

"Commander Simon would be furious with you," The Challenger said firmly.

Ivan gave a short, amused laugh. "How do you seem to know what I'm thinking? It's uncanny."

"I told you before. I just chose the most obvious." Sebastian sniffed.

It might've been near the truth, except Sebastian was a Dream-Prober.

"Who is this Kruse Hays?" Ivan shifted on the solid rock and took another bite of the apple he'd found on the bottom of the basket.

"He has served as Tereus's army commander for about six or seven years that we know of," The Challenger replied. "Just where he keeps himself and what he does when there are no conflicts, we don't know."

"But you can be sure he's been up to no good." Sebastian grunted.

Having finished his lunch, Ivan picked a tall weed growing next to him that looked much like a pale purple stalk of wheat. The nectar was sweet, hurting his teeth, and so he gave it a toss.

"Listen," The Challenger exclaimed. "I've just heard the first cry of a fallen soldier."

Shooting to his feet, Ivan cocked his head, concentrating on the sounds of blood-curdling war cries. The approaching horde, driven mercilessly by Kruse Hays, thundered their way into Zephyrus's Circle.

Through the buffer of trees, the reverberations of swords hammered into armored chests. Wounded cries from frightened soldiers collided with the high-pitched whinnying of their horses. Ivan covered his ears to block out the gut-wrenching noise. *War is horrible. Why do men fight—and kill?*

At first, he was only too glad to be isolated, safe from the action of battle. Time crept by as slowly as mushrooms grow on a dry rock. His stomach knotted. He wished his beagles would return. He wished Peter would come, and they'd all leave together. An icy surge of fear knifed up his spine, and Ivan shivered. *I can't just stand here like a coward, listening, imagining the worst—doing nothing. What would* she *think of me?* He stood and kicked at a pile of leaves.

"Stay put." Sebastian growled again. "This is not your war."

"Maybe I can help," Ivan blurted. He spun around defiantly, something warm in his belly driving him into action. He clutched Bounty's mane and leaped into the saddle. His decision was made though he didn't understand it. He was usually more cautious, more reasonable, less aggressive.

"And maybe you can't." Sebastian scrambled to his feet and made a grab for Bounty's bridle. He missed.

Ivan had made up his mind.

"Halt! Ivan. You wear no armor, no shield, and no warhorse." Sebastian's groan quickly turned into anger. "Simon has enough to worry about. He'll have you court-marshaled for this insurrection."

Ivan lifted his chin and said rebelliously, "I'm not in his army."

"Well, that's just it," Sebastian reasoned. "You're not in anyone's army. You're a civilian, a visitor, a-a guest here. For mercy-sake, will you please listen to me?"

"I know I can help."

"Ivan Kimble, you'll get yourself killed. You know nothing of fighting a war. Stop!" Sebastian cried.

"I'll stay at the edge of Zephyrus's Circle, near the trees, and observe," Ivan said over his shoulder. "I'll give a full report after the war is over, like the fenner whip."

Ivan knew his reasoning was weak, but he couldn't stop himself. He kneed Bounty forward and could still hear Sebastian harping.

Sebastian mounted, rushing to catch up while continuing to rant words of reproof.

"Wait! Ivan, wait for me. If anything happens to you, Zephyrus will have my head. Do you understand?"

Leaving the woods, Ivan urged his horse into a trot. *If only Anna-Iza could see my brave move toward the enemy. She would be proud of me.* He stopped at a fringe of trees near the battle site, trying to watch everything at once.

All were engaged in fighting, parrying, and thrusting their swords. Deafening clamor and slashing metal filled the air. Shields flew up, warding off a rain of arrows. Several of Simon's men, especially adept at archery, brought down the enemy in rapid succession. Some fell, crying in agony, meeting their doom. Horses whinnied in pain sustaining gashes from the soldiers' frenzied thrusts. Blinding dust kicked up from the battle and thickened the air.

Moving closer for a better view, Ivan encouraged Bounty. "Go just beyond the shelter of these elms." He stood in his stirrups, stretching his neck to see.

Bounty suddenly shot off, and Ivan was thrown back hard into the saddle. His horse screamed, shaking his head, terrified by the stink and the noises.

Overcome by fear, the horse raced closer to the center of battle. There, they became locked between several enemy soldiers and their lethal blades. They shoved Bounty forward and pushed him sideways.

"No, I don't belong here!" Ivan cried, but his words were lost. Soldiers with green, crimson, and blue plumes merged, fighting the cold black and silver of Hays's regiment. Jerking on Bounty's reins, Ivan struggled to find a way out,

He witnessed the horrors of war. A man wearing a silver metal collar over black armor suffered an arrow that passed through his cheeks. The soldier screamed and pressed his gloved hand against his face, soaking it with blood in moments. Then, the same enemy was struck from behind by one of Greendyn's men. The twice-wounded soldier toppled off his horse, wailing as he fell.

Another soldier with a crimson plume displaying an emblem of Zello on his breastplate pulled back his sword with muscled arms and thrust it through his opponent's belly. The stabbed man clutched at the blade as it was withdrawn, slicing his hands to the bone. He howled, staring first at his bloodied palms and then at the rush of hot liquid spilling over his belt and trailing down his groin.

Fighting a need to heave, Ivan's hand flew to his mouth. His own stomach burned thinking about the man's belly and the blade that cut his hands so deeply.

War. War is horrible.

The same crimson-plumed soldier who'd just stabbed the enemy, suddenly appeared beside Ivan. He recognized the name on the breastplate beneath the dragon's image. *This is the famous Commander*

Gifford. Ivan's eyes opened in astonishment.

Lifting his visor with a sharp snap, Gifford yelled angrily at the Dark Army, "You're a bunch of mad dogs, not worthy to trespass on Forest soil! Leave now, or you'll all be slaughtered for pig food." Gifford glared at Ivan. "*You there.* Get off the battlefield at once."

Ivan shivered, feeling vulnerable and inept. "Y-yes," he said, his voice quivering. Maneuvering his way through several sword fights raging in full force, he slumped against Bounty, embedding his face into his horse's hot, sweaty neck. "Please, Bounty, find a way out of this mess."

Shaking his head up and down, his horse shoved his way through a mass of warriors, finally leaving the thick of combat. They halted behind a group of trees. Ivan's breath came quick and shallow. His heart pounded hard. He released a deep sigh believing he was safe.

"Thank you, Bounty. You came through for me when it really mattered."

Approaching alongside on Old Bones, Sebastian growled through his teeth, shaking his fist at Ivan. "Just what do you think you accomplished by rushing into the middle of battle? You could've been killed. Don't you think the commanders have enough to worry about without you adding to their troubles?"

"You're right. I'm sorry." Ivan lowered his head, wondering what had possessed him to act so foolishly. "It was stupid."

"Yes, it was. Careless, reckless, and unthinking—just stay out of everyone's way. My spirit wasn't inside the cloak, so I couldn't help you if you'd gotten hurt.

After his stiff scolding, Sebastian's image melted

into swirling smoke, beginning with his horse's feet and ending at the top of the spirit's head. Bluish wisps trailed and disappeared into the garment. Angry, the spirit entered a little harder than was necessary, Ivan thought.

"Oomph!" Ivan grunted as he was shoved forward by Sebastian's harsh entrance.

Minutes crept by in a slow, gray fog nightmare. When a gust blew, it scooped up leaves and twigs and whirled them around. It caused a thrumming sound that swept up into the surrounding trees.

"What is this ferocious wind?" Ivan spit pieces of dirt that caught on his lips.

"I suspect it is the violent aftermath of the Ghost Warriors being called into the earth," The Challenger said. "You must appreciate how blasphemous this act of resurrecting the dead has been to the High Intervener. There will be severe consequences."

Chapter Nineteen

Zello

"Ah, yes," Sebastian agreed, "the High Intervener is trumpeting his wrath."

Ivan was about to point out that the windstorm had suddenly died away when something frightening raced toward them. Soldiers from the Dark Army galloped on sleek dark steeds decorated with extraordinary riding gear. Black blankets, edged with gold fringe, draped their horses. Their bridles were studded with jewels and swinging tassels. The new arrivals slashed their way into the thick of battle. Warfare intensified, bloodier and crueler.

"These are Commander Hays's most fearsome fighters." The deep voice resonated from the sword. "Hays must've called them to finish the battle and claim victory."

Before Ivan could turn and evacuate to his safe haven near the border of trees, Greendyn's men stampeded from the north for an ambush. Determined and aggressive, they shoved Ivan and his horse into the oncoming killers. There was no opening left to escape. Suddenly, Bounty was wedged between three horses.

"Get out of here," Sebastian yelled.

"Move quickly to the east!" The Challenger's strong voice commanded.

Bounty's nostrils flared as his sweaty muscles quivered. He lifted his head and whinnied to the point of screaming. Ivan jerked on the bridle, but his horse couldn't budge. He was trapped a second time in battle and was even more frightened.

"Move—*now!*" Sebastian shouted.

Frantic to find an opening and break free, Ivan pulled harder on Bounty's reins. No matter where he moved, a soldier blocked his path. Too late, an enemy raised his long, lethal blade, preparing to remove Ivan's head. He bent low, tucking his arms to his sides. In a flash, Private Hambuckle raised his unsheathed dagger and plunged it deeply into the attacker's ribs. The enemy warrior doubled over, gripped his horse's mane, and slumped sideways. Hambuckle raised his leg and gave the man a rough kick. The wounded soldier swore vengeance as he slipped off his horse and crashed to the ground.

"Get out!" Hambuckle shouted at Ivan. "You *must* stay alive."

Ivan's throat burned. His chest tightened until he couldn't breathe.

"Move from the warriors' path!" another soldier yelled.

Ivan couldn't tell who'd said it. Everyone was shouting. The noise, the dust, the smell of horse excrement and fear, and the blood of men assaulted him. Rivulets of sweat streaked down the sides of his face, stinging his eyes. *I want out of here. I want to go home.*

A loud, deep roar echoed from the late, gray sky. Then, the fighting stopped and went quiet. Ivan looked up through moist eyes. Something huge was flying toward them. It had wide wings, a long neck with a small head, and bright yellow eyes. A snakelike tail whipped behind the dark creature. Descending rapidly, its body undulated through the wide, vacant sky. The shape grew bigger and bigger, and a burst of yellow-orange flames shot from the beast's mouth.

"What in heaven's name?" Ivan tracked it, his brow lifting higher.

Enemy soldiers came to a standstill, their swords lowered and frozen. Some shook their heads in disbelief, watching the approaching shape. Others ripped off their helmets to get a better look. Their lips trembled.

"It's that blasted dragon," the enemy cursed and shouted. "Now we're done for."

They pulled back, crossing their weapons over their chests in gestures of submission.

"They've surrendered," Sergeant Berkel shouted.

"Don't trust them," Gifford warned. "Hold your swords in the ready."

Twisting in his saddle, facing his men, Greendyn screeched, "Watch them carefully!"

"*Zello! Zello! Zello!*" the garrisons shouted excitedly.

"Well, I'll be." Sebastian's voice rose from the cloak.

Ivan guided Bounty to a safer position. He was still in shock after nearly getting his head sliced off. "Z-Zello?" he repeated.

"Yep, that's our castle dragon, all right." Sebastian's voice was proud.

"But they said he wouldn't come. That he was angry."

"He must've changed his mind."

A dark-clad warrior, his face contorted with hatred, aimed and threw his lance skyward in a fruitless gesture of defiance against the dragon. The weapon fell pitifully short, and the warrior swore.

Pumping his fist wildly, Greendyn shrieked at the Dark Army warriors, "Weapons down!"

A blur against a darkening sky, the creature soared overhead trailing a gust of wind, leaving a musty after-smell like old fungus and dust.

Gliding downward, Zello's huge wings spread wide. He dropped lower and lower. Banking, he circled once. And then he plummeted toward the fighting field. Soldiers gasped while one sobbed loudly, begging for his life. "No, not me. *Pleassse.*"

Ivan wanted to bury his head against Bounty, but he couldn't take his eyes off the giant beast. The legendary dragon stretched out his sharp claws. Opening his mouth wide, Zello let out a long, booming roar. Bounty jumped. Lifting his tail, he defecated.

The dragon's hind leg muscles and tendons pulsated as he swept down, seizing first one and then another soldier of the Dark Army. Grabbing them from their horses, they swung midair like rag dolls. Powerful claws lifted and cradled the struggling men under his forearms. They shrieked, begging for mercy. Hissing into the night air, head elevated, Zello pumped his wings as he ascended, reaching a high altitude in only moments.

Enemy soldiers shrieked with anger and terror. They shook their fists and weapons, cursing the beast. Panicked, they attempted to break away and flee. Simon and Gifford's men turned swiftly, trying to corral the retreating Dark Army.

"Remove their weapons!" Gifford stood in the stirrups and waved his sword wildly.

"Take prisoners!" Simon grabbed a bloody mace from an enemy soldier, turned on him, and smashed it against his head.

Though the Dark Army struggled to pull away from the throngs of soldiers, they were surrounded, trapped. Some cast their weapons aside, hoping to keep their lives. Some pleaded to be released, while others swore and threatened to destroy the garrisons.

Ivan straightened from Bounty, trembling so hard he could scarcely speak. "W-who were the men Zello t-took away?"

"Hays's second in command, a great war strategist, I understand." Sebastian's face tipped upward, exhibiting a huge grin.

"I believe the other man is Hays's War Advisor," The Challenger informed.

Zello's ribbed wings caught the yellow and orange of sunset. He whipped a sharp turn, becoming smaller and smaller, taking the sky's warm colors with him. The dragon's image faded and soon disappeared.

"Will Zello return and take more soldiers away?"

"I don't think so." Sebastian spoke slowly, as though considering the question in greater depth. "I'm surprised he showed at all. His eyesight is very poor late in the afternoon. He could've snatched anyone from the fighting fields. I shiver to think."

Ivan swallowed loudly.

"That's it!" The Challenger exclaimed.

"What?" asked the other two.

"Don't you see? That's why the Dark Army

scheduled their battle near the end of the day."

"It's because of Zello's poor eyesight, isn't it?" Ivan said.

"Odd, because we didn't expect him to show at all." Sebastian didn't attempt to hide a grin.

"Good riddance," the sword scoffed. "I'm sure Hays and his army will fall quicker now that his two important officers have been removed."

"I have the feeling Zello may have aimed for Kruse Hays." Sebastian scratched his head, staring into the ether of the sky. "But I'm pleased those two have been eliminated. Let's leave and move toward the creek."

"I wouldn't trust them." The deep voice resonated from the metal. "Their commander has just arrived, and he won't accept surrender. Let's travel to a safer—"

Right then, a group of fierce riders dressed in black pounded in their direction. They were the men that Ivan had seen racing into battle only moments ago with fancy horse gear. A huge man with a wide chest pointed his glinting sword straight at Ivan. Fear raced upward from Ivan's knees to his heart. He read the name *Commander Kruse Hays* printed on his shield and breastplate. Ivan's attention froze on an image of a vicious bird clutching arrows in his bright, red beak. *Was Hays a Black Knight?*

Before Ivan could turn and leave, Sebastian screamed, "Pull The Challenger from its hold! Have a weapon for your protection. Then get out—*fast*."

The noise of battle escalated after the bloodthirsty commander arrived with fresh men. Soldiers lunged and parried their swords. The enemy hadn't surrendered after all, just as Gifford and Greendyn predicted. It had been a ruse.

Black-clad riders galloped toward him bellowing war cries of death and destruction. Thick arms pumped their weapons into the air.

How did I get into this? He clamped down on chattering teeth, too scared to move.

Commander Kruse Hays jerked his bridle so hard his horse shrieked in pain. Spinning the animal roughly, Hays came face-to-face with Ivan, glaring through his deep-set, fiery eyes. Matted brown curls made his big, helmetless head and heavy jaw stand out. Sweat and dirt caked the creases in his face and neck. Several of his teeth were knocked out recently, evident by the blood dripping down his chin onto his cold dark breastplate. His lips were pulled thin with a vicious expression. He didn't seem to notice the blood or missing teeth.

Trapped and paralyzed with fear, Ivan had no place to move.

Hays slammed his horse against Bounty, throwing Ivan forward with a jolt. Ivan swayed and grasped his saddle's pommel and struggled to stay seated. His opponent leaned forward, laughed menacingly, and bragged. "Brutality is our family's namesake, and I'm bloody proud of it."

A massive man, Hays's bare muscled arms glistened under leather armbands. He reminded Ivan of Burtack, the large Black Knight that he'd slain only hours before. Even the shape of their broad, flat noses mimicked each other.

Why am I getting all the big mean ones?

Kruse's bloody mouth widened into a vicious grin. He raised his sword and swung at Ivan's neck.

"Duck, Ivan!" Sebastian yelled. "Pull your weapon.

It's your only chance to stay alive."

Ivan saw the blade coming and pressed his chest and face against Bounty's coarse mane. The cold whooshing of metal passed overhead—dangerously close. With sweaty hands, Ivan reached to his side where The Challenger waited to be removed. His body was angled in the wrong position. He'd have to risk sitting up for a moment to access his weapon. *Why didn't I listen to Sebastian and drawn my sword when I first arrived? How careless of me.*

Hays glared with sadistic pleasure. He was like a fox pawing at a trembling vole until it was time to pounce and devour his prey.

Straining his arm and body, Ivan grasped the sword's hilt in its too-tight hold. Hambuckle's leather sheath was not designed for a heavy weapon like The Challenger. It wouldn't budge. He tugged, but still, it wouldn't pull free. Crying out, he twisted his wrist painfully, almost beyond endurance. It loosened slightly. He relaxed his burning fingers for a moment and then pulled sharply on the golden hilt. It released, and the length of metal pulled free.

"I'll bring this vermin down," The Challenger said with a fierce voice. "Hold on tight with both hands."

The magical sword rose. Ivan remembered The Challenger's moves from his fight with Burtack. A sizzling arc of silver swept skyward, making contact with Hays's armored shoulder. The smirk on his face was replaced by shock. Cutting through his armor, the blade had sliced into his arm, though it didn't appear to slow him down.

Something struck Ivan hard from behind. He let out a piercing scream and slumped forward in excruciating pain. One of Hays's warriors had slashed him across his back, through fabric and flesh. Hot wetness oozed from his wound and quickly soaked his back

The thick ridge of Hays's brow lifted with triumph. He threw his brutal soldier an approving nod. "You're in the Big League now, little boy," he snarled. "You have to play by the Big Boys' rules. And for me—there are none." Laughing, he spit blood where his teeth had been.

"I'll heal you," Sebastian assured, "but you're in grave danger."

"I know," Ivan said through clamped teeth and tearing eyes. "I can't escape from this. Sebastian, please help me." Within moments the heat and the tap of healing fingers caressed his back. The wound drew closed under his blood-soaked shirt. Burning pain eased and then disappeared.

"Watch your right side," The Challenger called. "Your attacker is coming again."

Ivan glanced in that direction. Commander Simon had shot forward and cut down the warrior who slashed Ivan's back.

"Get out, Kimble, or you'll die!" Simon turned to fight another Dark Warrior.

No time to dwell on unfair fighting practices. Ivan's hands gripped his weapon as it lifted once more, slamming against Hays's sword. Edges came together with a crash of metal. Ivan's forehead beaded while runnels of sweat crept down his neck, doing nothing to cool him.

Grinding his blade against Hays's weapon, Ivan pushed the man back into his saddle. Armor groaned. The man scrunched his face, baring yellow teeth. Then, righting himself with great effort, Hays forced Ivan back in his saddle. Veins pulsated in Hays's neck. His face flushed bright, his eyes set in a tight, baleful glare. But Ivan was the younger of the two with strong muscles, and—*he* held The Challenger.

Sebastian spoke, unwilling to resist goading words, just as he'd done to Burtack. "Hays, you should've spoken with your brother before you engaged this young man in combat. Burtack died because he was an arrogant bully just like you. Now you will suffer the same fate."

Stressed against The Challenger, Kruse Hays's outstretched sword froze. His eyes showed alarm. "What did you say about my brother?" The big man glanced around, scowling. "Burtack dead? Do you lie to me?"

Ivan ground his sword against Hays's blade. He couldn't stop now.

"Who killed my brother?" he howled.

"Now hold on tight, Ivan," his weapon instructed. "I'll guide you through."

In a flash, The Challenger released pressure against his opponent's blade. Hays lurched forward. Before he could catch himself, the great sword drew back, then back farther still, gathering momentum, singing as it swept toward Hays's neck. It met thick flesh with a slicing blow. The sharp edge cut deeply through tendons and veins, severing the commander's jugular. Blood poured hot down the sword's blade, causing Ivan's hands to become almost too slippery to hold the hilt. He tightened his grip. Hays's eyes bulged. Blood gushed from his neck onto his breast armor, blotting out the horrible bird image.

Ivan wiped his sticky hands on his trousers. Jerking the reins, he backed Bounty away.

The Dark Army's notorious commander slumped slowly. Gurgling blood, he slipped off his horse, hitting the cold earth with a loud crash.

"I can't bear it." Ivan looked for an opening to escape.

He'd killed Burtack's brother. They died the same fate. Ivan's sword had severed their jugulars. *I should've guessed it. They were so much alike—their size, their brutality, their eagerness to fight.* The shock of his ordeal sent Ivan reeling. He was afraid he'd pass out.

"What have I done? Help me. I have to get away from here."

"That's what I've been trying to tell you for an hour." Sebastian's voice held more fear than anger.

The Forest's garrisons divided and provided a path for Ivan, protecting him as he rode away.

A faceless soldier said, "I can't believe it. An outsider, a mere boy, has killed Kruse Hays."

Ivan kept his head low, unwilling to meet staring, questioning eyes. He gave Bounty his lead to go wherever he wanted. Ivan didn't care. His beliefs were tumbling, crashing, turning to ash. He stared at his slimy hands, his shirt and trousers splattered with another man's blood. The odor made him retch.

****

"Two men have died today because of me," Ivan mumbled to himself. Shaking his head, he pulled at his hair and pushed at his temples with the heels of his hands. The jarring memory festered and tormented him. He stroked his horse's sweaty neck, trying to suppress his dismal feelings. *"What have I done? Oh, Bounty, what have I done?"*

Slowly releasing held breath, his mood remained somber. He wanted time to clear his head, to think rationally, to be alone. He ached to leave this awful place, but he wouldn't abandon his beagles. He wouldn't give up until Peter was riding by his side.

"I was a fool, Sebastian. You tried to warn me, to stop me, but I got a real stubborn streak in me."

Sebastian materialized from the cloak along with his old horse and gave Ivan a rueful but shrewd look.

"I thought of Anna-Iza. I didn't want her to be ashamed of me. I wanted her to believe I was brave and strong. Why did I behave so stupidly? I don't understand."

"It's the confused actions of a boy who's becoming a man." Sebastian's furrowed brows softened. "Put such thoughts aside now. There will be time enough to discuss these hard-learned lessons. You're not out of danger yet, not as long as you remain here, and the enemy still surrounds us. Although, it seems the fighting has diminished for lack of a commander."

They rode side by side. Ivan turned a shamed glance at his companion, aching for reassurance for his defiant behavior, a sign that all had been forgiven. But Sebastian only stared silently ahead, his lips pressed together.

When they reached the creek, Ivan glanced upstream and then down. Something had caught his eye. There was movement behind some trees, not far away. *What is it?*

Sliding from Bounty with unsteady legs and a woozy stomach, Ivan moved toward the water to wash.

He stared to his right, but all was still. Finding dried blood behind his ear, he rubbed it away. *Now, how did that get there?* He cupped his hands, drinking until he had his fill. His mind cleared as the throbbing in his head eased. On the opposite bank, the rust color of a redstart's tail fluttered. She scratched in the earth looking for grubs or worms. A nightingale sang a sweet song in the distant trees.

Sebastian joined him. "I'm worried about you, Ivan."

Ivan raised himself from a squatting position, watching the swift rapids push over the rocks. "I need time to think."

"Of course, I understand."

The redstart stopped scratching the earth. The nightingale stilled.

Once more, an unexpected movement drew Ivan's attention. A tall, splendid man astride a shiny black steed stared in his direction. The horse had a fancy, decorated blanket with golden tassels swaying from the bridle. Wearing shiny black armor, the man held a silver-trimmed shield at his side. An enemy? *Is he the same person I thought I saw downstream moments ago?*

Shuddering, Ivan worried that the stranger was a mercenary.

The black-armored man lifted his visor and gawked at Ivan.

"Who is he? He seems familiar," Ivan asked.

Sebastian's mouth opened, but he didn't answer.

The stranger paused, his attention unwavering. Then he turned his horse with a harsh kick. Racing south, he disappeared from sight.

For just an instant, the man reminded him of Peter.

Of course, that was absurd. His brother would have recognized him and stayed. He would've called Ivan's name, laughed, and dashed toward him. They'd have thrown their arms around each other and cried with happiness. Peter would never fight for the Dark Army in spite of what Fungoda had told him.

Near exhaustion, Ivan could scarcely stay upright. Just then, the slow, heavy steps from a horse sounded behind him, and Ivan panicked. Grasping The Challenger with tight hands. His spine froze. He spun around and stared at the mustached-man gazing down at him.

To his great relief, he recognized Simon sitting atop his large bay horse. There was no expression on his pale face, only clinging dust and a small cut that had already clotted on his chin. His hair, soaked with sweat, lay flat against his head. The commander's helmet was tucked under his arm, his weapon sheathed, while his hand gripped his right thigh.

"You could be a good soldier," Simon said in a quiet tone. "You're quick, if not impulsive. You're focused, and you've learned the moves of the Forest's greatest weapon—The Challenger."

Ivan stared up at him, waiting for a scalding lecture.

"Maybe you'd consider joining my regiment. We patrol the Southern part of the Forest, you know. And…" Simon added, with a glint in his eye. "We'd be sure to win the Shield of Honor next year if you were on our team."

Ivan inhaled slowly, trying to calm his thumping heart. He studied the cloudless sky, pretending to consider Simon's proposal.

"I've lost good men here today." Simon hesitated and then continued with a sorrowful voice. "With strenuous training, you could become an exceptional soldier, maybe an officer. But you need to learn to follow orders. I can see that's your weakness."

Ivan felt frown lines bunch on his forehead. He realized the sounds of warring men had died down considerably. Only a few desperate cries filtered through the woods. Several evening birds twittered as though singing their praises for the end of battle.

"I'll think about it," Ivan muttered, but he would never be a soldier. No. He'd never be part of Simon's, or anyone's garrison. *I will never kill another man.*

"I actually came to borrow the Long Dark Cloak." Simon's face was pinched as he lifted his bloody hand from his thigh. His horse turned at that moment, and there was a long, deep gash. The flow of blood had stained the commander's trousers, marking a path to his tall leather boots.

Ivan's stomach turned queasy, but he undid the ties and handed it up as Sebastian swirled and dissolved into the cloak.

"The men from our garrisons need the healing cloak more than I do." Simon reached for the garment.

Draped over Simon's wound, the cloak's healing powers went to work. Relief was immediate, confirmed by a long exhale of the commander's breath. "I don't know what we'd do without this wonderful gift of magic. Thanks, Sebastian."

"My pleasure," the spirit softly replied.

Turning his horse to leave, Simon halted and then swung around. "The men will be gathering for the evening meal. Maynard and the kitchen servants are preparing a feast. I expect you to join us for a sumptuous Victory Dinner."

Ivan nodded. He was ravenous and thirsty again, which probably contributed to the light-headedness he felt. Or maybe it was numbing relief from a long, wearying day.

"I saw you take Commander Hays down." Simon emphasized his next words, "You were not authorized to kill anyone."

"But Simon, I didn't plan—"

"It's okay." His hand shot up in an abrupt gesture. "I understand it couldn't be avoided. Hays had his sights on you."

"But why? I didn't even know him."

"Several reasons, I reckon. First, you were in his path. Second, you stood out unprotected by armor, so he thought you'd be an easy kill. What's more, both Kruse and Burtack hated good-looking men." Simon shrugged and then snorted. "Probably because they're both so ugly. They were brothers, you know."

"I told him so," Sebastian spoke from the cloak.

"By the way, good job, Kimble." Simon saluted.

Ivan stood, blinking with confusion. *A good job? I won't hang for this?*

Chapter Twenty

Morning Feast

Ivan opened his eyes and blinked to focus out the cottage window. Feeling rested and refreshed, he fingered the sleep-gum from his eyes.

Maynard had readied comfortable accommodations for him in one of the many cottages. The small, cozy room was much like the guest cottage at Hurst-on-the-Vert. Clean, sparse, and most welcomed. When the servant had mentioned the feast that evening before, Ivan yawned wide and said, "I believe I'll pass. Give my apologies to the men for not joining them."

"But sir," Maynard argued, "that's how men bridge their nightmares of war into reality. By talking about them again and again until they become legend."

"Just the same," Ivan replied, "I don't care to relive the nightmare." Maynard finally conceded. Licking his teeth, Ivan swallowed the awful taste in his mouth. He remembered he'd had a terrible dream about Peter and Tereus that caused him to cry out in terror. *What was it?* He couldn't remember, but he was glad it wasn't real.

Sudden movements near his bed made him sit up with a start. Alfred and Canute looked at him wide-eyed and scampered to their feet. Leaping from his warm bed, Ivan squatted on the floor laughing, drawing his beagles into a happy embrace. They slathered him with their darting wet tongues over his face and neck, wagging their whole bodies.

Ivan laughed. "Maynard must have brought you back while I slept. Now, did you boys learn anything about chasing timmerlans and other weird things in the Forest? This place isn't like our outside world. There are different rules here. Strange people and dangerous creatures—including dragons."

Ivan grabbed his clothes that were draped over a straight-back chair. He assumed that Sebastian and the Long Dark Cloak were with Commander Simon healing the injured. He dressed quickly and left the cottage, his beagles bouncing playfully at his side. Hurrying toward the open meadow, and despite the horrors and blows he'd received in battle, he felt quite well.

Then memories flooded over him, and he lowered his eyes in disgrace. Shame penetrated his soul. He was not the same person. A boy forced to become a man, a man who'd killed two men. He sighed remorsefully. *How will I tell Peter?*

Ivan thought of Dirk Mackle, the bully in his school. Kruse and Burtack were proof of what a bully becomes when unstopped. It was just as Mrs. Hambuckle had said. Ivan knew things would be different when he returned to the Graydon Village School. Unclenching his teeth, he pushed away his angry thoughts. *Yes, things will be very different.*

Cutlery banged sharply against metal plates while cups clunked noisily onto the wooden tables. He could tell by the delicious aromas and the humming voices that breakfast was being served in the meadow—not far from Zephyrus. A mix of lighthearted bickering and laughter became louder as he drew closer.

Tentatively, Ivan entered the large open area where lanterns hung on low branches, lighting the blue-gray sky of morning. There, long rows of trestle tables and heavy benches were occupied with hundreds of seated men.

Servants dashed here and there carrying platters of hot food and porcelain pots of tea. Eustace, recognizable in his red bow tie, and Maynard busily orchestrated the hurried movements of the kitchen staff. They looked up as Ivan approached and gave him a welcoming smile and a brief wave.

Bolting from Ivan's side, Alfred and Canute beelined toward Simon. He was seated in the middle of the head table surrounded by men, probably his own garrison.

Simon lifted his eyes at the sound of barking. He broke into a boyish grin as he stood from his cramped bench seat. When he saw Ivan, he cleared his throat and began to clap. Soldiers, taking a cue from their commander, rose from their places, cheering and whistling through their teeth.

Ivan felt his face and neck heat. What had he done to garner such praise and recognition? He had disobeyed orders, rushed into battle unprepared, and killed the commander of the opposing army, all with no authorization. He was surprised that Simon wasn't waiting to toss him out of the Forest—or worse.

Simon motioned for the lad's attention. "Come join us here." Ivan veered in that direction.

The commander's face appeared worry-free, with the Dark Cloak resting over his shoulders and tied securely. He patted the seat next to him and then bent, leaning sideways to stroke the beagles. They snuggled close to the commander's legs, anxious to be fed.

"Men!" Simon shot up from his seat again, reaching his arms high over his head. "I want you to meet Ivan Kimble. Some of you know this good-hearted and brave soul is responsible for getting the sap that'll surely save Zephyrus's life." Simon rested his hand on Ivan's shoulder for a moment.

The men applauded wildly.

"Good job, Kimble!" someone yelled from a back table.

Bowing his head, Ivan said in a quiet voice, "I did what had to be done." He could've said more, much more. Like how he'd whimpered, nearly collapsing when he faced Burtack, or like how terrified he'd been when forced to fight Commander Hays. Ivan didn't feel like a hero on the inside, and he didn't want to be praised as a hero on the outside, either. He felt like a fraud and wished he could sit and eat his breakfast in peace. Ivan manipulated his long legs under the table and sat next to Commander Simon.

"The other commanders have taken several dozen wagon-loads of corpses and armor to the South Castle," Simon informed.

Ivan's brow puckered with sympathy. The men from the other tables returned to discussing the now-ended war. Their somber faces disguised by half-smiles of relief. Hands and platters moved quickly up and down the tables while heaping forkfuls of food were shoveled in one after another. Ivan's stomach gurgled with hunger.

Untying the strings at his neck, Simon handed over the cloak. "Here, put it on. When you stop to visit

Zephyrus, return it along with The Challenger to the Sanctuary of Truth. That is unless you plan to stay, and you're most welcome to do so."

"I'm sorry. I must find my brother and then leave."

Nodding, creases formed between Simon's eyebrows. His lips parted as though he was about to speak, but he must've decided against it.

Ivan twirled the cloak around his shoulders, pleased to see it was washed and mended. He exchanged greetings with Sebastian, who remained inside the cloak.

"Addie!" Simon hollered over the sea of heads. "Where's our breakfast? We're starving here." He gave a wry smile. "You'd think we were important enough to be served first, wouldn't you?" The outburst made Ivan jump.

"I was thinking the same thing," Ivan agreed. Dizzy from hunger, he licked his lips.

"I'll be right there," Addie yelled.

Ivan turned his head and studied Zephyrus. "How is he this morning?"

"Better." Simon glanced in that direction. "He regained consciousness during the night. We have positive expectations for his recovery. He had a short conversation with Sebastian earlier."

"That's right." Sebastian didn't elaborate.

Simon reached down, stroking his canine friends and scratching their ears with affection.

"What will it be here, sweeties?"

Ivan turned in his seat, glancing up to see a stout young female with a very pretty face. Her starched cap, edged in eyelet lace, was cockeyed. She held a large tray with eggs, piled with bacon and bangers, cooked to dark brown, along with heaped fried mushrooms and tomatoes. Ivan's nostrils widened.

Holding the tray near, the servant waited until Ivan slid a full portion onto his plate. He lifted a piece of buttered toast from the tray's edge and licked the dripping butter from his fingers.

"I was waiting for our guest of honor to arrive," she said in her defense and winked at Ivan.

"Meet Addie." Simon introduced her and clapped his hands. "She keeps us all in line—tolerates no rough stuff, no swearing, no food fights."

"Or leaving anything on your plate," Lieutenant Pezzuline called from the opposite side of the table.

"I'll remember that." Ivan grinned, knowing it wouldn't be a problem. He thanked her.

Addie's flushed, round cheeks puffed out. She was obviously enjoying their new guest's attention. "I'll bring you a fresh pot of tea in a minute or so." She moved to the next guest with her tray.

"Bring bowls for his beagles, too." Simon raised his hand for her attention.

"Sure thing." She glanced down at them and gushed, "What handsome dogs, just like their master."

Huffing, Addie soon returned and handed the dog dishes to Simon. Before she moved away, she gave Ivan an adoring look.

Simon jabbed him with his finger and snickered. "You have an admirer."

Ivan lifted one eyebrow and continued to eat, his affections belonged to someone else.

Rising from their seats, Berkel and Pezzuline offered their congratulations to Ivan.

"You're quite the swordsman." Pezzuline pumped

Ivan's hand. "I've never seen anything quite like it."

Sergeant Berkel chuckled and saluted. "Are you ready to leave, Commander?"

Saluting in return, Simon said, "Yes. Help the men put the tables and benches back into the storage sheds. Then go saddle up."

"Yes, sir." Pezzuline rubbed his reddened eyes vigorously with his index fingers and yawned.

Ivan hoped Addie would make a final round so he could take another helping. His appetite was strong, and since he'd not eaten the evening meal, his stomach seemed bottomless. He sliced his last two bangers into bite-sized rounds on his plate, allowing just the right distance between them.

Simon fidgeted, anxious to leave. "They're delicious sausages, aren't they?" he remarked politely, as though trying to pass the time more quickly without insulting his honored quest.

Murmuring his praise, Ivan's brow rose high in agreement.

"They're made by our very own Wolflords here in the Forest." Simon rested his elbows on the table and clasped his hands.

Ivan's fork stopped near his mouth. "A Wolflord made these?"

"Yeah, do you know about our newcomers to the Forest? They've been here about ten years or so."

"Sebastian has told me they were werewolves once, and they'd gone through a hideous transformation to become men." Thinking further on the subject, Ivan joined three very unpleasant images: A werewolf is carnivorous. Carnivores eat meat. Man is meat. *Oh, ghastly thought.* Were the sausages made from venison, pork, and man-parts? Metal pinged when he dropped his fork to his plate. He reached for his teacup and washed down the taste that lingered in his mouth.

Though most of the soldiers had left, Ivan paused, considering how to ask Simon a question.

"Let's go." Simon made a move to rise from his seat.

Ivan leaned closer and said in a low tone, "Tell me, did you know my brother Peter?"

Grimacing, Simon inhaled deeply. He seemed a little annoyed. "I knew it was only a matter of time before you asked."

"You knew him well?"

"Yes, and I liked Peter very much. He has many fine qualities. Easy to get on with, amusing and inquisitive. Smart…ah, just a likable chap, you know?"

Ivan beamed. "That's how I remember him, too. Why didn't he join the British Army?"

"Simple answer, really." Simon's brow rose, and a twitch appeared in the corner of his mouth. "He once told me he didn't want to get maimed or killed. No one wants that, but…"

After a long pause, Ivan rubbed his forehead.

Simon continued. "I've been worried about him. He keeps himself scarce and distant from us, and he didn't attend the games this year. I haven't seen him for a long time."

"What's he been doing since he's lived in the Forest?"

"He used to stay at the castle, now I'm not sure. I've asked him to join my regiment several times, but Peter insisted his aspirations were much higher than being in my garrison."

Ivan ventured his main question. "I've heard he's given his allegiance to the Dark Army." He hoped Simon would snicker and call the claim ridiculous.

The commander pressed his fingers around his teacup. A crease appeared between his angled brows, his mouth lifted into a snarl. "I don't know why Peter would even consider such a foolish thing. He has everything he could want. Lord Graydon and Zephyrus love him dearly. Sometimes we'd tease Zephyrus about his golden boy because of Peter's blond hair, light complexion, and his winning ways."

Ivan grinned. "That sounds like Peter. People have always loved him easily. He was my friend and protector as well as my brother."

Sliding his cup away, Simon laced his fingers and tightened them.

"Do you know where I can find him?"

"Sorry, I don't. If I knew, I'd locate him myself." Simon's jaw hardened.

A shadow of doubt and anguish flashed through Ivan's heart. *What is Simon withholding?*

"What proof was given that he joined the enemy?" Simon suddenly asked.

Ivan didn't answer at once.

Simon pushed. "I mean, what makes you believe that Peter changed his allegiance and joined the Dark Army?"

"Two things." Ivan bit hard on his bottom lip. "Just before you approached me at Red Fox Creek asking for the cloak, I saw a tall man on a fancy black horse. He wore shiny black armor with silver trim. He carried a long thin sword in his hand. When he lifted his visor and stared, though he was a fair distance away, he reminded me of Peter." Ivan faced the commander, his heart beating unsteadily.

"And was it?"

"There was something about how he sat so straight with his shoulders pulled back. I keep thinking about it and wondering."

Simon lifted his head and stared at Ivan. "And the other reason that caused you to believe Peter may have betrayed us?"

Ivan recoiled at the word, feeling his face drain of color. Averting his eyes, he replied, "Fungoda said as much."

"Did he? Well, then…"

"Do you think it's true? Is Fungoda ever wrong about the things he says?"

"I don't know. It's possible Peter was mistaken for someone else. There are lots of people in the Forest." Simon's knuckles clenched white. "If he did join the enemy, he has no idea how monstrous Tereus is. I truly hope he is smarter than that."

There was a long silence while Ivan digested the things Simon had told him. He was both distressed and elated by what he'd heard. *I'm sure that's it. Peter has been mistaken for someone else. This is all a colossal mistake, and as soon as I find him, everyone will learn the truth.*

"It's just that…" Ivan's jaw muscles twitched. He stared at the table's edge. "I've killed two men since I've been here. And I…"

"I understand the sickening feeling inside." Simon glanced at him. "You've realized that men have died and you were responsible. Like you were saying earlier, they're gone from this world forever, possibly without leaving their marks of greatness or any notable contribution." Simon's voice faltered. He looked in the distance and quietly added, "Nothing...a man's life means nothing."

With an outward sigh of remorse, Ivan knew that Simon did understand his feelings of regret and shame. Bowing his head, he repeated the words he'd heard his own father say, "It makes no sense, except war must be fought to keep our homes and families safe at any cost."

Simon rubbed his brow. "The message may be that a man must try to make his contribution early in life in case his end comes quickly."

Ivan's lips parted with astonishment. It was one of the most profound statements he'd ever heard.

"Before yesterday, I don't recall ever shouting with anger at a person." Ivan's voice was soft and thoughtful. "I'd never killed a man. Peter used to tell me that I had a passive nature, even cowardly." Ivan felt uneasy admitting his shortcomings to Simon.

Simon slapped him between the shoulders. "I'd never call you cowardly, my friend. Not after witnessing the brave things you've done. You put many of my highly trained soldiers to shame." He paused for several moments and then said, "Sometimes you have to do things that don't seem to fit your character. Today you can claim your own brave victory."

Thinking on it, Ivan had to agree. He'd been forced to fight and save himself, his beagles, Anna-Iza, and people he cared for. That's how people mature, Ivan decided. By taking responsibility and doing what's right. He sat up straight, drawing a deep breath filled with fresh new wisdom and hope.

Chapter Twenty-One

The Demon Rises

Ivan walked to the clearing where Zephyrus stood in dormant solitude. The massive oak's far-stretching branches now hosted every bird species living in the Forest, or so it seemed. Tipping his head, he saw blackbirds, wrens, jays, and toss finches, which would stay the winter, and even a family of fenner whips. He recognized small warbler blackcaps and jackdaws with their pearly eyes. They perched on Zephyrus's long tangled branches, singing sweet melodies and offering their gladness. A dozen soldiers on horseback, wearing breast armor with swords at their sides, lowered their shields to watch Ivan approach. Men also paced on foot, alert.

Lieutenant Pezzuline called, "Zephyrus has been asking for you."

"He's awake?" Delighted, Ivan saw Zephyrus's facial features pushing through his trunk. First, his eyes appeared, then his large nose, and lastly, his lips. Ivan drew closer, standing in awe before the Great Oak.

Zephyrus opened dull green eyes and managed to say, "Ivan Kimble, I have much to thank you for."

In a moment, Sebastian fully emerged from the confines of the Dark Cloak, standing with head bowed before Zephyrus. With a reverent voice, he said, "My

Lord, my King, The High Intervener has kept watch over you."

Zephyrus's red-webbed eyes scanned the group, and he went quiet for a time. Words thick and slow, he said, "How can I ever repay you for saving my life? Without the healing sap, I'd surely have died."

"I did what had to be done," Ivan muttered.

"A great many men lost their lives here during the battle." Zephyrus's voice sank with despair. "What did Tereus think he would gain by such treachery? He underestimated the strength and skill of our garrisons only to have men sacrifice their lives for his deranged ambitions. Madness, absolute madness."

Ivan had no answer, but he thought the words sounded a great deal like his own father's after he left his Russian homeland, and this comforted him. That every man's life was important, that every man could leave his mark and make the world a better place.

Suddenly, Zephyrus's eyes shot open. "I sense something ominous and dark is rising."

The earth trembled.

"What's happening?" Ivan blurted. The ground shook violently under their feet. "Are we having an earthquake?"

Bounty's ears flattened against his head. He neighed loudly as his forelegs rose. Reaching for the bridle, Ivan cooed to calm him. There was a rolling sensation and more shaking. An explosive crack reverberated through the trees, and the smell of sulfur filled the air. Every bird flew away.

A horrified look of disbelief solidified on Zephyrus's smooth bark face. "This cannot be. The Black Book of Pearls forbids Tereus rising from the fiery depths." His voice weakened. "I have no energy to deal with my evil brother."

Wood mice darted from under a thick carpet of leaves looking for a secure hiding place, while Alfred and Canute scampered away, yelping.

A bloodcurdling, deep-throated roar rose up from a lone tree stump at the edge of the circular clearing. Red and orange fire blasted out while black soot shot up between the thick forks of the stump's roots. Forming within the leaping flames were thousands of distorted agonized faces, screaming as though Hell itself had laid claim to them. In the blaze, burning miniature bodies clawed over each other, trying to reach higher. But there was no relief at the top. They sizzled in the fire with no reprieve, no release.

Ivan's belly tightened. Who were these poor souls being destroyed in flames? Then he thought he recognized some of them. Men from the past. Those monsters that had condemned others to die for their own selfish causes. They were evil leaders of countries, robbers, blasphemers, murderers of women and children. He closed his eyes, unable to look at them any longer.

Evil faces faded, consumed into billowing, acrid black smoke, pushing skyward.

A putrid smell, like rotting animal carcasses, scorching fur, and sulfur, caused Ivan's eyes to water. His throat burned, and his hand flew up to cover his nose.

A voice rose from the flames. "How dare you destroy my army. You will pay with your lives for this.

"Tereus," Zephyrus spoke his brother's name with disdain.

Ivan coughed, his eyes flushed with tears. A faint outline formed within the darkening inferno of a huge man with long thick horns curving into lethal hooks at the top of his head. Two pairs of smaller horns, black as ebony, protruded from his forehead.

Hot with rage, searing and powerful, the beast-man swore, "Where is he?"

It was the most frightening voice Ivan had ever heard.

"Where is the man who killed my commander?" the demon screamed, pumping his arm through the smoke, his big head swinging side to side, searching.

No one spoke.

"Be careful," Zephyrus whispered. "Tereus's specter could become dangerous."

Soldiers on foot and horseback cautiously circled the Great Oak with swords drawn from their scabbards. Berkel and Pezzuline moved to enclose Ivan within their protection.

"Why are you surrounding me?"

"Your life is in danger." Pezzuline shot him a terrified look.

"But it wasn't my fault." Ivan shook in cold panic. "Sebastian, what should I do?"

"Mind what the soldiers tell you," he said, looking alarmed. "Remain quiet and don't move. The demon has forced himself through a porthole." Sebastian stepped closer and also shielded him.

"Do not threaten my subjects," Zephyrus bellowed. You'll suffer everlasting fiery consequences."

"Have you forgotten, my brother? I live in the depths of blazing Hell every day of my life."

Tereus blew breath through the smoke. His words

were sharp like the cutting edge of the huge sword that he gripped in his blistered hand.

Teeth chattering, Ivan's fingernails dug into his palms. The acrid smoke choked him, stinging his nostrils and throat. Alarmed, he wondered, *What can I do against the power of a demon?*

"Stop! Ivan." Sebastian grabbed Ivan's arm when he turned with the notion to escape. "Stay in one place. This is only Tereus's specter, but he senses movement above ground. He may appear, and then his terror will spill forth, scorching the earth."

Ivan gulped and froze in place. "But what does he want of me?"

"He knows you." Sebastian's frightened eyes stared in Ivan's direction. "You are the stranger that killed his commander. Be still now."

Sweat collected on Ivan's forehead and neck. His heart pounded so hard he had difficulty breathing. Shaken by a terrifying thought, he suddenly remembered...

That's how my dream ended when I woke this morning.

I'm going to die here.

****

Tereus's ghostly form became clearer, growing larger as it rose from the blaze. Dense smoke obscured his feet and ankles. The beast-image vibrated, weaving yellow and orange flames through his terrifying specter that remained just as it did before. Hairless, Tereus's face was blistered red. His massive bare chest, shiny with sweat, was festered with scars and dark burns.

Ivan stood paralyzed with fear. He had never seen a neck so thick. His legs looked large as tree trunks. His leather mid-thigh skirt was studded with small golden disks that sparkled, throwing flashes of firelight. *He's not real*, Ivan reminded himself. *Only a phantom.*

Fixing baleful eyes on Zephyrus, the demon ignored the surrounding soldiers. Neither did he seem to notice Ivan wearing the Long Dark Cloak and gripping the hilt of The Challenger.

"You have destroyed them all, crushed my ancient warriors in the White Rock Corridor." Tereus pointed a muscular arm at Zephyrus, shaking his finger accusingly. "It was *you*, brother, who commanded the rocks to close." His face twisted with centuries of jealousy, hate, and anger.

Zephyrus answered, "I did not command the rocks to close, but I surely would have." He paused for a moment. "The Ghost Warriors were already dead, but you called them to rise and fight your cruel, pointless war. Now they rest in peace until the Great Eternal Rising."

Tereus snorted like a mad bull and released a deep roar. A firestorm exploded around him. "They were mine to command, Zephyrus! They gladly served me in battle a millennia ago and took up arms to fight for me again."

"You have violated the sacred laws of the Forest as set forth by the High Intervener." Zephyrus's voice was strong and shrill. "As it is written and known in the Black Book of Pearls, commanding the dead to rise is blasphemy."

"I don't abide by your foolish laws," Tereus sneered, baring silvery teeth. "I've never pledged myself to *your* weak and useless God. He condemned me to live underground. *He* is your protector. Not mine."

"Yes," Zephyrus defended. "*He* is my protector."

"You don't look so good, brother. Is *he* protecting you now?"

Going silent, Zephyrus appeared weakened.

"Then we shall see how powerful your God is when I rebuild Helvaka," the beast mocked. "I'll be the true king of the resurrected city as I should've been a thousand years ago. The throne belongs to me, but you stole my kingdom away."

"What was done countless generations ago was just and fair. The throne wasn't yours to sit upon. Our father made that very clear. You will be chained forever in the deepest, fiery caverns for your acts of treason."

Contemptuous laughter filled the Forest as though Tereus was amused by some inward joke. "Chained forever—I think not. I won't be imprisoned much longer in this damned inferno."

"Who will release you?" Zephyrus's mouth hung open.

"I have chosen my successor." Tereus's voice boomed. "You know better than I, dear brother, that according to the Black Book of Pearls, I will be granted full pardon if I find someone to take my place as ruler of the fiery deep."

"Who would be so senseless and agree to become your servant in the blazing underworld?" Zephyrus shuddered at the suggestion. "Surely, it's not one of my loyal subjects."

"You will know soon enough."

"You're a liar and deceiver. There is no such passage with an escape clause in the Black Book of Pearls," Zephyrus said with forced effort. "I helped to inscribe the words with the High Intervener after giving my solemn oath to become Master and Peacekeeper of the Forest. Nothing with that meaning exists in the passages for you. Only I will be granted a successor."

"I'm impressed!" Tereus snickered, his slit-eyes opened with surprise. He shoved his long, wide sword into its scabbard, folding his arms across his massive chest. "Then perhaps you've forgotten the chapter that I speak of unless you have the Great Book in your possession." He waited a moment, nostrils flaring. "Well, do you have it?"

Zephyrus did not answer. His twig-eyebrows came together with pain and doubt.

"Answer me!" Tereus shouted. "Where is it?" His face twisted viciously. "You hold nothing in your sanctuary. All relics are gone. Only the Long Dark Cloak remains, and it has no significant powers. There is nothing left to protect you. Everything's gone." Laughing cruelly, his lips curled. "The poison works that way…slow, with deep suffering. Today, I am the New King of the West Forest."

"*You* are responsible for the poisonous axe blows," Zephyrus managed to say.

"Why, Zephyrus, how can you blame me for such a terrible crime? You know I'm confined to the underworld. I can't escape my burning dungeon."

Ivan closed his eyes, sickened by the deceitful beast. Surely Zephyrus knew Tereus mocked him with his lies.

"Who did you commandeer to wield the Silver Axe against me?" Zephyrus asked sharply, his pale green eyes burrowed into the beast.

"Now, wouldn't you like to know, my dear

brother?"

"I am not your brother. I do not claim you."

Tereus scowled angrily, not expecting the rebuff. His rage swelled. Red flames shot higher, and dark smoke swirled around as his apparition grew more defined.

Several horses bucked and whinnied while the patrolling soldiers struggled to bring them under control. "Easy, easy boy."

"You won't be talking so mightily when Helvaka is rebuilt, and I rise again. I will sit upon the throne as the One and Only King of the Land. I shall be Master and Lord over the Great City and all the Forest."

"These fantasies will never be," Zephyrus replied icily.

The conniving beast feigned humility. "My dear Zephyrus. It's only because I'm confined to the darkest depths that I'm so cantankerous. Allow me to show myself in the flesh. You have the power and authority. Let me put my bare feet upon the cool grass, smell the fresh air, and watch the clouds move through the sky. Then, you'll see how agreeable I can be. I'll tell you the name of my future thrall."

"I strike no bargain with a traitor and blasphemer," Zephyrus shot back, his lips pulled into a snarl.

Thin trails of smoke, like ghostly fingers, slithered forward from the opening where Tereus's phantom image stood. The curling wisps found Ivan and wrapped their tentacles around him, seeking, evaluating. They thickened against the scabbard that held The Challenger and then hastily returned to the demon.

"Who stands cowering behind armed men and

horses like a wizened old woman?" Tereus shouted. "Show yourself."

Zephyrus spoke in Ivan's stead, "The lad is my friend. He is a guest of the Forest."

"Who are you?" Tereus's thundering voice exploded, his flaming eyes probed into Ivan.

Ivan quaked.

"I was told you'd left the Forest, but here you stand before me." A column of caustic smoke and fire shot up through the root's opening. Snapping and hissing, it rose higher and higher. Fire engulfed the image of the enraged demon but didn't appear to burn him. Ash and soot floated to the ground, settling onto the soldiers' hair and clothing. Their hands flew to cover their mouths and noses. Some turned away and gagged. Others fell to their knees in coughing spasms, scarcely able to draw breath into aching lungs.

Tereus's voice boomed, *"You* are the intruder from the outside! *You* fetched the sap from that pitiful old pile of wood they call Fungoda. *You* killed my commander." Incensed, the demon pulled his sword with quickness, leaning forward and holding it in an iron grip with both hands. *"You* will die for your interference."

Too frightened to speak, Ivan's legs lost their feeling. His brain iced over with terror. Then logic reigned. *How can a phantom have the physical strength to engage me in a sword fight? He's only a ghostly image.*

"I'm coming through!" the demon roared. Lightning cracked across the darkening sky, thunder rolled and crackled. "This intruder will die by my sword."

White-hot sparks flew skyward, sizzling as they reached new heights. Thick plumes turned black as nightmares. A sharp grating sound like dragon claws on glass cut through the air.

"You will not come forth," Zephyrus said hotly. "You will not violate the sanctity of above-ground."

"I will break through the barrier. The lad will not leave the Forest alive."

"*Ivan*," Zephyrus screamed, "withdraw The Challenger and drive its point into the center of the stump. Hold it there with all your strength. Don't let go. *Hurry*."

With trembling hands, Ivan removed The Challenger from the sheath, but his legs wouldn't move.

"Begin with one step," Sebastian said with urgency. "Now another. Do as Zephyrus orders. It's our only chance to ensure the demon won't break through and slaughter you."

Ivan gasped.

Soldiers jumped aside and allowed Ivan to pass. Abruptly he wondered, *with all these trained soldiers, why is it me to thwart the beast from coming through the porthole?*

"Closer, now, only a few more steps." Sebastian's voice quivered.

Smoke stung Ivan's eyes. Moving closer, the fire threatened to ignite the hem of the Long Dark Cloak, but oddly it did not burn him or the garment.

Tereus gripped his phantom sword with powerful hands. Smoldering eyes glared. Cocking his head, Tereus cursed Ivan.

"You remind me of someone. Who in thunder are you, anyway? You've spoiled everything—all of my long-laid plans."

The demon's sword swung with such speed that Ivan didn't see the heavy weapon coming in his direction.

He heard his own sharp intake of breath with the frightening sound of swiftly passing metal. Smoke swirled in the blade's path. The weapon, being part of the apparition, whizzed through Ivan's middle. He cried out. His belly muscles tightened with a hot, tingling sensation. He believed it was his last breath.

But the sword did not cut him.

I'm alive. He nearly fainted with relief.

"*Now, Ivan!*" Zephyrus shouted. "Drive in the point."

Ivan's knuckles turned white as The Challenger rose high. With both hands, he plunged the tip of silver into the wood stump.

The earth shook. Tereus exploded with a deep-throated roar just as an electric crack split the air. Ivan held the sword with all his might. His jaws clenched in bone-grinding agony. Arm muscles twitched, aching from immense pressure. Sweat drenched his body from fear and the flame's heat.

I feel as though I'm burning to ash. Yes, it's only a specter, just a ghost. But the demon is real. His slit eyes, his wide mouth twisted with fury, his hatred, and his need for revenge are as real as the tree stump he's materialized from.

The beast's final howl of submission cut through the blast of dark plumes. He screamed an oath, "You will all burn! I will destroy you, leaving only ashes for the wind to carry away."

Flames and smoke returned through the opening of

the stump root and pulled Tereus's fading specter into the cavity.

With the last of his strength, Ivan forced his legs to back away, leaving The Challenger impaled in the wood. His breath came in rapid, shallow gulps. Staring vacantly, too exhausted to go on, his chin dropped to his chest and his eyes closed.

Chapter Twenty-Two

Recovery

Zephyrus, the *Westwind*, true to his middle name, blew a steady stream of wind to force away the last remnants of filthy smoke and residue. His worried eyes stayed fixed on Ivan.

Next to the tree stump, Ivan stood dazed and disoriented with clenched blue-veined hands. Soot smeared his face and hair while particles of ash collected on the cloak that hung over his shoulders. He was scarcely conscious of it.

"You can remove The Challenger now," Sebastian said from the cloak. His voice was gentle and loving like that of a grandfather.

With the last of his strength, Ivan obeyed. Molding his hands around the hilt, he pulled the sword from the wood with ease. Just as he did, the ground shook. The action was followed by sharp snapping and popping. Moving back several steps, he collapsed to his knees. He stared at the sword's golden shaft, not knowing why he held it or where he was. He coughed.

Pezzuline and Berkel rushed to his side, wearing worried expressions. Pezzuline reached for Ivan under his arms and tugged him to a sitting position, then kneeled behind him. He rested Ivan's head against his chest.

Removing the ancient weapon from his grip, Sergeant Berkel patted him on his shoulder. "You'll be all right, lad." His tone was calm and consoling.

Zephyrus sighed weakly. "Can you help him, Sebastian?"

"I'm working on it," the spirit-voice replied. "I can't seem to go deep enough to purge the smoke. It's a tricky bit of work."

"What's wrong with me?" Ivan rasped, squinting through blurry eyes. "It's hard to breathe. Everything is dark. I feel like I'm dying."

"Don't give in to it," Sebastian encouraged from the cloak. "It's only temporary, caused by Tereus's wicked magic. God only knows what the horrible beast mixed into that bloody smoke."

Thrashing, flailing his arms, Ivan yelled, "Help me! Death is coming."

"Death will not take you." Pezzuline tightened his arms around him. "Our love will protect you."

Ivan wrenched in the embrace of the man who held him. He couldn't escape the fearsome cold voice that gripped him. The demon had threatened his life, and Ivan felt he would make good on his promise.

A lavender-gray haze appeared and shifted into the vague shape of Tereus's massive form, threatening and frightening. Gasping for breath, Ivan screamed. He swung his fists wildly, hammering at the empty air as the evil shape moved toward him.

"There now, I won't let him get you," Sebastian promised. "Away with you, blackheart of the underworld. The lad stays with us."

Tereus hissed. "I will consume your flesh and chew your bones if you enter my domain again." His scorching eyes snapped as his ghostly shape grew pale, slowly evaporating.

"You will do nothing of the sort, not while I live." Zephyrus's words cut sharp as jagged stone. The haze flashed dirty-white and then dissolved.

Inhaling several breaths, Ivan coughed, spitting blood into his palm. He wiped it on his trousers. He panicked. "The sword? Where is it?"

"Don't worry." Berkel extended the weapon in his hands. "I have The Challenger right here."

Slowly sitting up, Ivan looked around. "Where have I been? It was a horrible place."

"You're with friends who love you," Sebastian said firmly.

Peeking through the underbrush, Alfred and Canute dashed forward. They leaped at Ivan's chest, licking his face and neck. Recovering some awareness, he pulled his beagles close, embracing them.

Drugan and Mart-Mart landed nearby, making clicking noises with their beaks and flapping their wings. Mart-Mart asked, "What happened? Did you eat some smoke?"

Ivan didn't answer. His stomach felt as though he wanted to throw up. The strong spices in the Wolflord sausages he'd eaten earlier churned in him like wind gone wild.

Moments later, Ivan recognized the soldiers surrounding him and remembered the dream he'd just had. *Was it a dream?*

Calling to Pezzuline, his voice little more than a whisper, Ivan said, "Would you bring Bounty to me? I want to leave the Forest as soon as possible."

"Ivan, we…" Sergeant Berkel began, his tone laced

with apology.

Lowering his eyelids, the lad waved the words away. "I want to leave."

"What about finding your brother?" Pezzuline looked stricken.

Ivan blinked. "Brother? Do I have a brother?"

"His memory will come back soon enough," Sebastian assured them. The soldiers pulled Ivan upright on shaky legs.

"Be careful moving him too quickly," the lieutenant cautioned with his palms easing downward.

After several unsteady steps, Ivan stood erect. Filling his lungs with deep breaths, he coughed harshly.

"You should take him to the barracks to rest," Pezzuline ordered. "Have someone sit with him and see to his recovery."

Ivan shook his head. "I'm feeling much better. There's no reason to coddle me." Tereus's threats clamored through his brain. "I need to return these relics and have parting words with Zephyrus."

The Great Oak's tangle of branches drooped listlessly. He must've heard his name called, for his eyes opened slightly. Pezzuline and Berkel escorted him and reluctantly backed away.

Ivan raised his head. "Zephyrus, I must leave now."

Green eyes fluttered. "Ivan, my dear friend, I thank the High Intervener you are safe from the beast. You have been of great service to me, and I will forever be in your debt."

"I did what I had to when you needed me. Anyone would've done the same. But now it's time to leave."

"Are you quite sure you feel well enough?" Heavy

twig-brows shadowed Zephyrus's eyes.

"It's you I'm worried about." Ivan glanced up at the great tree.

"In time, I'll recover and preside over the Forest as I've done for a thousand years. Now, what can I do for you?"

"I'd like to return the cloak and The Challenger for your safekeeping." He made a half-turn toward Sergeant Berkel, who held the magnificent sword.

The sergeant placed the metal in Ivan's hands and nodded. "I'll go get Bounty." The lieutenant mounted his horse and raced away.

"Ah yes," Zephyrus said. "I accept them gladly."

After a moment, the large door in Zephyrus's massive trunk opened and grated on dirt. It pushed wet leaves away, just as it had when Ivan first entered the Forest.

It seemed like years ago. Ivan was a different person now. Remembering the Golden Lantern, he paused at the entrance and glanced behind him toward the triplets. The lantern was not visible on Dorset's lower branch where he'd left it, and so he assumed someone had hidden it in the grass for safekeeping. Stepping inside the tree's immense cavity, the spicy smells and rush of cool, damp air greeted him. Sadness flashed through him as he tugged off the garment and replaced it on the peg where he first found it.

Sebastian's form materialized from the cloak with only gray swirls of color. Concern and worry carved his face.

"I'll miss you as my guide." Ivan hesitated. His dry throat constricted with an unexpected sob. "You've been a great friend to me. I'm lucky to have known someone of complete goodness."

Extending a thin hand, Sebastian rested it on Ivan's shoulder. "Indeed, I've had a long time to practice. But it is *we,* the people, who are blessed by your visit. Perhaps it was fortuitous, but I believe the High Intervener sensed our need and sent you into our Forest to help us."

"I believe in the High Intervener. God is real," Ivan said, his eyes tearing. "He helped me stay alive just as he has helped Zephyrus."

"And so he did." Sebastian grinned widely.

Stroking The Challenger's decorative hilt, Ivan felt it vibrate in his hands. Since no one had told him otherwise, he placed it on resting hooks on the wall above his head.

"I'm grateful for your help," Ivan said to The Challenger. "If not for you, I'd be one of the many bodies being counted at the South Castle right now."

The sonorous voice rang from the length of thick metal. "It was my pleasure to serve you, Ivan Kimble. Any time you return to the Forest, please ask, and I'll be available to you."

"Yes, of course." Ivan stepped back, frowning.

"Something's bothering you?" Sebastian lowered his chin and looked up under his bushy eyebrows in a contrite way.

Ivan bowed his head. He smelled the woodsy fragrance, peppery with a faint whiff of fungus, much like the penny bun mushroom. The scowl lines in his forehead deepened. "Sebastian," he said and paused, considering his words carefully, "I don't belong here. I won't be returning to the Forest."

The tree's large hollow cavity became quiet.

"I see," Sebastian muttered with sadness. "Your feelings are understandable. I'm sure the shock of everything you've gone through has affected you profoundly."

Ivan lifted his eyes and gave a single nod.

"Come here and see me, Ivan, please." Zephyrus's low voice echoed softly through the sanctuary's cathedral-like chamber.

Stepping out into the early morning sunlight, Ivan met Zephyrus's kind eyes. "Sir," he said, bowing with respect.

"How are you feeling?"

Ivan rubbed the back of his neck. "I'm a little fatigued." Turning his head, he sniffed. "As though I'd been smoked like a slab of bacon."

Zephyrus chuckled lightly.

"Could Tereus come through the opening in the tree roots, again?" Ivan threw a nervous glance at the stump. A few languishing threads of smoke rose from the hole.

"No. I was deeply concerned that he had somehow managed to open a porthole to the above world, but that wasn't the case. He cannot enter onto sacred ground without my permission. He's bound to the underworld—for now."

Hands stuffed into his pockets, Ivan said, "That's comforting."

"But to my dismay," Zephyrus replied and wheezed, "Tereus suggested he'd found new powers. It bothered me when he said he had selected an ally, a partner, to help him. I need the Book of Pearls to check if there is, indeed, a *release clause*. I don't recall ever agreeing to such a thing with the High Intervener."

"I hope the book will be located, sir."

Just then, clomping hooves sounded in the distance. Pezzuline approached on Bounty from the south, his own horse in tow.

"The other relics, sir…" Ivan raised his face toward Zephyrus. "Where do you believe they are?"

Zephyrus winced, narrowing his heavy brows. "I suspect they're all here somewhere in this vast woodland. They'll likely stay hidden until the opportunity is ripe to use them for my destruction. Tereus hasn't been defeated. Nor has he lost his burning ambition to rule the Forest. For now, he's bound and limited to his underworld."

Nodding anxiously, Ivan pulled his hands from his pockets and was about to repeat his farewell.

"Ah!" the Great Oak suddenly exclaimed. "I've just received a burst of messages from the Forest trees. They have many stories to tell." His twig-mustache twitched, a small smile played at his lips. "They say that Peter is galloping on Foothill Road, and he will see you at the border."

With a burst of laughter, Ivan remembered Fungoda's prediction that Peter would meet him there. Joy rose up in him. He'd made many good friends and changed a great deal. If asked, Ivan couldn't describe the exact changes, but he knew he was different. He would never be bullied again, not by Dirk Mackle or his friends, or Tereus of the Underworld. He would do what was necessary to protect others who needed his help.

Raising the volume of his voice, Zephyrus said, "You will find an ample deposit in your account at Graydon Village Bank. It will help defray any expenses you may have incurred while risking your life to save mine."

"Thank you, but it's not necessary." Ivan lowered his head and stared at the ground. "It was my decision to journey into the Forest. There's no reason to pay me for helping when I was needed."

"Just the same, the bank draft has been deposited." Zephyrus's tone was insistent.

"Thank you," was all Ivan could say, afraid he might break down and weep.

Pezzuline swung off Bounty, his lips puckered with disgust. "Sassy horse if I ever saw one! How do you get this animal to obey?"

Ivan smiled bleakly, reaching for the bridle as the officer slid from the saddle. "We understand each other." His face crinkled. "Bounty *always* gets his own way."

The lieutenant burst into laughter.

Ivan had sudden doubts. Surely Fungoda had been misinformed about Peter's betrayal. What could he know, anyway? He was an ancient tree that stood unmoving for at least five thousand years. *I know Peter better than any old tree.* He took a deep breath and raised his chin.

"Will you return and visit us soon?" Zephyrus's voice was a bit wobbly. "We would welcome you. You may collect any amount of firewood you want—no living trees, of course." He winked and smiled.

Sebastian's voice boomed from inside the sanctuary. "I've invited him back, too."

Averting his eyes, Ivan shook his head and gazed into the distance. "I-I'll see."

"We wish you'd consider the invitation seriously,"

Pezzuline and Berkel said within seconds of each other.

"You need to come again." Pezzuline rolled his eyes. "Come when we can have fun together, hunting, fishing, and chasing the pretty noble girls at the South Castle. I know Lord Graydon would enjoy meeting you," he added as further enticement.

Ivan grinned at Pezzuline's humor. Slowly he opened his mouth, but words were stuck behind a lump in his throat.

"It seems all the harshness of the Forest fell upon your shoulders," Zephyrus said, compassion wringing in his voice. "We forget how young you are. You're only fifteen, and yet you've experienced battles and hardships that most men would not encounter in a lifetime."

Ivan's heart fluttered with surprise. "You know all about that?"

"Yes, I've heard most of what has happened." Zephyrus regarded his brother and sister trees that stood at the edge of the meadow. "*They* haven't stopped talking since Root-Underground reopened. I'm considering slipping back into dormancy just to gain a little peace." His smooth bark lips curved into a grin, and he cracked a bit of laughter.

Eyes from surrounding trees opened wide, staring curiously at Ivan. *They must know about the dumb things I've done.* Ivan turned his back on them and faced Zephyrus.

"You've handled dangerous circumstances like a courageous and sensible man. I admire your bravery."

Ivan tried to answer. There were so many things he wanted to explain, to ask, but nothing sounded quite right, and he was afraid he might break down and sob.

For the second time since entering the Forest, someone had called him brave, and the words strengthened him. "I…we'll see," he said again, releasing a pent-up sigh.

"Aaah!" Zephyrus gave a burst of surprise. "There's a message coming from the trees regarding Peter's location."

Ivan's heart pounded like a rain-engorged river over granite rocks. He moved closer to Zephyrus. "Where? Tell me, where is he?"

Zephyrus concentrated for some moments. "Soon, he'll swing south to meet you near the entrance." His eyes glowed, his brow rose. "It's just as Fungoda has told you."

Ivan threw his head back with full-throated laughter. He yelled, "Yes! I'll go meet him. Thank you. Thank you all very much." His grin stayed. He almost flew into the saddle and urged Bounty forward. He turned to wave and called, "King Alfred, King Canute, let's go meet Peter."

****

Watching silently, Zephyrus appraised the lad, his eyes shining brightly. He released a grateful sigh and whispered, "Yes, everything is as it should be."

Chapter Twenty-Three

Peter

Slowing Bounty to a stop, Ivan leaned forward in his saddle trying to look everywhere at once. His chest muscles tensed, his legs squeezed against his horse's ribs. He searched for Peter, but there was no sign of him. Alfred and Canute woofed, appearing confused as to why they'd stopped so near the border.

In the distance, the Forest's entrance came into view where the familiar wide-open heathland awaited him. Short yellow grasses were woven with touches of umber, crimson, and pale ochre. Heather spread its patterns of purple on both sides of the roadway as though welcoming Ivan's return.

Where is he? Zephyrus had said that Peter rode east at a steady canter and had turned south. "I'll stop here and wait," Ivan said, combing his fingers roughly through his dark hair. Sliding from his saddle, he listened for an approaching horse but heard nothing. He searched the branches above and saw the dried leaves scraping elbows with each other, but no facial features punctuated the dark-trunked tree.

"Do you talk?" Ivan asked the elm nearest him and waited. "I'm looking for my brother. His name is Peter—Peter Kimble. I was told he'd meet me here near the entrance of the Forest." The tree didn't reply.

Undeterred, he walked around the tree with Bounty in tow and said, "My name is Ivan. Did someone pass here asking for me? Peter is quite tall. He has blond hair, sharp features. Have you seen him?" No answer. Maybe not all trees spoke, or some were forbidden to speak with outsiders. He shrugged, unimpressed. Releasing Bounty, he warned him, "Don't wander too far."

Lowering himself on sprawling rocks nearby, he buried his boots in the tall grass. He absently plucked a weed that looked like ripe wheat with a pale purple head and separated it from its casing. Chewing the sweet juices hurt his teeth. He licked the pain away with his tongue and gave the weed a toss. He remembered he'd tasted the sweet nectar once before. Shortly, he eased his head back against an elm and studied the pale gray sky. *Will it burst open and rain this morning?*

There was a rustling sound not far in the meadow. Startled, he jumped to his feet. "Peter?" But it was only Bounty scratching his flank against a tall bush.

Calming the excited beat of his heart, he sat and leaned back once more, molding his shoulder blades against the tree and falling into a daydream. For an instant, he doubted the chain of events that replayed in his memory. His eyes closed tightly as shame flushed through him. "What will Peter say when he learns what I've done?"

Ivan already missed Anna-Iza. The ache of loneliness overwhelmed him. How had the sweet little goddess captured his love so easily? He visualized her beautiful blue-green eyes looking up at him, welling with pearl-bright tears. She had whispered softly, "I'll miss you. Please hurry back to me."

Even a swift shake of his head couldn't dissolve her dreamy enchantment. *It must be the Spell of Love.* Thinking of her, he smiled happily until the voice inside him warned, *"You have pledged your love to Anna-Iza, and this cannot be."*

"But…" Ivan protested.

"She is a High Goddess. It is as Sebastian has told you. She has responsibilities to her gods, to her sister goddesses, and to the Forest. Her loyalties belong to Zephyrus. He is her true Master."

Ivan lowered his head until his chin rested upon his chest. His shoulders sagged. The joy from moments ago seemed to leak out and fade with his newfound happiness.

Alfred and Canute raced to him, skidding to a halt, whining in sympathy. He reached to stroke their necks, gripping their fur in his fingers as though squeezing away the agonizing truth.

"What must I do?" Ivan mourned. Having no handkerchief, he wiped his tears on the sleeve of his jacket.

His inner voice urged, *"Release her."*

He sniffed loudly, bending forward with his elbows on his knees. "I have to think on it."

Soon, Peter will come this way. We'll ride home to our farm. Loneliness will be a thing of the past. Feeling relieved, Ivan drew several shuddering breaths and straightened himself. "Everything will be better when Peter comes home."

A breeze moved around him, followed by a grumble of thunder. For a moment, the sound reminded him of Tereus, and a chill crossed his neck, raising prickly goosebumps that traveled down his arms.

After a time, growing even more anxious, Ivan peered through the trees. Maybe Peter took another route and wouldn't come. *Has he changed his mind?*

Ivan snapped alert. A stomping sound, like that of a horse, moved north of him. From the gentle slope of lawn, to the dark stand of trees with color-changed foliage, to the cool lapping gurgles of the Red Fox Creek, he watched. And then…

Feet shuffled. Heavy breathing came from somewhere through a grouping of trees. A cold, threatening voice rippled across the air, "Move your weapon one inch, and you'll never blow a harmonica again."

"But, I-I don't play the harmonica," came a stammering and terrified response.

"Then maybe I should slash your throat for good measure. Drop your weapon, Nugent. *Now!*"

Panicked, Ivan grabbed Bounty's mane, swung up into the saddle, and urged him forward. *Where are the quarreling men? Is Peter one of the voices?*

"Someone caught a rebel," Ivan said quietly.

He guided Bounty to the north, where he found shelter behind a copse of trees. He gasped. Grazing in the meadow was the black stallion with a long, shiny mane.

"I know that horse. It belongs to a soldier in the Dark Army. Do you remember, Bounty? The rider reminded me of Peter."

Ivan strained to hear the angry voices. Drawing on his newfound courage, he followed the sounds. He suddenly remembered the cloak no longer draped his shoulders, and having no weapon for protection, his bravery waned.

Shortly, he came upon a small clearing. A tall man with slender legs held a silvery blade across his hapless victim's throat. Stretching to get a better look, Ivan's breath stuttered with shock. Blond hair reached the man's shoulders with his head turned away from view.

The blond man spoke through clenched jaws. "Do you hear me, Nugent? Either rejoin your regiment or leave the Forest for good."

"Yes, sir. Right away, sir." The veins in Nugent's neck bulged, and his face was sprinkled with perspiration.

"There won't be a second warning. I'll cut your throat next time, for sure." The tall man forced his knife's edge tighter against flesh. A thin line of blood trickled down the man's neck.

"I'll leave." The victim's terrified voice squeaked.

The tall man released his captive and gave him a shove. His foot shot forward, pinning Nugent's sword to the ground. "This stays," he snapped.

Nugent stumbled, falling to his knees. "But that's my sword. How will I protect myself?"

"You're lucky this time. You've lost your weapon but kept your head. Now move!"

It's Peter! I believe that's his voice. I recognize his high forehead and tumbled blond hair, his long straight nose. Ivan's heart expanded with excitement. Too frightened to speak, he forced himself to silence. The rebel picked up his hat and rose to his feet, swatting leaves from his jodhpurs. He raised his angry eyes and stared at Ivan. His mouth dropped open. Pointing excitedly toward the clearing, he stammered, "That's him! He's the one I was waiting for."

Peter twisted and took a quick glance over his shoulder.

"He's worth a lot of money—a huge reward." Nugent jabbed his finger in Ivan's direction, and Ivan's heart rate increased. "I'll split it with you half and half. What do you say?"

Peter's gaze met Ivan's, and there it stayed. His lips parted, his eyes grew wide.

Spittle foamed at the edge of Nugent's mouth. "We'll divide the reward. I'll even do the killing. Just let me have my sword." He stooped.

"Leave it," Peter said icily, his jaw tightened.

"But we could—"

"You won't be killing him."

"But the reward…"

"He's my brother."

"Your what? No, really?" Nugent leaned forward, frowning. "Well, you do look a bit alike."

"Go. Get out of my sight. Now!"

"Brothers. Who'd ever think?" Nugent tucked his shirt into his too-tight waistband, smoothing his hair. Taking a last scathing look at Ivan, he mumbled, "Brothers. Just my bloody luck." He swung around and rushed north on foot.

Ivan and Peter stared at each other as though in a trance.

"Ivan…little brother of mine."

"Peter." Ivan rushed forward, arms thrown open.

They came together, embracing and laughing. Peter clapped Ivan's back, calling his name over and over. "I've missed you, Ivan. Oh, heavens, how I've missed you."

Kissing his cheeks, Ivan buried his face against his

brother's neck. His eyes burned with tears, but he didn't care. They'd found each other at last. Now everything would be right. They were together again.

"Where have you been?" Ivan's voice faltered. "Why didn't you come home?"

"I have a lot to tell." Peter patted Ivan's back.

Barking madly, Canute left his hiding place and raced toward the stranger. Standing on hind legs, scratching at Ivan's trousers, he must have believed his master was in danger. Alfred kept his distance, peeking out behind a clump of rocks.

"This is my beagle, King Canute and his brother, King Alfred."

Peter flashed a knowing smile. "I have so many things to explain, so many things to tell you. But, let me look at you." He stepped back, grasping Ivan by his shoulders, staring into his face. "My little brother grew up. You're almost as tall as me."

Ivan nodded. "Very close."

"You've filled out." His hands squeezed Ivan's biceps. "Hard muscles. Must be from all that farm work." He tilted his head and laughed. "Not bad looking either. The girls must go wild for you." His white teeth sparkled when he laughed again, and he embraced Ivan tightly.

Wiping his eyes, Ivan studied the brother he thought he'd lost.

"Did I change much?" Peter crossed his eyes, twisted his mouth, and stuck out his tongue. He swept elegant fingers through his hair, emphasizing a moment of dramatic arrogance.

"Your hair is longer, darker blond than I remember. Thinner at your hairline, but only a little. I notice wrinkles at the edge of your eyes." Ivan traced the corners of his brother's mouth, following a crease down with his finger.

Peter swatted Ivan's hand away. "I didn't come here to be insulted and told I was getting old." He winked and chuckled softly.

Ivan turned serious. "Where have you been?"

"Wait, not here. Let's move farther away from these trees in case they're listening. Down there." He motioned. Taking long strides, he moved to where the horses stood grazing.

Following, Ivan soon kept perfect pace with his brother. "Who'd be listening, and why should it matter?"

"Oh, the trees and those nosy fenner whips. You probably don't know about the reporting birds, but they can be a real nuisance."

"I know about them," he answered, but Peter's attention drifted for a moment toward the meadow.

"You still have that disagreeable horse, I see. He was just a colt when I left."

"Bounty," Ivan reminded him.

"Yes, I remember his snooty disposition."

"He's gotten even worse these past years."

Peter's musical laughter caught Ivan's memories.

"It's good to see you." Peter draped his arm over Ivan's shoulders. "I've missed you desperately, and I'm very glad you're here." Then, as though the question just occurred to him, Peter asked, "Why did you come?"

"To find you, of course. I'd heard you were in the West Forest."

"Who told you?"

"Lars Benton. He was collecting firewood somewhere north of here when he saw you throwing wood into a farm cart. It was you, wasn't it?"

Peter turned away for a moment. "Oh, yes. Now I remember."

Pained, Ivan faced him unwavering. "Why did you hurry away when Lars called your name?"

"Hurry away? Well…" Peter shifted uncomfortably. "You know the wood was meant for veterans of the war—men who needed help—and I took it when I wasn't entitled. It was shameful of me."

His brother's face flushed pink, his embarrassment real. Even so, why hadn't he approached Lars and ask after his health? Or offer to help him load his cart? Peter must've seen the dark patch over Lars's eye, his stump for an arm.

"Poor soul," he muttered, meeting Ivan's frown. "I know his disabilities happened in the war."

"Yes, it's been difficult for him."

"Weren't you afraid to come into the Forest? After all the stories I'd told you about dragons and trolls and other vicious creatures?" He tapped his finger against the scar on his chin.

"Terrified." Ivan's eyes went wide. "But I'd go anywhere to find you." He bowed his head, feeling shy. "When we were young, you told me a troll had bitten you. Was it Maloof?"

"Oh, you've met the notorious horde of trolls and fallen wizards, then?"

"I've only met a couple of trolls while on my journey."

"It was Cecil, that vicious heathen-runt. Grabbed at my shirt, pulled me down, and sank his teeth into my chin. I've never learned why he did it."

"He didn't seem violent," Ivan said, remembering the troll waddling away from the Norman shed with a full load in his pants.

"Cecil can't be trusted." Peter swept his arm through the air as though that made his remark final.

At that moment, Ivan recalled the frightening sounds and shuffling feet of some strange animals in the back of their barn. He'd never told Peter about the intruders. Standing back, Ivan watched Peter's face. "Did trolls ever visit you on our farm?"

Peter's eyes dilated, his shoulders pulled back rigidly. "H-how did you know?"

"I heard something—them. Maloof has a nasty habit of snorting and bringing up mucus, spitting it away with a loud noise. It's sickening to hear. It happened early one morning before you came to help with the milking."

"You saw them?"

"No. I heard them where the calving pens are located. I didn't move an inch until you showed up and pulled the barn door open. Maybe you remember my terrified look."

Peter lifted his chin as though recollecting that morning. "Your face was white as milk, and you were jerking your eyelashes out from fear. I reprimanded you for that awful habit."

Ivan gave a single nod.

"You don't pull your lashes out anymore, do you?"
"No."

"That's good," Peter said. "You don't stutter, either."

Ivan nodded again. Proud of overcoming the two

bad habits his brother had scolded him about. He wondered if Peter was intentionally avoiding the subject of his long absence.

Looking off into the woods, Peter said, "It's forbidden for any creature to leave the Forest, but Cecil and Maloof came several times. Cecil tried to convince me to hide in the Forest until the war was over, insisting there were countless opportunities for me if I wanted them."

"What would he gain by offering refuge to you?"

"I don't know." Peter shrugged. "I thought he was trying to be helpful at the time, but I now realize his loyalty is tied to Tereus."

Icy fingers squeezed Ivan's spine.

Peter mussed Ivan's hair playfully and punched his shoulder. Then, scowling, he moved away and watched the horses chomp on grass. "As long as I'm admitting shameful things, I might as well tell you. I didn't go to war."

For a stifling moment, Ivan didn't answer. Then he replied gently, "I know."

Peter's eyes shot open wide, his mouth went slack. "How did you find out?"

"Fungoda told me."

"Oh, of course. He's just filled with all kinds of wisdom that's really none of his business. Meddlesome old grump."

Ivan caught the bitterness and wondered why.

Peter must've sensed Ivan's disappointment and quickly explained, "He was always telling me what to do, warning me through Root-Underground about my behavior. I got really tired of his interference."

Discouraged with his brother's comment, Ivan

studied the ground, trying to comprehend it all.

"It's true." Peter glanced at the horses who were nudging each other. "I didn't want to go to war and get blown to bits, to become disfigured like Lars. What good would I be to anyone if I had no arm and only one eye?"

Ivan felt the need to defend Lars. "He seems to manage."

Peter gazed at Ivan with what looked like a blank stare. He was about to speak but then closed his lips.

"It's all right." Ivan held up the palm of his hand. "You don't have to explain to me. I understand your hatred of war and killing."

When Peter didn't defend himself even though Ivan insisted he needn't, his feelings were hurt. "Why didn't you come home? The war's been over for nearly two years. I waited, hoping for the day you'd come back."

"I couldn't—couldn't face you, Mother and Father. They were so proud of me for going to war to fight for freedom." Peter eyed his brother. "You remember how they boasted?"

Ivan's brow rose briefly. "They talked of nothing else. I was proud of you, too."

"I'm sorry I disappointed you all. I just couldn't. War isn't for me." He strode toward a pile of flat rocks. Finding a suitable place to sit, Peter lowered his long torso with the grace that Ivan remembered. Ivan sat next to him.

"What's that look on your face?" Peter turned to ask.

"Mother and Father died in a terrible train accident just outside London almost two years ago."

Peter looked tortured. He wiped his hand over his face. "Yes, I know."

"You knew?" Ivan shouted. His eyes opened wide. "Why didn't you come home to attend the funeral?" He fought his anger and acid roiling in his stomach. "I needed you to be with me."

Shrugging, Peter shook his head slowly. He sniffed and cleared his throat. "I *was* there, disguised. No one guessed I was the bent old woman with a tattered coat and sagging brown stockings. I saw you, and I sobbed even louder."

Ivan moved closer and put a comforting arm around Peter. "Why?"

"I'd planned to contact you later. But watching you, I saw how brave you were during the ceremony. You handled all those people with your usual poise. I was too ashamed to approach you."

"Brave? Not hardly. I was in shock. I scarcely remember a moment of that day. They were our parents. Peter, you should've shown yourself. We needed each other—I needed you." He jerked his arm away. Fighting his anger and disappointment, Ivan bit his lip to keep from screaming. *Peter was there and didn't even offer his condolences, his comfort.*

Lowering his head, Peter sat silently, making no excuses.

"You abandoned me." Ivan shot to his feet, quaking.

"Ivan, I…"

Turning his back, Ivan squeezed his fists, more irate at his brother than he'd ever been.

Peter rose quietly from the rock, placing a hand on Ivan's shoulder. "I'm sorry, but…"

"Losing them was torture. I was so lonely after Mother and Father died." He shrugged his brother's hand away, trying to keep his tears in check.

They were quiet for a time, lost in their own regretful thoughts.

"You were always there for me when we were young. I could depend on you." Ivan backed away, grating his teeth. "I don't understand."

"I was negligent, selfish, and a real cad," Peter said in a whisper. "Will you forgive me?" When Ivan didn't answer, Peter took Ivan's arm and guided him back to the rock.

"I don't want to sit. I'm mad." He pouted.

"You have every right to be angry." He held Ivan's face in his hands, staring into his eyes. "Truly, I'm sorry."

Calming himself, Ivan let out a deep sigh and turned away. He didn't want to spoil their reunion by fuming. He sat again, leaning forward with elbows resting on his knees. Tears fought their way to his eyes, but he denied them. He wouldn't let Peter see him weep. Not this time. Not after Peter's total selfishness.

Peter sat and inched away, allowing more distance between them. Straightening, he said, "You know who we are?" His blond eyebrows rose with the statement.

Ivan cocked his head, wondering if Peter was trying to change the subject yet again. "We're Russian, aren't we?" He waited and asked again, "Well, is there something you know that I don't?"

"Then he never told you? He said he would when I left, in case I never returned."

By his tone, Ivan figured the comment would be a serious revelation and would shake his comfortable world.

"Can't you guess? Don't you ever wonder about your heritage, your fine table etiquette, the way you move and greet people, your clear speech? The manner in which you dress? I remember that you hate wearing the same clothing twice."

Bewildered, Ivan searched his brother's eyes to see if he was teasing. "But we've always been this way. Mother and Father were from high society Russia. They taught us respectable manners. What's odd about that?"

"Nothing odd." Peter faced him and grinned. "Ivan, we're related to the Romanovs, the powerful ruling family of Russia. They were czars. Our father was a cousin to Prince John."

He lifted his eyebrows but couldn't understand why it was important. He shrugged. "That was a long time ago, and it doesn't matter to me."

"Don't you see, little brother? We have royal blood. We could be rulers of the Forest—of all England, in fact."

Ivan stared at him with disbelief. "I know what kings can do, and I don't want any part of it."

Looking disappointed, Peter sighed and frowned. "I thought you might say that."

Bounty snorted, and they looked up, watching as he gave the black stallion a mean push with his head and then walked a few yards away.

"Your horse is a bully."

"He's spoiled and gets his own way most of the time." Forcing a steady voice, Ivan asked, "The black horse belongs to you?"

"He's a beauty, isn't he? I named him Darkly. Fits, don't you think?" Peter's smile went wide, his eyes filled with delight. It was as though he'd swept their strained conflict far behind him.

"I've seen your horse before, haven't I?"

Frowning, Peter blinked and nodded.

"You were armored in black and silver—enemy colors when I saw you."

"Yes." Peter peered up under light lashes, meeting Ivan's questioning stare. "I was worried that Nugent and his partner Wiley were in the area. I'd kill them both if they made a move to hurt you." He paused. "Haven't I always protected you?" He laughed as he leaned back on his hands.

"You're on the enemy's side, then?"

"Not exactly. It's more involved than that."

"How involved?" Irritated at the lack of explanation, Ivan tried again. "You were wearing enemy armor."

"And you!" Peter redirected his attention. "I've heard rumors about you, too. I couldn't—I don't believe it. Did you really kill Commander Hays?"

Ivan cringed, realizing how cleverly his brother changed the subject…again.

"I insisted the story wasn't true." Pete's brow creased deeply. "You wouldn't hurt anyone, not for any reason. How did the rumor start?"

"Please, I don't want to talk about it."

"Oh, then it must be true." His blue eyes rounded, his mouth twitched at the corners. "How on earth? You?"

"I had no choice. Hays had his sight on me. It was kill or be killed."

"Sure, I understand. We don't have to talk about it. The experience is probably quite raw right now." His face wore a stricken look. "I can't believe you killed him." His hand trembled when he plucked a thin stalk with a pale purple head next to his leg. Separating it from its casing, he sucked the sweet juice. "Know what this is?" He held another for Ivan.

Shaking his head, Ivan said, "I've already tried it."

"It's called whiffle-weed. Makes you happy when you're sad. Of course, it takes quite a few drops of nectar to fully do the trick, but it's been helpful to me." His sly grin told more of the story.

"It hurts my teeth," Ivan mumbled."

"Oh yes, I'd forgotten you never eat anything sweet." Peter chewed a second weed and then tossed it away. He pushed himself off the rock.

Ivan stood slowly, his voice quaking. "Tell me, did you join the Dark Army?"

Peter didn't speak for some time, and Ivan waited. "I don't know how much I dare tell you. It might endanger your life."

"Tell me all of it."

"I...ah, well. There are many secrets I shouldn't divulge." His eyes moved amongst the trees, seemingly expecting them to comment.

Grimacing, Ivan shook his head. "I'd never tell. I never have."

"It's complicated." Peter licked his lips as though considering his options.

"You must tell me. I have a right to know."

"Don't breathe a word of what I'm about to share with you." He lifted his head, checking his surroundings again. "Be careful of those fenner whips. They carry messages to the Elftens. And the trees have ears."

Ivan's jaw muscles twitched, anxious to hear the truth.

Peter leaned closer. "I...well, I mean, Lord Graydon hired me to infiltrate the Dark Army and learn their secrets. I report only to him. He's afraid others would be in danger if I shared the information. In order to be convincing, I had to join Hays's regiment by buckling on armor and strapping a sword at my side. I became part of their hideous war. Honest, I've never killed anyone in battle." His hand went up, shielding a whisper. "No one suspected that I hid myself in the woods to avoid fighting. That's how I happened onto you and Nugent, but I couldn't come home, nor could I reveal myself to you."

"Why?"

"Because Nugent might blab the information, especially if he thought he would get paid for it."

Ivan listened intently. He felt a rush of joy and pride. His brother wasn't a traitor but an important spy to Lord Graydon.

"I told you." Peter's voice rose adamantly. "I'm not a soldier. I don't want to go to war and be slaughtered or maimed. But I wanted to do my part."

Ivan straightened his shoulders. He knew Peter's character better than Fungoda. His brother would never become part of enemy forces. Instead, he was gathering information to defeat them.

"The war is over now," Ivan reminded. "You're not Lord Graydon's secret agent any longer."

Peter's forehead knitted worry lines. "I'm not sure. I have to give a full report, and he hasn't officially dismissed me."

"I'm proud of you." Ivan grinned. "You've done

more than your share to help Zephyrus and the West Forest."

"I don't know about that." Peter looked away, scraping his teeth over his bottom lip.

"What's wrong?" Ivan took on a worried look once again.

"There's more. This is the part that frightens me. It keeps me from a peaceful night's sleep."

"What is it?"

"I've had dealings with Tereus."

Ivan choked. "Oh, no, you haven't."

"Let me finish, and you'll learn why I needed to do this. Tereus shared his plans with me to conquer the West Forest. He believes we're allies and that I'll help him gain control, even destroy Zephyrus."

"Peter, you must not!"

His brother held up a halting hand. "Tereus has ambitions to become the new ruler of all the land. He wants me to sit upon the throne as King of Helvaka. Imagine that." Offering a quirky smile, Peter winked. "Me, a king."

"What are you doing, Peter?" His nostrils flared. "You must break your allegiance with him. He's evil, vicious, and very dangerous."

Peter's blue eyes flashed. After a moment, his face relaxed. "I know you're right. Tereus sought me out and shared his scheme to conquer the Forest. I thought I could gather information and pass it on to Richard Graydon. But now…"

"Go to Zephyrus right away. He'll help you break your pact with that horrible demon. He's not to be trusted—*ever.*"

"I can't. Zephyrus will question me. He'll be

furious and believe I betrayed him."

Ivan scrunched his face. "The Great Oak is the true power, he can help you."

"You must know all about Tereus, then?" Peter exhaled deeply.

Nodding once, Ivan replied, "Sebastian told me. I've come to believe it now that I've experienced it." He turned a tight face. "Please, listen to me. You must not meet with Tereus. He has powers you can't even imagine. He'll destroy you in the end."

Peter whirled on his feet, shaking, his fists jammed into his sides. "Who are you to tell me what to do? You've only been here—what, a few days? Already you think you know it all."

Ivan jerked back. They'd never had angry words between them. "I'm sorry. I didn't mean to order you about. I love you. I don't want you hurt or killed."

"Little brother." Peter visibly calmed himself and spoke more kindly. "I know what I'm doing. Tereus won't get the better of me. I'm too smart for him."

Ivan's jaw muscles flexed. "Don't underestimate him. The beast showed his specter, threatening the lives of everyone, especially me. I was nearly destroyed by the toxic smoke and fire he spewed forth. His very voice chilled me to the bone."

Peter stared at his brother, lips trembling, his face turned stone-white.

"I nearly died after inhaling the poisonous gas. He meant to kill me."

"I…I didn't realize."

"Does he know who I am?"

"No. He only knew you'd killed his commander, and he swore revenge. I wish you hadn't done that."

"You told him I'd left the Forest?"

"Yes, so he'd stop stalking you." Peter's hands shook, he raised his head and gazed at the sky.

"He knows I'm your brother?"

"No." Peter shook his head wildly for emphasis.

"You must have nothing to do with that hideous monster. His powers are beyond our understanding. Please, Peter. Come home with me, now."

"Home?"

"Alfred and Canute are ready to leave, as I am. We'll travel together to our farm."

Peter turned away as if to hide his face. "I can't go yet. I have things that need to…um…be resolved."

"Resolved?

"Well…" His speech stumbled. "I have to report, you know, give Lord Richard the information I've gathered."

"In a couple of days, then, will you come home?"

"It depends on how long it takes." He looked at the ground and kicked at a small stone. Then he took a step back.

Disheartened, Ivan asked, "Soon, then? I'll clear away the things stored in your bedroom. It will be just as before."

"I must see Lord Richard and then say my goodbyes to many friends. But…"

"But what?"

"I don't know about being a farmer again. Not my cup of…well, you know."

"Come home, and we'll talk about it." Ivan hoped his brother would change his mind.

"Sure." Peter's smile was grim.

"It's lonely on the farm, what with Mother and

Father gone. And even more lonesome as winter approaches." Ivan rubbed his eyes. "Please, don't stay away too long. I miss you."

Peter yanked his brother into a tight embrace. "I miss you, too. Sometimes I wish I'd simply gone to war, gotten it over with, and returned home to my family."

"I've wished for your return every day."

Peter released a strangled moan. "I'm sorry I had to leave, sorry about Mother and Father, and especially for leaving you."

Ivan waited for further explanations, but Peter merely slumped. He stared into the open field where Darkly browsed.

After a moment, Peter faced him. His expression lightened, his smile broadened. "You've never been cross with me before. You've changed."

"I didn't mean to, I—"

"You've grown up, become more aggressive, even brave. I like that. You know how I always told you to fight back, not to be so passive. Now you can defend yourself." His eyes blinked moisture. "I won't worry about you quite as much."

"There's no need to worry. Just come home, and we'll watch out for each other."

Peter suddenly tensed. "Do they know who axed Zephyrus?"

"I haven't heard for certain. Apparently, the attacker was disguised in a gray hooded cloak, and he made a quick escape."

Peter's face pinched.

"What is it?"

"Listen to me, little brother of mine." His eyes

went dark. He gripped Ivan's upper arms. "You must leave now and never come back to the Forest."

"Why?" Ivan felt the wind knocked out of him. He'd decided he wouldn't return to the Forest and had announced this to Sebastian and Zephyrus. Then he'd changed his mind because of his feelings for Zephyrus and his pledge to Anna-Iza. Now, Peter was demanding that he never set foot on Forest soil again.

There was a frightening set to Peter's face. "I— let's go get the horses." He bolted from where he stood, leading the way.

Ivan followed. "Why can't I return?"

As they approached their mounts, Peter slowed and halted. Turning swiftly, he hissed. "Don't come back, or Tereus will kill you. I may not be able to protect you again."

"Protect me?" Ivan gasped air. "How will Tereus know? He's confined to the underworld. Zephyrus said he's more restrained now than ever because of the crimes he's committed."

"If only you hadn't killed his commander—but you did. Tereus is furious. He howled like a rabid animal for your blood." Peter covered his eyes with his hand. "He swore to burn your hide over a slow fire with an iron bar impaled through your body."

Ivan gave a cold cry of fear. In his dream, the demon had told him he'd eat his flesh and chew his bones. *Which punishment is worse? Or are they one and the same?*

"Promise me. You must promise." Peter gripped Ivan's arms, pressing hard. "Never return to the Forest for any reason, or you'll die."

Ivan turned from his brother's glare. In spite of

Peter's frightful warnings, he couldn't—wouldn't—make that promise. He wanted to return and see his many friends, to learn that Zephyrus had fully recovered. He would see Anna-Iza and withdraw his pledge of love. His heart grew heavy with dread at the thought. He'd never had many friends before, but now…Sebastian, Zephyrus, Simon, the soldiers, Anna-Iza, and her retinue—all of them were special to him.

Minutes passed, and Ivan found his courage. "I've made promises too, and I intend to keep them." He forced a confident grin. "Don't worry. My new friends will keep me safe." After hesitating, he asked, "Will you come home?"

"Now that we've found each other, do you really think I wouldn't?" Peter chuckled. He grabbed Ivan and threw his arms hard around him. "I love you, Ivan. I love you more than any person on earth—ever. I can always count on you and trust you."

"I do care, and I love you, too," Ivan replied. "That's why I need you to be with me. You promised we'd travel the world and have fun together."

"Yeah. Yeah, we could." Peter released him and drew a long breath, like an inward sigh.

"I'll be waiting for you."

"I really must go." Peter's lips pulled taut as he mounted easily. "I'll see you in a few days. It will be interesting to see the farm again." He turned to wave, showing a wide grin, and galloped off toward the south.

Ivan settled into his saddle. He gave in to a feeling of great happiness as he guided Bounty toward the Forest's exit. Whistling for his beagles, he called, "We're going home, boys."

****

Standing close to her flying silver stallion, Anna-Iza watched Ivan leave the Forest. Her heart warmed and beat a little faster. A stream of tears cascaded down her cheeks. Why must their affection be forbidden? "Please, hurry back to me."

****

Zephyrus raised his eyes. He thanked the trees at the entrance for informing him that Ivan had now left the Forest. He hoped Peter would keep his promise to follow in a few days. He watched the puffy clouds collide as though nudging each other in triumph. A good rain would help wash these toxins away, he was sure.

Reviewing the past several days, he managed a smile. *All is as it should be.* In time, everything would be revealed. The Black Book of Pearls had prophesied it.

A dark-haired lad will come seeking and find maturity, wisdom, and friendship. He will risk his life for the Forest's survival. He will find himself in his search. Your duty is to keep him alive.

- The Black Book of Pearls. Chapter 77, Verse 7.

A word about the author...

In an earlier career, Vicki Price was a freelance fashion illustrator in Los Angeles, working for both wholesale and retail fashion houses. After she retired from her business, she taught watercolor classes to young people for over a decade. Now, she's an active fine art watercolor artist as well as a passionate writer of young adult fantasy.

Vicki and her husband live in the lovely Sierra Nevada Mountains, not far from Yosemite National Park. The deer, quail, and wild turkeys visit and eat the cracked corn they've provided, next to the ravens that squawk for their peanut treats.

Printed in the USA
CPSIA information can be obtained
at www.ICGtesting.com
JSHW010138240724
66689JS00009B/95